D0257987

HOW WILL I KNOW?

Also by Sheila O'Flanagan

Dreaming of a Stranger
Caroline's Sister
Isobel's Wedding
Suddenly Single
Far From Over
My Favourite Goodbye
He's Got to Go
Too Good to be True
Destinations
Anyone But Him

How Will
I Know?

Sheila O'Flanagan

headline

Copyright © 2005 Sheila O'Flanagan

The right of Sheila O'Flanagan to be identified as the Author of
the Work has been asserted by her in accordance with the
Copyright, Designs and Patents Act 1988.

First published in 2005
by HEADLINE BOOK PUBLISHING

4

Apart from any use permitted under UK copyright law, this
publication may only be reproduced, stored, or transmitted, in
any form, or by any means, with prior permission in writing of
the publishers or, in the case of reprographic production, in
accordance with the terms of licences issued by the
Copyright Licensing Agency.

All characters in this publication are fictitious
and any resemblance to real persons, living or dead,
is purely coincidental.

Cataloguing in Publication Data is
available from the British Library

ISBN 0 7553 0753 4 (hardback)
ISBN 0 7553 0756 9 (trade paperback)

Typeset in Galliard by Palimpsest Book Production Limited,
Polmont, Stirlingshire

Printed and bound in Great Britain by
Clays Ltd St Ives plc

Headline's policy is to use papers that are natural, renewable and
recyclable products and made from wood grown in sustainable
forests. The logging and manufacturing processes are expected
to conform to the environmental regulations of the country of origin.

HEADLINE BOOK PUBLISHING
A division of Hodder Headline PLC
338 Euston Road
London NW1 3BH
www.headline.co.uk
www.hodderheadline.com

It takes more than me at the computer to get the print on the pages so thanks to:

Carole Blake who makes me feel like I know what I'm doing

Marion Donaldson who reminds me of what I'm meant to be doing

Team Headline who know what they're doing (thankfully)

My family who have always supported me doing what I'm doing (even when it means forgetting them sometimes – sorry about that)

My friends who let me get on with doing what I'm doing and who very kindly buy the end result

Colm who often makes me do something else

And special thanks all of you who buy my books, who make doing what I do, and what I always wanted to do – writing them – so wonderful by your support and encouragement. Extra thanks to everyone who has taken the time out to sign the guestbook on my website www.sheilaoflanagan.net. Whenever I worry about how things are going I read the comments and feel energised again. I really appreciate it. Thank you again!

Chapter 1

Anchusa (Summer Forget-Me-Not) – Blue, white, pink or mauve star-shaped blossoms cover branching stems. Water in dry weather.

Claire woke up earlier than usual on the morning Georgia was due to go to summer camp for a month. She lay in bed with her eyes closed for a couple of minutes while she tried to figure out what was different about the day and then it struck her. It was the absence of noise – more especially the absence of the gentle hiss of rain which had been present every single morning for the last two weeks – that had woken her. The only sound was of the birds singing in the apple trees outside the house.

She opened her eyes and slid out from under the sheets. The early-morning sun – something she hadn't seen in ages – filtered through the chink in the heavy damask curtains. She pulled them open and blinked in the unexpectedly bright light. Then she took her white silk robe from the back of the bedroom door and tiptoed downstairs so that she wouldn't wake her fourteen-year-old daughter. Not, she thought, that there was really much chance of that. Most mornings a pickaxe wouldn't have gone amiss when trying to prise Georgia out of bed – Claire would spend ages shaking her and calling out her name before Georgia budged. But she felt that this morning might be different, because Georgia was thrilled about her trip to the Irish College in Galway and had been wildly overexcited the night before. It had taken all Claire's powers of persuasion to get her to bed in the first place, and she knew that Georgia had spent at least an hour reading or listening to her shiny pink iPod in her room after-wards because she'd been able to see the glow of the light from beneath her door. So she didn't really want her waking up too early now.

She went into the kitchen and opened the back door. Phydough, their two-year-old mainly Old English Sheepdog (his mother was pure-bred and beautiful but his father had legged it after his moment of illicit lust), barked happily at her. Claire had chosen the quirky spelling of Fido from a children's book that Georgia had once loved, believing that a dog of his undoubted intelligence and dignity needed a special name.

'Quiet, Phy,' she whispered. 'Don't wake the entire neighbourhood!'

The dog gave a small woof and then wagged his tail enthusiastically. Claire scratched him behind his ears and took a pouch of food from the cupboard. Phydough jumped up on his hind legs and leaned against the cupboard doors, his soft brown eyes eager with anticipation.

'Down, Phy,' she said. 'Sit.' She filled the bright blue ceramic bowl which Georgia had bought him the previous Christmas and put it down in front of him. The dog snuffled his way happily through the chicken and vegetable mix while Claire filled the kettle and plugged it in. Then she walked out on to the patio behind the house and surveyed the bedraggled garden.

It was long and narrow and right now it was also a total mess. The lawn badly needed to be cut and the evergreens that lined the walls were growing out of control, choking the rose bushes which had been forced to thrust their stems high into the air in the fight for light. The flowerbeds were overrun with weeds and the two apple trees desperately needed pruning. Part of the problem, of course, was that the incessant rain of the past fortnight had caused everything to shoot up by an extra couple of inches as well as flattening some of the flowers and giving them an appearance more suited to autumn than midsummer. But the real reason the garden was unkempt and overgrown was that it had always been Bill's domain, not Claire's. And she hadn't been able to face tackling it in the past three years, so the only job that had been done, even on a half-regular basis, had been mowing the lawn. She bit the inside of her lip as she looked at the weeds encroaching on the patio area and the sodden bamboo grasses along the near wall. Soon, she promised herself. Soon I'll do something about it.

The kettle clicked off and she spooned coffee into her favourite yellow mug. She took a blueberry muffin out of the bread-bin and peeled away the waxy paper as she tucked her legs beneath her and perched on a chair at the kitchen table. She pulled the previous day's paper towards her and glanced through the news. But her mind wasn't really on the task. She was thinking about Georgia and her trip to the summer camp in the Irish-speaking Gaeltacht and hoping that she'd have a good time in her month away. And, if she was really, really honest with herself, she was wondering how the hell she herself was going to cope on her own for a month.

The closest she'd ever come to living on her own before had been the few weeks she'd spent as an au pair in France. And that didn't really count because, even though she hadn't had any family or friends around her, the house had been full of the shouts and squeals of the two Carmichael children and she was never actually on her own. Admittedly their parents hadn't been around that much, but at least Amy and Raul had taken up her time.

I will *not* obsess about being alone, she muttered as she threw her half-eaten muffin out of the open kitchen door and on to the grass beyond the patio; loads and loads of women live on their own all the time. I only need to get through the next month. It won't be that difficult. And besides, I've lots of work to do and some very tight deadlines to do it in. I'm always complaining to Georgia about how much work I have to get through. With her out of my hair I'll be able to concentrate on getting stuff done instead of moaning about how hard it is to find the time.

She drained her mug and refolded the newspaper. Then she began the task of tackling the mountain of ironing piled up on the rocking chair in the corner of the kitchen. This was her second major batch of ironing in the past twenty-four hours. Yesterday had been the critical stuff – all the clothes that Georgia wanted to take to camp with her. Claire had wailed at her that she hardly needed to take a T-shirt for every day she'd be there and that seven pairs of identical jeans was surely a bit excessive, but Georgia had given her that pitying look that teenagers use when faced with hopeless parents and reminded her that it was important to have the right stuff and that she had to cater for goodness knows what social events and that there was no way she was going to be the only one who had nothing to wear.

'But Georgey – you're bringing eight white tees and they're all the same,' cried Claire. 'And I know you need different things for different events, but different doesn't just mean another pair of jeans.'

Georgia had pointed to an overlooked stack of brightly coloured miniskirts. 'And you can't complain about those because you bought them for me,' she'd said triumphantly.

Now Claire pulled one of her own T-shirts towards her and began to iron it. Actually she didn't really mind doing the ironing too much, she found it comparatively restful. She switched on the radio and listened to an early-morning chat show as the iron glided across the cotton material.

She'd finished the three T-shirts and a couple of pillowcases and was just starting on her king-sized sheet (she hated doing sheets; even though there weren't any awkward parts they were just too big to fit over the ironing board properly) when Georgia walked into the room wearing her blue pyjamas, rubbing her eyes and yawning widely.

'You're awake early.' Claire glanced at the wall clock.

'Couldn't really sleep,' said Georgia. 'I texted Robyn and she's up too.'

'Are she and her mum still calling here around ten?' asked Claire.

'I guess so.' Georgia shrugged as she opened the fridge door and took out a fruit smoothie.

'You'll have to have more than that for your breakfast,' remarked Claire.

'I know, I know. Don't fuss.'

'D'you want me to make you something?'

'Don't be daft, Mum.' Georgia put her arms around Claire's waist. 'I *can* boil an egg, you know.'

'Is that what you're having?' asked Claire sceptically.

'Yeuch.' Georgia leaned against Claire's back so that her red-gold hair cascaded over her mother's shoulders. 'I'm going to make some toast. But to be honest with you, I'm not very hungry.'

'Excited?' Claire turned to look at her daughter. Georgia's eyes – amber-flecked like Claire's own – were sparkling with anticipation.

'It'll be fun,' said Georgia. 'It really will.'

'Though how on earth you're going to make yourself understood in Irish at the college when I can hardly understand your English these days I'll never know,' teased Claire gently.

'Oh, like, you're so not with it.' Georgia grinned at her mother. 'Though I'm not sure about the Irish either. I can see myself not speaking at all!'

There was a sudden, awkward silence and the two of them looked at each other. 'Not like that,' said Georgia hastily, seeing the flicker of concern in Claire's eyes. 'Not . . . you know . . . just not knowing what to say.'

'Sure, sure.' Claire nodded vigorously. 'But I bet you'll get the hang of it in no time.'

Georgia made a face. 'I hope so. I know it's my native language and I do want to understand it, but it's bloody difficult.'

'Only because we don't speak it every day,' said Claire. 'It's like anything, once you get used to it it'll be no bother to you.'

'Your faith in me is very touching.' Georgia grinned.

'Go and make yourself some breakfast,' Claire ordered. 'And stick the kettle on again for me, I'd love another coffee.'

Leonie O'Malley and her daughter, Robyn, who had been Georgia's best friend since primary school, arrived exactly on time to take both Claire and Georgia to the train station where Georgia and Robyn would catch the train to Galway. Some parents had chosen to drive their children to the Irish College, but the group who were going from Georgia's school had elected to take the train. A teacher from the college had come to Dublin to supervise them on the trip west.

'I think it's a great idea,' said Leonie. 'Makes it all the more exciting for them. Plus, the idea of driving to Galway and back on a Saturday, whether it's in the so-called height of summer or not, is too awful for words.' She grimaced as she spoke, but Claire simply nodded and called up to Georgia and Robyn – who'd decamped to Georgia's bedroom for reasons unknown – to get the hell down here now, Leonie was ready to go.

'Are you sure you want to come to the station with us?' asked Leonie.

'Absolutely,' replied Claire. She picked up Georgia's case, made a face at the weight of it, and lugged it to Leonie's 4X4. 'Just as well this case has wheels,' she told Georgia when her daughter reappeared. 'It weighs a ton.'

'That's *why* I picked the one with wheels,' said Georgia.

'That's why they tell you not to pack too much,' retorted Claire, but she grinned at Georgia all the same.

'All aboard!' cried Leonie.

'Are you sure you want to come?' Georgia echoed Leonie's words.

'Of course I'm sure,' said Claire. 'I have to see you off safely, don't I?'

'You could do it from here,' said Georgia. 'Robs's mum will make sure that we get on the train OK.'

'I know.' Claire moistened her lips. 'But I want to see you off myself.'

'OK.' But Georgia's eyes were anxious.

Claire took a deep breath and got into the Subaru. She wedged herself up against the door, Georgia beside her, while Leonie and Robyn got into the front seats.

'Everyone all right back there?' asked Leonie.

'Yes,' said Georgia. Her hand slid across the seat and held on to Claire's as Leonie turned the key in the ignition.

Claire felt her heart beat more rapidly in her chest as the car moved away from the kerb. She closed her eyes and kept them closed. She knew that she would be more or less all right if she didn't open them again, if she didn't admit to herself that she was in a car. And, she told herself, as she always did on the rare occasions she needed to be in one these days, it wasn't cars she should panic about. It wasn't a car that had been the problem. But somehow it was cars that set off the panicked feelings inside her.

She felt the pressure from Georgia's fingers increase as they picked up speed and she wrapped her own fingers around her daughter's in response. I really need to do something about this, she told herself for the hundredth time. I can't spend the rest of my life terrified of something so basic as being a passenger in a car. And it's very hard for me to lay down the law to Georgia about anything when she knows that such a simple thing has the power to render me rigid with fear. Surely she must lose all respect for me.

But, Claire acknowledged, that didn't seem to have happened so far. In fact Georgia was a great daughter, although Claire did worry because she hadn't yet turned into one of the snarling monsters that most teenagers eventually became. Give it time, Leonie, who had two sons and a daughter older than Robyn, had told her. It'll happen eventually. Though Georgia's such a great girl it might not be as bad as you think.

Claire hated to think that the bond between herself and Georgia might come under pressure as her daughter started to grow up even more. Right now, Georgia was the best thing in her life. It wasn't fair, Claire sometimes told herself, to think of her daughter as her rock, as the most important part of her existence. But it was a fact all the same.

The car slid to a halt at traffic lights on the quays. Claire allowed her eyes to flicker open and then clamped them closed again. I *will* get help about this, she promised herself. I will.

'OK, Mum?' whispered Georgia.

'Sure I am,' Claire responded. 'I'm fine if I keep my eyes closed, Georgey-girl. You know that.'

'I know.' Georgia's voice was full of reassurance and Claire squeezed her hand again.

She knew that she was shaking as she got out of the car at Heuston station. Leonie looked at her enquiringly, but she assured the older woman that she was absolutely fine. She hefted Georgia's case out of the boot and dumped it on the pavement.

'Are you sure you don't want to take out a few things?' she asked.

'Mum!'

'You know you exceed the recommended clothing essentials by a factor of about ten?'

Georgia laughed. 'OK, Mum, but those recommendations were obviously for refugees from the fifties or something.'

Claire laughed too. Her heartbeat had slowed down again and she was feeling much better. They walked into the station concourse and towards the platform for the Galway train. A short, dumpy, grey-haired woman, dressed in a navy tracksuit with a school crest on the sweatshirt and carrying a massive clipboard, looked at them appraisingly.

'*Coláiste Cian?*' she asked.

'Yes,' said Leonie. 'Robyn O'Malley and Georgia Hudson.'

The woman consulted her clipboard. 'Robyn *agus* Georgia. *Fáilte*,' she said as she ticked off their names. The girls looked at each other and giggled.

'Go on,' said Claire. 'You've got to get on the train. And not another English word out of you for a month.'

Georgia put her arms around her mother and hugged her tightly. 'I'll miss you,' she said, her voice suddenly younger and a little anxious.

'I'll miss you too,' said Claire. 'But you'll have a great time.'

'I know I will,' Georgia told her. 'You'll look after yourself, though, won't you? You won't do anything mad or crazy?'

'Me? Mad or crazy?' Claire grinned at her. 'When do I ever?'

Georgia's smile wobbled. 'Well, you know, now that you have an empty house you might start living some hectic social life.'

'I might.' Claire chuckled.

'So no sleazy nightclubs or picking up unsuitable men or anything,' said Georgia.

'Absolutely not,' said Claire. 'Although maybe the odd seedy night-club . . .'

Georgia smiled at her. 'You'll be OK, won't you?'

'Georgey, it's *me* who's supposed to worry about *you* being OK,' said Claire. 'I'll be at home. I have Phydough to look after me. Don't fret.'

'I won't,' said Georgia. 'It's just . . .'

'I'll be fine,' Claire assured her. 'And so will you. I hope you have the most wonderful time.'

'You don't mind me going or anything, do you?'

'Georgia! Of course not. And I think it was fantastic that you decided you wanted to go yourself. It'll be great fun. You probably won't want to come home.'

'Can't see me wanting to stay in the wilds of the west.' Georgia grinned. 'I'm a city girl at heart!'

'*Brostaigh oraibh*,' said the grey-haired woman impatiently.

'You'd better hurry all right,' said Claire. 'Take care, honey. Have a good time. Keep in touch.'

'I'll text you,' promised Georgia.

'*As Gaeilge*?' asked her mother.

'Ah, listen, you don't understand half my texts in English,' protested Georgia, 'so I can't see you having a clue about the Irish ones.'

'You might be right,' agreed Claire. She hugged Georgia again. 'OK, pet, off you go.'

'See you, Mum.'

Georgia and Robyn walked through the barrier and towards the train. Claire kept her smile fixed firmly on her face as she watched them get into the carriage.

'I suppose we'd better stay until the train goes just in case either of them has an abrupt change of heart,' she said to Leonie.

'If Robyn has an abrupt change of heart I'll kill her,' Leonie responded. 'Leaving aside the cost of the college, she made me buy her an entire new wardrobe for the summer. She'd better get plenty of wear out of it in Galway!'

Claire laughed. 'At least I only had to buy a few skirts for Georgey, although heaven knows whether she'll wear them or not. She's going through a jeans phase at the moment.'

'Jeans are good,' said Leonie darkly. 'Jeans mean that they're covered up. You should see some of the tops Robyn thinks are acceptable items of clothing.'

'Oh, I know.' Claire nodded. 'You'd never be able to keep up with them and what's fashionable and what's not. And I don't want to be a nagging sort of mother, but sometimes . . .'

The two women exchanged looks of understanding. Then the train pulled out of the station and they sighed with relief.

'Excellent,' said Leonie. 'I know I'm supposed to miss her for the month, and of course I will, but it does give me a bit of space to reclaim my life.'

Claire smiled noncommittally.

'What about you?' asked Leonie. 'Anything wild and wonderful planned?'

Claire shook her head. 'Up to my neck in work,' she told Leonie. 'And I'm reckoning that this month will be a great opportunity to get down to it without Georgey barging in and asking me where the TV remote is or what I've done with her iPod or whether there's anything to do because she's bored out of her mind.'

Leonie laughed. 'But it's an opportunity for you to get out and about without having to worry about her too.'

'Oh, sure,' said Claire dismissively. 'Not that there's anywhere I need to get out and about to.'

'Well, look, if you're at a loose end or anything . . .'

'That's really good of you, Leonie. But I'll be fine.'

For a moment it seemed as though Leonie would pursue the issue, but in the end she nodded briefly and simply asked Claire if she could drive her home.

Claire shook her head. 'No thanks. I think I'll wander downtown and do a bit of shopping.'

'Well then, would you like a lift as far as O'Connell Street?' asked Leonie.

'No thanks, all the same,' said Claire. 'I could do with the walk.'

'Are you sure?'

'Absolutely,' she said. 'Absolutely.'

Chapter 2

Dianthus (Sweet William/Annual Carnations) – A wide variety of colours especially reds and pinks. Water in dry weather.

Claire didn't spend as long as she'd anticipated in town because her navy leather shoes had started to chafe at her feet and ankles thanks to the fact that the temperature continued to rise steadily and her feet swelled up in response. So after an hour she caught the 44A home, trying to ignore the pain of the blisters that she knew were getting bigger with every passing second. By the time she'd got off the bus and made the five-minute walk to the tall, narrow house close to the seafront she was yelping under her breath. She pushed open the front gate, pulled off the offending shoes and stood gratefully on the still-damp grass beside the front path, looking up at the house.

When she'd first told people she and Bill were buying a three-storey-over-basement property, they'd looked at her in complete amazement and then whistled that it must be huge and costing them a fortune. They were right about the second part of it, she admitted, but the house had been built to take advantage of a narrow strip of land and so it was smaller than most people imagined despite its height. They'd bought it because it was in a great location for Bill's surgery and the basement was ideally suited for conversion, given that it had a separate entrance at ground level while the main entrance to the house was up a flight of steps.

When they'd moved in the kitchen had been in the basement. It had taken time and effort to convert it to a surgery with waiting room and toilet and then move the kitchen up a floor next to the dining room. The first floor had been made up of a living room, a bedroom and a bathroom, while the top floor had two bedrooms (one of which was now Claire's office) and another bathroom. Renovating the house had been a messy and difficult job, especially constructing an exit from the new kitchen to the garden, but eventually it had been completed. Even if there'd never been a need for a surgery Claire knew that she would have changed the location of the kitchen anyway. The basement was far too gloomy for what she always felt should be a cheerful family room.

She walked towards the house through the grass, enjoying its comforting coolness on her hot feet. And when she opened the front door and stepped into the hallway she was glad of the coolness of the black and white tiles underfoot too, even though she normally felt they were a bit cold and unwelcoming and was longing to change them when she got the time.

Phydough, who'd stayed in his basket when she'd gone out with Georgia, padded over her to greet her. She patted him absently then opened the enormous green first-aid box on top of the fridge and took out two plasters which she stuck over her blisters. 'And that'll teach you to walk in unsuitable shoes,' she said out loud. At the word 'walk', Phydough barked hopefully.

'I can't,' she told him. 'Not yet. My feet are too sore. Later.'

He understood the word 'later' and looked at her reproachfully.

'Honestly,' she said, scratching him in his favourite spot under his chin. 'Later.' The dog walked off in disgust and plopped back into his basket, while Claire opened the back door to allow air into the kitchen before filling the kettle and switching it on.

The sound of the doorbell – loud and insistent so that it could be heard in both the house and the garden – made her jump. She walked barefoot into the hall and peered out through the spyglass. Then she opened the door.

'Hi, Eavan,' she said. 'What brings you here?'

'That's all the welcome I get?' Eavan Keating raised an eyebrow and looked quizzically at her friend from her bright blue eyes.

'Sorry,' said Claire. 'I didn't mean to sound unwelcoming. It's just that it's ages since you dropped by.'

'That's because you're always too busy.' There was a note of disapproval in Eavan's voice.

'Oh, Eavan, you know how it is with Locum Libris,' said Claire. 'Always so much to do and so little time to do it in!'

'Huh.' Eavan was sceptical.

'No, really!' Claire shook her head so that her burnt-cinnamon waves brushed across her face and she had to push them out of her eyes impatiently. 'They've got a new text coming out on the role of some bloody bacterium in the gut and it's taking me for ever to get through. I've a stack of papers the size of Everest on my desk and I know that when I open my e-mail there'll be more incomprehensible stuff for me.'

'You work too hard,' said Eavan sourly, 'and they don't pay you enough.'

'But they're good to me,' Claire pointed out. 'They let me keep my own hours. I do so much from home. It suits me.'

'And you're a soft touch to them, you know that?' But Eavan's tone was teasing. 'Anyway, I came to tell you that we're meeting for drinks later tonight. The club crowd. And don't say you can't come. Your excuse is always that you have to be home for Georgia. Now she's away for a month, you can get out and about a bit.'

Claire looked at her doubtfully. 'I *will* get out and about,' she said. 'But I'm not sure about tonight. I do have lots of things that I need to catch up on.'

'You have all weekend to catch up on things,' said Eavan. 'We want to see you tonight. No excuses.'

'It's just . . .' Claire poured boiling water into mugs from the kettle which had switched itself off while they were talking. She swirled the tea bags around and then dumped them in the sink. Then she opened the fridge and took out a carton of milk. 'You know I love the people in the club, Eavan. But I don't feel like I have much in common with them any more.'

'That's nonsense and you know it.'

'It's not nonsense,' said Claire. She looked at her friend. 'I can't play so I haven't been at matches or anything, and I really don't feel that I can drop in the way I used to.'

'You can play,' said Eavan. 'Not as well, maybe, but you can play.'

'Me and Paul Hanratty won the mixed doubles tennis and badminton before the accident,' said Claire harshly. 'Now I can't move properly on court. You know that. I can't run and I'm not fit enough.'

'Oh, Claire, you were always the fittest of us!'

'That was then,' said Claire.

Eavan sipped her tea and said nothing.

'I'll do my best to come,' said Claire eventually. 'But I don't want to be pressured by you.'

'I never pressure you,' said Eavan. 'Never. But come on, Claire – you've got a whole month to live a little. And it'd be about time.'

'Don't say things like that to me,' said Claire fiercely. 'I have a good life now, Eavan Keating. Me and Georgey – we've worked it all out. And it's not like I sit home at night and sob into my whiskey glass or anything. I get out and about. I go to Georgia's events, I take Phydough for walks, I get across to Locum Libris. I have a full, busy life and just because I don't spend it in clubs and pubs with people that I used to be friends with doesn't mean that I haven't managed to get myself back on an even keel!'

Eavan stared at her. 'Claire, what you've described is fine. But it doesn't include going out with the girls or sitting round doing nothing or any of the things that make life worth living.'

'I lost the one person who made my life worth living,' said Claire angrily. 'And it wasn't easy to get over that, you know. But I have. In my own way. And I really don't need you coming round here getting at me just as soon as I'm on my own for half a second because you don't believe I can function as a normal person by myself.'

'I don't think that!' cried Eavan.

'You do. Everybody does. You think that I'm going to go to pieces, but I'm not. I was a doctor's wife, for God's sake! I know about grief and bereavement and everything else. There isn't anything you can tell me that I haven't already heard.'

'It's different when it's you and not some patient,' said Eavan.

'Oh, give me a break.'

'Have you seen anyone about your phobia yet?'

'For your information, Leonie O'Malley drove me and Georgia to Heuston station today,' said Claire. 'So if you're thinking that I'm still not able to get into a car, you're so wrong.'

14

'Leonie called me,' said Eavan. 'She said that you wouldn't take a lift home. And that you had your eyes closed the whole way there.'

'Who the hell does that woman think she is, interfering in my life!' cried Claire. 'OK, yes, my eyes were closed. Some people keep their eyes closed on planes. I keep them closed in cars. No big deal, Eavan! And I didn't take a lift home because I wanted to go shopping.'

Eavan took her half-empty mug to the sink and rinsed it out. 'There's no talking to you, is there?'

'If you were talking *with* me that'd be fine,' said Claire, the anger gone from her voice. 'But you and everyone else still talk *at* me. You all have great ideas about what I should be doing, but it's my life. Mine. And I'm perfectly OK with it.'

'Don't you want someone else in it?' asked Eavan. 'It's nearly three years, Claire.'

'Oh, for heaven's sake!' Claire looked at her friend impatiently. 'Of course I don't want anyone else in it. I had Bill. There is no one else. There never will be.'

'Never say never,' said Eavan softly.

'In this case it's easy.' Claire ran her fingers through her hair. 'Look, Eavan, I appreciate your concern, I really do. But you're worrying about nothing.'

'So are you going to come tonight?'

'I'll do my best,' said Claire.

'OK.' Eavan picked up her bag from where she'd left it on the kitchen table. 'I'll see you later then.'

'Yes,' said Claire. 'See you.'

She let Eavan out of the house. As she held open the heavy front door, the Tesco delivery van with the grocery shopping she'd ordered over the internet pulled up outside. Claire waved at Eavan and smiled at the delivery man, pleased that at least he was someone who wouldn't lecture her about her life.

Glenn Keating was playing in the back garden with Saffy, their soon-to-be three-year-old daughter, when Eavan returned laden with the shopping she'd done on the way home from Claire's. He strode into the kitchen and smiled at his wife.

'How's Claire?' he asked.

Eavan made a face at him. 'I don't know,' she told him. 'I asked her to come for a drink with us tonight and she flipped her lid and told me to stop interfering.'

'I suppose I don't blame her for that,' said Glenn. 'I'd hate it too if people were on and on at me all the time.'

'I'm not on and on at her!' exclaimed Eavan hotly.

'I know. But from her point of view I guess that every time you call her you're asking her somewhere and then ticking her off about it when she doesn't come.'

'I haven't asked her anywhere in ages,' protested Eavan. 'And when I do she always uses Georgia as an excuse. But she can't now with Georgia away.'

'So what did she say this time?'

'Oh, that she was up to her neck with editing some medical book and that she had to tidy the house.' Eavan snorted. 'But she also said that she isn't mad keen about meeting people from the club because they all knew her from before, when she was fit. I tried to tell her that she's fit enough but she wasn't having any of it.'

'Well, maybe she'll turn up later.'

Eavan sighed. 'Perhaps. But I doubt it. I dunno, Glenn. There she is hanging on to a house that's far too big for her and working her guts out for people who really don't give a stuff! She pretends she doesn't have time to do anything and whenever she does come out it's always fleeting because she's so busy and she has to get back to Georgia, but she doesn't have anything to be busy about and Georgia isn't a baby any more. It's all horseshit.'

'So she's keeping busy to . . . well, to deal with it.'

'Fine, but dealing with it should also include getting a life again. I'm fed up with her throwing friendship back in my face. There's only so much of that anyone can take. It's been three years.'

'You're a good friend,' agreed Glenn. 'Anyone can see how hard you've tried.'

'She was good to me too,' Eavan reminded him. 'When we were working and I went through a bad time . . . she supported me.' Suddenly she found her eyes flooding with tears.

'Hey, there's no need to get upset about her!' Glenn looked at his wife in surprise. 'She's your friend, she's been good to you, and that's why you're still being good to her – sometimes too good to her, Evs – even when she doesn't bloody well appreciate it.'

'You're right.' Eavan wiped the unshed tears from her eyes. 'Of course. But Claire . . . used to be fun. She used to let her hair down with the best of us. She didn't need Bill beside her to have a good time. She had no qualms about leaving him at home with Georgia to come to the club two nights a week, for example. So it's a bit rich of her to not want to come out now when there's absolutely nobody at home. It's such a waste.'

'Great-looking woman too,' said Glenn pensively. 'She still looks as though she's in her twenties.'

'OK, that's being a bit extreme,' said Eavan edgily as she checked her own appearance in the reflection of the glass opposite.

Glenn laughed. 'But she *is* attractive,' he told her, 'in a waif-like kind of way.'

'She wouldn't have anorexia, would she?' wondered Eavan. 'You're right about the waif-like appearance, but she wasn't always like that. I remember the two of us going on some insane diet one time – you know, like cabbage and beetroot or something – because we'd both piled on a few pounds. Claire was really pissed off that she couldn't get into a particular pair of trousers. Of course Bill would get at her if she went on mad diets, that's the problem about having a doctor for your husband!'

'Isn't anorexia something teenage girls get?' asked Glenn. 'I'd have thought that if either of them had an eating problem it'd be Georgia.'

'I saw Georgey in the shopping centre last week,' said Eavan. 'She looked the picture of health. If only Claire was as sensible as her daughter . . .'

'Give her time,' said Glenn gently. 'She has to deal with things in her own way.'

Eavan kissed him. 'You're a wonderful man,' she said. 'Caring, understanding . . . every woman's dream.'

'As long as I'm *your* dream, that's all that matters,' he told her.

'Oh, you're very definitely that,' she assured him as she slid her hand under his shirt. Then she abandoned the procedure because Saffy, who'd been watching them from her sandpit in the back garden, yelled that she wanted a drink of juice and she wanted it now.

Chapter 3

Helipterum (Everlasting Flower) – Usually white, pink or yellow daisy-like flowers on slender stems. Can be dried for winter decoration.

After she'd unpacked the groceries and put them away, slamming the cupboard doors closed in her anger about Eavan's visit, Claire stomped up the stairs to the home office which she'd kitted out at the top of the house. She'd told Eavan the truth when she'd said she had a lot of work to do – stacks of papers surrounded her ice-white Apple computer and almost completely covered the large maplewood desk. Claire's office also contained a bright orange typist's chair, a wood-effect filing cabinet, a small fridge (which deep down she felt should be stocked with champagne but usually only contained mineral water) and an assortment of bookshelves on which dog-eared medical manuals fought for space with the chunky blockbuster novels she secretly preferred to read.

Claire liked her office. The truth was that she liked being there whenever she was alone in the house. It was a space which was exclusively hers; designed by her, furnished by her, used only by her. It had never been anything other than her office, and somehow that made her feel comforted and secure. Sometimes she sat on her orange typist's chair with her knees drawn up under her chin and told herself that her life had become particularly dreary if she felt her office was a comforting place to be. But it was.

She sat at her desk but she didn't bother pulling the manuscript she'd been working on towards her. Instead she stared at the blank computer screen and thought about Eavan's visit.

Eavan Keating was her closest friend. Claire had met her on her first day at Locum Libris, a company which published a range of medical textbooks as well as printing specialist medical magazines. Claire hadn't had any specialist knowledge when she'd joined as an office junior, but she'd learned a lot as time went on and, of course, being married to a doctor helped. Only she hadn't been married to Bill Hudson when she joined Locum Libris. But she had known that she *would* marry him. She'd known that from the start.

She closed her eyes and allowed herself to remember the first time she'd met Bill. It was her fifth birthday, and her mother had invited all the children in the small cul-de-sac where they lived to her party, sending out invitations on pink paper in pink envelopes. Claire could recall the excitement of her new pink dress, of the huge birthday cake with fat pink candles, of the pink-wrapped presents from her parents and the pink balloons tacked around the room. The other children had brought presents wrapped in pink too. Except for six-year-old Bill Hudson from two doors down. He'd handed her a box with no wrapping at all.

'I tore it off,' he said gruffly. 'It was too girly.'

Funnily, she couldn't remember now what was in the box. Sweets, she thought. Or maybe crayons. Something colourful. But she didn't take any notice because she'd felt something in her heart tug as she looked at Bill Hudson, his caramel-brown eyes defiant as he watched her carefully.

'It doesn't matter,' she'd said. 'You can have cake anyway.'

She took him by the hand and led him to the table, where she asked her mother to cut the cake so that Bill could have a slice.

'Not till all your guests are here,' Eileen had told her, and Claire had snorted and said that everyone who mattered was here and she wanted to do the cake and candles now.

It had almost become a scene because she'd seen the look in her mother's eye, but Bill had suddenly squeezed her hand and said he didn't want cake just yet, but lemonade would be nice and maybe some crisps if that was OK? And Eileen had poured him lemonade and handed him crisps, for which he thanked her graciously before trotting into the garden followed by Claire.

She'd never stopped following him.

19

Soulmates, her mother had once said. She'd told Claire that she'd grow out of her devotion to Bill Hudson eventually, though, and warned her that Bill would one day find someone else too. She had been anxious about the fact that neither of them had ever seemed to want to find someone else, and then very, very relieved when Bill had gone the fifty-odd miles from Dundalk, where they lived, to Dublin to study medicine while Claire had opted to spend a year au-pairing in France (even though Eileen hated the thought of her only child being away from her for any length of time).

'It'll be good for you to be apart for a while,' Eileen had told her that first weekend when Bill had gone to Dublin and Claire was waiting to go to Montpellier. 'You need to meet other people.'

Claire hadn't told Eileen that she and Bill had decided that too. That they'd agreed that knowing each other for so long, loving each other for so long, wasn't a good thing. Nobody married the almost-boy-next-door they'd known since they were five. It just didn't happen. And if they didn't play the field, Claire had told Bill seri-ously one evening as they sat on the low wall in front of her house, their two heads, one fair, one dark, close together, they'd regret it for ever.

So Bill had gone to Dublin and Claire had flown to France and they'd promised each other they'd keep in touch but not get too upset when, as would be bound to happen, they met other people.

Claire had been first. She hadn't expected it, stuck in the tiny town of Floret, about ten kilometres south-west of Montpellier, and being worked to the bone (so she wrote to her mother) by the Irish couple she was living with. She'd met him in the village square one day, Roger Simenon, classically tall, dark and handsome and as unlike the attractive but amiable Bill Hudson as it was possible to be. Roger, Claire decided, was already a lady-killer. He knew the moves, he knew the right things to say, he flattered her ceaselessly until she finally agreed to go to the cinema in Montpellier with him. And dinner afterwards, he promised. At a really good restaurant.

There was no doubt that Roger was charming and gorgeous and made her heart beat faster. And then one night he told her that he had booked a room for them in a little pension.

She'd stared at him wordlessly.

'You do want this, don't you?' he'd asked. 'I won't do anything you don't want, *ma mie*, but I think it's time, no?'

'What was the name of the goldfish my dad flushed down the toilet?' she asked him abruptly as they stood outside the restaurant, which had been the best so far.

'Huh?' He looked at her in astonishment.

'What's my favourite colour?'

'Claire, *chérie*, I don't—'

'Who was my teen pop idol?'

He laughed. 'Claire, Claire. None of this is important!'

'Goldie,' she told him. 'Not very original, I know. Magenta. George Michael. I still like him, though I'm not entirely convinced he'd be interested in me somehow.'

'So now I know.' Roger laughed. 'And for your information, I never had a goldfish but we had a rabbit called Déjeuner. My favourite colour is black. And I think Siobhán Fahey is pretty hot.'

'I don't love you,' she said. 'And I don't want to sleep with you.'

'Well then what the hell has the last month been all about?' he demanded.

'Making sure,' said Claire.

When she got back to the house in Floret she rang the number of Bill Hudson's Rathmines bedsit in Dublin.

'What was the name of the goldfish my dad flushed down the toilet?' she asked when he eventually came to the phone.

'Claire!' Bill blinked a few times and looked at his watch. 'It's one o'clock in the morning and you're phoning me from France. Why are you asking me a question like that at one in the morning?'

'What was its name?' she demanded.

'Goldie,' he replied. 'Like the goldfish he buried in a matchbox under the gooseberry bush and every other goldfish you possessed too, as far as I remember.'

'My favourite colour?' she asked.

'Pinky-purple,' he said. 'Darkish.'

'My teenage pop idol?'

Bill laughed. 'I was sort of hoping I was your teenage idol.'

'Pop idol,' she said urgently.

'George-bloody-when-will-he-come-out-Michael,' said Bill.

21

'I love you,' she said.

'I love you too,' replied Bill. 'Now, any chance I can get back to bed? I've an exam tomorrow.'

'I'm sorry.' Claire suddenly realised how stupid she'd been.

'Don't be,' said Bill softly. 'I've missed you, Claire. I'm glad you called.'

'I'm coming home,' she told him. 'I can't live without you.'

She told the Irish family in Floret that she'd had enough au-pairing. Niall and Theresa Carmichael were devastated to hear that she was going because Claire was good with Amy and Raul, who both adored her, and extremely hard-working around the house. (Their previous au pair had utterly refused to do any of the little light jobs Theresa had given her, like polishing their heavy oak furniture or washing the floors every day.) They offered her more money to stay. But Claire's mind was made up. Six months without Bill Hudson was six months too many.

Con and Eileen Shanahan were devastated at her return too. They might not have particularly liked the idea of her disappearing to France for a year, but they'd believed it was good for her to get away from Bill for a while. Now she was coming home and she'd informed them she was going to get a job in Dublin. If she can, Con had said sourly to Eileen. The jobs market wasn't exactly flourishing at the time.

It took Claire two weeks to get the job at Locum Libris. Her typing skills were good, thanks to the course Eileen had insisted she go on while she was in her last year at school, she had an easy, pleasant telephone manner and she picked up the medical jargon really quickly.

'You pissed me off,' Eavan told her later. 'You were too damn quick for all of us.'

But the two girls got on well together, even though Eavan had shrieked in disbelief when, a couple of weeks after joining the company, Claire had arrived at the office wearing a sapphire ring on the third finger of her left hand and told them that she and Bill would be getting married the following year.

'It's not that I don't think you should get married if you truly love this guy,' she'd told Claire after work that evening when they'd gone for a celebratory drink. 'It's just that I don't see why you need

22

to tie yourself down to one man. You're in the prime of your life, Claire. You should be hitting the clubs and having a good time.'

'Hitting the clubs and desperately seeking Mr Right,' Claire informed her. 'But you see, Eavan, I've found him already.'

And indeed, when Bill had turned up at the Locum Libris Christmas party with Claire, looking breathtakingly handsome in his rented tux, Eavan had conceded that maybe Claire had a point in marching him up the aisle as quickly as possible. Because, Eavan told her, he was so damn cute and gorgeous that unless she got a ring on his finger pretty quickly there was no doubt some other woman would make a play for him.

'I wouldn't be interested,' he told Claire when she repeated the conversation to him that night. 'I've never been interested in anyone but you.'

She was nineteen. He was twenty. She had never, for one second, regretted marrying him.

She cupped her face in her hands and willed herself not to cry. She'd allowed herself to cry at first. Bill had always told her that tears were an important part of the body's healing mechanism and she knew that he was right. But there came a time, she thought, when the tears should stop. And she was damned – she bit her lip fiercely – she was damned if she was going to cry for the first time in months when she was by herself in the house. It would be like giving in to Eavan's interfering words. She just wasn't going to do it.

Eileen had cried at her wedding. Her father, Con, hadn't. He'd squeezed her hand very hard as they got out of the car at the church and told her that he hoped she'd be very, very happy and that Bill was a great man who'd be a wonderful doctor and that she couldn't have chosen better. And he smiled at her and said that when Eileen cried, as she was bound to do, Claire wasn't to think it was because she harboured any doubts about them. Just that everyone cried at weddings.

The night before, Eileen had asked her whether she was absolutely sure that this was what she wanted to do. She was marrying someone who was still studying medicine. Her job was their main income. It was going to be a terrible struggle.

'I don't care,' Claire told her. 'I love him.'

'I don't doubt that for a moment,' agreed Eileen. 'It's just – oh, darling, you're tying yourself down, running into debt, having to worry about so many things when you should be having fun.'

'Eavan said something like that,' Claire told her. 'Bill Hudson is the best time I ever had. He always will be. He's going to be a brilliant doctor and eventually the money will come.'

Actually it had taken time before the money started to come. The week that Bill joined a general practice in North Strand, Claire discovered she was pregnant. She never told Georgia that she'd been unplanned – after all, as she once said to Eavan, they'd always intended to have children, just not at the time Georgia was conceived. But she accepted the fact that it had happened and, besides, her daughter was without doubt the most beautiful baby in the world. She'd grown into a pretty child and a stunning teenager, thought Claire, a lucky mixture of her good features (like thick hair and good cheekbones) and Bill's big brown eyes and long lashes. She was a happy, well-adjusted child too. They'd done well with Georgia.

Claire felt the pain grip her again. Bill had been so proud of his daughter. She remembered the day Georgia had started in a new school and he'd looked at her in her uniform, hair pulled back into a fat Lara Croft plait, and he'd been quite unable to speak until Georgia had kissed him on the cheek and told him they'd better get going because he was dropping her off or had he forgotten.

It's not fair, thought Claire. It's not fair that he won't get to see her grow up and have a career and hopefully a wonderful marriage of her own; it's not fair that he'll never get the pleasure of this house and garden when buying it was his dream come true for the present and for the future; it's not fair that someone who was so damn good all his life had it cut short so horribly.

She closed her eyes and bit her lip. Sometimes it seemed as though no time at all had passed since it had happened, and yet she knew that it had. But it was almost impossible to figure out what had gone on in the intervening period. Those days had merged into a jumble of time when she knew that she'd kept going but couldn't remember how. But she remembered the day everything had changed. Because it had been at the end of a wonderful week. In fact, after marrying Bill and after the birth of Georgia, the best week of her life.

Chapter 4

Dicentra (Bleeding Heart) – Locket-shaped flowers, mainly pink or red, on arching, slender stems. Can be damaged by cold winds.

They'd been on their first overseas holiday in five years and it had been an utterly wonderful ten days in an all-inclusive five-star resort in Jamaica. The best bit about the whole thing was that it had been free – to Claire's utter astonishment and amazement she'd been the winner of a competition on the back of a cornflakes packet. She had never quite believed that anyone really won competitions on the back of packets of anything. But the letter had dropped on to the mat on a particularly dreary November day of low clouds and drizzling rain and told her that the family holiday had to be taken in the next twelve months and to contact the tour operator directly.

Claire had hardly been able to wait for surgery to end that day, and events had conspired against her because there had been a steady stream of patients presenting themselves with the hacking coughs and runny noses that were always a feature of November. It was on days like this that she wished she hadn't given up her job with Locum Libris to work full-time as Bill's receptionist and administrator. Joe Halpin, the office manager at the printing and publishing firm, had tried very hard to persuade her to stay. Over the years Claire had become a valuable member of the company, with her knowledge of proof-reading and copy-editing, not to mention her quick grasp of the computer software which had transformed the industry. But she told Joe that her husband's need was greater. His latest receptionist had just handed in her notice (she'd decided to take a year off to backpack through the Himalayas) and had already started to wind

25

down. The responses to the ad he'd put in the paper had been decidedly underwhelming – although there were plenty of people prepared to work part-time, nobody really wanted the fulltime surgery hours – and in the end Claire had decided that it made more sense for her to stop commuting across the city to the new offices of Locum Libris in Dun Laoghaire when she could simply walk down the stairs and into the basement and be at work. Besides, she'd told Bill, it would give her more time with Georgia.

Eavan (who'd got married herself a few years earlier, despite telling Claire that nobody would drag her up the aisle before her thirty-fifth birthday), had told Claire that a husband and wife working together wasn't always the best idea, that they would be sick of the sight of each other. And, she said darkly, if Bill spoke sharply to her or said that her work wasn't good enough or something like that, how the hell was Claire going to react? How could she tell Bill to sod off, that she was up to her neck and entitled to spend a bit of time gazing into space if she wanted?

Claire had laughed and told Eavan that her work would always be good enough and that she rarely gazed into space. After all, she reminded her, hadn't Joe Halpin and his deputy, Trinny Armstrong, both begged her to stay because they said they couldn't do without her? They'd hardly have offered her a pay rise, stingy and all though it might have been, if they hadn't thought she was good enough.

Eavan's direst prophecies hadn't come true. Claire loved working with Bill and the practice ran more smoothly than ever before. Sometimes, as they lay beside each other in bed at night, Claire wondered how it was that she had been so lucky to meet her soulmate when she came across so many people who hadn't. Like Margaret Reilly, who regularly came to the surgery claiming to have walked into the corner of the door when everyone knew that after a couple of pints Terry Reilly would thump her. Despite Bill's advice, the woman wouldn't report her husband and wouldn't leave him. And Claire's heart would go out to her every time Margaret walked in with a bruised cheek or forehead. Samantha Walton was another regular at the surgery who hadn't been lucky with her choice of husband. Martin Walton was a serial philanderer who'd given Samantha trichomoniasis. And Bill had then had to talk to her about

26

the very real possibility of Martin picking up a more serious sexually transmitted disease and infecting Samantha with that too. There were other women, women who'd left their husbands, whose husbands had left them, who were in unhappy marriages . . . they all came to the surgery with illnesses that were sometimes physical but often a result of the stresses of their lives, and every time Claire saw Margaret or Samantha or Fiona, Sharon, Esther, Lillian or Beatrice, she thanked her own very lucky star that she had Bill Hudson.

But the only thing about Bill was his work ethic – how much effort he put into the practice and how little time they had to spend together as a family. So when she'd ripped open the envelope that November morning and had seen the amazing news that she'd won the competition, there was no doubt in her mind that this would be the trip of a lifetime. And that they were going.

Bill had agreed. He'd picked her up and swung her in the air, and Georgia had come into the room and looked at her parents in total astonishment and then had been caught up in the whooping and hollering of the excitement of a week in Jamaica.

They went in February, leaving behind a city caught in a freezing cold snap where people's breath hung in misty clouds in front of their faces and where running the central heating all day still didn't make the house completely warm. (Especially a house like Bill and Claire's which, despite all their renovations, still allowed heat to escape somehow.) It had been even colder in London, where they had to get the connecting flight – the skies were heavy and grey with yet-to-fall snow, and when their huge plane lifted off and pushed its way through the clouds Claire had closed her eyes and gripped tightly to the arm-rest of her seat, terrified by the bumping and shaking of the aircraft and convinced that they were all going to plummet to their deaths.

Both Bill and Georgia had laughed at her. Bill had started to explain about the safety of air travel and engine thrust and lift, while Georgia had said happily that it was just like being on a roller-coaster and wasn't it great fun, but Claire had continued to hold the arm-rest and begged them not to move just in case they tipped the plane over.

She'd managed to recover once they punched their way through the top of the clouds into the clear blue skies above and the turbulence eased off. By the time they were over the Atlantic she'd managed to let go of the arm-rest. And as they landed in Jamaica she'd almost got over the terror.

'But you flew to France on your own,' Bill told her when she'd explained that she'd hated every minute of the flight from Dublin to London too. 'I didn't realise you were scared.'

'I didn't really think about it when I was going to France,' she said. 'I was too busy missing you to care. And coming home I was too excited to notice. Besides,' she added, 'both times the weather was great and I don't think we bumped even once.'

'You're such a fool.' But he kissed her on the lips anyway while Georgia tried to pretend that she didn't know them.

The resort near Montego Bay was absolutely wonderful. Even though the hotel had nearly two hundred rooms and was almost full when they arrived, its huge gardens and long stretch of private beach meant that it never seemed too crowded. Bill, Claire and Georgia spent their days sunbathing, windsurfing and snorkelling, and their nights eating their way through a menu of jerk chicken, wahoo and lobster while happily (in the case of Bill and, to a lesser extent, Claire) drinking a variety of exotically named and brightly coloured cocktails. Georgia was equally happy to order vibrant fruit punches garnished with maraschino cherries and pineapple pieces. Bill told them that it was healthy eating. Claire, who reckoned that she'd put on at least a stone over the course of the week, had raised an eyebrow at him in disbelief. 'Of course it's healthy,' he said. 'Fresh food, fresh fruit and loads of vitamin D from the sun. How much healthier do you want?'

'When you put it like that . . .' Claire snuggled up to him.

'We need to go on holiday more often,' he told her. 'It's my fault, Claire. I've been so caught up in the practice and making it a success that I haven't given enough time to you or Georgia.'

'You give us plenty of time,' said Claire. 'You're always there for us.'

'No,' Bill objected. 'I'm there because the surgery is in the house, but it's not the same thing. It's not that I want to drastically cut back the surgery hours or anything, but I need to get a better balance in my life. And yours. And Georgia's.'

28

'She won't say no to seeing more of you,' agreed Claire. 'And I guess I'd be happy to see more of you outside the working relationship too!'

'Well, you will,' said Bill firmly. 'This has opened my eyes, Claire. Work isn't everything.'

'I'm glad you think so.' She kissed him very gently on the ear. 'Because I think the home balance is going to shift a little regardless.'

'Huh?' He looked at her.

'Call yourself a doctor!' She grinned. 'Why do you think I've been circumspect with the cocktails?'

'Claire!' Realisation suddenly dawned. 'You're pregnant!'

'Well done, Dr Hudson.' She laughed.

'But this is great,' he said. 'Absolutely wonderful! Georgia will be pleased.'

'I hope so.' Claire looked at him a little ruefully. 'She's been on her own for so long . . .'

'I blame myself for that too,' said Bill. 'I know we said we'd wait after Georgia but I didn't mean us to wait so long.'

'It's hardly your fault that I didn't get pregnant straight away when I stopped taking the pill,' said Claire.

'Maybe not, but . . .'

'And it doesn't matter now because I am,' she told him.

'I should have known.' Bill frowned. 'I must be a really shit husband not to have known. And a shit doctor too.'

She laughed again. 'You're always the worst patients,' she told him. 'So maybe you're entitled to be crap at diagnosing family stuff too.'

'I love you,' he said.

'I love you too.'

'I've loved you since the moment I first set eyes on you.'

'I know,' she said. 'Because it was the same for me.'

'I wonder how many people can say that they met their future partner at their fifth birthday party.'

'I wonder how many people stayed with them if they did.'

'I'm so glad we make it work,' he said.

And she kissed him.

*   *   *

29

The last time she kissed him was as they lay on the pontoon off the bay of the hotel. The three of them had swum out to it on the final morning of the holiday so that, as Claire had told them, when they got back to the frosty February air at home they could close their eyes and remember toasting themselves in the Caribbean sun. Georgia, especially, loved lying on it, allowing the sun's rays to warm her body as the floating deck beneath her bobbed up and down. When she got too hot she would stand on the edge and dive neatly and cleanly into the crystal-clear water below. Sometimes she would challenge Bill or Claire to a race back to the beach and eventually one or the other of them would rise to her taunts. On the day of the accident, neither of them felt like moving.

'I'll race her,' Bill said eventually. 'And just for once I'm not going to hold back. That girl's getting too cocky by far. I'll whip her little ass!'

'Macho bully,' said Claire. 'Don't worry. You stay there. I could probably do with working off some poundage. I'm sure the baby will be grateful.'

'You'll lose,' he told her.

'I know,' she said and kissed him.

She was vaguely aware of the roar of an engine as she stood on the pontoon and dived into the water. What she didn't know was that the engine sound was from an out-of-control jet-ski which was heading straight for them. Almost as soon as Claire had struck out for the shore, the jet-ski crashed into the wooden pontoon, flinging its seventeen-year-old driver into the air, slicing the wood from beneath Bill Hudson and then careering madly into the rock and concrete jetty a few yards away.

Claire was aware of the enormous tidal rush that dragged her under the water, the sudden silence and fizz of bubbles and then the loudest bang she'd ever heard in her life.

And that was the last thing she remembered until she woke up in hospital with Eileen sitting beside the bed.

Her first frantic thought had been of Georgia. Eileen had taken her by the hand and told her very, very quickly that she wasn't to worry, that Georgia was alive and that she'd be all right. She had injuries,

Eileen said, but they were mainly superficial cuts and bruises. Although – Eileen swallowed hard when she said this – Georgia had lost a finger in the accident. The little finger of her left hand. It had been crushed between the rock and a piece of debris and it couldn't be saved. Claire had stared at her mother in silent shock as she heard the words. Then she whispered, 'Bill?' even though she knew there was no point in asking. She'd known, from the moment Eileen had told her that Georgia was all right, that Bill wasn't.

'He . . . his neck was broken,' Eileen told her. 'The jet-ski caught him and . . . well . . . it was instantaneous, Claire. He didn't suffer. The driver of the jet-ski died too.'

Claire couldn't speak and she couldn't cry. She stared at her mother, dry-eyed.

'It was pandemonium.' The tears had begun to roll down Eileen's face. 'At first people thought you and Georgey had been drowned. They couldn't see you. There was the explosion, you see, when the jet-ski hit the jetty. Some of the tourists took photographs. They gave them to us, for the insurance. It was . . . unbelievable.'

'You're OK,' Con told her. 'Your main injury is your leg. It was hit by flying debris and your knee is damaged. You've hurt your hip too.'

'My baby,' whispered Claire. 'What about my baby?'

'Besides her finger, Georgey has lots of scrapes and bruises,' Con said. 'She was furthest away but the huge wave knocked her against the jetty.'

Eileen took hold of Claire's other hand. 'The unborn baby,' she said with difficulty. 'Oh, Claire, I'm so, so sorry. You lost it.'

And then Claire cried, at first with silent, heaving sobs and then louder and louder so that eventually a nurse hurried into the room and shooed Con and Eileen out before sedating her.

She opened her eyes and looked at the computer screen again. She rarely allowed the memories of the accident to come to the surface of her mind any more. Doctors, friends of Bill, had recommended counselling for her, but she'd refused. Claire had often suggested that some of Bill's patients needed counselling when they discovered they had serious illnesses, but she never felt it was anything that could help her personally. She had reserves, she once told Bill, to draw on. And when he'd asked what they were, she'd replied that they were knowing that there was someone like him who loved her. Now Bill was gone, she still clung to the feeling that she had her own reserves and that she didn't need to talk to anyone. Besides, she'd muttered to Eileen who'd asked about it, she didn't want to relive that day over and over again. She wanted to forget it. She didn't want to talk about how she'd felt when she discovered that her husband was dead. She didn't want to remember what it was like to walk unsteadily into Georgia's room and see her little girl a white face against a white pillow in the hospital bed, the cut on her cheek standing out because of the livid purple bruise around it and the six stitches it had needed. Georgia had opened her dark eyes when Claire had come in to see her and had smiled faintly despite her swollen lip.

Claire had put her arms around her daughter and told her that she was all right. Georgia had sighed deeply and gone back to sleep without saying anything, and Claire had felt only relief that her daughter was awake and, despite her injuries, in no danger. It was on the second visit, when Claire had to tell her about Bill's death, that Georgia looked at her silently and then cried. At first Claire hadn't even realised that Georgia wasn't speaking. Words seemed unimportant. But when all of her questions to her daughter were responded to by a shrug or a squeezing of her hand, Claire suddenly realised that something was badly wrong.

The doctor had told her that Georgia was traumatised by the accident and that she would speak again as soon as she'd managed to deal with everything. He'd given Claire the impression that Georgia would talk in a day or two, when she felt able. When a week went by and still her daughter hadn't uttered a word, Claire began to feel more and more panicked. At the same time she had to help with the arrangements to get them all home. And then there was Bill's funeral, although she left most of that to his parents, Jessie and Seamus, happy to go along with whatever they decided. Very few people were aware that Georgia didn't say anything that day, although Jessie had remarked to Claire that the little girl was very quiet. Claire left it until after the funeral to tell Bill's parents that the shock of the accident had left Georgia temporarily unable to speak. They'd looked at her in horror, their faces mirroring her own fear that Georgia might never speak again.

Nobody could really give her much information on Georgia's sudden silence. The doctors – and she'd had the best because of Bill – said that there was nothing physically wrong. Georgia was checked by a leading neurologist. A psychiatrist told Claire that Georgia needed time to come to terms with what had happened. It wasn't unheard of, he explained, for people to retreat into silence when confronted with a life-changing trauma. But he wasn't able to tell her when, or if, Georgia would talk again. He suggested time with a therapist which Claire (even though she wouldn't have anything to do with one herself) had agreed to immediately. And Georgia had gone along to every visit and had stayed perfectly silent the whole time. Claire knew that her daughter could understand everything that was being said to her. She knew that she wasn't in any way brain-damaged. But she was fearful all the same.

The weird thing was, she remembered, that Georgia had developed a way of communicating with her almost immediately. Of course Claire spoke to her daughter all the time, but Georgia herself responded with hand signals and gestures which were breathtakingly easy to understand, even when the issue was complex. Claire had to work hard to stop herself from using signals in return. She also tried to ask Georgia difficult questions, hoping it would force her to speak, but Georgia had remained obstinately silent. It wasn't as though she didn't *want* to talk, Claire conceded, but somehow she simply wasn't able to put her thoughts into sounds.

The breakthrough, when it came, was sudden and unexpected. They'd been sitting together in the living room watching an episode of *Malcolm in the Middle* when Phydough, bought by Claire a few weeks earlier in the hope of unlocking Georgia's silence, had trotted into the room wagging his tail excitably. Georgia's bottle of orange juice had been balanced precariously on the arm of the sofa in defiance of a request from Claire to put it somewhere safer. The dog's tail caught it and upended it on to Georgia's lap. She'd jumped up in dismay and cried out Phydough's name.

Both Phydough, who'd never heard her voice before, and Claire, who, for a moment, didn't realise what had just happened and was watching the bright orange liquid stain her pale green sofa, looked at Georgia in surprise. And Georgia herself had whispered Phydough's name over and over again as though she was afraid to stop. They'd had a family party to celebrate the return of Georgia's voice. A small party – both sets of grandparents, Bill's younger brother, Graham, and his wife Colette, and his older sister, Lissa, and her husband Matthew. Georgia had talked to them all in a voice that was still a little croaky and they'd all laughed and joked with her as they'd done when Bill was alive.

'I miss him,' she'd told Claire hoarsely later that night when they'd all gone home. 'I wish it had been me that was killed.'

'Georgia!' Claire was horrified. 'Your dad wouldn't have wanted you to be killed. You're young – you've got your whole life to lead.'

'But he only led half of his,' she said sadly. 'It's not fair.'

'No.' Claire hugged her close. 'It's not fair. But life isn't fair, Georgey-girl.'

'You miss him too,' said Georgia. 'I can see it. You didn't want him to die.'

'Of course not,' said Claire into Georgia's long wavy hair. 'But I certainly wouldn't trade you for him either. It was a terrible thing for all of us. But you and me – we've got to go on living.'

And that was why, she thought to herself as she hit the keyboard and woke the computer from sleep, she'd gone back to work with Locum Libris. She'd called Joe Halpin, who had already sent her a card expressing his condolences because news of Bill's tragic death had been reported on TV and in the newspapers. She'd asked him if there was any copy-editing she could do for them because she needed to be at home for Georgia but she also needed to earn some money. There was insurance, she told him, and a further claim still to be settled. But as far as she was concerned she couldn't sit at home with nothing to do. She wouldn't be able to do that without remembering day after day, and she didn't want to remember. Not like that.

Joe told her that he'd be delighted to have her back. She could do copy-editing at home, he said. And if she wanted to come in a couple of mornings a week there was always work to be done on the trade magazines.

She thanked him profusely and went back to work. She'd used

some of the insurance money to kit out the office, taking Georgia with her to choose the ice-white computer and the maple desk as well as the other furniture. The orange typist's chair and multicoloured filing trays had been Georgia's choices. And now Claire truly was busy. Joe had taken her at her word when she said that she was prepared to do as much work as he could throw at her.

So when I tell someone like Eavan Keating that I'm too busy to go out drinking with people from the Smash & Grab club I'm not lying, she muttered as she looked at the various files on the computer's desktop. I have loads of things to keep me going. Whether Georgia is here or not. She blinked away the tears that had welled up in her eyes and opened the email programme. She knew that Joe had planned to send her some additional files the previous night and she hadn't bothered to log in that morning. So she wanted to download them now.

Along with Joe's files was a picture sent from Georgia's mobile phone of herself and Robyn standing outside the college building. *As u can c here now*, Georgia had written, *all OK. Bibifn*.

I love her, thought Claire as she looked at the photo of the two smiling girls. I don't want anything ever to happen to her. She's the most important thing in my life. To be honest, the only important thing in my life any more.

Chapter 5

Ligularia (Golden Rays) – Yellow and orange flowers. Needs space and some shade. Water copiously in dry weather.

The white fluffy clouds that had dotted the sky in the morning had gradually disappeared during the day, leaving a vast expanse of unbroken blue. Eavan Keating, and the rest of the people from the Smash & Grab club who were meeting for drinks, decided to get to the pub as early as possible so that they could stake a claim to some seats in the beer garden which they knew would be crowded. Eavan and Glenn (who didn't play either tennis or badminton but who regularly called in to the clubhouse near Sutton Cross) arrived first and bagged a table.

'I do hope Saffy doesn't act up on Candida tonight,' said Eavan as she checked her mobile to make sure she hadn't missed a message from their eighteen-year-old babysitter. 'She's been a devil all day!'

'Like her mother,' said Glenn. 'Contrary.'

'Shut up.' Eavan pushed him gently. 'I'm not in the slightest contrary. I'm a wonderful person to live with.'

Glenn laughed and went into the pub to get some drinks. He returned with a glass of white wine for Eavan and a sparkling water for himself.

'I was thinking of doing a water crawl tonight,' he remarked as he sat down beside her. 'They're offering two for the price of one on flavoured ones.'

'What flavour is that?' she asked, nodding at the drink in front of him.

'Plain,' he said. 'I'd ordered it before I saw the special offer.'

'So you'll overdose on cranberry and apple?' she asked in amusement.

'Maybe.'

He took a sip of the sparkling water and Eavan smiled at him. When she'd first started going out with him she'd been surprised that he didn't drink alcohol at all. Then he'd told her that it was simply that he didn't drink it now and hadn't for the last five years. He was an alcoholic, he said, and some of the worst moments of his life had been spent in pubs.

Eavan had been horrified that she'd suggested meeting in a pub in the first place but Glenn told her that he still liked the atmosphere and the social nature of it all and that he hadn't stopped going to them just because he'd stopped drinking alcohol. At first she hadn't quite believed him, but after five years of marriage she realised he'd been telling the truth. And that he wasn't the kind of reformed drinker who lectured everyone else about the evils of alcohol. Although, as he told her, it was sometimes hard to keep a straight face when people around him got drunk.

'And you never want any yourself?' she'd asked.

'Oh, sometimes I crave it,' he'd admitted honestly. 'Sometimes I think there's nothing I'd like more than to crack open a beer and chug it back. But it would be a very fleeting pleasure compared with what would happen to me afterwards.'

'So if you say that you want just one drink . . .'

'That's not an option,' he'd said firmly. 'Never, ever let me have just one drink.'

Now she leaned across the table and kissed him on the lips.

'What was that for?' he asked.

'Just because,' she told him.

'And just as well you got it in now,' he said. 'The gang is starting to arrive!' He stood up and waved at the people who had just walked in to the beer garden, then helped them to drag wooden chairs across the flagstones so that they formed a group together.

'So, Paul, come on – tell us all about Oz,' demanded Eavan as a tall man in his early thirties joined them. He was wearing baggy cargo pants and a Day-Glo-green T-shirt. 'Was it worth the year off?'

'It was absolutely brilliant,' Paul told her. 'And totally worth chucking in my job for. I had a great time.'

'I admire your nerve,' said Glenn. 'I can't imagine just packing it all in.'

'That's 'cos you have Eavan and Saffy to worry about,' said Paul. 'I've no ties, so why shouldn't I get around a bit?'

'I don't mind having family ties,' admitted Glenn. 'But I've rather missed my chance to travel the world.'

'I didn't quite manage the world,' Paul said. 'But the funny thing is, no matter where you go, people are still looking for the perfect person to settle down with.'

'What about those Aussie women?' teased Eavan. 'None of them get their claws into you?'

'I'm waiting for the perfect woman to come along,' Paul told her.

Glenn chortled. 'You'll be bloody waiting, mate – ouch!' He winced as Eavan hit him lightly on the back of the head.

'Henpecked,' said Paul as he lifted the glass in his hand. 'Well, cheers, mates!'

'Cheers!' cried the group in response.

Eavan looked at her watch and frowned. 'Still no sign of Claire,' she said to Glenn.

'We got here early,' he reminded her. 'She could still show up.'

'I bet she won't,' said Eavan.

'It's her first day on her own,' Glenn said. 'You don't have to fret just because you haven't managed to get her out tonight.'

'Do you think I'm interfering too much?'

'No.' He put his arm around her shoulders. 'I think you're a great friend and she's lucky to have you.'

'Oh!' Suddenly Eavan's hand flew to her mouth in dismay. 'I've just thought . . .'

'What?'

'I told her we were meeting for drinks. But I didn't say here. She might think it's at the club. She might be in Sutton instead of Howth.'

'She won't think that,' said Glenn. 'Whenever we meet for drinks it's here.'

'Yes, but it's so long since she's met the whole gang,' said Eavan.

'D'you want to call her?' asked Glenn.

'Maybe I should,' replied Eavan. 'But we had a bit of a go at each other . . . I'm not sure whether it'd be a good idea. Talking to me again might put her off altogether.'

Claire had spent most of the afternoon in her office ploughing her way through a tract on *Helicobacter pylori*, a bacterium which had been found to cause stomach ulcers. She wondered why it was that people who were experts in certain fields had to write in such a boring way. Surely the information about *Helicobacter pylori* could be made more interesting? But maybe it wasn't meant to be interesting because it was only going to be read by other medical people. All the same, Claire thought, they could make it a little less soporific, if only for the sake of proof-readers.

She was still reading through the papers when she heard the padding of paws on the stairs and Phydough pushed the office door open. She kept reading until the dog put his head on her lap. And then she realised that he had his leash in his mouth.

'Oh, Phy!' She looked guiltily at him. 'Your walk. I forgot.'

He barked at her.

'I know, I know. I'm a horrible person,' she told him. 'Can you wait until I finish another five pages?'

The dog barked again and Claire rolled her chair back from the desk. 'You know, you're right,' she said. 'I promised you a walk later, and it is later. Much later.' She looked at her watch. 'Nearly seven, Phy. I completely lost track of time. Probably because it's bright and sunny. Let me change into my tracksuit bottoms and trainers and we'll go out.'

Still with the leash in his mouth, Phydough followed Claire into her bedroom where she took off her navy trousers and patterned blouse and stood near the full-length mirror in her bra and knickers. She glanced at her reflection and made a face.

Too skinny. When people talked about it not being possible to be too rich or too thin, they weren't talking about her type of skinniness. They were talking about tall, reed-like models with flawless complexions and toned bodies. Her skin wasn't flawless (how on earth could you be the wrong side of thirty-five and still break out in spots, she wondered – what kind of trick was that for nature to play on anyone?) and her body certainly wasn't toned. Besides, she might be skinny these days but she somehow managed to have dimply thighs and a low-slung belly with the zippered scar of her Caesarean section still visible after fourteen years. And, of course, the more recent scar from her knee surgery and the other tiny scars on her legs were still achingly visible. She reached for her T-shirt and track-suit. Better to hide it all, she thought. Anyway, most people looked better with their clothes on. Claire had never quite understood the allure of a nudist beach. Surely anyone with any degree of concern about the way they looked would be turned into a quivering wreck at the idea of displaying themselves in all their glory for people to see!

Phydough watched as she laced up her trainers and checked to make sure they weren't rubbing her blisters. He hurried down the stairs ahead of her and waited impatiently at the front door while she set the alarm and took her keys from the hall table.

'Slow down,' she cried as he hauled her down the garden path and immediately made for the coast. 'Phydough! Heel!'

He was well trained but eager to get out and about. She allowed him to drag her down the road and towards the sea front. The grassy walk along the north side of the bay was thronged with people taking advantage of the change in the weather. Claire kept a firm hold on Phydough's leash, conscious of the other dogs being walked in the area too. He hadn't had his morning walk because of Georgia's depar-ture for the Gaeltacht and she was finding it difficult to keep him under control. She hadn't intended to make this a long walk either, but now she was filled with guilt and decided that the bacterium could wait while Phydough had some much-needed exercise.

'We'll go to Dollymount,' she told him, 'and then you can have a run in the sand dunes.'

What does he hear when I talk to him? she wondered. Just a jumble of sounds, or does each word sound different? And if he can under-stand *walk* and *sit* and *no*, how come he can't understand other things?

The breeze, blowing from the south instead of from the bay as usual, was warm. Claire felt her spirits lift as she matched her pace to that of her dog. She'd spent too long at one go in front of the ice-white computer and her neck was sore. It was good to stretch out and walk in the fresh air.

By the time they reached the sand dunes, though, her legs were tired and her ankle was beginning to hurt a little again. She took off her trainers and socks and walked in the still-damp sand while Phydough raced enthusiastically through the dunes.

Her mobile rang as she abandoned the task of trying to keep up with him and flopped down on the spiky grass.

'Hi, Mum!' cried Georgia. 'How's it going?'

'Great,' she replied, happy to hear her daughter's voice. 'How are you? What's it like there?'

'It's brilliant,' Georgia said. 'Me and Robs are sharing a room in a lovely house. It's a bit Laura Ashley but it's cute. Sive and Emma are staying here too. The rest of the gang are in a house about five minutes away. Did you get my e-mail?'

'Of course,' said Claire. 'Thanks for sending it.'

'The weather's great here,' continued Georgia. 'We've done registration and stuff this afternoon and there's a big get-together in the college this evening.'

'How's the Irish coming along?' asked Claire.

'Oh well, we haven't had classes or anything so far,' said Georgia, 'so it's really only having to say things like please and thank you. They won't let us have our mobiles switched on during the day apparently, so that we can't be tainted by outside influences.'

'Oh.'

'And we're not supposed to keep ringing home and talking *as Bearla*. The *Bean an Tís* keep an eye on us. It's a great expression, isn't it? Woman of the House?'

Claire laughed. 'It has a certain charm.'

'But I'll call when I can and text you every night,' promised Georgia.

'Don't get into trouble calling me,' said Claire. 'A text is fine. All I need to know is that you're OK and having a good time.'

'I think it's going to be fun,' said Georgia. 'And there's some really good-looking blokes too.'

'Georgia Hudson! I didn't send you to the Gaeltacht to pick up boys.'

41

'It's not my main game plan,' Georgia assured her. 'But you never know, do you?'

'Indeed.'

'I've got to go,' Georgia said. 'What are you doing now?'

'Actually, I'm walking Phydough,' said Claire. 'I forgot this afternoon when I got home and he came and prised me away from my desk.'

'Poor Phy.' It was normally Georgia's responsibility to take him for a walk in the afternoons when she got home from school. 'Is he missing me?'

'I'm sure he is.'

'Well, look after yourself, Mum. Don't work too hard. Don't forget to take him for his walks.'

'I won't,' promised Claire.

'And remember what I said about the sleazy nightclubs!'

Claire laughed. 'Sure will.'

'Talk soon,' said Georgia.

'Take care,' said Claire and put the phone back in her pocket. She pulled on her socks and trainers again and then whistled for Phydough, who was frantically chasing seagulls but who loped up to her, tongue hanging out of his mouth.

'Come on,' she said. 'Time to go.'

She clipped his leash back on to his collar and headed towards home. Her phone rang again and she slid it out of her pocket.

'Hi,' she said, without looking at the caller ID.

'Claire Hudson, where the hell are you?' asked Eavan.

'Oh, Eavan, hello.'

'Claire, we're all out here in the beer garden. You didn't go to the clubhouse, did you?'

For a moment Claire was tempted to lie and to say that she had gone to Sutton instead of Howth. She knew that if she said she'd forgotten about the drinks that evening her friend wouldn't believe her. And she hadn't exactly forgotten. She'd just pushed it to the back of her mind.

'Um, no, I didn't,' she admitted finally.

'Well, where are you?' demanded Eavan. 'I thought you were going to come tonight.'

'I didn't promise,' said Claire. 'I'm walking the dog. I got caught up in some stuff after you left and I forgot about walking him. So I'm doing it now.'

'Oh, Claire! Listen, I'm sorry if you thought . . . well, if I was a bit abrupt with you earlier.'

'It's OK,' said Claire.

'Anyway, look, it's not that late. Why don't you come and join us? It's lovely and balmy and the gang's all here. We're having great fun. Paul Hanratty's back from Oz. He was asking about you just now. Oh, hold on, Claire . . .'

Claire heard a scuffling noise and then Paul's rich, deep voice. The sexiest voice in the club, someone had once said. That was definitely true, thought Claire. Pity about his skinny legs, though.

'Paul, hi, how was Oz?'

'Had a fantastic time,' he told her. 'How are you keeping?'

'Pretty good,' she said. 'Walking the dog.'

'I thought you were coming out for drinks with us. You're the only reason I turned up.' But he laughed to show he was joking.

'Sorry, Paul. I know I half said I'd come, but I got busy.'

'Well, look, I'd love to see you again. Catch up on old times.'

'Oh, I don't know if there's much to catch up on.'

'C'mon, Claire. You were my partner. We were the best team in the club!'

'Flattery will get you nowhere,' she told him sternly.

'Show you my Oz photos,' he added. 'In which I look fit and tanned and much healthier than the pasty bloke you knew and loved.'

She laughed. 'You weren't at all pasty,' she told him. 'You know quite well that there was a small army of women who thought you were rather attractive.'

'Not you, though, unfortunately.'

Claire said nothing.

'Shit, sorry, Claire. I didn't mean it like that.' Paul sounded uncomfortable. 'I was joking. Not very sensitive of me.'

'That's OK,' said Claire briskly.

'One drink, then. To show you forgive me.'

'Well, maybe. Can I let you— Oh hell! Phydough!'

'What's the matter?' asked Paul.

'Nothing. I let the leash go by accident and now the dog's gone frolicking ahead of me. I gotta go, Paul.' She hung up abruptly and hurried after Phydough.

'That's that,' said Paul as he handed the phone back to Eavan. 'She's gone chasing her dog.'

'That bloody dog!' Eavan made a face. 'She's nearly as cracked about it as she is about Georgia. So no luck with the drink?'

Paul frowned. 'She said maybe.'

'Really?' Eavan's face brightened. 'That's a big step.'

'Is it? I thought she might just be trying to get rid of me.'

'Let's wait and see,' said Eavan. 'If you haven't heard from her—'

'Hey, I like her, she's a friend. A good friend, we used to click on court, you know. But I'm not calling her again. If she doesn't want to come for a drink, that's her business.'

'Perhaps she *will* call. I know there wasn't anything between you 'cos she was married and she's older than you . . . and you were going out with someone else then . . . but . . . could there be?'

'God help us, Eavan, you're kind of jumping the gun a bit. Like I said, she was a friend and I liked her. That's all.'

'Should I just butt out?' Eavan turned to look at Glenn, who'd been listening to them. 'Am I trying too hard? I mean, if she wants to rot at home for a month on her own, isn't it her decision?'

'Probably,' said Glenn. 'And you're a hopeless matchmaker anyway!' He grinned at Paul. 'Sorry, mate, she can't help herself.'

'No worries.' Paul smiled back. 'C'mon. Let's forget about Claire and have some fun.'

'Phydough!' called Claire as she ran after him. 'Heel! Heel! Oh, fucking hell . . .'

The dog had been running in a zigzag across the grass and had raced across the path in front of a pair of joggers. One, a girl in her twenties, had managed to sidestep him, but her male companion had tripped over him and now lay sprawled across the grass, Phydough happily licking his face.

'Get off!' said the man on the ground as he hauled himself upright. 'Get the hell off of me, you mad mutt.'

'I'm so, so sorry!' gasped Claire as she caught up with Phydough and grabbed the leash. 'It was an accident. He wouldn't have bitten you or anything, he's a complete softie.'

'People with Rottweilers say that,' said the man, who Claire estimated was closer to her own age, and who was brushing grass from his body, 'just after they've savaged some poor kid.'

'Phydough wouldn't savage anyone,' said Claire defensively. 'He was just a bit overexcited.'

'He's gorgeous.' The girl leaned down and petted him. 'Oh, come on, Nate – he's cute.'

'He's a miniature elephant. He's not cute,' snarled Nate. 'I think I've twisted my ankle.'

'You are such a baby!' The girl winked at Claire. 'I must apologise for him,' she said. 'He's not normally such a grouch. But we've been under a bit of stress lately what with getting our business off the ground and everything. And of course Nate's had a lot of stuff of his own to worry about. You just wouldn't believe how . . .'

'Sarah!' Nate looked grimly at her. 'This woman doesn't need to know our entire history.'

'Sorry.' This time Sarah looked abashed. 'I do ramble a bit.'

'It's OK,' said Claire. 'And it was my fault entirely. I let go of his leash. I hope you're not hurt.'

'If you can't control the dog then you shouldn't have him out,' said Nate, who was rubbing his back gingerly. 'Come on, Sarah. Let's get on with it. I know we were making really good time before being knocked over.'

'I said I was sorry.' Claire was pissed off with him now. 'You can see he's harmless.'

'He's lovely.' Sarah tightened a scrunchie around what Claire guessed was a mass of flaming red hair securely tied behind her head. The sunlight glinted off a huge ring on her engagement finger. Claire couldn't help noticing a gold wedding band too. 'And Nate is being unaccountably rude. The only thing hurt is his pride.'

Claire smiled at her, and Sarah's green eyes sparkled. Her husband (though Claire couldn't understand why such a grumpy man was married to such a friendly girl) had finished brushing the grass from his clothes and looked at Claire in annoyance. She was surprised to see that one of his eyes was green, like Sarah's, and the other a vivid blue. It made his irritated look even more disconcerting.

'My pride isn't hurt,' he said. 'My back is. And so's my ankle.'

'Oh, you're fine,' said Sarah. 'Honestly. Men. You'd swear you'd fallen fifty feet or something.' She laughed suddenly. 'Just as well you're not any taller. You'd be even crankier.'

He was tall enough, thought Claire. At least six foot, and broad-shouldered. But a complete wuss to be knocked over by a dog as gentle as Phydough. Even if Phy probably weighed as much as him.

'I'm all right,' he conceded, abruptly looking away from Claire. 'But you need to be able to control a dog that size.'

'I do!' Claire was about to protest even more, but Sarah grabbed Nate by the arm.

'Come on, you big lug,' she said cheerfully. 'I'll race you.'

Claire shivered as they ran off. She could never hear anyone say the words 'I'll race you' without thinking of diving into the water to race Georgia just before the jet-ski hit the pontoon. She exhaled slowly. The sequence was still running in her head – the engine sound, the dive, the rush of water . . . then the hospital and finally the taxi ride to the airport on the day they were due to go home. It was the taxi ride that had sparked off her loathing of cars, because it was then that it had all suddenly hit her. The fact that she'd nearly drowned. That Georgia was maimed for life. That Bill, the only man she'd ever loved, was dead and about to be shipped home in a box; and that she'd lost, not only her husband, but also their longed-for second child. She'd started to shake in the taxi, her teeth chattering and her body suddenly cold despite the perfect temperature. And still the moment before the accident flashed through her brain; the moment when everything was exactly right, when she and Georgia and Bill were having the holiday of a lifetime; the moment before everything changed completely.

Eileen had noticed her trembling and had put her arm around her. Georgia, on Claire's other side, hadn't seemed to notice anything. She was sitting staring out of the window in the silence that would last for three anxiety-ridden months. And Claire had struggled to get herself under control so that she could be strong for the daughter who needed her, even though she felt like collapsing in a heap on the floor of the cab.

She'd been fine on the plane. She hadn't cared when they hit a patch of turbulence because right then she'd thought that if the 747 did plunge into the sea it wouldn't make any difference to her. Or to Georgia. The whole family would be together again. And though she tried not to think like that, she really couldn't help it. But in the car on the way back from Dublin airport she began to shake again as the memories came back, sharper than ever. Over the next few weeks it seemed to her that even the idea of getting in a car made her tremble. She knew she certainly couldn't drive one.

Nobody noticed at first. She and Georgia had stayed for a week with Eileen and Con and they hadn't gone anywhere. When it was time for them to come back to Dublin, Claire had said that she wanted to get the train.

'Why?' Con had looked at her in utter astonishment. 'You need to bring home your cases.'

'Bring them down next time,' said Claire. 'It's mostly holiday stuff. We don't need it.'

Eileen had told Con to let Claire and Georgia take the train if that was what they wanted, but to drive down himself with their things.

Eventually Claire sold Bill's gold Toyota. She told Georgia she wouldn't be able to drive for ages because of her leg. Georgia had shrugged her shoulders and gone back to watching the TV. She'd never once asked about getting another car.

The flashback faded and Claire was back on the seafront again. Phydough sat quietly at her feet.

'You know, don't you?' she said, bending down to him, her eyes filling with tears. 'You know when I'm upset. You don't act up and run around like a lunatic then, do you? You're a good, good dog.'

Phydough barked.

'I'm OK now,' she said. 'Let's go home.'

Chapter 6

Torenia (Wishbone Flower) – Flowers abundantly in a variety of colours.
Needs support. Prefers sun or partial shade.

Almost a week later, Georgia Hudson sat cross-legged on one of the two single beds in the small but warmly decorated bedroom of the house in Galway where she and Robyn, plus four other girls who were attending the Irish College, were staying. She was playing Triple Pop on her mobile phone, spinning the coloured balls around with an ease that would have bemused Claire if she'd been there to see it. On the other bed, Robyn O'Malley was tapping out messages to their friends who were still out.

'The great thing about texting is that you don't have to do it in Irish,' she murmured to her friend. 'Although I think I'm getting better at it.'

'I'm getting better at speaking it.' Georgia didn't look up from her game. 'Even after a week. But I can't spell it for nuts. Not that I'm much at spelling anyway. Mum is forever giving me grief about it. But like I tell her, with spell-check, who needs it?'

Robyn nodded as she sent a group message to the other girls from Dublin who'd come with them to the west of Ireland. 'Still, it's a bit of fun, isn't it?' She finally looked up at Georgia.

The other girl ended the game and nodded. 'And I'm sorry about tonight. I know you were looking forward to the céili.'

Robyn shrugged. 'Are you feeling OK now?'

'Yes,' answered Georgia. 'I'm sorry if I messed it up for you. But my stomach really hurt.'

Robyn put her phone on the bedside locker. 'Was it honestly

your stomach or was it Jamesie and his mates?' she asked matter-of-factly.

Georgia made a face at her friend. 'It really was my stomach. The other thing – it's their problem really. I think it's that Mum doesn't cook half as much red meat as we get here and those meatball things at lunch were pretty gross. I wanted to go out too, you know. I liked the session on Wednesday even though . . .' She rubbed her left hand absent-mindedly. 'It's his problem, not mine. It wasn't him that made me want to stay in tonight, Robs, honestly. Some people are just ignorant pigs. No, I just felt sick. I'm sorry, 'cos I'm fine now. You shouldn't have stayed with me. You might have done OK with Peadar . . .'

'If he's interested he'll still be there tomorrow.' Robyn shook out her mane of strawberry-blonde hair. 'And there are other blokes out there for you. Stiofán Ó Sé, for example.'

'Oh, come on, Steve's not interested in me.' Georgia blushed.

'Yes he is.'

'Not really,' said Georgia. 'Be realistic, none of them fancies me after a while.'

'Nonsense,' Robyn told her. 'Anyway Steve said it to Annelise McNally and she told Laureen Keogh . . . he definitely fancies you, Georgia.'

'It won't last.'

'Don't be so stupid.' Robyn shook out her hair again and then picked up a hand-mirror to examine the minuscule spot on her cheek. 'You're by far the best-looking of us, and you've got great tits.'

Georgia giggled and blushed again.

'Well you have.' Robyn picked at her spot. 'I wish I had a chest like yours.'

'No you don't,' said Georgia. 'I mean, what if it doesn't stop? What if I'm totally huge in a couple of years?'

'Like that's a problem?' Robyn looked at her in astonishment.

'I don't want to be kind of top-heavy,' said Georgia. 'Like Jordan or someone. It's gross.'

'You'll be gorgeous,' Robyn assured her.

'No way.'

'Absolutely,' said Robyn.

'Gorgeous girls don't have scars that mean stupid blokes make rude comments.'

'Georgia Hudson, you've a mark on your cheek that you'd need a microscope to find,' said Robyn sternly. 'It hardly counts.'

'And what about this?' Georgia held up her hand. 'Not that I care any more but Jamesie and Co weren't very nice about it, were they?'

Robyn looked at it blandly, accustomed to the sight of Georgia's missing little finger. 'Like you said, it's his problem,' she said dismissively. 'And anyone who makes a comment about it isn't worth knowing. Doesn't stop you from doing anything yourself, does it?'

'Messes up my keyboarding,' Georgia told her.

Robyn snorted.

'Look, I know that I'm not a complete hag or anything,' Georgia agreed. 'Though the finger makes a difference, no matter what you say. I know. I know,' she added as Robyn opened her mouth to speak. 'He's a moron. Only . . . I thought he was nicer than that, and now . . . Anyway, it's not only my face that has scars, it's my arms too.' She extended them so that Robyn could see the network of tiny white marks that criss-crossed her slim, tanned limbs. 'And so . . . well, Robyn, why would anyone want me when they can have someone without marks and who isn't missing any bits who their mates can't make fun of?'

'"Cos it isn't the marks or the missing bits that count,' Robyn said.

'I wish you were right.' Georgia sighed. 'But somehow I don't really think so.'

'I told you – anyone who cares about the way people look isn't worth knowing,' Robyn said firmly.

'But Robs, that's just about everyone when you really think about it,' said Georgia ruefully as she began another game on her phone.

Claire was sitting outside a pub at the Pavilion in Dun Laoghaire. She couldn't remember the last time she'd been in a pub (or even outside one) at eight o'clock on a Friday evening, but when she'd dropped over to Locum Libris that afternoon with a bundle of work, Trinny Armstrong had invited her for drinks with the rest of the production department. They were celebrating Trinny's thirty-fourth birthday. Trinny, with her usual panache, had ordered a bottle of champagne and Claire was sipping the celebratory drink and trying not to remember that the last time she'd drunk champagne had been on the Jamaican holiday with Bill.

She listened idly to the conversation of her colleagues as they admired the delicate pendant with a single drop diamond that Trinny's boyfriend, Josh, had given her for her birthday and then teased her about the fact that the next diamond he bought her might be an engagement ring. Trinny, as always, insisted that she'd no interest whatsoever in getting engaged, declaring that she was still far too young to even think about it, that there were lots more things in her life she wanted to do before being hauled up the aisle. Claire drained her glass and regarded Trinny thoughtfully. The other girl wasn't that much younger than her really. And yet she seemed to be a completely different generation. Is it only me, Claire wondered, who thinks that being in love was the most important thing that could ever happen in my life? Or is that simply because of Bill? If he hadn't been around would I be like Trinny now – like almost everyone else here – wanting to have a good time and hating the idea of settling down with one man?

'Here you are!' Joanna Harris put a glass of wine in front of Claire, who looked at her in surprise.

'You were in a world of your own when we ordered,' Joanna told her.

'I'm not sure . . .' Claire protested.

'Oh, c'mon, Claire.' Trinny's tone was persuasive. 'You hardly ever come out with us. It's my birthday! Celebrate.'

'I . . . of course,' said Claire. The unaccustomed glass of champagne had gone to her head and she didn't really want anything else. But she couldn't say no. She was always saying no. She raised the glass half-heartedly. 'Happy birthday again, Trinny.'

'Thank you.' Trinny grinned.

'I don't know why you celebrate them at all,' muttered Joanna. 'I try to pretend they don't happen these days.'

'So do I,' said Trinny's assistant, Rosie, gloomily. 'You might want to be footloose and fancy free, Trinny, but it's been six months since I've gone out with anyone and I'm a year older than you!'

Hah! thought Claire, a little triumphantly. It isn't only me who thinks love is important. Rosie does too.

'Tch, tch.' Trinny shook her head. 'Men tie you down.'

'I wouldn't mind that,' said Rosie with amusement. 'I believe those fur handcuffs can be a great turn-on.'

'I like them.' Petra Matthews admitted with a smile while the others laughed raucously. 'And I like being blindfolded too.'

Claire looked at Petra in surprise. Fur handcuffs! And blindfolds! She wouldn't have thought that Petra would've gone for something like fur handcuffs or blindfolds. She looked far too ordinary for that sort of stuff. And now Celia, the final member of the production team, was nodding knowledgeably as Trinny outlined the merits of vibrators and other sex toys in the bedroom. I'm so hopeless and out of touch, thought Claire despairingly. And me and Bill must have had the world's most mundane sex life ever even though it seemed pretty all right to me at the time!

'All the same . . .' Rosie continued more seriously, 'I'd like to have someone in my life again. It's six months since me and Steve broke up and to be honest with you all it seems to me that it's abso-fucking-lutely impossible to find a decent bloke out there. I'm fed up with flitting from one-night stand to one-night stand.'

'At least you're having one-night stands,' muttered Petra. 'I can't remember the last time I even had a date, let alone a one-night stand. And I really, really miss a bit of sex.'

Joanna laughed harshly. 'Depends on the sex. David's perform-ance in that department got rapidly worse and worse. I mean, he thought he was great, he thought that going at it hammer and tongs was what I wanted even though I told him a little bit of finesse wouldn't go amiss from time to time.'

'Is that why he ended up with the blonde?' Petra asked.

'Oh, darling, there were loads of blondes,' cried Joanna. 'Redheads and brunettes too, I'm sure. Unfaithful bastard.'

'What exactly went wrong?' Claire couldn't imagine living with an unfaithful husband.

'Serial womaniser. But fuck him.' Joanna sniffed and pulled a crum-pled hanky from her bag. She blew her nose noisily and then looked defiantly at Claire. 'I know we don't see you much, but what about your love life these days?' she demanded. 'Anyone new on the horizon?'

Claire stared at her in astonishment.

'I mean, it's been quite a time, hasn't it?' asked Joanna. 'Have you gone out with anyone else?'

'No,' said Claire shortly.

'Don't you want to?' asked Rosie.

'No,' said Claire.

'I wish I could think like that.' Petra sighed. 'I wish I could put men out of my mind for ever. But I like them too much, even if I know it's all going to go horribly wrong. At least there's always that brief stage when you think maybe it'll all go right. And when you're excited just about seeing them!'

'I've got to go.' Claire stood up quickly and the steel chair clattered across the flagstones. 'I need to get home and walk the dog.'

'Stay,' said Trinny. 'You haven't even finished your wine.'

'I can't,' said Claire. 'Poor old Phydough will be going nuts at home.'

'Hey, Claire, I'm sorry if I upset you.' Joanna looked at her anxiously. 'Don't go because of me, for heaven's sake.'

'I'm not upset,' said Claire. 'Not in the least. Honestly. I enjoyed the drink. I must do it more often. But I really have to get home now. It's nothing to do with you, Joanna.'

'Well, look, before you do . . .' Rosie stopped her. 'If you're interested in getting out and about, Claire, I might have just the thing for you. For anyone who's trying to meet someone, in fact.'

'I'm not trying to meet someone,' said Claire.

'I am,' Petra said. 'What's the story, Rosie?'

'A new dating thing,' said Rosie. 'It's called Dinner in the Dark.'

'Sounds like dinner in my house,' said Joanna bleakly. 'I'm usually on my own because Antonia's off with her friends. So I sit there with the telly on and the lights off.'

'Don't be ridiculous,' said Rosie. 'This is totally different. You buy tickets and it's basically this big get-together where you're sitting at a table with total strangers in the dark.'

'OK, Rosie, I think you've lost the plot,' said Trinny.

'Listen,' said Rosie impatiently. 'The idea is that it's for singles and you have to get to know the person beside you without judging them on how they look.'

'Where on earth did you hear about this?' asked Joanna in astonishment.

Rosie was sheepish. 'I joined an internet dating agency.'

The girls looked at her sceptically and Trinny muttered that Rosie could be letting herself in for something completely dodgy. But Rosie shook her head and said that it was completely above board. Petra and Celia listened with interest as Rosie outlined the merits of the agency and the Dinner in the Dark night.

'You know, it's not a bad idea,' said Petra. 'Let's face it, girls, we know it's difficult to find any man, let alone the right one! So I think you're very brave, Rosie, and I'm going to go to your Dinner in the Dark thing. Besides, it might work for me. I mean – my nose! I bet it's because of my nose that blokes don't hang round. It's the world's ugliest.'

'No it's not,' said Claire, who was still standing beside her pushed-back seat. 'And the whole idea sounds daft to me. You're going to see people anyway when they eventually put the lights on.'

'Yes, but by that stage you've decided you like them for their personality,' said Rosie.

'I think it sounds a hoot,' said Celia. 'I see myself sensually winding pasta round a fork—'

'You eat with your fingers,' Rosie told her. 'It heightens the sensual experience, apparently.'

'Well, count me in,' said Celia.

'Um – I think you might have to register with the agency,' Rosie told her. 'It's called HowWillIKnow.com.'

'Oh, Rosie! It's not one of these scams where you have to sign up loads of friends so that you get free membership, is it?' cried Trinny.

'Not at all.' Rosie looked at her in annoyance. 'I guess you just have to register so that they can find you in case you do turn out to be a complete nutter or something. I'll e-mail you the website. Besides, it's worth checking out. There are loads of guys on it.'

'Probably all taking the piss,' said Trinny.

Claire was pleased that somebody else was sceptical too.

'I don't care.' Petra said. 'It's worth a shot. I'm in too.'

'And me,' said Joanna. 'I hope they cater for the older woman.'

'For everyone,' Rosie assured her.

'I really have got to go,' said Claire. 'Rosie, I can't wait to hear whether you meet anyone in the dark, but I honestly wouldn't hold my breath.'

'It's better than not trying to meet anyone at all,' said Rosie hotly.

Claire said nothing. The girls exchanged glances.

'I'll see you all in a week or so.' She smiled briefly and pulled her bag over her shoulder, then walked quickly towards the train station, breaking into a jog as she saw the snaking green of an approaching Dart in the distance. She flung herself into a carriage and winced because the run had made her flat tan shoes rub against her week-old blisters again.

She leaned back in her seat and sighed. The evening had been enjoyable until they'd all started talking about men. Why was it, she wondered, that everyone seemed to think she needed someone else in her life when they did nothing but complain about their own love lives? It seemed to her that, in general, men caused nothing but trouble and her experience had been totally unique. If you had a bloke, you were always worried about the state of the relationship; if you hadn't, you worried because you weren't attractive enough or clever enough to get one. It was a war zone out there and now Rosie was even bringing technology into the whole thing! She was better off not getting involved. Things were good for her the way they were. Although, she admitted, it might be nice to socialise a bit more. For a short while tonight she'd felt like a grown-up again, in the company of women who just wanted to chat and wind down, even if the conversation had become ridiculous. Maybe she should give in and take up some of Eavan's invitations. At least they wouldn't be something as daft as internet dating and Dinner in the Dark.

Claire nibbled at the inside of her lip. It was hard to know what she should be doing with her life. Suddenly she was beginning to measure it against other people's and she could see how it might appear empty and unfulfilling. Yet she wasn't on that roller-coaster of emotions that the other women in Locum Libris seemed to ride. Which was better? she wondered. Dull and boring but at least keeping your heart intact? Or rushing out and about trying to find someone or something to light up your life? She smiled wryly. Once you'd had that someone already you could never find them again. If it was so difficult for most women to find the right bloke once, how on earth could they possibly find him twice? And what was the point in getting your heart bashed around while you were looking?

Phydough was asleep under the enormous Californian lilac bush in the back garden, but he jumped up and bounded over to her as soon as she opened the kitchen door. She sank to her knees and buried her face in his fur. The great thing about animals was that they never said anything to hurt you, never criticised you, never made you feel there was something in your life that wasn't quite right.

'Let my change into my flip-flops,' she told the dog, 'because I've been stupid and worn leather shoes again, even though they're flat. And then we can go for your walk.'

Phydough barked his approval at her plans. He sat patiently in the hall until she came downstairs again and clipped the lead on to his collar.

'Just a quick one round the block,' she told him. 'I took you out at lunchtime, don't forget.'

Am I a bit demented, she wondered, that I can have a better conversation with my dog than with people?

When they got to the end of the road, Phydough turned towards the seafront, but Claire jerked the lead in the opposite direction. 'I need to get milk,' she told him. 'Besides, last time we went down there you disgraced me by knocking someone over. And he might have been very rude but these days we were probably lucky that he didn't threaten to sue you for emotional damage or something.'

Phydough trotted alongside her, happy to listen to the sound of her voice and not at all worried about what she was actually saying.

'Oh hey, Phy, look at that.' She stopped in front of a shop in the cluster at Marino Mart. 'That's new.'

The shop front was painted in sea-green with a stencil of multi-coloured flowers trailing over it and through the letters of the name, which was 'Taylor's Florist'. Claire peered in the window but it was impossible to see much through the green security mesh. There was a sign in the window which said, 'Ask about our gardening service.'

'Should I?' She looked at the dog. 'I mean, Phy, that bush you were under today used to be a neat and tidy little thing. But it's almost totally out of control.'

Phydough tugged on the leash to let her know he was bored with standing outside a florist's, even one as decorative as Taylor's.

'Thing is,' she continued, 'it was Bill's garden. It would be awful seeing someone else working there.'

Phydough barked.

'But I know he'd hate to see it in the mess it is now,' she said sadly. 'And I can't let it get more and more overgrown, can I? All right, all right,' she added as the dog barked again. 'Let's go.'

When she got home again she realised she'd missed two calls on her mobile because she'd forgotten to bring it with her (which amazed her, because she'd got used to taking the phone with her wherever she was going, even though part of her resented always being in touch); and there were two messages on her answering machine in the house. The first was from her mother, wondering how she was. The second was from Eavan, wondering the exact same thing. Both of them sounded slightly anxious and surprised that she wasn't there. She looked at her mobile more closely and realised that the missed calls were from them too. Why the hell couldn't they leave her alone for five minutes?

She hadn't minded so much in the aftermath of Bill's death; in fact it had comforted her then to know that they cared so much. But now they were driving her crazy. It's not as though I'd do anything stupid on my own, she muttered under her breath. Even though being without Bill is like being without part of myself.

Georgia had once told her that the hardest part of losing her finger was sometimes not realising that it wasn't there any more. That sometimes it itched even though there was nothing to scratch. 'I have to check and see that it's really gone,' she'd told Claire. 'It's hard to believe that something that's missing can seem so real.'

Claire picked up the phone and dialled her mother's number. As she'd expected, Eileen had been concerned that there'd been no reply earlier.

'I was walking Phydough,' Claire told her. 'Before that I was over

57

at the printer's with some work, and I went for a drink with the girls.'

'You what?' Eileen sounded utterly shocked.

'I do still function as a human being,' Claire told her. 'It's not that I never go anywhere.'

Eileen's silence told Claire that she didn't quite believe her.

'Why don't I drop up and see you and Dad next week?' asked Claire suddenly. 'I haven't been to Dundalk in ages.'

'Next week?' Eileen sounded slightly distracted. 'Do you – I – well, yes, why not. Yes, Claire. Come as soon as you like.'

Claire frowned. Her mother's confusion over something so simple wasn't usual.

'Is everything OK?' she asked. 'Are you sure you want me to come?'

'Oh Claire, darling, of course!' cried Eileen. 'And it's such lovely weather. We can sit in the garden or something.'

'Great. I'll do that so,' said Claire.

'Why don't you stay over?' asked Eileen.

'Sorry, Mum, I can't,' Claire replied. 'Phy would go berserk if I left him on his own.'

'I suppose.' Eileen didn't want to get into an argument with her daughter although she didn't think it would matter if Claire left the dog on his own for one night. 'I'll see you next week.' Her voice softened. 'I'm looking forward to it.'

'So am I,' said Claire,

When she hung up from her mother, she called Eavan.

'Where were you?' demanded her friend.

'You're just like my mother,' said Claire. 'She rang this number and my mobile too.'

'It's usually easy to get hold of you,' Eavan said. 'I was worried.'

'Why do people worry about me so much?' demanded Claire. 'I don't worry about you, you know.'

'Claire—'

'Anyway, it doesn't matter. Was it anything special?'

'Just reminding you that it's Saffy's birthday soon and me and Glenn are having a birthday tea for her. We thought you'd like to come.'

'Who else is coming?' asked Claire.

'Well, no one,' admitted Eavan. 'Just you, me, Glenn and Candida. That's her babysitter. Wednesday at six.'

'OK,' said Claire.

'OK?' Eavan sounded astonished. 'I was sure you'd find a reason not to come.'

'Why would I?' asked Claire. 'Saffy's my god-daughter. I want to come.'

'I know,' said Eavan. 'It's just that you're normally working. Or something.' Her tone conveyed the fact that she didn't think much of Claire's usual excuses.

'Do you want me to come or not?' asked Claire tightly.

'Absolutely.'

'I'll see you there so,' said Claire.

'Great.'

'OK then,' said Claire. 'I'm off to have a cup of tea.'

'Right,' said Eavan uncertainly.

'See you,' said Claire, and hung up.

Eavan turned to Glenn who was sitting beside her and looked at him in astonishment.

'She said yes. Just like that.'

'So I gathered.'

'That's so unlike her.'

'I thought you'd be pleased,' said Glenn.

'I am.' But Eavan frowned. 'And she was out earlier tonight but didn't say where.'

Glenn raised his eyebrows. 'Secret lover?'

Eavan laughed. 'There'll never be one of those,' she said. 'Claire might rejoin the human race and come to three year olds' birthday parties, but I know for sure that she'll never let someone else into her life. She's turned Bill Hudson into a model of perfection and no one will ever be able to match him.'

'What would you do if I died?' asked Glenn suddenly.

Eavan stared at him.

'If something happened to me?' he asked. 'If I got cancer or was run over or something?'

'I don't know,' said Eavan.

'Would it depend?' asked Glenn. 'If I died from an illness, would that make you more likely to find someone new than if I was killed like Bill?'

'Don't talk like that,' said Eavan uncomfortably.

'I wouldn't want you to be lonely,' said Glenn.

'I'd have Saffy,' Eavan told him.

'Just like Claire and Georgia,' said Glenn.

Eavan said nothing.

'Would you go out with someone from the Smash and Grab?' asked Glenn.

'I've no idea,' replied Eavan. 'I don't look at it like that.'

'If I wasn't here would you find someone, though?'

'Glenn Keating! You *are* here. I love you. Stop talking like this.'

'But do you depend on me?' asked Glenn.

'Of course I do.'

'Could you manage if I was gone?'

This time Eavan looked at him anxiously. 'What the hell are you going on about?' she asked. 'You're scaring me.'

'I'm sorry.' He put his arms around her. 'I didn't mean to. I was just . . . well, you know . . . thinking.'

'Don't think at all if you're going to think like that,' said Eavan as she snuggled closer to him. 'If you must think, think of me in bed wearing that new lacy number I bought last week.'

'Too hot to wear anything in bed!' Glenn chuckled and kissed her. And Eavan sighed with relief that they'd got off the subject of Glenn's mortality at last.

Chapter 7

Oenothera (Evening Primrose) – Mainly pink and yellow flowers; this is a night-flowering plant. Thrives in lots of sun.

It was nearly midnight when the phone rang yet again. Claire had been sitting watching TV and drinking a glass of wine. She was, in fact, slightly tipsy – owing to the fact that she so rarely drank alcohol these days, it didn't take much to influence her. And even though the small amount of wine and champagne she'd had earlier hadn't really affected her too much she supposed the effect might be cumulative. As the phone rang she was thinking, somewhat ruefully, that she might have a headache the next morning. It amused her to think that she could be hungover. Those were the days, she thought, when me and Bill could get plastered on a huge bottle of Pedrotti and feel fine the next morning. But the instant the phone rang she felt herself sober up. Nobody rang at midnight unless there was something wrong. She'd been used to it, of course, when Bill was alive. There were some patients who thought nothing of ringing him at any time of the day or night requesting a house call. But it was different now.

She picked up the phone and cautiously said hello.

'Mum.' Georgia's voice was faint, and Claire felt nervous adrenaline rush through her body.

'What's the matter?' she asked.

'Nothing,' said Georgia softly.

'Why are you whispering?' Oh God, thought Claire, maybe it's her voice. Maybe someone's said something to her and triggered off something in her speech again. She tightened her grip on the receiver and tried desperately not to panic.

61

'Robyn's asleep,' explained Georgia.

'Oh.' Claire felt herself relax slightly. She picked up her glass and took a sip of wine. 'Is something wrong?'

'Not really,' said Georgia.

'Not really?'

'It's silly.' Now that she'd rung Claire, Georgia was beginning to wish she hadn't. But she'd been lying in her single bed unable to sleep and she'd suddenly needed to talk to her mother.

'Nothing's silly, Georgey-girl,' said Claire gently.

'I wish you wouldn't call me that!'

'Sorry.' Claire waited. There was something wrong and Georgia needed to tell her at her own pace.

'I was wondering, Mum,' said Georgia slowly, 'how did you know Dad was the right person for you?'

Claire stopped herself from asking why on earth Georgia had rung at this hour with that particular question. She waited for a moment before she answered. 'I just did,' she said finally. 'That's not very helpful, is it, Georgia?'

'See, people say that, but I don't understand how you can "just" know,' complained Georgia. 'There must be something a bit more definite.'

'I wish there was,' said Claire. 'Maybe in other people's cases there is. It might just be that me and your dad . . . well . . .'

'I know, I know. Soulmates.'

'Sorry,' said Claire. 'I know that's a kind of hopeless thing to tell you. It happened for us but it really doesn't happen that often. I was talking to some women today and none of them was exactly ecstatic about their love lives. All the same, honey, you'll meet someone and you will know. People do.'

'I met someone.'

Claire held her breath. There was an image in her mind of this boy, whoever he was, with Georgia now. In her bed. It wasn't supposed to happen. But maybe it did. How the hell will I cope, she wondered, if she tells me she's having underage sex? At fourteen? She couldn't be. She really couldn't. Could she?

'I thought it might mean something,' said Georgia. 'But it didn't.'

Claire exhaled slowly. 'How come it didn't?' she asked.

'He wasn't the sort of person I thought,' replied Georgia.

'Georgey . . . Georgia . . . he didn't . . . try anything, did he?'

'Oh, Mum!' Suddenly Georgia's voice was at nearly normal volume and laden with disgust.

'Well, pet, how would I know?' asked Claire. 'You've rung me here really late at night and asked me questions . . .'

Georgia giggled suddenly. 'I suppose it's a bit weird,' she agreed. 'Sorry. But I wanted to talk to you about it.'

'I'm very glad you felt able to ring me,' Claire assured her. 'So, go on, spill the beans.'

His name was Jamesie, Georgia said, and she'd met him on the very first day. He was absolutely gorgeous-looking, Georgia added. They'd been standing beside each other in the college cafeteria and got talking. Later she'd spoken to him again and she'd liked him a lot. He'd asked her if she'd be at the next céili. She'd said she would and he'd told her he was looking forward to seeing her there.

'And did you manage all this in Irish?' asked Claire curiously.

'Sort of,' Georgia answered. She told Claire that everyone had been at the céili and that there'd been lots of traditional dances, which had been surprising fun. But when she went to find Jamesie he was talking to some of his mates and he ignored her. When she'd tried to catch his attention he deliberately turned away. Later she'd spotted him deep in conversation with another girl, Zoë King, who'd put her arm around his waist when she'd seen Georgia looking at them. Jamesie had put his arm around Zoë too and turned away from Georgia again. And then one of the other blokes had told her that she was wasting her time with him – a guy like Jamesie O'Sullivan didn't need to be seen with someone who didn't even have a full hand.

'Georgia!' Claire was horrified. 'He didn't say that!'

'Apparently so.' Georgia's voice trembled. 'Thing is, Mum, he was dead nice before. He really was. And he must have seen my hand. So I thought . . . I mean, I know I couldn't really be in love with him but . . . it's just – if I got that so wrong, how the hell will I know in the future?'

'Oh, Georgia, nobody really knows,' Claire told her. 'And that bloke needs a good thump.'

Georgia laughed shakily.

'Honestly,' said Claire, 'I can't believe such crap!'

'Mum!' Georgia laughed a little more. 'You never let me say that.'

'I know. I don't like it as an expression. But still.' Her voice softened. 'You've got to expect some fellas to be morons.'

'I know,' said Georgia. 'But I wish I had some idea how to tell who's a moron and who isn't. And I thought that maybe there was a way. Maybe you knew.'

'I wish I had good advice for you,' said Claire. 'I'm probably the worst mother in the world for that sort of thing.'

'Ah, you're not,' said Georgia. 'You and Dad were too good an example, I guess.'

'Are you all right there?' asked Claire. 'You're not so devastated that you want to come home, are you?'

'Nah!' Georgia's voice lifted. 'I'll be fine. I think I . . . well, honestly, I was just a bit homesick. And I suppose I was a bit upset that he kissed me even though he apparently hates me, but I suppose I'll get over it.'

'He kissed you!'

'That's what people do,' said Georgia. 'And it wasn't a proper kiss. Just a kind of lip thing.'

'You're only fourteen. I can't get my head around you kissing anyone.'

'Get with it, Mum,' said Georgia. 'Earlier you seemed to think that I was up to much worse. And there are plenty of girls who hop into bed with blokes at fourteen.'

'I sincerely hope not,' retorted Claire. 'It's illegal for one thing. And besides, it's – well, it's not something you'd want to do.'

'How old were you?'

Claire couldn't quite believe she was having this type of conversation when Georgia was two hundred miles away. She'd assumed it might happen in a quiet and thoughtful way at home sometime. Certainly not over the mobile. Times have changed, she thought. They really have.

'I didn't rush into it,' she said. 'Though quite honestly I think that was a good thing. There's far too much emphasis placed on having to jump into bed with people these days.'

Georgia laughed. 'Only if you want to,' she told her mother. 'We have the right to say no.'

'You'd better exercise it while you're still below the age of consent,' Claire told her. 'And besides, sex is—'

'Don't bother to tell me it's gorgeous and wonderful and best with the right person,' Georgia interrupted her. 'We get that at school. And I've absolutely no intention of hopping into bed with anyone, Mum. He kissed me, that's all. I know that as a teenager I'm a seething mass of rebellious hormones, but a kiss was just a kiss, you know. I just wondered when you first did it?'

'I was nineteen,' said her mother. 'So you have a way to go.'

'And – and did you sleep with anyone else except Dad?'

Claire thought about Roger Simenon. He'd wanted to, of course, but she'd been so horrified at the thought of anyone other than Bill that she'd gone home in a panic. She wasn't sure whether she'd just been naïve or whether the bond that she and Bill had had was so strong it would have been impossible for her to sleep with anyone else.

'No,' she told Georgia honestly. 'I didn't.'

'Do you regret that?'

'I guess I should,' she replied. 'After all, it's all about experience these days, isn't it? But when I was with your dad it was enough for me.'

'And now?' Georgia asked the question casually.

'Now I have a different life,' said Claire.

'I wish Jamesie hadn't been so shitty,' said Georgia, risking another word that Claire normally wouldn't allow.

'I wish I could give you a hug,' said Claire.

'I love you, Mum.'

'I love you too. And I miss you.'

'Really?' Georgia laughed. 'Last year you were always trying to get me out of the house.'

'That was when you were going through your irritating phase,' said Claire in amusement, although the real reason she had wanted Georgia out of the house was so that her daughter would mix with other people and wouldn't be weighed down by Claire's own feelings of depression. 'These days, I miss you when you're not around.'

'Just wait til I go through my moody teenager phase,' Georgia told her. 'I mean, I haven't done that yet, have I? And it's bound to happen.'

'I'll be ready for it,' promised Claire. 'Now, darling, you'd better get to sleep. I bet you have a busy day tomorrow.'

'Yeah. I do. I will. Thanks, Mum.'

'Goodnight, Georgey-girl,' said Claire.

'I asked you not to call me that,' said Georgia. 'It was my baby name.'

'Goodnight, Georgia,' amended Claire.

'Goodnight,' responded Georgia. 'Sleep well.'

It was unbearably hot in the bedroom, even with the window wide open. Claire lay naked on the king-sized bed, half covered by a white cotton sheet. A shaft of silver moonlight fell across Phydough on the floor beside her, his big pink tongue hanging out of his mouth. The dog had jumped on the bed when Claire had finally climbed between the sheets but had jumped off again almost immediately, sensing the stifling heat.

Claire stared up at the ceiling, too hot to sleep. She couldn't remember it ever having been too hot to sleep when Bill had been beside her. Not in Ireland at any rate. There'd been the holiday to Majorca one year where the temperatures had soared into the mid-forties and the tiny apartment they were renting had turned into a mini-furnace. They'd asked for the air-conditioning to be turned on but it transpired that none of the units were connected. And so they'd ended up pulling the two single beds out on to the tiny balcony every night where the breath of breeze made it possible to doze off but where the mosquitoes snacked on them incessantly and they woke up each morning covered in red weals. In the end, as Claire told Bill, they were getting more gratification out of scratching each other's bites than having sex. It had been their second holiday together and it had been a last-minute cheap deal. They'd wondered how it was that everyone they'd ever known who'd done the last-minute cheap deal found themselves in gorgeous bougainvillea-covered low-rise apartments which would have cost the earth normally; whereas they'd ended up in a soulless high-rise with no air and plenty of insects. But it didn't really matter. It was all they could afford and the summer in Ireland had been wet and cold. So let's not complain, Bill had said as they sweltered through the night. We still haven't got the heating fixed at home!

Claire shivered suddenly and got up off the bed, pulling on her long cotton T-shirt. Phydough looked up at her and gently banged his tail on the floor. She stepped over him and walked down the stairs to the kitchen. Her heart thudded as she pushed open the door. She hated walking around in the dark but she made herself do it sometimes. To prove, she told herself, that there was nothing spooky about being in the house on her own and that there were no ghosts to frighten her. She also told herself that any ghosts that might visit her should be welcome ones. But she didn't quite believe that somehow. She didn't need to turn on the light in the kitchen, though, because the silver-white glow of the full moon was bright enough to see by. She exhaled slowly and then squeaked in fright as Phydough pushed past her.

'Sorry,' she told him as he whined at her. 'I didn't mean to frighten you. Just like I know you didn't mean to frighten me.' She watched him as he padded softly to his food bowl. He sniffed at the remnants of his lamb mix and then looked at her expectantly.

'Eat what's there,' she ordered sternly.

Phydough whined again.

'Honestly, you pack away more than me and Georgey combined,' she told him, nevertheless reaching into the cupboard and taking out a pouch of beef and vegetables. 'And it can't possibly be good for you to have a meal in the middle of the night.' She tore open the pouch and emptied the food into the bowl. The dog snuffled happily as he ate and Claire smiled at him.

She poured a glass of water for herself and then unlocked the back door. It was soup-warm despite the fact that it was three in the morning, and there wasn't a breath of breeze to rustle the leaves of the apple tree halfway down the lawn or whisper through the long bamboo grasses nearer the house.

Claire sat in one of the garden chairs and sipped her water. She hoped that, in Galway, Georgia had finally fallen asleep. Claire was still bristling with rage on behalf of her daughter. How dared that pup of a boy (probably some acne-riddled teenager, even though Georgey had said he was good looking) make an issue of her disfigurement! Didn't they know the kind of effect that could have on her? OK, Claire conceded, she seemed to be dealing with it really well, but who knew whether careless or hurtful remarks wouldn't trigger off a reaction in her again. It truly could be enough to stop her speaking!

Claire shivered in the warm air. She couldn't bear the thought of Georgia retreating into her world of silence again. Yet she had to be pragmatic about it. Kids – teenagers – could be impossibly cruel. She remembered a girl in her class at school being teased unmercifully about the ugly teeth braces she'd had to wear. There were times when the child had gone home in tears. And of course wearing glasses, particularly the awful NHS style of the day, had been an open invitation to everyone to mock you.

Claire sighed. Georgia would have to deal with it. She *was* dealing with it. But she hoped she'd be able to cope. And what about the other questions her daughter had asked? What about the whole concept of falling in love? Claire had felt particularly inadequate in answering them. How did anyone know they were in love? How should you behave on your first date with a guy? How did you deal with rejection? How did you tell someone you didn't love them any more? The last was the only question she had even half an answer to because she'd given Roger Simenon the push, but it wasn't really the same thing. She hadn't fallen in love and out of love again. She'd never really cared about him at all.

I can't really help her, thought Claire miserably. I haven't done all the things that other mothers have. I haven't sat home waiting for the phone to ring. I haven't worried that my boyfriend might be cheating on me with someone else. I don't have any real experience of that whole dating scene. Because of Bill. She stared out over his untidy garden again. Because of Bill she'd had an easy time. They'd grown up together, knowing everything they needed to know about each other, trusting each other. So she hadn't had to learn any of the other stuff. But now, for Georgia's sake, maybe she should.

Only how could you do that? she wondered.

Suddenly she got up from the chair and went back into the kitchen.

She'd tidied the pile of magazines into the rack earlier in the week. Women's magazines mostly, which Bill had taken on subscription for the waiting room. She'd never got round to cancelling the subscriptions so the magazines still arrived every month, even though she didn't bother reading most of them. But she knew that they were a mine of information. As she flicked her way through them, she could see there was plenty of advice there. But was any of it really practical? Did any of it work? When it came to advice, could you really depend on some fashionista in a London office block?

To help Georgia she should really have gone through some of these experiences herself. To help Georgia maybe she should try to have them now. After all, it was her fault that Georgia didn't have a father any more. Her fault that Bill had been the one who was lying on the pontoon when the jet-ski crashed into it. She was the one who'd entered the competition; it was because of her that they were in Jamaica in the first place; and she was the one who'd stopped Bill from racing Georgia. If she'd allowed him to be the one to race then it would have been her that had been killed. She tried not to think about that very often but sometimes she couldn't help it. And sometimes she wondered if Georgia wouldn't have been better off with Bill still around instead of her. But would he have been any good at this part of her life? Would he have had a better take on how girls of fourteen should behave with boys? Being a doctor had meant him dealing with lots of female physical problems as well as angst. He'd probably met more teenage girls than Claire ever had.

But he wouldn't know how it felt as a woman to be laughed at by a bloke. And Claire could empathise with Georgia about that even though it had never happened to her. So if she got some experience in the dating game . . . Admittedly it wouldn't be easy to find dates on whom to try out high-gloss lippy or the latest short skirt. And she was too old for a lot of that stuff anyway. But if she tried going for a drink with some men? Just to get an idea? Was that possible? Surely it wasn't that hard to meet someone? Or was it? She knew that women complained that men were hard to find – none of her colleagues at Locum Libris were happy with the men, or lack of them, in their lives. Would she have to do what Rosie had done and sign up with an agency? After all, she'd be competing with lots of young, gorgeous women for men, and how the hell did you meet someone available in your age group when you didn't do pubs and clubs? Maybe things like Dinner in the Dark were actually a good idea in a city where you struggled to find the right person.

She could try, couldn't she? After all, she wasn't going to find anyone like Bill. There was no chance of her falling for someone. She knew that she would never fall in love again. This would be research. And it would be worth it, for Georgia's sake.

Chapter 8

Ipomoea (Morning Glory) – White, blue, purple and red trumpet-shaped flowers that last for only a day. Damaged by cold winds.

She woke up later than she'd expected the following morning because it had been after four when she'd gone back to bed and the rising sun had already begun to tint the edges of the eastern sky with hues of golden pink. But she'd closed the damask curtains tightly so that no light would get through, and it was the sound of Phydough barking at a low-flying bird in the garden outside that finally woke her. She felt surprisingly refreshed and she had her breakfast – a fruits-of-the-forest smoothie and half a muffin – out on the patio again.

The forecasters had finally decided that the country was in the grip of a heatwave which they expected to last for at least another week. Every evening the TV weather showed comparisons with other hotspots in Europe as viewers were told that Irish and UK temperatures were higher than some of the best Mediterranean resorts and perspiring camera crews were sent to crowded beaches to interview families who smugly told them that Spain and Italy just couldn't compete this year.

After she'd finished her breakfast she took the magazines out into the warmth of the garden and went through them all again. She vaguely remembered having seen an article about modern women spending a fortune to find the right man through the internet but she hadn't bothered reading it. Now she thought it might have useful information. Not that she had any intention of spending a fortune on finding anyone. But perhaps it was an exposé of the whole internet dating scene, warning readers about being ripped off.

The piece *was* about internet dating, but not the sort Rosie had talked about. This was top-of-the-range internet dating, designed so that you met only the most eligible of eligible men. Rich men. Men who earned over a million a year. And the article didn't give out the name of the agency – you had to find out by word of mouth. Claire made a face. There wasn't the slightest chance of her finding out the name of such an agency by word of mouth because she didn't know anyone rich enough to possibly be involved with it. Besides, she realised as she read further, it cost €75,000 to be a member. Bloody hell, she thought, as she stared at the glossy picture of an attractive woman sitting on a yacht moored off San Tropez, I could go on a hell of a lot of dates in Dublin for that! In return, she read, the agency would assign her a personal dating adviser who would set up dates for her at prestigious events (she nodded in interest at the idea of premium seats at Wimbledon; she'd always wanted to go!) or whisk her away to meet the man of her dreams at a dinner for two in New York.

Somehow it all seemed even more slick and businesslike than she'd ever imagined. Last night, when she'd thought about dating men for Georgia's sake, she'd supposed that she could just meet someone locally. She hadn't quite thought through how she'd actually accomplish that, and now she realised that simply bumping into a man wasn't a real option any more. You had to get out there and work at it. And it was like everything else. If you wanted a premium service you paid a premium price!

But I don't want a premium service, she reminded herself. I just want to dip my toe in the water and see what it's like when a woman goes out with a man she barely knows. So maybe Rosie's down-to-earth, common-or-garden internet dating is a good idea. Or am I losing my marbles altogether? She wished she knew.

She gathered up the magazines and went back into the house. Upstairs, in her office, she switched on her computer and logged on to the internet. She typed in howwillIknow and looked in utter amazement at the page in front of her. Somehow she'd expected it to look sleazy and desperate, but it didn't. A big banner headline welcomed her to the world of HowWillIKnow.com and told her that her circle of friends was about to expand for ever. Once she registered, she read, she would be able to access chat rooms, message rooms and event boards and would be invited to official HowWillIKnow nights out during the year.

She clicked on the tab marked 'Search' and filled in the boxes, saying that she was looking for a man between 35 and 45 (as if, she thought, any thirty-five-year-old would go out with a woman a couple of years older; the thirty-five-year-old men were probably busily looking for twenty year old women!) and that she didn't care where he came from.

She was astonished to find that a long list of potential HowWillIKnow candidates, all with nicknames, appeared on the screen. An icon told her that there were pictures of each man available but that she had to be a member to access them.

The first name was 'Stargazer'. She clicked on the 'More Information on Stargazer' button and discovered that he was a thirty-five-year-old man who lived in Dublin. He was a non-smoking Scorpio whose weight was 'average' and who had dark hair and blue eyes. He was, according to the information, a management consultant. Claire frowned. She never quite understood what a management consultant actually did. Although Glenn Keating now worked in sales and marketing, he'd had a job as a management consultant in the past and had once told her that his main function then had been to bill client companies for telling them the blindingly obvious. So, she thought, as she scrolled down the page, Stargazer could be anything really. He described himself as easy-going and romantic (which made her wince) and his favourite activities were travelling and music. As far as she could see he was covering a whole range of possibilities, as he enjoyed pubs, clubs, cinema, restaurants and art galleries as well. His reading material was travel books and thrillers. His CD collection included Simon & Garfunkel and Dido. His favourite film was *Casablanca*. (Why do so many men think *Casablanca* is a great movie? she wondered. Is it to prove that they can watch weepies?) He'd stay in to watch travel programmes and Formula One and he wanted an equally easy-going woman who enjoyed good food, good wine, adult conversation and visiting new places.

Claire was peeved that she couldn't see Stargazer's picture. He was totally unsuitable as a potential person to meet, since travelling anywhere wasn't on her agenda because of Georgia. And because of the fact that she couldn't get into a car, she added to herself. But having read so much about him it irked her that she couldn't actually see him!

She clicked through a few more names: Tiger (fearless and romantic, who liked spicy food and garage music); Adonis (yes, I'm attractive and I don't mind you knowing it, who liked blockbuster movies and fast cars); Tai-Pan (an airline pilot who was ready to come back to earth) and JustMe (pretty normal, easy-going, middle-of-the-road, who liked sports and music). Of them all, JustMe sounded the most likely person to go out with. And also, she admitted, the most boring. But at least he was probably telling the truth about himself. Most people were middle-of-the-road!

HowWillIKnow allowed members to register for a monthly fee, for which they could put up their own profile and access others'. Claire nibbled at her fingernail. Could she do this? Was it absolutely crazy? She opened her bag and took out her credit card. The monthly fee was a hell of a lot less than the €75,000 needed to join the exclusive agency whose name she didn't know and was unlikely to ever learn. And an investment of €20 on the other hand wasn't much to be able to learn things for Georgia. She didn't have to go out with anyone if she didn't want to. She hesitated, the credit card between her fingers. Phydough, who'd followed her upstairs as usual, began snoring gently in the basket under her desk. How many of these men would even consider going out with a woman with a kid and a dog? she wondered. What if nobody wanted to go out with her at all?

That was learning too, she told herself. That would mean that she could tell Georgia that all men were shallow bastards just like some of the Locum Libris girls seemed to think.

'Oh, what the hell,' she said out loud. She clicked on the 'Register Now' button and filled in her credit card number. She decided against putting up a profile of her own. She was the one who'd decide when, how and if she'd make contact with anyone. But at least this way she had the choice. A short time later she checked her e-mail for her personal registration number and went back on to the site to look at the photos. Stargazer was so incredibly good-looking, with his olive skin, dark hair and smouldering eyes, that she didn't for a second believe his photograph was real. Tiger looked like any blond member of a boy-band. Tai-Pan's face was almost completely hidden by the brim of the Miami Dolphins baseball cap he was wearing. JustMe, like his profile, seemed pretty middle-of-the road, with mid-brown hair, blue eyes and an open, friendly face.

So can I do this? wondered Claire. Can I actually contact him? Or would it be better to wait until the Dinner in the Dark and meet someone there? She rubbed the back of her neck at the realisation that she was seriously considering the Dinner in the Dark event.

I'm going completely bonkers, she thought. From someone who last week didn't have the faintest intention of ever going out with anyone again to suddenly thinking it's OK to e-mail complete strangers and want to meet them – this really isn't what my life is all about. She looked at the screen again. And then glanced at the framed photo on the window-ledge beside her desk. It was of Bill and Georgia, taken on her first day at school. Georgia was wide-eyed and expectant. Bill's expression was ferociously proud. He'd want me to do this, she thought. He'd want me to be able to help her in the best possible way. But she hesitated. She still wasn't sure whether this *was* the best possible way.

Her email programme pinged to let her know that she had a message. Claire downloaded the new batch of work which Trinny had sent her. Internet dating could wait a little bit longer, she told herself. There was no need to rush into it when she had much more urgent things to do.

The following day, another one of blistering temperatures and cloudless skies, Claire decided to visit her mother. She dressed for comfort in her flattest sandals, a light skirt and the kind of low-cut strappy top that she wasn't sure was suitable for a woman whose next significant birthday would be the big four-oh but which was nice and summery. She bought herself a first-class ticket for the Enterprise train, reasoning that the amount of money she saved by not owning and insuring a car meant that she could spend it on upgrading her travel arrangements whenever possible, then settled into her comfortable seat and took out a selection of magazines from her sunflower-yellow straw bag.

Although her intention had been to trawl through the pages to get further ideas about dating men (because she still hadn't plucked up the courage to contact JustMe), her immediate attention was drawn to the glossy pictures of A-list celebrities at an awards function and the incredible clothes they were wearing. Some of them were undoubtedly gorgeous (Claire felt that Nicole Kidman would look stylish in a sack) but some of them were complete frights. And she wondered whether men really did like women to wear dresses slashed to the waist from the neck down and the leg up. She thought it looked tarty but maybe she was completely wrong. Maybe it was just that Bill had liked it when she made what she called her 'elegant effort' of sweeping her hair up and wearing fitted but not too flirty dresses. Would I do better in a miniskirt and boots? she wondered fleetingly, before remembering that it wasn't her own appearance she was worried about but Georgia's, and that she'd kill her daughter if she went out in a skirt that didn't cover her knickers.

Meeting men, she thought as she continued to flick through the pages. How do you do it if you haven't the nerve to go on-line? Of course it would be different with Georgia, she realised. After all, she was already meeting them (even if they were insensitive little shits) at the Irish College. Presumably as soon as she was old enough she'd be hurrying to bars and clubs where there were probably far too many men all waiting for her. Claire bristled as she imagined unsuitable blokes vying for her only child's attention, showing off like young men always did, trying to look cool. She smiled wryly. Everyone wanted to look cool, though, didn't they? Especially in their teens. If she started criticising guys just because no one would ever really be good enough for Georgey, she'd be acting like an old fogey. And she wasn't ready to classify herself as an old fogey just yet. Besides, Georgia had to live her own life. Claire just had to hope that she was bringing her up the right way, so that, in the end, Georgia would meet someone and fall in love and have the same kind of wonderful relationship she herself had had, and that her parents had too.

She looked up and caught the eye of the passenger opposite, a man in his early twenties who was relaxing in his seat and listening to a personal stereo. He smiled and she smiled back at him, feeling unaccountably pleased that someone younger than her and fairly attractive (lean face, almost jet-black hair, very blue eyes) would even notice her.

There you go, she told herself. I've met a perfectly attractive man on a train. OK, this one's too young for me and too old for Georgia, but he's here and if I wanted I could chat him up. Because he's noticed me. And that's quite flattering really.

The man smiled at her again and then leaned forward. This time Claire felt herself recoil slightly. OK, she thought, it's nice that he smiled at me. It's nice to be noticed. But what the hell does he want?

'Excuse me.' He took the earphones from his ears, reached out and touched her strappy top just above her right breast.

God Almighty, thought Claire frantically, I'm being assaulted on the train.

'Got him!' The man grinned and Claire gasped. He was holding a small, but long-legged, spider between his fingers. He opened the carriage window and let it go. 'Sorry,' he said. 'I was afraid you'd shriek and jump around if I told you. It might have fallen down that top and you'd have gone mad. I couldn't kill it. I'm a softie like that.'

'Thank you,' she said breathlessly. 'But I wouldn't have shrieked.'

'I have a sister,' he told her. 'She can't bear creepy-crawlies. She could shriek for Ireland. I based all women's reactions to spiders on her!'

'Can't say I'm very fond of them myself,' admitted Claire. 'But I've got used to them.'

'Anyway, apologies if you thought I was some kind of pervy freak.'

'No, of course not,' lied Claire.

He laughed and replaced the earphones while Claire hid herself behind her magazine again and thought that if she could misinterpret their actions so badly, she surely needed lessons in dealing with men before she tried dating one.

But really, she thought, I'm not as bad as all that. Not in a casual way. I had lots of male friends in the Smash and Grab club and we got on well. Guys like Paul Hanratty, for instance. I don't have problems relating to men as people. Just as sex objects.

It was nearly three years since she'd had sex. She sighed deeply. She didn't think she missed it. Why would she when in her head sex and love and physical pleasure were all part of the Bill Hudson package, just as she'd told Georgia. After the accident, sex had been the absolute last thing on her mind. And with every passing day it became easier to dismiss it as irrelevant in her new life. She knew that she missed the intimacy but that was different. All the same, she thought, as she glanced over the top of the magazine at the attractive bloke opposite, experiencing the physical pleasure again would be nice.

She blushed furiously. What the hell would he think, she asked herself, if he realised that the woman opposite him, the woman who was at least fifteen years older than him, was imagining making love to him? And what the hell is going on in my own mind, she wondered, that for the briefest of moments I could even think it?

He glanced up and saw her looking at him. He smiled again, but a little uncomfortably this time, and Claire blushed. Am I losing it altogether? she asked herself. This is a stranger on a train. I can't go round having sex fantasies about men on trains. Especially gorgeous young men.

Would it have been OK to have a fantasy about an older man? she wondered. Although wasn't that the problem for women of her age? There were no available men. Wasn't that why Rosie and Petra were so concerned with finding someone before they hit thirty-five? Because they thought that once you'd got past your mid-thirties there was no hope? She suddenly recalled an e-mail that Trinny Armstrong had once sent to all the female employees of Locum Libris and which had made them laugh but then nod their heads knowingly.

The nice men are ugly. The handsome men are not nice. The handsome and nice men are gay. The handsome, nice and heterosexual men are married. The men who are not so handsome, but are nice men, have no money. The men who are not so handsome, but are nice men with money, think we are only after their money. The handsome men without money are after our money. The handsome men who are not so nice and somewhat heterosexual don't think we are beautiful enough. The men who think we are beautiful, that are heterosexual, somewhat nice and have money are pigs. The men who are somewhat handsome, somewhat nice and have some money and thank GOD are heterosexual are shy and NEVER MAKE THE FIRST MOVE! The men who never make the first move automatically lose interest in us when we take the initiative. NOW, WHO IN THE WORLD UNDERSTANDS MEN? Men are like a fine wine. They all start out like grapes, and it's our job to stomp on them and keep them in the dark until they mature into something you'd like to have dinner with.

Her phone beeped with a text message alert. She rummaged in her bag and looked at it. The message was from Georgia. *A1 2day*, she read. *Hvg gr8 time. Luv G.*

Well, at least Georgia was OK again, even if she had had an encounter with a guy who would end up being one of the pigs in Trinny's e-mail. Claire felt herself prickle with anger again on her daughter's behalf. That was why, she mused, it was important for her to find out things about men even if their circumstances were totally different. Because only then would she be able to advise Georgey about the right way of going about things.

She continued to flick through the magazine but it wasn't terribly interesting and she was pleased when the train arrived in Dundalk exactly on schedule. The concrete platform was actually hot underfoot, making Claire feel as though she were on holiday abroad. She bought a huge ice-cream from a shop near the station and licked it happily as she walked towards her parents' house. She'd just finished it as she arrived.

Eileen was in the front garden, dead-heading pink roses from the bushes that lined the path.

'Isn't that Dad's job?' asked Claire as she pushed open the gate. 'He'll go mad at you for interfering. How're you?' She dropped a kiss on her mother's cheek. 'And where is he?'

Her mother smiled shortly at her. 'Not here right now. I'm almost finished. Why don't you go inside and put the kettle on. D'you want something to eat? There's the makings of a salad in the fridge.'

'Salad would be lovely,' said Claire. 'It's about the only thing it's possible to eat in this heat.'

'You're still too thin.' Eileen's words were sharp and she smiled more warmly at Claire to take the sting out of them.

'I know.' Claire made a deliberate effort not to argue with her mother over her weight and walked up the path to the house.

'There are some granary rolls in the bread-bin,' Eileen called after her. 'I'll be in in a minute.'

Claire dumped her bag on the kitchen table and opened the cupboard door. The same old plates were stacked inside, a delicate willow-pattern in blue and white. She recalled asking her mother to buy new plates once, showing her an ad in a glossy magazine for a more modern design. But Eileen had told her that the willow-pattern plates were perfectly serviceable and that she'd no intention of being a slave to fashion. Some of them were cracked now, Claire noticed, as she took down both dinner and side plates as well as the matching cups and saucers. They were nearly forty years old. It was amazing that they'd lasted so long.

The salad ingredients in Eileen's fridge were old fashioned too. Lettuce, tomato, hard-boiled eggs and some slices of cooked ham. It was a summer meal straight out of an Enid Blyton children's book . . . No rocket or radicchio which Claire normally used. No mozzarella or pine nuts either. Standard tomatoes and not the cherry variety which she preferred. Claire wondered a touch ruefully whether she'd simply succumbed to the lifestyle choices of celebrity chefs or whether she really did like the fashionable ingredients more.

Eileen walked into the kitchen and threw her gardening gloves on the draining board.

'Would you like this outside?' asked Claire.

'Oh, I think so,' agreed Eileen.

Claire filled two long glasses with water from the fridge and carried them outside while Eileen brought out cutlery and condiments. They sat down and Claire slid her feet out of her flat sandals so that she could wriggle her toes in the sun. She brushed a stray wasp from in front of her face.

'Eat up,' said Eileen as she buttered a bread roll and pushed it towards Claire. 'You could do with a bit more weight.'

'Oh, for God's sake, Mum. We've already done the thin conversation.'

'I worry about you,' said Eileen. 'You know I do.'

'Yes,' said Claire. 'But there's no need. Honestly.'

'Are you and Dad going anywhere nice for your holiday this year?' she asked in order to change the topic of conversation. 'You haven't said anything about it yet and you've usually headed off somewhere warm by now.'

'No need this year,' said Eileen. 'Warm enough here for anyone.'

'True,' said Claire. 'But getting away would be nice.'

'Yes.' Eileen stared into the distance.

'Is something wrong, Mum?' Claire suddenly felt anxious. She looked at her mother, noticing that the frown lines on her forehead were a little deeper than usual and that the expression in her eyes was uneasy.

'Well, in a way,' said Eileen.

This time Claire felt a tendril of terror wrap itself around her. It wasn't that her parents were old by today's standards, but they were getting on a bit. She didn't want to think that they'd reached the age where they'd begun to be afflicted by various ailments. They'd both been very healthy people until now. She looked enquiringly at her mother, keeping her expression as bland as possible.

'Don't look like that,' said Eileen. 'There's nothing wrong with your dad or me.'

Claire sighed. She'd never been very good at bland expressions.

'What then?' she asked.

'You'll laugh,' said Eileen. 'Although I'm not sure that laugh is the right word under the circumstances.'

'What circumstances?'

'We'd have told you soon anyway if you hadn't rung to say you were coming.'

'Told me what?' asked Claire.

'Told you that we were splitting up,' said Eileen.

Claire looked at her mother in utter astonishment. A wasp landed on the side of her plate and explored a juicy tomato but she ignored it. 'Splitting up?' she repeated incredulously. 'Splitting up?'

'Yes,' said Eileen.

'But – but you've been together for years!' she cried. 'What on earth would make you split up? That's the silliest thing I've ever heard. You're having me on.'

'Why would I have you on about something like this?' asked Eileen.

Claire was speechless.

'Your dad and I have decided,' said Eileen, 'that the best thing to do is split.'

'But why?' cried Claire again. 'I always thought you were happy together. Why on earth would you want to split up now?'

'Because we've reached the last quarter of our lives,' said Eileen. 'And we don't want to waste them together.'

'Huh?' Claire stared at her.

'We've wasted so much time together. Why waste any more?'

'You haven't wasted time,' exclaimed Claire. 'You were happy.'

Eileen raised an eyebrow and Claire looked at her in bewilderment. 'You weren't happy?' she said. 'No. I can't believe that.'

'It depends what you mean by happy,' said Eileen.

'I mean happy!' Claire said forcefully. 'You enjoyed each other's company. You went places together. You didn't fight . . . I don't understand this, Mum. I really don't. We were always a good family, weren't we?'

'I married your father because I was pregnant,' said Eileen.

'With me. Yes. I know,' said Claire. 'It's not like you tried to keep it a secret from me. But you also said that you and Dad worked hard at your marriage. You were always banging on about it when I was a kid, telling me that it was all about give and take.'

'Maybe that was to convince myself,' Eileen told her wryly.

'No.'

'I never loved your father,' said Eileen. 'And he never loved me.'

'Mum!' This time Claire was truly shocked. She could make herself believe that somehow her parents had drifted apart over the years, but that they'd never loved each other at all was impossible to accept. Hadn't they always told her that she was a love-child, a product of what they'd felt for each other?

'Well of course we said that,' said Eileen testily when Claire reminded her. 'What else could I tell you? You were thirteen. I didn't want you thinking you were the result of a quick shag behind the electricity sub-station.'

'Mum!'

'I'm sorry.' Eileen sighed. 'That's a terrible expression and I've picked it up from watching those dreadful *Ibiza Uncovered* programmes on the telly. They're absolutely trash TV but when I turn it on I just can't help myself. I don't know why—'

'Mum!' Claire interrupted Eileen's wayward thoughts. 'You and Dad? Never loving each other? At all?'

Eileen twisted a fork between her fingers. 'Oh, I suppose to say that I didn't love your dad and that he didn't love me . . . maybe that's unfair. We – we were good together. You know.'

Claire squirmed uneasily in the chair as she thought about her parents' sex-life. This is more information than I need, she told herself. But she said nothing.

'So I thought I loved him,' the words were tumbling from Eileen's mouth now, 'but it wasn't a long-term thing. And then I discovered I was pregnant.' She shrugged. 'There wasn't any real choice back then, Claire. We got married.'

'But everything seemed OK to me,' Claire protested. 'I mean, Jacinta O'Brien's parents got married because of her older brother, didn't they? But I remember they were forever fighting. Shouting at each other. Mr O'Brien hit Jacinta's mother at one point, didn't he?'

Eileen nodded. 'It wasn't like that with your dad and me,' she said. 'Of course it wasn't. Your father isn't a violent man, Claire. It was nothing like that. At the start we told each other that we were in love. After you were born . . . well, we definitely thought we were in love—'

'So you must have been,' interrupted Claire, 'It's not something that you pretend, for heaven's sake!'

'We wanted to love each other,' said Eileen. 'And we wanted the marriage to work too, for your sake as much as anything else. So we stuck with it. But we were very different people, darling.'

Claire rubbed her temples. She knew that was true at least. Her mother was a quiet, home-loving woman who enjoyed domestic things. Her father had always been the outgoing one, the one for a laugh, the last to leave a party. But she'd believed that they complemented each other, not that her mother had hated every moment she was out with her father, or that he had detested staying in. It seemed like the foundations of her life were shifting underneath her and she was powerless to do anything about it. It's happening again, she thought frantically. Just like three years ago. Everything I thought about my life and the future is all turning to dust. She clamped down on the feeling of panic that threatened to overwhelm her.

'We got used to it, though,' continued Eileen. 'Besides, from my point of view, what could I do? The only job I'd ever had was in a factory. If I left your father – there were no options, Claire. He wasn't earning enough to support two households. We did what lots of people of our generation did. We lived separate lives.'

'But you went on holidays together,' Claire protested feebly once again. 'And then later, when I was older – what was to stop you splitting up then if that was what you wanted?'

'The longer time goes on the harder it is,' said Eileen. 'And, of course, I was still in the situation where I was dependent on your dad.'

'But when I left home?'

'We should have split then,' agreed Eileen. 'Though at that point we had an arrangement that worked. And although we didn't love each other we didn't hate each other either. It was easier to stick with the status quo. But it was wrong.'

Claire was horrified to find that a tear was beginning to slide down her cheek. She wiped it away quickly. 'So why change now?' she asked shakily.

'The thing is, your dad has found someone else,' said Eileen.

This time Claire actually felt her jaw drop.

'He's in his sixties!' she cried. 'For God's sake, Mum. This is ridiculous.'

'Well, life doesn't pass you by just because you get older,' said her mother acidly. 'And your dad is entitled to find someone if he wants.'

'I can't believe you're telling me this.'

'They want to be together,' said Eileen. 'And I'm tired of putting up with it.'

'Putting up with it?' Claire looked at her in astonishment. 'You mean it's been going on for a while?'

'Over four years,' said Eileen.

Claire was silent.

'Her name's Lacey Dillon,' said Eileen. 'They met at his bowling club.'

Claire stared at her. 'My father is in a relationship with someone called Lacey? What sort of name is that for a grown woman?' Her eyes widened. 'Don't tell me she's a busty twenty year old! He couldn't be having an affair with a twenty-year-old girl, could he?'

'Oh come on, Claire!' Eileen looked at her daughter impatiently. 'Don't be so silly. I told you he's known her for four years! She's fifty-two years old and she runs a recruitment agency.'

'But—'

'She's been good for him,' Eileen continued. 'He's a different man because of her.'

'He's your husband!' Claire protested. 'My dad. He can't possibly—'

'Why not?'

Claire stared at her.

'Look, I know it's a bit of a shock,' said Eileen. 'But I had to tell you.'

Claire said nothing.

'I don't want to carry on living with him,' said Eileen. 'It was different before Lacey. There were other women but nobody serious.'

'Other women!' Claire found her voice again. 'Mum, I just can't believe what I'm hearing.'

'Well, what do you expect?' asked Eileen. 'I wasn't interested any more and he – he was.'

'Oh, God.'

'Not that I might not have been interested if the right man had come along,' said her mother blandly. 'But he didn't. If he had, maybe it would have been me making the first move. As it is, it's your dad.'

'So he's moving out to be with this Lacey woman?'

'She's actually quite nice,' said Eileen.

'I just can't believe it.' Claire finally swatted away the wasp from her plate. 'Why now, after four years with her? Why can't they continue on the way they were before?'

'Because I don't want it that way,' said Eileen. She looked at Claire thoughtfully. 'Besides, they had talked about it way back. We all had. We were going to tell you. But then . . . the accident happened. And we didn't think it was something you could cope with at the time.'

Claire raised her amber-flecked eyes to look at her mother. 'So you're telling me you stayed together to protect me? That you've always stayed together to protect me?'

'Not always,' said Eileen. 'When you were young, yes. Afterwards I could have left him, but I didn't want to. I was protecting myself. But there's no point any more. I have to move on.'

Claire leaned her head in her hands. 'I wasn't expecting this,' she said slowly. 'Of all the things you could have told me . . . this is . . . unbelievable.'

'I always thought you'd guess,' said Eileen. 'You know, when I'd drop in to see you and Bill without your dad. Or when you'd call and he was out. I was surprised you never asked.'

'It never, ever occurred to me.' Claire looked up at her. 'I was so certain of your marriage. Only today . . .' She bit her lip. 'Only today, I was hoping that Georgey would have the kind of marriage that I had. And that you and Dad had.'

'What you and Bill had was obviously very special,' Eileen told her. 'What me and your dad had was . . .' She shrugged. 'A lie, I suppose.'

'I still can't believe it.' Claire frowned. 'Are you absolutely sure? I mean, is this Dad going through some ridiculous male menopause kind of thing?'

'No,' said Eileen shortly.

'And all through your marriage, when I was small . . . there were other women?'

'He wasn't sleeping with someone new every week,' Eileen told her. 'It wasn't like that, Claire, of course it wasn't. But he's different to me and he wanted different things, and at first I thought I was the right person but then I realised I wasn't. So there were women, not all the time, but they happened. None of them was serious, though. But now one is.'

'Lacey Dillon.' Claire could hardly keep the contempt out of her voice.

'She's a nice woman, Claire.'

'Have you actually met her?'

Eileen nodded.

'This is so ridiculous!'

'No,' said Eileen. 'Staying together when we don't love each other is ridiculous.'

'Where's Dad now?' Claire looked around as though he might emerge from the shrubbery behind them.

Eileen shrugged.

'Has he moved out already? Does he know you're telling me this?'

Eileen nodded.

'And he didn't want to be here?'

'He didn't see the point. He said he'll call you. He was afraid there might be a scene, and you know how he is about scenes.'

'Typical!' Claire snorted.

'Don't take sides,' begged Eileen. 'It was both of us. We both made the mistake. We both want to fix it.'

'But what about this house?' asked Claire suddenly. 'What will happen to it?'

'We've put it up for sale,' said Eileen. 'The estate agent has been around already with a couple of prospective purchasers even though they haven't put up a sign yet. Lacey has a home of her own near Lusk. She's selling that. Herself and your dad will buy somewhere between them. And I'll buy somewhere else too.'

'But you'll never have a home like this again!' Claire looked around at the big garden, bursting with the colour of the flowers and shrubs that her father had planted over the years. 'Or a garden like this either.'

'I don't want one,' said Eileen. 'The garden was your dad's domain as well, you know. Anyway, this is a four-bed detached house. It's far too big for me.'

'I don't believe it,' said Claire. 'I really don't.' She waved away another wasp. 'You know, when Bill and I argued, I used to tell him that we should be like you and Dad. Solving everything.'

'You and Bill hardly ever argued,' Eileen reminded her.

'I know. But when we did . . .' Claire found her eyes welling up with tears again. 'I used you and Dad as role models.'

Eileen bit her lip. 'I'm sorry to disappoint you,' she said.

'I'm sorry too,' said Claire. 'I really am.' She picked up her glass and took a long drink of water, unable to look her mother in the eye. It seemed so unreal to her, as though all of her childhood had been based upon a fantasy. She hadn't known that her parents weren't happy together. Even as an adult she hadn't suspected. Is there something wrong with me, she wondered, that I can't tell how other people feel? 'Georgia won't like it either,' she said eventually.

'But it can't be helped, darling,' her mother told her. 'All my life I've done things because it was expected of me or because I was worried about how other people might react. I don't want Georgia to feel hurt, but she's a modern girl growing up in a modern environment. She expects this sort of thing.'

'Not from her own grandparents!'

'Perhaps not. But it's happened, Claire, and neither your dad or me wants to go back.'

Claire bit her lip. 'It's like all of my memories are being ripped apart,' she said slowly. 'All the things I believed in. All the places that meant something . . .'

'Not really,' said Eileen. 'The places are still here. It's just the people who'll be different.'

'Since when have you become so damn sensible?'

'I've always been sensible,' said Eileen.

'Maybe.' Claire rubbed the nape of her neck. 'Does anyone else know?' she asked. 'About you and Dad?'

'We've lived here all our lives,' said Eileen drily. 'They knew about your dad long before I did. And it was accepted, you know. That he had an eye for the ladies.'

'No one ever said anything to me,' protested Claire.

'Why would they? Didn't you kick the dust from your heels and hare off to Dublin to be with Bill as soon as you could?'

'Went to France first,' observed Claire.

Eileen shrugged.

'Why don't you move to Dublin when you sell the house?' asked Claire suddenly. 'You'd be nearer to me then. I could keep an eye on you.'

This time Eileen laughed. 'Keep an eye on me! What are you expecting me to get up to?'

'Nothing,' said Claire hastily. 'I meant—'

'You meant that now that I'm an abandoned old woman you feel you should pop in with some soup for me every day?'

'No.' Claire suddenly laughed too, surprising herself. 'It's just that – well, it isn't easy being on your own.'

'Somehow I think it's better than living with someone who doesn't love you,' said Eileen.

'Was it that bad?' asked Claire.

'It saps your confidence,' confessed her mother. 'OK, the magic had gone for both of us. But you still can't help wondering why he doesn't find you attractive any more.'

'Oh, Mum.' Claire put her arm around Eileen's shoulders. 'It seems such a waste.'

'I know,' said Eileen. 'But at least we're finally doing something about it.'

Claire looked at her watch. 'Does Dad expect me to meet him? Here? Somewhere else?'

'I said I'd ring him if you wanted to see him tonight,' said Eileen. 'It's up to you. You can meet him wherever you like.'

'I want to talk to him,' Claire said. 'But maybe not today. I'm not sure I'm ready to talk to him today.'

'It's all right for you to still love him,' Eileen told her.

'I understand that,' said Claire. 'And of course I still love him. So you can tell him that. I'll phone him later. Or maybe I'll text him and tell him that myself.'

'He'd like that,' said Eileen. 'He's worried about how you'll react.'

'What can I do?' asked Claire blankly. 'You've both obviously had a long, long time to think about it. All I can do is hope that you're doing the right thing.'

'We're doing the right thing,' Eileen assured her. 'Your glass is empty, darling. Would you like more water or d'you think you need something stronger?'

Claire and Eileen sat in the garden until it was time for Claire to catch her train. Eileen chatted about estate agents and moving house and the weirdness of looking at townhouses and apartments at her stage in life. But, she said, some of them were lovely. Ideal for one person. And decorating would be fun, wouldn't it? Claire suddenly realised that her mother seemed much more light-hearted than before and that her eyes twinkled and sparkled in a way she hadn't seen in a long time.

'Were you so desperately unhappy?' she asked again as she hugged Eileen goodbye.

'You don't notice it until you change things,' said Eileen, 'and then you wonder how you coped at all.'

'I wish I'd known.'

'What could you have done about it.' Eileen smiled faintly. 'It was our mistake, not yours.'

'A long-term mistake because of me.'

'We should have done something about it before now,' agreed Eileen. 'I blame myself for letting things drift.' She caught Claire by the hand. 'Don't ever let things drift,' she said. 'Get out there and live your life, Claire.'

Claire swallowed hard. 'I'm doing fine,' she said to her mother.

'I don't want you to have regrets,' said Eileen.

Claire looked at her ruefully. 'There'll always be regrets,' she said.

'Let him go.' Eileen tightened her grip. 'It's time to let him go.'

Claire wanted to be angry with her mother for saying those words, but she couldn't be. Not today.

'If it makes you feel any better,' she told Eileen suddenly, 'I'm meeting a guy for a drink.'

'Claire!' Eileen's eyes lit up. 'Really?'

Claire chewed at her lip. She wasn't meeting anyone. But she could. She could e-mail JustMe tonight and suggest a date. She could call Eavan and ask for Paul Hanratty's number and meet him for the old-friends' drink he'd asked about. She could meet men and have a social life which would stop Eileen looking at her in despair every time they met, and her mother would never need to know that it was all for Georgia's sake.

'I have to call him.' Claire was thinking of Paul. 'He's an old friend. It's just a drink.'

'But Claire, this is fantastic.'

'It's not fantastic,' said Claire. 'It's a drink. And I only told you so that you can see I'm fine. Georgia's fine. We're all fine. So don't worry about us. Worry about yourself.'

'You need to see other people,' Eileen told her. 'Find someone new.'

'I wish you could get it into your head that my life isn't about finding someone,' said Claire. 'Georgey and I are still a family.'

'But it's nice to have someone to love,' said Eileen gently.

'You're a great one to talk,' retorted Claire, 'given that you've just told me you've lived most of your life with a man you *didn't* love.' She picked up her bag. 'I've got to go. I'll call you. And I'll call Dad too.'

'Claire—'

'I'll let you know how I get on,' said Claire. 'But it's only a drink. Please believe me.'

'OK,' said Eileen. 'Have a nice time.'

Suddenly Claire smiled. 'I haven't confirmed it yet,' she said. 'And if I do, I won't have a thing to wear. He's used to seeing me in sports gear.'

Eileen smiled too. 'Wear a skirt. Stretch out your legs in front of him and I bet he falls for you.'

'Mum!'

'You have great legs, Claire. Everyone says so.'

'For heaven's sake!' But Claire looked at her in amusement.

'Go for it.'

'I won't be showing off my legs,' said Claire. 'Not in their naked state anyway. There are too many scars on them to be attractive. But if it makes you happy, I'll think about wearing my tightest jeans. They make me look like a beanpole.'

'Wear whatever you like,' Eileen told her. 'Just have a good time.'

'Sure.' Claire kissed her quickly on the cheek. 'I'd better go. I'll phone you.'

'OK,' said Eileen. 'Don't forget.'

Chapter 9

Lavatera (Tree Mallow) – Pink/white flowers all summer. Quick-growing but should be pruned hard every year.

The journey home seemed to take much less time than the journey to Dundalk. Claire sat in her seat and gazed out of the window as the coastal scenery flashed by, recalling everything her mother had told her about her relationship with her father. It beggared belief, thought Claire, that Eileen and Con hadn't been happy together. They'd seemed an ideal couple to her. There had never been any arguments in the Shanahan household, no high dramas, nothing to indicate that they weren't living the lives they wanted to live. And now her mother was saying that it had all been a sham. That those happy family evenings in front of the TV or sitting together in the flower-filled garden had been nothing more than an illusion. It was simply unacceptable, Claire thought helplessly. She couldn't believe that her entire childhood – and indeed her entire life – had been based on a fiction. Con and Eileen didn't love each other. They never had. They'd only married because of her.

She bit her fingernail. That was what was most difficult to accept. Because of her, they'd lived for more than thirty-five years together. Years of clinging on to something that wasn't true. Years in which they'd have been happier apart. How could she not have guessed? And particularly how could she not have guessed that her father had apparently been seeing a plethora of other women? Now – at this ridiculously late age in his life – he'd apparently found one he wanted to live with for ever. And that was truly unbelievable. Her father was nearing retirement age. She couldn't quite visualise him tripping up the aisle with someone else at this point in his life. And what about this woman – this Lacey person? In her fifties, she remembered. Had she been married before too? Was there another family in the background? Would her father expect her to like the new woman in his life and accept whatever baggage she was bringing with her?

Was Lacey someone like her? Claire wondered suddenly. A widow who had finally decided to make a new life for herself? Or was she a woman who had seen an opportunity and seized it, not caring that Con was already married? Which was she? A saint or a slut?

She supposed she'd better phone him when she got home. Eileen would undoubtedly have been on to him already, letting him know that Claire had been told. It was all far too civilised, she told herself. All too matter-of-fact. She supposed she should be happy that her parents had made the decision if that was what they wanted but even so . . . it went to prove that even if you did manage to navigate that minefield of men, you couldn't be guaranteed to have got it right. No matter how great it might appear to everyone else.

Although she never would have admitted it aloud to anyone, Eavan Keating loved being a housewife. Being a stay-at-home mother had never been on her agenda in her early days with Locum Libris, when she'd sat opposite Claire Shanahan and wondered why on earth Claire would want to marry Bill Hudson and struggle with married life and a mortgage before her twenty-first birthday. Eavan had argued vociferously with Claire about tying herself down and committing herself too soon – getting married, she'd often said, was for when you'd finished playing the field a bit. And staying at home – well, that was for women who had no pride in their own achievements. She conceded that Claire wasn't selling out completely since she was acting as Bill's PA, but, she told her friend, it really wasn't quite the same thing when you didn't have a job of your own that was completely separate from anything your husband might do.

Eavan had never considered herself to be an all-out career woman but she'd never expected to decide to give up her job and devote her time to her husband and her daughter either. However, as she'd struggled to find a crèche with room to take baby Saffy and allow her to go back to work, she'd felt increasingly desolate about the choice she was making. She didn't want to leave her gorgeous, smiling baby with strangers for the best part of the day. She didn't want to have to rush home through stress-making traffic jams to pick her up and then find herself too tired to play with her in the evenings. She didn't want anything in her life to be more important than Saffy's welfare and happiness.

So, with only a couple of weeks to go before she went back to the printing and publishing firm, she'd sat on the sofa beside Glenn and asked him if it wasn't possible, with some cutbacks on their part, for her to give up her job with Locum Libris after all. She'd known that it was a tricky proposition. Over the years she'd done well with the company so that she'd ended up being promoted a number of times. Even allowing for the costs of childcare they'd be taking a significant cut in income if she stopped working. And their dream house in Howth already took a huge chunk out of Glenn's salary.

'I know it'll be difficult,' she'd whispered (because Saffy was sleeping in her Moses basket beside the sofa and she didn't want to wake her), 'but surely we can manage?'

The anxious look that crossed Glenn's face was fleeting.

'Whatever you think best,' he told her, and then he'd kissed her softly on the mouth. They'd ended up making love on the sofa while Saffy slept. And Eavan knew that they'd made the best possible decision for their family even if it did mean that Glenn had committed himself to working even harder.

Eavan was still surprised at how easily she'd taken to being a mother. And at how simple it had been to swap staff meetings for coffee with other mums and proofing deadlines for pooling childcare. Of course it drove her crazy sometimes – Saffy was still going through her Terrible Twos phase and was sometimes the most impossible child in the universe to deal with; she'd insisted on listening to her CD of 'The Wheels on the Bus' over and over again one Thursday afternoon until Eavan had wanted to get on the damn bus and drive it off the nearest cliff; there'd also been the day when Saffy had taken Eavan's entire collection of make-up and thrown it all down the toilet. Those were the times, Eavan thought, when being at work was the easy option.

But mostly, like now, she was blissfully happy in her chosen role.

She sat in the back garden and allowed herself the luxury of a glass of chilled white wine to reward herself for giving the kitchen a really thorough cleaning earlier. Saffy and her best friend, Rachel Gorman, were playing happily in the sandpit in the shadiest corner of the garden, engrossed in their world of make-believe. Eavan had agreed to take Rachel for a couple of hours while her mother, Ruth, was having her hair done. Ruth usually returned the favour.

It doesn't get much better than this, Eavan thought, as she sipped her wine. She closed her eyes and wallowed in her moment of pleasure and satisfaction at having the perfect house and the perfect husband. It's not wrong to be satisfied about it, she told herself guiltily, as she opened her eyes again. We've worked hard. Glenn still works hard. We're entitled to nice things.

And it *was* nice. She looked proprietorially around at her neatly trimmed lawn and carefully tended evergreens, as well as the blazes of colour that were her beds of alyssum and flax in vivid yellow, blue and bright, bright red. Then she bit her lip as she gazed at the beautiful flowing burgundy tree mallow which had been a present from Bill Hudson a few years earlier. Poor old Claire, she thought sadly. I can understand why she doesn't like to come here very often. The four of us used to have such good times together. And seeing the shrub probably reminds her of him too. I never thought of that before.

She looked at her watch and frowned suddenly. Nearly four. Glenn was late. He'd had to go in to the office that day because there was some really important staff meeting. Eavan hadn't been overly pleased about the fact that he was working on a Saturday, but it often happened. The thirty-five-hour working week was a thing of the past, especially in Glenn's industry. He'd promised that he'd be back by three, though. He was often late home, but he usually phoned to tell her first. It was part of the rules they had for living with each other. Keep each other informed at all times. Don't let worry and suspicion crowd into the marriage. It wasn't, they agreed, that they had to know where the other person was every single second of the day, but they'd let each other know about variations in their routines.

It hadn't actually seemed that important when they were both working but since Eavan had given up her job to stay at home it mattered more to her. She didn't like to think that Glenn was managing to keep on with his old lifestyle while hers had changed. And despite the fact that she couldn't have been happier with the change she was aware that there was still a general agreement in the working environment that stay-at-home mothers didn't quite contribute as much as people who slaved away for the corporate good. They would pay lip service to the work of women who stayed at home, she knew. But they never quite believed it. Until she'd made the switch she didn't quite believe it herself.

She looked at her watch again. The meeting had probably gone on a bit – she'd been at those types of meetings herself, where you thought that everything was sorted and then someone would pop up with a stupid question and the whole thing would start all over again. And then there was the traffic. Glenn's office was in Blanchardstown, where traffic was notoriously heavy, especially on a Saturday, with everyone going to the huge shopping centre. All the same, he usually phoned if he was stuck in some tailback. I'm not his keeper, said Eavan firmly to herself. But now that she'd noticed the time she knew that she'd be conscious of his lateness until he finally made it home. And she'd worry, very slightly, until she heard the car pull into the driveway.

She wondered if Glenn ever worried about her. He didn't need to, of course. Her life was so bound up with Saffy that there was nothing she could do that could cause him to worry. She frowned again and bit her lip. Whenever she worried about Glenn – and, she had to admit, those times were rare – it was that he had somehow been lured into accepting an alcoholic drink again. And that the whole fabric of their lives would collapse because of it.

In some ways she wished she'd known Glenn in his alcohol-filled days. Because of not knowing, she was acutely aware that in her mind she'd built them up into a period of hedonistic excess and black despair. And she was terrified that they might happen again. Of course they might not have been that bad. But she knew from the newspaper articles she'd read and the TV programmes she'd seen that living with an alcoholic was complete hell. She didn't think she could cope with it. I'm living with one now, she reminded herself sternly. Just because he doesn't drink hasn't changed that fact. I'm living with him and it's not complete hell. It's perfectly fine. And I have to stop panicking every time he's a few seconds late and thinking the very worst of him. Why the hell should I think the worst when, as far as I'm concerned, he's always been the best?

The sound of the car pulling up outside the door made her relax suddenly. She recognised the tone of the engine, the slamming of the door and the beep of the alarm. Glenn was home. Everything was fine.

Claire was still reeling from her mother's news as she sat in front of the computer and opened her web browser again. She still found it impossible to take in the full impact of her parents' split. And she felt more stupid and ignorant about the relationships between men and women than ever before. She was worse than hopeless, she told herself. Georgia didn't stand a chance with her as a mother. She had to do something.

She would give herself two options, she decided. She would contact JustMe and then she'd call Paul Hanratty too. If she had two dates her mother could hardly get at her for staying home too much. Plus she'd gather twice as much information on dating men!

She logged on to the HowWillIKnow site and found JustMe, then clicked the 'Contact' button and started an e-mail.

I'm easy-going, non-smoker, drink wine, work from home. Average height, red-gold-blonde hair. She paused for a moment. What did she really want to tell him? Did it matter if she was only going to see him once anyway? *I like warm weather, animals and sport.* She paused again and then shrugged her shoulders; there was no point in not being truthful. *I have a daughter.* But she wasn't going to tell him Georgia's age. She wasn't going to put any information about Georgia on the net. *Please contact me if you WLTM.*

Her finger hovered over the 'Send' button for almost a minute before she finally hit it.

Everything wasn't fine. Not really. Eavan wasn't sure exactly what the problem was, but she knew something was bothering Glenn. He'd come into the house and left his briefcase on the kitchen counter as usual. He'd said hello to her, looked out the window at where

97

Saffy (alone now since Rachel had gone home a little earlier) was demolishing the sandcastles they'd built; then he'd walked upstairs and into the bathroom, where she'd heard the sound of the shower being turned on. She'd stood outside the bathroom wondering what on earth the matter was and what on earth she was supposed to do about it.

Glenn had spent ages in the bathroom and she'd gone downstairs again before the hum of the shower ceased. By the time he came to join the family, she and Saffy were rebuilding the sandcastles again.

He looks tired, she thought. There were shadows under his eyes and his brow was creased. But he smiled as he saw both of them and stretched his arms open wide for Saffy to rush into. He whirled her round in the air while she shrieked with laughter and begged him to spin faster and faster.

'I'll fall over if I do much more.' He put her gently on the ground and staggered slightly. 'I'm totally dizzy as it is.'

He sat on the wooden patio bench.

'Are you OK?' asked Eavan.

'Of course,' he said. 'Just dizzy.'

'Can I get you a drink of water?'

'Sure,' he said. 'Water'd be lovely. It's still so hot, I'm dying of thirst.'

Eavan brought him a long frosted glass filled to the brim.

'You're late home,' she said.

'Oh, you know how it is at meetings,' said Glenn easily. 'Everyone has to have his say. We're expanding the network but we still have to cut costs. I'm going to be out of the office for the next few weeks.'

'Out where?' she asked.

'With clients,' he told her. 'Don't even bother ringing me on the landline. Just call the mobile.'

'Are you happy about it?' she asked.

'What can I do?' he returned. 'The pressure is on to increase business. I've got to do what I've got to do.'

'Well, don't kill yourself,' she told him.

'Darling, it's not a question of killing myself or not. Whatever it takes to pay the mortgage I'll do.'

Eavan looked worried. 'Is it a problem?' she asked.

'Of course not,' he said firmly.

'Because if it is . . .'

'Don't worry so much,' said Glenn. 'Everything's fine. Now come on, do you want to go out to dinner tonight?'

'Out?' Eavan looked surprised.

'You and me and Saffy. A family night out.'

'Where?'

'The Mexican in Howth is nice,' he suggested. 'And child-friendly.'

'OK.' She smiled at him and then kissed him on the cheek. 'I do love you, you know.'

'I love you too,' said Glenn as he hugged her close to him.

Claire didn't ring her father until much later that night, after she'd taken Phydough for a long walk along the seafront, during which she'd talked through the whole issue of her parents' broken marriage with him. He'd barked from time to time as though he was agreeing with her that the situation was incredible. Then she told him about registering with HowWillIKnow. He barked at that too. She felt better afterwards, but when she came home she still hadn't plucked up the courage to call. She wasn't sure that she really wanted to listen to what Con had to say, to discover that Eileen had been telling the truth when she said that there had never been real love in the marriage. Claire didn't want to believe that.

So she'd sat at the kitchen table, flicking her way through yet more magazines (this time Georgia's teen mags) and wondering whether all girls between the ages of twelve and seventeen really did spend their entire lives worrying about spots on their foreheads and bad breath and not being able to kiss properly and lusting after some bloke whose name they didn't even know. They worried about their clothes being wrong, their hair being wrong, about being too fat, too thin, having big breasts or small breasts. They worried about everything. That all passed me by, she thought, as she read an article about 'How To Tell If He Really Means What He Says'. I always knew what Bill meant.

She stacked the magazines in a pile and then picked up the cordless phone. She couldn't put it off any longer. She walked out into the dusky evening with the receiver in her hand. Mars, low on the horizon, shone orange-white with reflected light in the sky. A creamy crescent moon hung sideways above it. She dialled her father's mobile phone.

'Hello, honey,' he said on the first ring.

'Hi, Dad.'

'How are you?'

'I'm OK. You?'

'Grand,' said Con. 'I'm glad you called.'

'I had to call,' said Claire. 'To hear your side of everything.'

'I thought your mother would have made it clear that there aren't any sides.' Con sounded testy. 'It's a mutual decision, Claire.'

'I know,' she said. 'Mum was very explicit on that point. It's just that I find it so hard to believe. I thought you loved each other.'

'Look, I know your mother says we never did,' Con told her. 'But that's not entirely true. We did at the start. And after you were born. But we weren't the right sort of people to be married to each other.'

'Seems to me that if you managed to stay together for this long there doesn't seem to be much point in changing now,' said Claire.

'Ah, Claire, you don't really mean that.'

'I do,' she snapped. 'I mean, Dad, you're talking about moving in with another woman. At your age! I thought you'd have more sense.'

'It's precisely because I've reached this age that I think I *should* do it,' said Con. 'Me and your mother lived a lie. It wasn't always an uncomfortable lie. I have a lot of affection for Eileen, you know. But I don't love her. I do love Lacey and I want to marry her.'

'Oh, surely you've got past that stage in your life by now!' cried Claire.

'Past wanting to love someone and be with them? I don't think so.' Con sounded defiant.

'It's not that I don't think you shouldn't have someone to love . . .' Claire found it difficult to express how she really felt. 'It's just that – well, I don't see why you need to rush into marrying her.'

'Hardly rushing,' said Con drily. 'It's been a long relationship.'

'Oh, I don't care,' said Claire as dismissively as she could. 'Do whatever you think is right.'

'I am,' said Con. 'So when will you come and meet her?'

'I'm busy at the moment,' said Claire. 'I've got some work on hand, I'm using the opportunity to get a lot done while Georgey's away . . . and . . . and I've people to see . . . plus . . . um . . . there's someone coming to see about tidying up the garden. So, you know, I'll call you.'

Con said nothing.

'I *will* call,' promised Claire.

'I'm in town at lunchtime on Monday,' said Con, 'and I thought it would be the ideal opportunity.'

'Oh.'

'After all, it'll only be a couple of hours. Lacey will be able to spare the time then too.'

'You've talked it over with her already?'

'When your mum told me she'd gone through it all with you today I talked to Lacey about meeting you. She'd like to see you, Claire. She really would. I've told her a lot about you.'

'I still don't know why there has to be this big rush to meet up,' said Claire sourly.

'Come on,' urged Con. 'A quick lunch, meet and greet, no big deal. Honestly.'

'It's just that—'

'Please, Claire.'

'Oh, all right.' She wished she hadn't sounded so ungracious, but she couldn't help herself. She felt as though her parents were steamrollering her into a new phase of their lives. A phase she wasn't ready for yet.

'Great.' Con sounded relieved. 'Lacey works off Nassau Street. Why don't we meet in Fitzer's at one? We might be able to get a table outside. I'll book it anyway.'

Claire had never heard her father sounding so decisive before. 'OK,' she said.

'Thanks, Claire.'

'That's OK.'

'So we'll see you then?'

'Yes. Sure.'

'I'm looking forward to it,' he told her. 'It's ages since I've seen my favourite daughter.'

'Your only daughter,' she reminded him automatically, carrying on the verbal ritual that had started years ago.

'That's why you're my favourite,' he said.

She felt her eyes fill up with unexpected tears. 'I love you,' she said.

'I love you too,' he answered, before hanging up.

She walked back into the kitchen and sat in the wicker chair. It seemed to her that she was the only one upset over the break-up of her parents' marriage. Eileen and Con both seemed happy. And that, she supposed, was the most important thing. But she still couldn't quite get her head around the fact that at this stage in their lives they were both prepared to change things completely. I suppose, she thought, I can see how Dad would be happy, and him with the fifty-two-year-old woman waiting in the wings! But Mum? She'll be on her own. And being on your own isn't exactly a bed of roses.

She frowned. She was on her own too. And it was all right. She got by, didn't she? If she ignored the nagging sadness of missing Bill, the rest of her life was OK. But then, she reminded herself, she had Georgia. Eileen had nobody. Surely, despite whatever she might say, her mother needed someone in her life too?

Chapter 10

Tellima (Fringecup) – White frothy flowers on a semi-evergreen plant. Lift and divide every few years.

W hen the alarm went off the following Monday morning Eavan rolled over in the bed and hit the off button, squeezing her eyes tightly closed so that she didn't wake up properly. Saffy had taken to sleeping till around seven, and Eavan wanted to catch up on every extra minute she could in bed. She waited for Glenn to get up so that she could pull the sheet more tightly around her. Even in the hottest weather she liked having the sheet practically over her head.

She drifted in the half-world between sleep and waking, expecting to feel the movement of Glenn getting out of the bed. And then she realised that he hadn't moved at all and she was suddenly wide awake.

She sat up and yawned, then shook him by the shoulder. 'You'll be late,' she hissed. 'Get up.'

He blinked a couple of times, then looked at her in surprise. 'Whassa matter?'

'The alarm went off fifteen minutes ago,' she told him. 'You didn't hear it.'

Glenn closed his eyes. 'I'm tired,' he said.

'Glenn!' Eavan looked at him in astonishment. 'You have to get up. You said that you had a full schedule today.'

'Mmm.' He lay immobile on his back while she looked down at him. Then he opened his eyes wide and sat up. 'God, sorry. I wasn't properly awake. I didn't realise what was going on.' He pushed the sheet to one side. 'You're right. I *will* be late.'

She watched as he opened the door of the en-suite bathroom and went inside. Soon she could hear him singing in his rich baritone over the sound of the shower. She ran her hands through her sleep-tousled hair. Something wasn't quite right. Glenn had been acting strangely ever since his Saturday meeting. It couldn't just be worries about work. Eavan knew that the phone business was going through a cut-throat phase at the moment, but Glenn was good at his job and she was certain that if he'd been set targets by senior management he'd have no trouble in meeting them. Maybe, though, he was concerned about the long-term future of the Trontec, the company he worked for.

She twirled the ends of her hair around her fingers. Maybe, like so many companies that had been set up over the past few years, Trontec's viability was under question. And Glenn didn't want to worry her with it because if Trontec went under . . . Eavan shuddered . . . if Trontec went under, then the Keating family was in big trouble financially. She felt her stomach constrict with tension. Or maybe, she told herself as she released the breath she'd been holding, maybe she was just getting everything out of proportion. She needed to chill out a little. Not worry so much.

That was the one disadvantage of not having a paying job of her own to worry her, she realised. She worried about everything else instead.

Claire was awake early too. She'd opened her eyes at about six and, instantly alert, had got up and gone downstairs. It was too early for the sun to hit the patio area of the house, but it was pleasantly warm, even in the shade. She sat on the edge of the table, her feet resting on the wooden bench, and thought about her coming lunch date with her father and his new girlfriend.

My dad and his girlfriend. God, she thought, how on earth am I going to get my head around it? How the hell am I going to behave with her? I don't want to like her but that's because I don't want to accept what's happened. But it's not fair to Dad to be nasty to her. What if she's nice? What if I think she's perfect for him? But how can I think that? After all, I'm the eejit who thought my mother was perfect for him!

She heaved an enormous sigh, and Phydough, who'd settled under the bench, looked up at her.

'People should stick to dogs,' she told him as she stretched her legs to tickle him with her bare toes. 'Much less trouble.'

She gazed out over the garden and then frowned as her eyes stopped at a bank of weeds which suddenly came into focus. She'd told her father that she was getting someone to come and look it. She'd said it because it had been in the back of her mind for ages, and because it made her time sound occupied so that Con wouldn't think that she could just drop everything and meet this Lacey person. She hadn't actually planned on doing anything yet. But now, looking at it, she knew that it needed tending sooner rather than later. The combination of the heavy rain earlier in the month and the hot sun of the last week or so had made it grow all the more rampantly and out of control. The wonderful red-hot pokers looked tall but anaemic in their patch along the side wall, and the beds of Galaxy sweet peas were parched through lack of care. In the height of summer, when the garden should have been a testament to Bill, it looked ragged and forgotten.

But who to get? She knew that Eavan and Glenn had contracted a big and (they thought) prestigious landscaping firm to do their garden a few years earlier but that they hadn't been a hundred per cent happy with the work. Gardening-lite, Eavan had called it sniffily, and had remarked that they were more interested in charging for unusual features than putting down plants that would thrive.

Claire slid from the table and walked, barefoot, through the too-long grass. The lawn was full of clover, she realised, and under the apple and pear trees it was being taken over by moss. Dry now, though. She scuffed at it with her heel and a cloud of dust and moss floated into the air. She ducked as a wasp flew past her, and then another. She frowned slightly. They were all going in the same direction, towards the house. And now that she noticed it, she could see that they were flying with a purpose and disappearing under the gutter. Shit, she thought. A nest. They'd had a wasps' nest a few years earlier and had had to get someone out to deal with it after Bill's DIY attempts had nearly had him stung to death. When the expert had called to the house, dressed in protective clothing much to Georgia's

105

amusement and delight, he'd told them that a nest could contain as many as fifty thousand wasps. The thought of fifty thousand wasps in the eaves had appalled Bill but intrigued Georgia. Nevertheless, they'd all been relieved when it had been destroyed.

So, she thought. Garden things. Either decide to do it myself or get someone else to do it. And find a wasps' nest exterminator. As soon as possible. But not today. She couldn't concentrate on anything other than lunch today. What she had to keep in mind, she mused as she allowed her thoughts to drift back to her father and Lacey, was that this woman had been in his life for four years already. So she had all the advantages. Claire knew that her father would have told Lacey about her and her life with Bill. Lacey had been around at the time of the accident and its aftermath. She would know things about Claire that Claire herself probably didn't want her to know.

She went back into the house and upstairs. She decided to take Phydough for an early walk so that she could have plenty of time later to get ready. The dog was only too pleased to get out and about early, and she allowed him to choose his favourite route along the seafront. Already a snake of commuting cars stretched along the main road. My life isn't so bad, she thought suddenly. I'm here on a sunny morning with my dog while all those people are stuck in hot cars. Quite suddenly she felt incredibly cheerful.

'Come on Phy,' she called. 'Let's run.'

So the two of them loped along the grassy walk while her hair flew out behind her and her legs stretched further with every step. Eventually they stopped and she sank to her knees.

'I'm not fit,' she told the dog. 'Really I'm not.'

But, she admitted to herself, she had been able to run. She hadn't fallen over and it hadn't hurt her and it had been fun. Phydough barked softly at her.

'I can't do it again,' she said. 'I'm in a lather, Phydough. Let's be a bit more circumspect on the way home.'

Phydough would have liked to run again. But he trotted happily beside her as they turned back towards the house.

When she got home, Claire went into the bathroom and ran herself a lukewarm bath. She crumbled some rose-scented cubes into it and then slid into the silky water. She leaned her head back and closed her eyes. It was a long time since she'd luxuriated in a bath, and she allowed her mind to drift as the delicate perfume of the cubes soothed her. If I can run like that, she thought, maybe I can play tennis or badminton again. I know it's different and I know I wouldn't be as good as I was before, but is that such a big deal? To my pride, maybe, because I was always one of the good players. But so what if I can compete again? Isn't that more important?

After her bath she went into the office and checked her e-mails. She'd checked them a couple of times since sending the message off to JustMe although so far she hadn't had any reply. But now a new message appeared in her in-box. She was surprised to realise that she was nervous about opening it.

Hello, Soft Cell, she read, wincing as she saw the user name she'd given herself in print. It looked and sounded stupid. *Thanks for your message. You sound really nice and sweet. Only thing is, I went out with someone last week and I think she's the right person for me. So I'm taking my name off the list. Plus, to be very honest, I can't stand kids. Best wishes, JustMe.*

She stared at the message. He'd turned her down. She couldn't quite believe it. All that agonising about picking the right person and writing the right message and he'd turned her down! She was surprised at how offended she felt. And rejected. She highlighted the message and hit 'Delete'. She thought about accessing the HowWillIKnow site again and finding someone else. But, right now, her heart wasn't in it. She closed down her e-mail program and opened her work file instead. Sometimes life was better at the molecular level.

At twelve o'clock she stopped working so that she could get ready for lunch.

'So, Phy, what d'you think?' she asked the dog, who'd followed her into the bedroom. 'I'm meeting Dad's girlfriend. Should I look chic and sophisticated or down-to-earth?'

Phydough watched her, his brown eyes half hidden by his white and grey fur.

'Maybe I should check out the magazines and see what's hot in make-up,' she continued. 'Though most of mine is years old.' She frowned. Having just been reading about bacteria in the document she was working on, she suddenly remembered that you were

107

supposed to throw out make-up after a few months because otherwise it became a playground for the microscopic life forms. Oh well, she thought, as she rummaged in her nylon bag for her two-year-old wand of mascara. I'll have to go out with my eyelashes crawling. Yeuch!

She opened the wardrobe door and looked at her clothes. They were a dismal collection, she acknowledged. Not that she'd ever really been a slave to fashion, but every single skirt or top or pair of trousers was at least two years old, if not more. Some of them – the pre-accident skirts in particular – were both too loose to wear now and too short to hide her scarred knee. The trousers were wide, whereas this year's look was narrow. And her T-shirts were nearly all plain white, which at least didn't date but was hardly daring. Though why do I want to look daring? she asked herself moodily, as she took one from the drawer beneath her blouse rail. I'm meeting a middle-aged woman who wants to marry my dad. Did that make Lacey her potential stepmother? wondered Claire suddenly. Was that the appropriate word for adult children to use for the second wife after a divorce? We need more terms, she muttered, to deal with ever more complicated lives.

In the end she settled for a soft cotton leaf-green dress which brought out the amber in her eyes and the golden glints in her hair and which was long enough to cover her knees. She brushed bronzer over her face (definitely less pale, she knew, than a week ago, thanks to the sun), dabbed some grey eye shadow on her lids and touched up her lips with a tinted salve. She left her soft curls loose around her face, slid some gold earrings into her ears and fastened the locket which Bill had given her for her twenty-first birthday around her neck. She chose a low-heeled pair of sandals which didn't rub against her now-healed blisters but which gave her enough height to carry off the rather clingy dress. 'I'll have to do,' she told Phydough. 'Let's face it, it doesn't much matter. She's going to marry Dad regardless of how I look!'

She caught the bus at the end of the Malahide Road and then walked along the quays and up Westmoreland Street, past Trinity College, towards the restaurant. The city was thronged with tourists and Dubliners alike, all enjoying the warmth of the sun on their backs as they walked the twisting streets. Claire crossed the road at Trinity, continued along Nassau Street and turned up Dawson Street. The restaurant was nearby; she could already see the tables and chairs on the pavement outside, and she hoped that her father had managed to book a table.

In fact he was sitting there already, but he was alone. Claire's heart skipped a beat. Maybe Lacey had changed her mind. Maybe bringing everything into the open had changed their relationship and she didn't want to be involved with Con any more.

'Hi.' She sat down opposite her father, who smiled at her.

'Hello, darling,' he said. 'You're looking well.'

'Thanks.'

'No.' He nodded at her. 'I mean it. You do look well. Better than I've seen you look in ages.'

'It's the sun,' she told him. 'I've got a bit of colour.'

'It suits you,' said Con. 'You've been far too pale for far too long.'

A waitress arrived at the table and Claire ordered a mineral water. Con already had a glass in front of him.

'So,' she said, when the waitress had gone. 'Where's your new woman?'

Con looked at her. Claire had tried to sound light-hearted but had only succeeded in sounding brittle. He knew that this was difficult for her, but he wasn't going to have her judging Lacey before they'd even met. He took a sip of his water.

'She's hardly new,' he said carefully. 'I've known her for a long time.'

'New to me.'

'She'll be here in a minute, and I'd really appreciate it if you lost the tone of disapproval.'

'Dad, I don't approve or disapprove,' cried Claire untruthfully. 'It's not up to me, is it? I'm just still a bit taken aback.' She stared at the table for a moment and then lifted her eyes to look at him. 'And I wish it was different.'

'I wish it was different too,' said Con. 'At least – well – oh, Claire, I wish your mum and I had done this years ago.'

'I do understand.' But Claire could see that her father's attention had moved from her to the woman who'd just entered the restaurant. She stopped at their table and smiled.

Claire didn't know what she'd expected her father's girlfriend to look like. She'd had two mental images, one created immediately when Eileen had said the woman's name – the brash image of a big-busted woman years younger than her father who'd seduced him with her physical charms. But then when Eileen had told her that Lacey was fifty-two, Claire had readjusted her mental picture into a slightly younger version of Eileen herself – comfortably plump, dark hair gone grey, casual clothes and a relaxed air.

Neither image was remotely correct. Lacey Dillon was a tiny woman, five foot tall at the most, Claire reckoned. She had ashblonde hair cut in a neat bob around a heart-shaped face. Her eyes were aqua blue. She wore a turquoise shift dress accessorised with matching backless shoes and offset by a chunky crystal necklace and equally chunky earrings. She could have been anywhere between thirty-five and fifty-five, though Claire would have put her at the lower end of the estimate. In fact, she thought, she doesn't look much older than me at all. Which is a bit depressing!

'Hi there.' Lacey kissed Con on the cheek and then turned to Claire. 'I'm Lacey,' she said as she held out her hand. 'I'm delighted to meet you at last.'

Claire had no choice but to accept it. The handshake was firm and decisive.

'Sorry I'm late.' Lacey sat on the empty chair. 'Phone rang just as I was leaving the office. You know how it is.'

'You work too hard.'

Claire opened her eyes wide. She'd never heard her father speak in that tone of voice before. Solicitous and caring and, very slightly, chiding. Lacey laughed.

'I know. I know. But I can't help it.' She waved at the waitress, ordered a water, and then smiled at Claire. 'Your dad says that you work for yourself. From home.'

'Not exactly,' said Claire. 'I do a lot of work from home but it's all for the same company and I call in there a couple of times a month. I'm a sort of freelance, I guess.'

'I used to work from home myself,' Lacey told her. 'When I set up the recruitment company first. But then it was taken over and they asked me to stay on as managing director. It's fine but not the same.'

'I suppose not.'

'I want her to retire,' said Con. 'Travel the world with me.'

'You can't afford to travel the world,' said Claire shortly.

Lacey picked up the single-sheet menu and looked at it. 'I'm going to have the Caesar salad,' she said. 'It's perfect for a hot summer's day.'

Both Con and Claire picked up their menus too.

'Same for me.' Claire put the menu back on the table.

Con's glance flickered between the two of them. 'The Dover sole,' he said. 'With a side salad.'

'Dad!' Claire looked at him in astonishment. 'No wedges?'

'No,' said Con. 'I'm trying to look after myself these days.'

They gave their orders to the hovering waitress and then sat back in their chairs.

'So, Claire,' said Lacey. 'I guess you want to know about me.'

'I suppose so,' said Claire.

'Well, it's all fairly straightforward. I'm fifty-two, a single mother of two grown-up children, I live near Lusk but your dad and I want something smaller and closer to the city. As I said earlier, I'm the managing director of a recruitment company. I first met your dad when I went to the factory in Dundalk where he worked, but I didn't actually talk to him until months later. We started seeing each other and have been seeing each other ever since. I love him very much and I want to marry him.'

Claire gulped. She'd never met anyone so matter-of-fact in her life before. And, as far as she could see, there was nothing in common between Lacey and Eileen. Except the children. She frowned and looked at the other woman.

'A single mother?' she asked. 'Are you divorced? Or widowed?' Her tone softened slightly.

'No,' said Lacey. 'When I said single I meant single. I never married the fathers of my children.'

'Fathers!' squeaked Claire.

'I got pregnant with my first child when I first started working,' said Lacey. 'I was very young at the time. It was a dreadful mistake. But I'm Irish and Catholic. I had the baby. Dylan is thirty-four now. He's married with a daughter of his own, Melanie. She's a year and

111

a half old and a little dote. A few years after Dylan was born I met a wonderful guy and we had a great relationship. But he forgot to tell me that he was married already. I was pregnant when we split up. I told him, but not until after the baby was born. Solange is twenty-four. She's living in Canada right now.'

Claire stared at her. 'And so now you've moved on to my dad.'

Lacey laughed. 'It's not like that at all,' she said. 'I know when I tell it baldly I sound like a social worker's case-load, but really and truly, Claire, when you've lived your life you have to expect certain possibilities. Getting pregnant the first time was through ignorance and stupidity. Getting pregnant the second time was sheer bad luck. I'm a good mother to my kids, I know I am. And I love your father. Very much.'

'It's not that I don't think you love him,' said Claire. 'But I don't see why you have to split up our family.'

'You know that's not true,' said Lacey. 'I had nothing to do with the split.'

'I'm finding that difficult to deal with at the moment,' said Claire. 'You see, I didn't realise there was a problem in Mum and Dad's marriage. I must be very stupid.'

'No you're not,' said Con. 'Besides, for most of your life you were caught up with Bill Hudson. Your mother and I were bit players.'

Claire looked at her father. 'That's not true.'

'Claire, from the moment you set eyes on him he was the most important person in your life.'

Claire said nothing.

'Now I have someone important in mine,' said Con. 'Your mother is happy for me. I want you to be happy too.'

'Of course I'm happy for you,' said Claire. 'And I know that you and Lacey have been together for a long time. But for me this has only just happened.'

'I do understand that,' said Lacey. 'I don't like to think of you feeling overwhelmed by it all. But your dad and I have made our decisions.'

'I'm worried about how Georgia will react,' said Claire.

'I know,' Con said, 'but Eileen thinks she'll take it in her stride.'

'There's only so much she can take!' cried Claire. 'She's already had to put up with a hell of a lot.'

'Yes.' Lacey's voice was soft. 'I'm really sorry about everything that happened to you. I'm sure it was a very difficult time.'

Claire swallowed and bit her lip. She wished she didn't always feel like she'd been hit in the stomach whenever anyone referred to the accident, even obliquely. But she couldn't help herself. She was saved by the waitress, who arrived with their food. By the time the plates had been placed on the table, she'd regained her composure.

'She sounds great, your daughter,' said Lacey as she ground black pepper on to her salad.

'She is,' said Claire.

'Away at the moment?'

'She's having a ball.' Claire couldn't help smiling. 'But I'll be glad to see her home. I miss her.'

'I miss Solange too,' said Lacey. 'I know she's having the most wonderful time abroad – she's working for a film company and they're shooting some TV series in Canada because they get great tax breaks over there – but I'd much rather she was at home.'

'Does she have much to do with her father?' asked Claire.

Lacey grimaced. 'No. He made it quite clear to me that he had a family and that he didn't see a place in his life for Solange. When she was eighteen they met up for the first time. She didn't think much of him. She told me that my choice of man was pretty poor.'

'So what will she say when she hears about you and Dad?'

'She knows already,' said Lacey calmly. 'I told her a little while ago.'

'And your son?'

'He knows too.'

'Am I the only one who didn't know?' Claire demanded as she turned to Con. 'Mum and apparently all the neighbours . . . and Lacey's family . . . is it just me?'

'Claire, love, we wanted to tell you before now. But we didn't think you were up to it.' Con reached out and grasped her hand. 'You know we were going to tell you before . . . when . . . when . . .'

She freed her hand and spoke brutally. 'When Bill was so inconveniently killed.'

'We needed to give you time after that,' said Con gently. 'To get over it.'

'But everyone seems pretty sure I'm not over it,' snapped Claire. 'Mum nagged at me about it again. Eavan keeps on and on at me about going out and meeting people and getting on with my life.'

'Haven't you?' asked Lacey softly.

'Oh, butt out.'

'Claire!' Con looked at her angrily.

'Sorry,' she said. She pushed away her plate. She hadn't eaten any salad but she really wasn't hungry. 'I'm truly sorry, Lacey. I want to be OK with you and Dad. I am OK with it. Just a bit taken aback, that's all. It's your life. And Mum's. You do whatever it is you like.' She stood up.

'Claire—'

'Everything's fine,' she interrupted her father. 'I'm fine. Don't worry about me. I'm just not hungry and I'm really not ready for this type of conversation all over again. Lacey, I'm glad to have met you. You know I'm still a bit shocked, but I hope things work out.'

'Nice to have met you too,' said Lacey calmly.

'Claire—'

'Dad, I'm not insulting you or Lacey by leaving now. Honestly I'm not. I'll call you.' She picked up her bag and walked out of the restaurant without looking back.

Claire strode up Dawson Street and then cut through Duke Street into Grafton Street. It was crowded with people, street artistes, hair-braiders and tarot-readers all jostling for space outside the department stores and boutiques. It was ages since she'd been in town and had braved the throngs of Grafton Street shoppers. Her heart was still hammering in her chest as it had been ever since meeting Lacey and her father.

The woman was OK, she conceded, but so different from her expectations as to be difficult to accept. She'd never have thought that her father would go for such a brisk and businesslike person, so completely and utterly different from Eileen. And then Claire suddenly realised that maybe it was precisely because Lacey was so different to Eileen that Con wanted to be with her. God above, though, she muttered under her breath as she stood at a bank machine to get some money, she hadn't expected someone with two kids. And a grandchild too! *And* two different fathers to the children – Lacey had been right about sounding like a social worker's case. But she seemed to be a very together woman. She seemed to have sorted out her life. She probably despises me, thought Carey, as she tucked her euros into her purse. Whining about my parents' marriage as if there was anything I could possibly do about it anyway. Behaving like a stupid child. Only . . . only . . . She tightened her grasp of her purse . . . everything is changing on me again. It's all going pear-shaped and I can't do anything to stop it!

She gulped at the warm summer's air, suddenly finding it difficult to breathe. I don't want things to change, she thought desolately as she leaned against the red-brick wall of the bank building. I want to know that some things never will. I want my parents to still love each other. She blinked in the afternoon sunlight and stared unsee-ingly down the length of the street, suddenly recalling the nights when her mother sat in front of the television, knitting needles clicking determinedly, while her father was working late. She wondered how many times he really had been working late. And what it had cost Eileen to keep up the pretence. A serial womaniser, just like Joanna's husband. And she knew that Joanna had been right to get a divorce.

I can't force them to love each other, she murmured to herself eventually. I can't make them stay together. And nothing ever stays the same.

The feeling of panic ebbed slightly. She moved away from the banklink machine and stopped by a flower-seller's bright and colourful display. There were scorching tiger lilies, yellow sunflowers and multi-coloured carnations. She thought of the empty vases dotted around her house and reached for her purse. Flowers would help. Flowers always helped.

She was handing over the money when she suddenly spotted Glenn Keating. He was sitting at a table outside a bar, an almost empty glass in front of him, reading the newspaper. Claire was so aston-ished at seeing him there that she almost forgot to take her change from the flower-seller.

She walked up to the bar and stopped in front of him. 'Hi, Glenn.'

He looked up from the paper, clearly startled. 'Claire!' he exclaimed. 'What are you doing here?'

'I met my father for lunch.' She frowned. 'And you?'

'Oh, me? I was meeting clients,' he told her.

'In town?' She looked surprised. 'I thought your clients were all around Castleknock.'

He laughed. 'We've spread our wings a lot over the last few years,' he told her. 'And we're doing a big marketing drive. Didn't Eavan tell you? I thought you two shared every little thing.'

'Not quite. So you're busy?'

'Up to our necks,' he said. He looked at his watch. 'In fact, Claire, I'd better get going. I've another meeting in a few minutes' time. I'm late already.'

'Yes. Sure,' she said.

He reached into his pocket and took out a mauve silk tie.

'Better get kitted out,' he said as he knotted it round his neck.

'Absolutely.'

'So, see you around.' He grabbed his briefcase and walked briskly down the street.

'You forgot your paper,' she called after him, but he was already swallowed up by the crowd.

Chapter 11

Laurus (Bay Laurel) – Glossy oval leaves. This grows best in a container. Can be damaged by frost.

Later that week, as she sat in front of the ice-white computer reading about a new, less invasive surgical procedure which was replacing a tried and tested old one and meant that patients spent a good deal less time in hospital, it suddenly occurred to her that sometimes change was a good thing. Obviously the changes that had happened to her hadn't been good. Her life had been devastated. But, in a totally different way, Eileen's had too. And Joanna's. And Georgia's, of course. In fact her family and friends had all encountered difficult times. Yet all of them, including her daughter, were facing up to new challenges. But in her case she was fighting against them.

Was that so terribly wrong, though? When she'd had it all before why shouldn't she remember it? It could never be as good again no matter what happened. She would always miss Bill at night. She would always be alone. She would always cry in the dark. Even if she won the lottery, or if Georgia became a world-wide successful superstar or businesswoman or whatever it was that she wanted most, or if she met a stinking rich and remarkably handsome man from HowWillKnow – even if any of those things happened none of them could make her happier than she'd been before. And that was why she didn't want anything else to change. Because no change could ever recapture the past.

The screen dissolved into screensaver mode because she'd been staring at it for so long without doing anything. She pushed the keyboard away from her and walked into her bedroom. She opened the wardrobe and looked at her rail of clothes. A miserable, boring collection, she thought as she stared at them. She should have gone shopping while she was in Grafton Street, made a bit of use of her time in town.

The sleeve from a jumper slid from the shelf above the rail and she pushed it back up. As she did so, her badminton racquet – which had been shoved on to the shelf and ignored for the past two years – was suddenly dislodged and fell down, hitting her on the head.

She massaged her crown and picked up the racquet. She tested the strings. Still taut – she'd had it restrung the year of the holiday in Jamaica. She remembered, quite suddenly, that she'd missed a match while she was away, had apologised repeatedly to the team for winning her holiday and being unavailable to play. And Eavan, who'd been the team captain that year, had told her not to worry about it, sure wasn't it only one match and wouldn't they manage without her just for once. Only, of course, it hadn't been just for once. She hadn't played again.

There were shuttles on top of the wardrobe too. She took one out of the tube. Then she bounced it on the racquet over and over, switching from bouncing it on her forehand to bouncing it on her backhand but never letting it fall. She'd once held the record in the club for the most bounces before dropping it but now she couldn't even remember how many that had been. She'd won a bottle of wine for her efforts.

She smiled at the memory. Then she stopped bouncing the shuttle and caught it. What would happen if she went back? What team would they put her on? Would they put her on a team at all? You had to be fit to play in the higher sections. She wasn't fit. She'd never be properly fit again. She stood uncertainly in the room, the racquet in one hand and the feathered shuttle in the other. It's not like you're a bloody international, she muttered to herself. It's not like it really matters. You could go back for the social part of it, just like Eavan's always asking you to.

She picked up the tube and stuffed the shuttle back into it. The season didn't start until September. There was plenty of time to think about it. Heaven only knew what other things might have cropped up by then. There was no point in getting into a state over possibly playing a stupid game. Even though her heart had suddenly begun to beat faster at the thought of winning a match again. She put the racquet and the shuttles back in the wardrobe. In the meantime, she told herself, there were plenty of things she could be getting on with instead of thinking about her life in a melodramatic sort of way. She had to get someone in to do the garden, didn't she? She'd told Con that she was going to do it and so she should. And . . . and she'd told Eileen that she was going to go for a drink with an old friend. Well that was something she could organise too. And there was the wasps' nest. She had to deal with that – or at least get an expert in to deal with it. Plus there was the social engagement of the week – Saffy's third birthday party at Glenn and Eavan's. She couldn't say that her life now wasn't busy. There were plenty of things going on.

She went back into her office and sat down at the computer again. She didn't have any work to do but she dialled up her e-mail programme.

There were more e-mails than she'd expected, all about the same thing. Rosie had forwarded the e-mail about the Dinner in the Dark event to everyone on the Locum Libris production team a couple of days earlier. So far all of them, except her, had decided to go.

Claire thought it sounded awful. She couldn't imagine eating in the dark with a selection of complete strangers. She certainly couldn't imagine enjoying it. But would she have to enjoy it, she wondered. Couldn't she put it down to researching men for Georgia? Maybe events like this were the future of dating and Georgia would go to them. If she went to this, at least she'd know what they were like. Although . . . she looked gloomily at the computer screen . . . internet dating was supposed to be the thing of the future too. And that had been singularly unsuccessful as far as she was concerned.

Much to her disgust, the two other messages she'd sent off (Danno – energetic, fun-loving, interested in sports, books and music; Guru – thoughtful, happy, interested in the everyday things in life) remained unanswered. She couldn't help feeling that if she wasn't able to get a date through the internet she was possibly the most hopeless person on the planet. She stared at the diary and wondered whether Dinner in the Dark was an entirely crackpot scheme. At least there'd be men there and they'd have to talk to her whether they wanted to or not.

She'd bought heaps more magazines and it certainly seemed as though even half-eligible men were in short supply, especially for women of her age. In fact, going by some of the articles, she should simply forget about the whole idea and leave the available men for desperate younger women. Others, though, insisted that women in their late thirties and early forties were in the prime of their lives, sexually experienced (which men loved) yet not stupid enough to believe the fairy-tale stuff. They gave the standard, non-technological, options for meeting men but Claire was pretty sure she was too old for nightclubs (she'd never really been into that whole scene anyway, though she did wonder whether she should check some out to see what Georgia might be getting into in the future); she'd mentally ruled out sports clubs because she wasn't yet ready to admit that she would have to hack around at a lower level than she was used to although bouncing the shuttle on the racquet earlier had definitely tugged at her competitive instincts for the briefest of moments; there was the possibility of the gym – she'd read somewhere that gyms were full of men and women checking each other out. But would she want to be checked out by someone when she was hot and sweaty and wearing gear that was guaranteed to highlight all the most undesirable aspects of her body?

In which case, she thought, coming round full circle, wouldn't Dinner in the Dark be quite a good thing, because nobody would be looking at her body? And wouldn't it be a good way of doing some of her dating research, because she'd definitely get to talk to men who were looking to go out with women? Maybe events like these would become more and more popular and Georgia might get invited to one. Better to check it out and discover whether it really was, as the HowWillIKnow homepage claimed, A Novel and Enticing Way To Meet the Man or Woman of Your Dreams. Claire couldn't help feeling that eating your way through a three-course meal beside perfect strangers in total darkness was a recipe for ending up with soup stains on your dress and no way of escaping from the bore beside you. But it was certainly a better bet than sweating in the gym or being ignored by men in cyberspace.

120

She typed a reply to Rosie saying that she'd joined HowWillIKnow and that she'd go to the dinner, and sent it before she could change her mind. This whole dating thing was a complete minefield, she decided. It was no wonder so many single women were neurotic about relationships. She'd be neurotic too if she really cared. Yet it was a minefield that had been navigated successfully by Lacey Dillon, hadn't it? She chuckled ruefully. Maybe Lacey was the person to give Georgia tips about men, not her. Lacey was the one with all the experience.

Anyway, there was a bit of time before Dinner in the Dark and there was always the remote possibility that Danno or Guru would contact her. In the mean time there was Paul. She frowned. Was there really any point in calling Paul when her motives weren't entirely honest? But they had been friends. It wasn't wrong to call a friend, was it? She picked up her mobile phone and checked its phone book. When they'd played in the club together she used to call him regularly about matches or team practices. She hadn't looked at the phone book in ages. But his number might still be there.

It was. She stared at it, smiling to herself as she remembered winning the mixed doubles tennis tournament with Paul and him lifting her into the air, high above his head, while yelling, 'We are the champions' at the top of his voice. The memory was a happy one and, for the first time, she could recall the day without a tinge of regret for how things were now. It had been fun. She could still remember the fun of it all.

She bit her lip. She would ring him. Today. Not now because she needed a bit of time to work up to it, but definitely later. She stared out of the open window, happy to have made a decision. The sky was still the same brilliant blue as it had been for the last week, broken only by a few straggly clouds high up in the atmosphere. The birds where chattering loudly in the branches of the trees and the scent of honeysuckle lingered in the air.

'The garden,' she said out loud. 'I'll ring someone about the garden as well.' Then a wasp flew through the open window and zipped past her ear. OK, she muttered to herself as she flapped a newspaper and tried to usher it through the window again, I also need to deal with this. But a garden centre might have someone to get rid of a nest too.

She took out the Golden Pages and was about to look up Garden Centres when she remembered the sign she'd seen in the florist's window. She'd liked the look of it and she always believed in giving business to local firms whenever she could. So she decided to take a stroll down to the shops and check it out first. If she didn't think they seemed up to scratch, then she'd go through the telephone directory.

Phydough looked at her hopefully as she came downstairs but he knew that despite the fact that she'd put her bag over her shoulder it wasn't time for his walk. She rubbed him on the head and gave him a Bonio, which he took out to the garden and the shade of the escallonia bush.

'See you later,' she told him and closed the door behind her.

Hot, hot, hot. She couldn't remember such heat. Not even in the summers of her childhood, which, up to now, had always seemed warmer and sunnier than those of her adult life. Her bright pink flip-flops thwacked softly on the cracked pavement and her flimsy cotton skirt swirled around her legs. Once again she was wearing a white strappy top. A teenage girl, with colt-like tanned legs and wearing a vivid orange belly top and matching short skirt, strode past her. Claire looked at her enviously. It would be nice, she thought, to be able to walk around the place in skimpy clothes and feel good about your-self. And then she laughed, because skimpy clothes were all very well when you were nineteen, but pushing it when you were the mother of a fourteen-year-old and had dodgy knees and silver-scarred legs – even if your mother insisted they were good legs!

The door to the florist's was open. Claire hurried across the main road, following behind the teenage girl. She was still watching her, still envying her youth and beauty, as she made her way towards the florist's. Which was why she collided heavily with the man who was leaving, carrying a bay tree in a large terracotta pot.

'Oh, shit!' He staggered backwards, then forwards, and then dropped the pot containing the tree on the pavement just outside the shop, where it cracked and came apart in five large pieces.

'Oops!' Claire looked at the broken pot and upended tree in horror. 'It's my fault. I'm so sorry.' Her eyes widened as she looked at the man with whom she'd collided. 'Oh,' she said again. 'It's you.'

122

'What is it with you?' demanded Nate. 'Are you a kind of one-woman knocking-men-over campaign? And where's the mutt this time?'

Honestly, thought Claire, why is it that I keep meeting such a disagreeable bloke? If he was nice maybe I could bat my eyelids at him and turn him into a research project, but as it is he's just annoying!

'I said I was sorry,' she said. 'For then and for now. And I didn't knock you over before, it was my dog. You're still on your feet this time, it's only the pot that's broken. So chill out.'

'The tree could go into shock,' he said. 'Tell *it* to chill out.'

'If it dies I'll pay for it,' said Claire. 'Does that make you happy?'

He contemplated the smashed pot, the pile of soil and the fallen tree, then looked grimly at her. 'I suppose it's not a disaster,' he said, although his tone implied that in fact it was. 'I'm sure the tree will be fine really, and we have lots of pots. Now were you actually thinking of going into the shop or was your plan just to stand outside and attack the customers?'

She frowned. 'Don't you want to get them to repot it for you now?' she asked.

'I'll do it myself,' he said.

'Yes, but how will you get it home?'

Realisation dawned on his face. 'I work here,' he said. 'I was bringing it outside for display purposes.'

'Oh.' Claire felt foolish.

He continued to look at her, his gaze disconcerting.

'Were you looking for something?' he asked.

'I . . . um . . . I . . .'

His look became impatient.

'Gardening,' she said finally. 'I wanted to enquire about gardening. You had a notice in your window saying you did it and I need someone to do some work in my house.'

'In your garden, I presume you mean,' he said. 'Not your house. We're not talking about some kind of indoor gardening, are we?'

'No. No. Of course not.' She stared at him tetchily. He was an extremely annoying man, and those odd-coloured eyes looking steadily at her were quite unsettling.

'So what do you want?' he asked.

'Someone to look at it. Tidy it.'

'Not design it?' His tone was disappointed.

'No,' she said. 'It's fine the way it is. It's just overgrown.'

'I see.'

'Is it something you do or not?' she asked impatiently. 'It says gardening on the notice. Look!' She pointed at it. 'So that presumably means you prune trees and bushes and weed flowerbeds and mow lawns. If it doesn't, fine, just say so.'

'I can do those things,' he said.

Suddenly her heart sank. If she employed him to do work for her then a man she didn't like would be wandering around Bill's garden, messing with Bill's stuff, cutting back Bill's trees and shrubs. Suddenly she didn't think this was such a good idea.

'Come inside,' he told her. 'Let me look at our book.'

She had no option but to follow him into the colourful interior of the shop. Flowers crammed every available space – the shaded store was brightened by enormous yellow and orange sunflowers, wonderful red-tipped white Habanera Blush daisies, amazing black and red annual poppies and a vast selection of budding roses.

Behind the counter sat his extraordinarily beautiful wife. Sarah, Claire remembered. Her glorious red curls were piled on top of her head and secured by multicoloured clips decorated with flowers and ladybirds. The low shaft of sunlight glittered off the diamonds of her engagement ring as she created an eye-catching display, using gypsophilia as a backdrop to the other blooms she was inserting carefully into a green sponge oasis. Claire wondered why she hadn't come to investigate the noise of the crashing pot, but then realised she had earphones in her ears and an MP3 player on the counter.

She looked up as they walked inside and her eyes narrowed in partial recognition when she saw Claire. As she removed the earphones, Claire recognised the tune that was playing as one that Georgia liked.

'Gardening book please, Sarah,' said the man briskly.

She reached underneath the counter and handed him an A4 diary in a Perspex binding covered with floral cartoons.

'Hi,' she said to Claire. 'Have we met?'

124

'Her dog attacked us when we were jogging.' The man opened the diary.

'Oh yes.' She grinned at Claire. 'Hardly attacked us though, Nate,' she added. 'More like he looked at you, saw a soulmate and decided to make your acquaintance.'

'Not likely.' Nate squinted at the diary. 'Though he obviously gets his greeting techniques from his owner. She crashed into me when I was bringing the bay tree outside. We need another pot.'

Sarah laughed. 'Sweetheart, I *told* you you'd drop it.'

'I didn't drop it,' retorted Nate. 'At least I wouldn't have if I hadn't been banged into.'

'Look, I came here to ask about gardening,' said Claire. 'Not to be got at. I told you I'd pay for your damn pot and I will. So just forget it, OK.'

A stricken look crossed Sarah's face and she glared at Nate.

'I told you that you have the customer services skills of a particularly dense rhino, you arse,' she snapped. 'You're not supposed to accuse the customers of assault!'

'Please,' said Claire. 'Forget about it. It was my fault. I wasn't looking where I was going. I was distracted. I've said I'm sorry about a million times but that doesn't seem to keep him happy. Given that he appears to be in charge of the whole gardening thing it wouldn't be a good idea to hire you. Like I said, forget it.'

She walked out of the shop and back into the blazing sunshine, quivering with rage. It was all very well to want to support local businesses but not when they were owned by complete tossers like him! She glanced back at the shop and at the mess of earth outside and felt a pang of guilt. Then her attention was caught once more by the magnificent display in the window. There was no doubt that Sarah was an accomplished florist. Maybe Nate was a great gardener. But Claire wasn't prepared to give him the opportunity. She looked at the colourful carnation and freesia bouquets in metal containers outside the shop. Some fresh flowers would be lovely at home, she thought. But not from here. She paused. There was a Spar shop a few doors down. Normally she never bought flowers from convenience stores or garages. But today that was exactly what she planned to do.

She almost changed her mind as she looked at the pre-packed flowers in the containers outside the shop. They weren't half as dramatic as the ones in Taylor's Florist. But she didn't care. Sometimes you didn't need drama, you needed comfort. And the warm red and yellow sprays were both comforting and pretty which was just what she wanted.

Sarah Taylor looked at Nate, her eyes flashing fury.

'You complete and utter tosspot!' she snapped at him. 'Honestly, do you want to put us out of business before we even start? You were impossibly rude to her and she wanted to be a paying customer. You plonker.'

'She wasn't looking where she was going,' retorted Nate. 'She walked straight into me. I had a fucking bay tree in front of my face! How the hell could I see her?'

'It might have been her fault, but haven't you ever heard that thing about the customer always being right? What *is* it about you?'

'Excuse me?' He looked at her angrily. 'What it is about me is that I'm here in this shop in the arsehole of Europe because, despite everything, I care about you and that's what you wanted.'

Sarah looked at him without saying anything.

'Oh God, Sarah . . . I'm sorry.' He sighed deeply. 'I really am. It's just—'

'I know what it's just,' she said quickly. 'I really do, Nate. But you've got to get it all into perspective. You can't blame everyone else for things. And you certainly can't blame me.'

'I don't blame you,' he told her, his voice softening so that he suddenly sounded like a different person altogether. 'Jeez, Sarah, you're the one person I can depend on. You're right. I am an arse.'

She laughed and put her arms around him. 'I know,' she whispered. 'But it's quite a neat, firm one all the same.'

'Sarah!' He laughed too.

They were still laughing when Claire walked by again. She'd bought quite a lot more flowers than she'd intended and she could barely see over the top of them. But she could see enough to make out the shape of Nate and Sarah Taylor hugging each other in the darkened shop.

God knows what they've got to hug each other about, she thought tartly; if he continues to treat customers like that they'll be out of business within a month. She sniffed self-righteously and continued down the road, holding the flowers in front of her, their coloured heads dancing in the breeze.

Eavan couldn't find the keys to the garden shed. They were usually kept along with all the other keys in the bottom drawer of the kitchen unit, but despite having tipped the entire contents of the drawer on to the breakfast counter, she hadn't been able to locate them. She remembered Glenn had had them at the weekend when he'd taken the lawnmower out. There was a small puncture in the inflatable paddling pool and she knew that there was a repair kit in the shed. Not that it was a major disaster, she conceded, as she looked out of the kitchen window at Saffy happily sitting in the sagging pool and skimming her bright yellow plastic duck over the inch of water, but it would be nice to fix it before things got worse.

She picked up the phone and dialled his mobile number.

'Yes?' he said as he answered it.

'Am I interrupting you?'

'No. Not really.'

She frowned. 'Where are you? Sounds like you're in the middle of a road somewhere.'

'On my way to a meeting,' said Glenn.

She grunted in acknowledgement and asked him about the shed keys.

'I don't believe you're ringing me to ask me this,' said Glenn tightly. 'The keys are where they should be.'

'I can't find them.'

'Look, woman, I've better things to do than spend hours talking to you about keys,' snapped Glenn. 'Honest to God, you'd think that the only things that mattered went on in the house.'

Eavan's grip tightened around the phone. Glenn never raised his voice to her. Usually if they argued he was almost excessively polite, keeping his temper when she was beginning to lose hers. She wasn't used to him being shirty with her.

'I only asked,' she protested.

127

'Why don't you look properly first?'

'I did look properly. I emptied everything out.'

'Then you must have taken them yourself earlier. It's nothing to do with me. I'm busy.'

Eavan stared at the receiver in her hand. He'd cut her off, just like that! She was tempted to ring him back and give him a piece of her mind but she stopped herself. He'd been under pressure lately, she knew that. This whole marketing drive was taking up his time and energy. OK, so he didn't have to take it out on her. But maybe this time she'd cut him a little slack. She replaced the receiver and walked back into the kitchen. If she thought about it long enough she'd surely remember where the damn keys were herself.

Glenn stood at the junction of Trinity Street and Dame Street and wiped away the beads of sweat that had appeared on his forehead. He didn't want Eavan ringing him during the day like this. Asking stupid questions. Thinking any of it mattered. He couldn't cope with it and sooner or later she'd be bound to guess. He wasn't able to face up to her guessing just yet. He wasn't sure exactly when he'd be able to face up to it himself. And how she'd expect him to deal with it when he did.

Chapter 12

Tithonia (Mexican Sunflower) – Orange, red or yellow blossoms and can grow up to 1.5m tall. Thrives in full sun.

When Claire got home she arranged her flowers in a couple of glass vases. Then she took a banana and mango smoothie out of the fridge and drank it back. What a complete asswipe, she thought as her encounter with Nate Taylor re-ran in her mind. There's the thing. You could go through the whole dating scene and still end up with someone like him!

She opened the glossy magazine that she'd also bought in the Spar.

'How to Meet Extraordinary Men in Ordinary Places' said the tag-line. The article suggested that you could pick up suitable men in garages (ask him to open the bonnet of your car); at bus stops (ask him what the number of the approaching bus is); in the super-market (ask him if he knows where the dog food is). Claire snorted. What kind of woman were you supposed to be, she wondered, if you couldn't open the bonnet of your own car or find the dog food in the supermarket yourself? The dog-food thing (according to the magazine) would make him realise that you were a loving and caring kind of woman but not the obsessive kind who owned a cat. The flaw in the article, Claire thought, was that if you had a dog you should know where the dog food was and if you didn't then he was going to find out about it soon enough! She rather liked the sugges-tion about the bus number, though. It was reasonably sensible. Although she was uncertain how on earth you were supposed to strike up a relationship with a bloke in the ten seconds before the

44A arrived at the stop. There was always her own recent experience of bumping into men at florists' shops. If Nate had been a nicer bloke then maybe smashing the terracotta pot and upending the bay tree would have been a great way to meet him. But he was appalling (although not entirely unattractive once you got used to the odd-coloured eyes) and, of course, he was married to the very beautiful Sarah. Claire felt that the unwritten rule of meeting Extraordinary Men in Ordinary Places was that they should actually be available.

Anyway, before she did any meeting of men at all, she was going to call Paul. She realised that she was putting it off, afraid to ring him in case he said no. She wasn't sure whether she could take a fourth rejection. I suppose this is a kind of nervous dating thing, she thought suddenly. If I was a woman looking for a date and I thought I'd met someone and I wanted to call them, isn't this how I'd feel? Nervous and apprehensive.

She didn't know why she was nervous or apprehensive this time. Paul was her friend. He'd been in her house. He'd known Bill and he knew Georgia. And this was purely and simply a drink. Besides, she thought suddenly, it would be nice to see Paul again and to find out how his year's break in Australia had gone.

She pressed the speed-dial button on her phone and listened to it ring. She was just about to hang up, thinking suddenly that his number could easily have changed, when he answered.

'Paul here.'

'Oh. Hi. Paul.' She was nervous again.

'Is that really you, Claire Hudson?'

'Yes,' she said.

'I couldn't believe it when your name flashed up!' His tone was pleased. 'How the devil are you?'

She smiled. 'I'm fine. How are you?'

'Good,' he said. 'Enjoying the summer.'

'An especially long one for you, I guess,' said Claire, 'given that you're just back from Oz.'

'It's great,' he told her. 'It's weeks since I've seen rain. Not that I want that to change in a hurry.'

'Did you have a good time?' she asked.

'Wonderful.'

'Is it good to be back?'

He laughed. 'Kind of. It's good to hear from you again, Claire.'

'Thanks,' she said. 'I was wondering, you know, if you'd like to meet up.'

He was silent for a moment and Claire suddenly felt the stab of rejection shoot through her again. Not you too, she thought. I was depending on you!

'I'd love to meet,' he said. 'I missed you at the drinks do.'

'I know. I was going to go and I didn't. Eavan was pissed at me,' said Claire.

'Not really,' Paul told her.

'I bet she was,' said Claire. 'It doesn't matter though. So you'd like to meet?'

'I'd love to,' he repeated. 'Where?'

This time it was Claire who was silent.

'Claire?'

'I've no idea where,' she said. 'I haven't been out in a while and . . .'

'I'm living on the other side of town right now,' Paul said. 'So how about we meet in the city centre? Say Thomas Read's, opposite Dublin Castle.'

'I've never been there before,' said Claire.

'It's nice,' said Paul. 'And if we go early it won't be too crowded.'

'Tomorrow?' suggested Claire. 'Or later in the week. Whatever.'

'I can't tomorrow,' replied Paul regretfully. 'I'm out to dinner with a few friends. How about Thursday?'

'OK.'

'Great,' said Paul. 'See you there. About seven thirty?'

'OK,' said Claire again.

When she'd said goodbye to Paul she flipped down the top of her mobile phone triumphantly. She'd done it. She'd made a date with a bloke. OK, it was Paul. OK, it wasn't going to lead anywhere and she didn't want it to lead anywhere. But she'd done it. So basically what she could tell Georgia was that you just had to take your courage in your hands and phone. No big deal really!

'Come on, Phy!' she called, and the dog looked up at her. 'I feel like walking.'

131

He barked in approval and went to get his leash. Claire looked at the pile of magazines again. Ask him where the dog food is, she thought. What a load of rubbish. And as for internet dating – a complete waste of time!

Georgia was sitting on the grass beside the outdoor basketball court watching the game. She'd lathered herself with heavy-duty sunblock because the sun was beating relentlessly from the azure sky. She tugged at the brim of her navy blue baseball cap so that it shaded her face.

Robyn and Sive – another of the girls from her school – were both playing in the match and every so often she roared a few words of encouragement at them. Her match had finished earlier and her team was through to the final of the competition. Georgia liked basketball. Her height gave her an advantage over some of the other girls of her age and she knew that, despite having the same lanky frame as her mother, she was strong. And, of course, it wasn't badminton. She was good at that too (Miss Grainger had told her that she was naturally athletic) but she wasn't sure that Claire would be keen on her playing badminton competitively now that she didn't play herself. Although what if she got picked for the higher team next term? She couldn't let them down, could she? She chewed a blade of grass and wondered why her life had to be so complicated.

The team were huddled in a time-out at the side of the asphalt court. Georgia idly picked a few daisies from the grass where she was sitting and fashioned them into a chain. She smiled at herself for doing it. It was a long, long time since she'd made a daisy chain. A memory flashed into her head like someone sliding a photograph in front of her. Herself, at around four or five years of age. A glorious day like this one. She was wearing a white organza dress, white socks and white shoes. She couldn't remember the occasion but obviously it was some kind of family do where Claire had dressed her up. And then her father had walked over to her and plopped a small daisy chain on her red-gold curls. 'My little princess,' he'd said, and picked her up and kissed her. She remembered putting her arms around him and hugging him close, and the smell of him – a musky, male smell

132

so different to her mother. And her heart had almost burst with love for him.

She missed him, of course. But not with the same intensity as Claire, she knew. Even now the memory of him was fading and the pain at losing him was fading too – though sometimes she felt guilty about that. And she still felt bad about the months after the accident where she hadn't talked and where Claire had tried not to let her know how worried she was.

'Can I sit down?'

She looked up. Before she could answer Jamesie O'Sullivan plopped down beside her.

'How are you?' he asked.

'Mr Ó Dálaigh is about five yards away,' she told him. 'Whatever you want you'd better say it *as Gaelige* or we'll both be in trouble.'

'I wanted to say I was sorry,' said Jamesie.

'For what?' She made a slit in the last daisy with the edge of her fingernail and joined the chain together.

'I said I'd dance with you at the céili. But I didn't. And I know Nicky Carr made some sort of comment to you which wasn't very kind . . .'

'You'd said something about meeting me at the céili, that's all,' Georgia told him. 'The fact that you didn't dance with me is neither here nor there.'

'But I wanted to,' said Jamesie. 'Only Zoë . . .'

Georgia got to her feet and brushed cut grass from the grey shorts she was wearing. 'I don't care about you and Zoë,' she told him. 'Look, I've got to go. I need to change. There's a group of us going to Spiddal tonight.'

'Georgia . . .'

She looked at him enquiringly.

'I wondered if you'd like to come to the movie at the college with me tonight.'

'Didn't you hear me say I was going to Spiddal?'

'Yes, but . . .'

'I like you, Jamesie,' she told him evenly, 'but you're not mature enough for me.' She brushed non-existent grass from her shorts again. 'Thanks for the invite all the same.'

She walked away from the basketball courts and back towards the college building. Her heart was pounding in her chest and she was finding it difficult not to turn around.

OK, she told herself as she pushed open the blue-painted door and let herself into the college building, so I think I dealt with that all right. Jamesie is probably a nice enough guy really; and coming over to apologise was kinda nice too 'cos he didn't have to, he didn't make any real promises about the céilí and it's not his fault that Nicky Carr is a shit, but he's the type, isn't he, who follows the gang line on things. So that if the blokes in the gang don't think I'm good enough then he'll just drop me. Like he did, actually. Better off that he sticks with Zoë really. Though . . . she thought about it again for a moment . . . Zoë is easily the most gorgeous girl here. Maybe she's dumped him. So he came running back after me. She tossed her head so that her hair danced around her face. Well, nobody comes to me because I'm second choice. Nobody! She rubbed the back of her neck and exhaled slowly. She didn't really want to be anyone's second choice. But would there ever be a time when she was someone's first?

'Hey, Georgia!'

She turned around in the corridor and saw Steve Ó Sé standing there.

'Steve,' she said.

'I was wondering if you're doing the kayaking today,' he asked. 'I didn't see your name on the list.'

Steve wasn't as good looking as Jamesie but according to Robyn he fancied her. Why? Georgia wondered. Why would anyone fancy her really? It was all very well for Robyn to say that it was because she had big tits, but she didn't want blokes to fancy her for her big tits.

'Sure I am,' she said. 'I put my name down late.'

'Great,' said Steve. 'I heard your team is through to the basketball final. Well done.'

'Thanks.' She smiled at him. 'Plus I heard you got full marks for that stupid grammar thing they set us last Friday.'

'It'd be difficult for me not to,' said Steve. 'My family speaks Irish at home most of the time. This is a bit of a busman's holiday for me.'

134

'Oh.'

'My parents have gone to the States for three weeks,' he told her. 'Visiting my sister. This was a convenient way of getting rid of me.'

'I see,' she said.

'It's not that bad.' He'd noticed the sympathetic expression flit across her face. 'Three weeks with my folks would've been excruciating, and I didn't want to go on a hiking holiday through Scotland with my aunt and uncle and nerdy cousin, which was the equally excruciating alternative.'

'Wouldn't be my thing either.' She stopped outside the door marked *Mná*. 'Well look, see you.'

He stood there and watched her.

'I really don't think you can follow me into the ladies' loo,' she added, nodding at the plaque on the door.

'No. No. Of course not. Sorry.'

She grinned. 'See you on the bus to Spiddal?'

He nodded. 'Great.'

'Great,' she repeated and pushed the door open.

Chapter 13

Antirrhinum (Snapdragon) – Tubular flowers in a variety of colours. Dead-head faded spikes.

By Wednesday afternoon it looked like the spell of fine weather might break. Dark, heavy clouds had rolled in over the country although the temperature stayed warm, making it muggy and airless. Claire took two Anadin for the headache that was pressing down on her before getting the bus out to Eavan's house for Saffy's birthday tea. Claire had agreed to be Saffy's godmother when Eavan was pregnant and had asked her if she'd take on the honorary role because, she said, there was no one she'd rather have. She didn't have any sisters who might be offended if they weren't asked, and besides, Claire was one of the most spiritual people she knew.

'Me, spiritual?' Claire had rolled her eyes and looked at Eavan in amused disbelief.

'Not religious,' said Eavan. 'Just – well, content.'

Saffy had been born a couple of months before the accident, and afterwards Eavan had asked Claire whether she still wanted to be the baby's godmother. The christening had been arranged, she'd said uncomfortably, but she knew that it might be difficult for Claire. Eavan hadn't known then about Claire's own lost baby. Claire hadn't told anyone before leaving on holiday and she hadn't felt there was any point in talking about it when she got back. So she didn't say anything to Eavan but did agree that she was happy and honoured to be Saffy's godmother. Only it had been very difficult to hold the baby in her arms and not think of what might have been. What should have been. And every time she saw Saffy she couldn't help

136

thinking of the baby she'd lost and how they would have been friends.

She let the memories wash over her once again as the bus trundled along the coast road. But she put them firmly out of her mind as she walked up the driveway to Glenn and Eavan's home.

She was always awed by the sheer size of the house – big, modern and double-fronted, with huge rooms and every possible convenience. She preferred her own tall, narrow house nearer the city but she had to admit that there was a spaciousness and light about Glenn and Eavan's place that was wonderful. She rang the doorbell and her friend answered.

'We're in the garden,' said Eavan as she kissed Claire on the cheek. 'I know it's probably going to piss rain and crash thunder at any second but it's so warm that we couldn't stay indoors.'

'Hi, Claire.' Glenn Keating got up and kissed her on the cheek. 'Lovely to see you. This is Candida, Saffy's babysitter.'

Claire smiled in acknowledgement at the younger girl.

'Claire! Claire!' Saffy clambered down from the bench table and flung her arms around her legs. 'I love you, Claire.'

Eavan laughed. 'She's loving everyone today because of the gift-giving,' she told Claire.

'Just as well I brought one then.' Claire handed Saffy a brightly wrapped parcel and the little girl tore at the paper excitedly to reveal a scarily realistic doll.

'She loves dolls,' said Eavan. 'Part of me worries that I should be making her play with Meccano or something to stimulate a different area of her brain.'

'Plenty of time for that,' said Claire. 'Georgia went through a doll phase too and subsequently dismembered all of them.'

'Good old Georgey,' said Eavan. 'How's she getting on?'

'Pretty well.' Claire sat down at the table. 'She's having her ups and downs, but as far as I can make out more ups, which is a good thing.'

'And you?' asked Glenn. 'How are you getting on?'

'I'm fine.' Suddenly Claire recalled seeing Glenn in town when she'd met her dad and Lacey Dillon. It had gone completely out of her head. 'Did you get to your meeting on time?'

Eavan's glance flickered between her husband and Claire.

'Oh yes, absolutely.' Glenn turned to Eavan. 'I forgot to tell you that I bumped into Claire one day,' he said. 'I was in a mad rush though.'

'Oh.' Eavan looked surprised and Claire frowned.

Glenn's description of their meeting was accurate in fact but not in nuance. They hadn't really bumped into each other. He'd been sitting in a bar. And then suddenly she realised that he didn't want Eavan to know he'd been in a bar. She nibbled at the inside of her lip. Was there a reason? Surely not. Surely he couldn't be drinking again. She wondered whether she should say something to Eavan and almost immediately dismissed the thought. It was none of her business and there were other things she wanted to talk to Eavan about. She hadn't spoken to her friend yet about the break-up of her parents' marriage. Part of the reason she'd agreed to come to Saffy's birthday tea was so that she could confide in her. It was absolutely ages, she thought, since they'd talked about something which had nothing at all to do with Bill or the accident or how everyone was coping.

'Will I get the cake, Eavan?' Candida asked.

'Cake!' cried Saffy.

Candida's intervention effectively stopped Eavan from asking Claire about meeting Glenn, although Claire knew her friend was curious about it. But she decided that if and when the topic arose she'd leave all the talking to Glenn. Meanwhile she oohed and aahed with Saffy over her chocolate cake shaped like a caterpillar with coloured Smarties as its feet. Once Saffy had blown out her three candles twice (the second so that Glenn could take a photo of the event because she'd done it too quickly the first time) they all had a slice. Eavan brought out a bottle of champagne.

'I know this is a bit silly given that it's Saffy's birthday and we're eating chocolate cake,' she told Claire and Candida. 'But I thought it'd be nice.'

Glenn opened the bottle and filled their glasses. He was drinking Ballygowan, Claire noticed.

Saffy ran around the garden in an overexcited fervour. That was why they hadn't had a proper party, Eavan explained. Far too much hysteria, and there'd be plenty of time for that in the years ahead. Besides, she told Claire despairingly, you couldn't just have a party with cake and lemonade any more, you had to provide entertainment. A bouncy castle at the very least, preferably accompanied by a conjuror or puppet show.

Candida agreed. She did a lot of babysitting in the area and went to a lot of the children's parties too. The goody-bag at going-home time was equally important, she reminded Eavan. At the last party she'd gone to, each child had received a stylish wristwatch.

Glenn snorted in disgust and muttered under his breath about people with more money than sense. When Eavan agreed that it was silly but you had to do it, he snorted again and then got up from the table, telling them that he had a filthy headache and needed to lie down.

'I've a bit of a headache too,' said Candida. 'It's the weather, I'm sure. In fact, I think I'll head off now if that's OK, Eavan.'

'Sure.' Eavan smiled at her. 'See you on Friday.'

'See you. Bye, Saffy.' Candida hugged the little girl and kissed her. 'Bye, Claire, nice to meet you.'

'Do you need me to run you home?' asked Glenn.

'No thanks,' said Candida. 'It's only a ten-minute walk and it might help clear my head.'

She waved goodbye to everyone and walked into the house. Glenn followed.

Eavan turned to Claire. 'What about you? Do you want to go inside too?'

Claire shook her head. 'I know it's dark and gloomy out here but I still prefer to be outdoors.'

'I don't know what's got into Glenn.' Eavan refilled their glasses with the last of the champagne as they settled back into their seats.

'Busy at work?' suggested Claire.

'There's something going on there,' agreed Eavan. 'He's out and about all the time now and I know that's not his thing. So maybe that's it.'

'Have you talked to him?' asked Claire.

'I don't know what to say.' Eavan bit her lip. 'I know that sounds ridiculous, but I can't quite bring myself to ask him.'

'Maybe you should.'

'Probably.'

They sipped the champagne. Claire wondered whether she should tell Eavan about seeing Glenn outside a bar. But that wasn't a crime. And she didn't know whether he'd been drinking anything stronger than 7Up. She didn't want to worry Eavan unnecessarily. Besides, why would Glenn start drinking again?

The silence between them grew. Saffy had followed Glenn inside and was now watching her *Finding Nemo* video.

'My mother and father are splitting up.' Claire hadn't intended to blurt it out just like that, but she couldn't help herself. Eavan looked at her in stunned amazement.

'What!'

Claire told her about calling out to Eileen, and her assertion that they'd never really loved each other. And then she told Eavan about lunch with her father and Lacey Dillon.

'Lacey Dillon?' Eavan's eyes opened wide. 'Isn't that the recruitment crowd?'

Claire nodded. 'How did you know?'

'They're quite well known,' Eavan told her. 'They do work for Trontec. But I always thought it was two people's surnames.'

'Yeah, well, it's not. And I think she sounds like a porn star!'

Eavan giggled. 'She does rather. But doesn't look it from your description.'

'No, she was the coolest, most businesslike person I'd ever met. Still, two kids by two different fathers . . . and my dad wants to marry her.'

'I can see how it might freak you out. I can't believe it either.'

'It's more than freaking me out.' Claire twirled the stem of the champagne glass between her fingers.

'I guess if your parents were unhappy . . .'

'They never seemed to be. That's the whole point.' Claire looked at her friend. 'I never bloody guessed. So it makes me feel particularly stupid.'

'Sometimes we don't know what's going on at all in other people's lives,' said Eavan. 'We think we do, but we don't.'

'I've decided that I haven't got a clue,' said Claire. 'About relationships. Georgey rang me to tell me that she'd had a bit of an upset over some guy at camp and I realised that I hadn't the faintest notion what to say to her.'

'Georgey and a boy!' Eavan laughed. 'Good for her.'

'Not good that she was upset,' said Claire. 'But good that she rang me. Anyway, she wanted to know how I knew that Bill and I loved each other.'

'Yeuch.' Eavan made a face. 'How do you answer that one?'

'I couldn't,' replied Claire. 'But I've had an idea since. I've even started it in a kind of way.'

'What are you talking about?'

As Claire explained her plan to go out with men to get some experience so that she'd know what Georgia was going through, Eavan sat in amazed silence.

'Claire, much as I know I've been on at you to get out, and even though I'm madly supportive about you doing new things, I'm really not sure that trying to meet a production line of men is a good idea,' she said when her friend had finished speaking. 'It's a bit uncaring, don't you think?'

'Uncaring?'

'Well, you're talking about going out with blokes just for the hell of it.'

'I know.' Claire smiled. 'But why not?'

'Well . . . what about someone who's looking for something more than whatever it is you're giving them?'

'If you read your magazines you'll find out they're all looking for more than you want to give them.' Claire laughed. 'I'm not going to meet anyone and pretend that I love them. I just want to suss the whole thing out, so that when Georgey says that a bloke has said this, that or the other to her I'll know what he really means.'

'What on earth makes you think that boys of Georgia's age will act in the same way as grown men?' asked Eavan.

'Oh, come on,' said Claire. 'Don't we always say that boys never really grow up!'

'Even so.' Eavan sighed. 'Claire, it's not that I don't think going out with men isn't great for you. But you have to do it because you want to, not as part of a mad plan.'

141

'Why?' asked Claire.

'Because . . . oh, Claire.'

'I thought you'd approve,' said Claire. 'Though it's supposed to be impossible to get a date in this town anyway. That's why I tried the internet – which is a complete wash-out! Nobody wants to go out with me. The damn dinner is my last resort! What's the point in deciding to date men if you can't find them? All the same, I've finally set up my first.'

'Claire! Who?'

'Paul Hanratty,' said Claire.

'Paul?' Eavan's eyes opened wide. 'I didn't realise you fancied Paul.'

'I don't!'

'Claire, you can't hurt Paul's feelings.'

'I won't,' said Claire. 'It's just an old friends sort of drink. Nothing more.'

'You know he had a very messy break-up with his last girlfriend,' warned Eavan. 'That's partly why he went to Australia. He was gutted by it.'

'I didn't know that,' said Claire. 'But I'll look after him. Eavan, I've known him for years. He's a friend. I don't consider him a date and he doesn't consider me one either. We were partners, for heaven's sake. It's like having a date with my brother.'

'I can't help feeling you're playing with fire,' said Eavan. 'And I don't think it's going to help you understand Georgia at all.'

'Who knows,' conceded Claire. 'But don't you see, Eavan, I have no experience at all when it comes to men. Not in the make-up or break-up departments. None. Anything might be useful.'

'If you think so,' said Eavan. But her tone was highly sceptical.

It was still highly sceptical when she told Glenn about Claire's plan later that evening. Glenn shrugged and said that he thought she'd be glad Claire was getting out of the house at last.

'That's what she thinks,' cried Eavan. 'But you must see that it's completely different.'

'No,' said Glenn. He closed his eyes again.

'Did you take something for your headache?' asked Eavan.

'Those stupid natural cure things,' Glenn muttered. 'I wish I could pop a few pills.'

'Yes, but—'

'I know, I know. I'm an addictive personality. I'd probably get hooked on Solpadeine.'

'Glenn—'

'I'm tired,' he said irritably. 'I'm tired. I have a headache. I don't feel like talking.'

'Is everything all right?' asked Eavan.

'I just have a headache,' he snapped. 'For God's sake, woman, give me a break.'

'OK, OK.' Eavan turned on her heel and walked out of the living room. She grabbed a book and went into the conservatory instead. But the letters jumped around the pages and she finally closed it with a snap. When she went back to the living room, Glenn was asleep. She thought it better not to wake him.

Chapter 14

Lunaria (Honesty) – Flat seed heads like pearly discs. Can be cut and dried.

It started raining at midnight. Claire, who was reading in bed, got up at the sound of the rain against the window-pane. It was still suffocatingly warm so she didn't close the sash to the very top but simply hoped she wouldn't wake up to a minor flood on the window-ledge the next day.

The thunderstorm started around three with a loud rolling crash that woke her from her fitful sleep. Claire liked thunder and lightning and always enjoyed the spectacle of a storm, but that night's was a minor affair – more noise than action, she murmured to Phydough, who'd come back up to her bedroom at the first bang. I don't think it's going to be enough to clear the air, she told him. But you never know.

It was still raining the next morning, which made it easy for Claire to sit at the computer and work through the day, although she stopped every so often to check her mailbox and make noises of disgust when she realised she was still being ignored by Danno and Guru.

Maybe I should put my own profile up, she thought. If I made it interesting enough perhaps people would contact me. After all, I sounded really boring in my messages. It's no wonder they couldn't be bothered.

She finished work late in the afternoon. She took a spiral-bound notebook from her desk and opened it to the first page. Although she hadn't actually gone out with anyone yet, she'd gained a certain amount of information. And even if Paul was a friend she could still use him as research material. But, she promised herself, she wouldn't hurt his feelings.

ALL ABOUT WOMEN AND MEN, she printed carefully.

1. *Women are flattered when men notice them. So maybe it's the same the other way round. Should we tell them that they look good in stuff? (Bill never cared, but he's hardly the best person to judge by!)*
2. *It's awful making a phone call to ask someone for a date. So if you're not going you'd better be really nice about saying no.*
3. *Being rejected hurts.*

She chewed the inside of her lip. She'd been hurt by the fact that JustMe had someone else and that neither Danno nor Guru had called. And the stupid thing about her feelings was that it didn't even matter to her! So what must it be like for someone who really cared?

4. *But you've got to pick yourself up and start again.*

She looked at her watch. There was still plenty of time for Paul to ring her and cancel their drinks for that evening, and, given the bucketing rain, she wouldn't be surprised if he used it as an excuse. After all, why would he bother with her really? Surely everyone had told him what a waste of space she was these days? But she knew that if Paul cancelled on her she'd feel his rejection worst of all.

5. *You never meet Extraordinary Men in Ordinary Places. You meet irritating tosspots.*

She looked at the last point and sighed. She'd been thinking of Nate Taylor as she wrote it. But she couldn't judge every man on the basis of someone like him. More likely, she thought, you met Ordinary Men in Ordinary Places. And you were probably better off that way!

Her mobile buzzed and she picked it up, convinced that it was Paul about to cancel.

'Hello, Georgey – Georgia,' she said, seeing her daughter's name on the display. 'How are things?'

'Not bad,' said Georgia. 'There's the most terrific storm going on here. I might get cut off. Thunder, lightning, everything! It's wonderful.'

'There was thunder here last night,' said Claire.

'We had a bit of that too,' Georgia told her. 'And the teachers thought that it would blow everything away, but now it's a million times worse.'

'Are you scared?' asked Claire.

'Mum!'

'Well, I thought that's why you were phoning.'

'No,' said Georgia. 'It's 'cos I have some time on my own and I desperately needed to talk in English.'

Claire laughed. 'You'll be home before you know it and you'll probably never speak a word of Irish again.'

'It's ingrained by now,' said Georgia. 'I guess part of me will be glad to get home, but it's fun here.'

'Any more news on that boy?'

'Jamesie?' Georgia giggled. 'He apologised to me.'

'Did he indeed?'

'Yes. And I was cool and collected and said it didn't matter.'

'You're amazing,' said Claire with feeling.

'And last night at the céili I danced with a guy called Steve who's very sweet.'

'Do you do anything other than have céilis there?' demanded Claire.

'I have to write an essay now,' wailed Georgia. 'There's plenty of awful things to do.'

'Good,' said Claire.

Georgia giggled again. 'How about you? What are you doing?'

'Well . . .' Claire hesitated. 'I think I'm going out.'

'Out!'

'Don't sound so surprised,' said Claire. 'I do go out, you know.'

'But not much,' retorted Georgia. 'Where? Eavan's?'

'No,' said Claire. 'I'm supposed to be meeting Paul Hanratty.'

'Your tennis partner,' remembered Georgia. 'Knobbly knees.'

'Georgia Hudson! He doesn't have knobbly knees.'

146

'You said he did,' Georgia pointed out. 'Dad asked what you saw in him and you said not his knees anyway.'

'When did I say this?' demanded Claire.

'One night before he called for you. You were playing a match and he was driving.'

'Really?'

'Yes,' said Georgia. 'And Dad laughed and so did you.'

'I don't remember that.'

'Well it happened.'

'Thanks for reminding me,' said Claire.

'So why are you meeting him?'

'He's back from Australia,' said Claire. 'The club met up for a few drinks and I missed it. So I'm meeting him separately.'

'Tell him I said hello,' said Georgia. 'But best not mention the knobbly knees.'

'I won't.' Claire laughed. 'I really wish I remembered that.'

'Trust me,' said Georgia. 'And have fun.'

'I will,' said Claire. 'Oh, by the way, I figured out the music program on the computer. It's good, isn't it?'

'Only now!' Georgia's voice was laden with sarcasm. 'You've had the computer for years, Mum. I can't believe you never bothered with it before.'

'When you get to my age things take longer,' Claire told her.

Georgia snorted with laughter, said goodbye and hung up.

Robyn O'Malley walked up to her just as she was putting her phone back in her pocket.

'How's it going?' she asked. 'Who were you talking to?'

'My mum,' said Georgia. 'Just checking on her. Letting her know about the storm.'

'You and her really get on, don't you?'

'Not always,' Georgia replied. 'But she's easy to live with. And I have to keep in touch to make sure she's OK.'

'Do you?'

'Of course. She's on her own in the house and I know that she isn't mad keen about it. She was extra cheerful when she was saying how much she didn't mind, so that's how I knew.'

'She'll be all right,' said Robyn.

'I know.' Georgia sighed. 'But I can't help worrying about her. She still misses my dad so much.'

'But it's ages since the accident,' said Robyn.

'I know,' Georgia conceded. 'But with Mum it's still like it was yesterday. And she tries to pretend it doesn't matter and she doesn't miss him but of course she does.'

'Do you?' asked Robyn curiously.

'Yes,' said Georgia. 'He was good fun.'

'Do you think your mother will ever get married again?'

Georgia considered Robyn's question carefully. She nibbled at her bottom lip as she continued to watch the sheets of lightning flash across the darkened sky.

'Georgey?' Robyn's voice was anxious. 'Are you OK?'

Georgia turned her fudge-brown eyes with their glints of amber towards her friend and smiled slightly.

'Worried about me?' she asked.

Robyn looked rueful. 'No,' she replied. 'Well, a little, I suppose,' she added.

'I won't stop speaking again,' said Georgia. 'Honestly I won't.'

'It's just . . .' Robyn shrugged.

'That was shock,' Georgia told her. 'It happens. They said so at the hospital.' She made a face at her friend. 'I know it was weird for everyone. It was weird for me too.'

'Did you *want* to speak?' Robyn looked at her curiously. By an empathic mutual consent they'd never talked about Georgia's silence before. But now Robyn thought her friend might be prepared to discuss it.

'I don't know,' Georgia answered her. 'Part of me did. But another part of me – inside me – well, it just seemed like what was the point? There was nothing I wanted to say.'

'Even to your mum?' asked Robyn.

'I know it's odd,' said Georgia. 'But I just couldn't.'

'She was worried,' Robyn told her. 'We all were. Everyone said there was nothing physically wrong with you, but I know that inside they thought that maybe there was.'

'As if this wasn't enough?' Georgia held up her maimed hand.

'Oh, Georgey! I'm sorry.'

'It's OK,' said Georgia. 'Really it is. And I got over the talking thing. But it does seem to terrify everyone whenever I don't answer them right away.'

Robyn looked shamefaced. 'I shouldn't have even asked you about your mum. It's none of my business.'

'That's all right,' said Georgia. 'It's just something I never even thought about before. Not seriously.' She rubbed the side of her hand and then looked at Robyn again. 'I joked about it before we came here, you know, I told her not to go clubbing and meet unsuitable men, but it *was* a joke, Robs. I'm not sure I'd want her to take it seriously.'

'How would you feel about it if she did?' asked Robyn.

'How did you feel about it when your mum got married again?'

'That was different,' said Robyn. 'She's divorced. And Mike is kind of cool really. I like him.'

'So I guess it would depend on the man,' said Georgia. 'But to be honest with you, I can't see anyone measuring up to Dad. Not for my mum. She was crazy about him. They were childhood sweethearts.' She made a face. 'I always said it was a bit naff, but they didn't think so. They were the ultimate lovey-dovey couple.'

Robyn nodded. 'I suppose it's different,' she agreed. 'You know my dad was a total slimeball. Anyone would've been a step up as far as Mum was concerned. But your dad . . .'

'I know.' Georgia's teeth nibbled at her lip again. 'He was OK really.'

Robyn nodded. 'Your dad was a good person, not like Slimeball Pete.'

'That's why I think it'd be really difficult for Mum to find someone else. Besides, Robs, she's too old to be meeting new men anyway.'

'Would it be a good thing, though, if she found someone?'

'She might stop looking at me like I was a fragile piece of china all the time,' conceded Georgia.

'There's always hope,' said Robyn. 'Remember when my Aunt Kathy got married? She was forty. Forty! You'd think she'd have given up by then, wouldn't you?'

Georgia nodded in agreement.

'So I guess you never know.'

'He'd have to be right for her, though,' said Georgia thoughtfully. 'He needs to like dogs. And sport – she watches it on TV a lot even though she doesn't play any more.'

'You need to make a list of requirements,' Robyn told her. 'So that your mum knows how you feel.'

'But, Robs, that's only if there was anyone. And there isn't.'

'Be prepared for the possibility, no matter how remote,' said Robyn sternly. 'So . . . someone incredibly rich,' she continued. 'Who'd try to buy his way into your affection.'

Georgia grinned. 'Someone with a gorgeous son would be nice too.'

'Absolutely.' Robyn laughed 'And a brother for me.' She pushed her friend playfully. Georgia pushed her back. And they giggled like the children they no longer considered themselves to be.

Later that day, when they were supposed to be writing an essay on the person they admired most, Georgia took her diary out of her denim bag. She opened it to a blank page and considered for a few moments before she began to write.

REQUIREMENTS FOR MUM'S BOYFRIEND
1. *Reasonably good-looking (no facial hair/back hair/not too much chest hair).*
2. *Clean (fingernails especially/also ears).*
3. *Not patronising (no heavy sighs when I say something).*

She nodded at the first three points. A good start, she thought. Then she began writing again.

Chapter 15

Pernettya (Prickly Heath) − Masses of early summer flowers then showy pink or white berries. Low-growing prickly bush.

It continued to sluice rain into the early evening and, growing more and more convinced that her date with Paul might end up being a casualty of the weather, Claire eventually called him to see if he still wanted to meet.

'Why not?' he asked in surprise.

'It's so wet,' Claire explained. 'I thought maybe it would be too inconvenient.'

'If we'd planned a picnic,' he said. 'But we're going to a pub. It's indoors. It's dry. What's the problem?'

'None,' she said hastily. 'It's fine. I'll see you there.'

She turned off the computer, made sure that Phydough's bowl was filled with dry food and that he had a fresh supply of water, and then went upstairs to change into a pair of comfortable jeans and a long-sleeved T-shirt. It wasn't until she was dabbing a touch of bronzer on to her cheeks that she suddenly thought that jeans and a T-shirt wouldn't look as though she'd made a lot of effort. She stood indecisively in front of the mirror. The thing was, she thought, this was Paul she was meeting. Paul was so used to seeing her in a sweaty T-shirt and tracksuit bottoms that anything at all would look like she'd dressed up for him! Besides, she couldn't dress up for him. She'd feel ridiculous. She added a slick of tinted lip salve on her lips but decided against her bacteria-ridden mascara, even though she knew that colour on her lashes made her eyes look bigger and brighter.

Her charcoal-grey coat was on the rack in the hall. Before putting it on she picked off some of the balls of fur which Phydough deposited on it every time he walked past. It was easy enough to catch the white hairs but the grey ones were almost a perfect match. She knew she'd be still picking them off on her way to the pub. Finally she rummaged under the stairs for an umbrella and emerged with a red telescopic one which had one broken spoke. She remembered the last time she'd used it, a few months earlier, rushing from the train station in a gale-force wind which had turned it inside out more than once and left it in its current state. She had, of course, vowed to get another but had almost immediately forgotten. It'll have to do, she muttered, as she let herself out of the house. As long as it keeps me dry that's all that matters.

The earlier drumming of the rain subsided to a gentle hiss as she walked down the road to the bus stop, stopping every so often to remove more dog hairs from her coat. It seemed as though the Irish summer had come and gone in ten days and that the country had now reverted to type after its Mediterranean flirtation.

She stood at the bus stop for five minutes before the bus arrived and threw a minor wave of muddy water over her feet as it came to a halt in the puddle which had formed in the gutter. Claire was glad she'd worn ankle boots with the jeans, even though they weren't completely waterproof and she could feel a damp sensation around her toes.

The passenger complement was young, she noticed, as she looked around for a seat. The girls were dressed up for a night out while the men were sporting carefully cultivated designer stubble and a contrived casualness that didn't deceive her. They were all on the pull! She wondered what the chances were of any of them finding their perfect partner tonight. But if they were all off to pubs or clubs she reckoned they must be pretty low. She didn't know what the top meeting venue actually was (I should find out, she thought, it'd be worth knowing for Georgia's sake) but she was pretty sure that most people didn't bump into their future wife or husband in a pub let alone a club. Meeting Extraordinary Men in Ordinary Places hadn't mentioned either of them as useful hunting grounds at all.

It was a fifteen-minute walk from the bus stop in town to Thomas Read's but she was still a little early. She folded her rickety umbrella and pushed open the door of the pub, surprised to find that it wasn't as jam-packed with people as she'd somehow expected it to be. According to all the lifestyle pieces she read about Dublin, the city was meant to be a heaving mass of people socialising at every available opportunity, and anyone sitting at home was a sad loser in a vibrant town. She bagged a couple of seats by the table at the front window and draped her coat over one of them, then ordered a glass of white wine from the barman and sat back in the seat.

So, she told herself, here I am, finally out on a date just like everyone wanted, and it wasn't that bloody difficult. It's all about how you think of it really. And it doesn't matter that Paul and I often had a drink together in the club when Bill and I were married. It's still a kind of date. She stared into space and wondered whether he thought of her as a date, or an old friend too. She hoped the latter. It was only everyone else's expectations that had her thinking of drinking with Paul Hanratty in terms of a date in the first place! Being a single woman, an available woman (no matter how unavailable she really felt) changed everything. It changed how people thought of her and now it was changing how she thought of them. But she didn't want to change how she felt about anyone. Least of all people she regarded as friends. She tried to remind herself that she was only here to get tips for Georgia but suddenly that seemed a silly reason to be in a bar in the city surrounded by younger, more attractive people who had a completely different agenda.

The door to the pub open and he walked in. Claire saw that Paul was as studiously casual in appearance as the male bus passengers had been. He's made an effort for me, she realised in surprise. And he looks great. The tan really suits him. Her heart lurched and suddenly she felt very nervous.

She waved tentatively at him and he joined her, apologising for being late.

'No problem,' she told him. 'I was sitting here people-watching.'

He smiled at her and ordered a drink. There was a moment's silence between them which was just beginning to slide into awkwardness when he suddenly asked her whether she would be rejoining the Smash & Grab club when the badminton season began again in September.

'Remember when we won the tennis and badminton?' he asked. 'Bet we could do that one more time.'

She shook her head. 'I'm not mobile enough.'

'I bet you could be if you put your mind to it,' he said.

'It's not my mind, it's my body,' said Claire. 'If I ever go back I'll ease my way into it and that'll take ages. It's a remote possibility, not worth talking about. Tell me about your year off, I'm sure that's far more interesting.'

He shrugged his shoulders slightly but launched into a description of his year's travels while Claire's attention moved in and out of the people and places he talked about. Despite telling Paul that she didn't want to talk about the Smash & Grab club any more, being with him now was bringing back memories for her. Of winning matches, losing matches, going for practice sessions, drinking in the bar afterwards. Sometimes Bill and Georgia had come to support her by shouting vociferous encouragement, celebrating with her when she won, commiserating when she lost. It had all been remarkably social, she remembered. She'd tried to get Bill to take up a racquet sport too but he'd contented himself with stints on the running or rowing machines in the gym, telling her that he wasn't competitive enough to want to play anything to win. And she'd laughed at him and said that winning was great but of course taking part was all that really mattered. Then he'd laughed back at her and kissed her and told her that he knew how much she hated losing! He understood her so well, thought Claire. He was the only person who understood all of her. Most people only saw part of the bits that made up the whole person. Bill had seen everything.

She sighed deeply.

'Am I boring you?' Paul raised an eyebrow quizzically.

'Of course not,' she said hastily, dragging her attention back to the story he'd been telling about someone who'd found a spider in their tent when they were camping. 'Sorry. I was just thinking that it would be utterly awful to find a spider like that.'

'I was talking about the snake in the boathouse,' said Paul.

'Oh, yes, sorry,' she said, realising that he'd moved on from the spider story and embarrassed at being caught out. 'I meant snake.'

She sighed again. I'm a cow, she thought. Paul has been really nice in asking me out and all I'm doing is thinking about Bill. Which is not what this was meant to be all about. She bit her lip. Coming out with Paul had been a mistake. It was wrong of her to use him no matter how important she thought it was to be able to find out things for Georgia's sake. She felt guilty now.

'Are you OK, Claire?' He looked at her quizzically.

'Sure,' she said briskly and took a large gulp of wine. 'I guess talking to you has made me remember some stuff . . .'

This time his look was sympathetic. 'I've hardly seen you since Bill's accident,' he said gently. 'I'm sure it's been awful.'

'Oh, I'm OK now,' she told him. 'What's awful is that everyone keeps telling me how awful it is.'

'Sorry.'

'I didn't mean you,' she said hastily. 'You're fine.'

'I didn't know whether to mention it before now or not.'

'Not,' she said. 'I'm tired of people feeling sorry for me and trying to be sensitive about my feelings.'

'I guess I'm a bit sensitive about things myself,' he admitted. 'You heard that Bryony and I broke up . . .'

'Eavan did mention it.'

'She was sleeping with my best mate.' Paul couldn't keep the bitterness out of his voice.

'No!' Claire was horrified. 'I didn't know that.'

Paul nodded. 'It's not something I actually boast about,' he told her. She nodded.

'So I understand when you say you don't want sympathy,' he said. 'I know that what happened between me and Bry was completely different, but you do tend to feel that people are looking at you and talking about you and feeling sorry for you . . .'

'Yes,' she agreed.

He glanced at her almost empty glass and ordered another drink. 'I've moved on now, though,' he said after the barman had brought their order.

'Did you meet anyone in Oz?' she asked.

To her horror Paul suddenly began to cry. She looked around the pub in embarrassment. She wasn't sure what she was supposed to do.

'Paul?' She looked at him anxiously.

'I met a couple of women and I slept with them but it didn't mean anything to me and I lied to you, I haven't got over Bryony at all.'

Claire gulped.

'And so I'm here under false pretences because I always liked you and everything but I don't want to meet anyone yet and if I did, well to be honest, Claire – you and Bill . . . I wouldn't be able to deal with that either.'

She didn't know what to say. In the end she put her arm tentatively across his shoulder and told him that she understood perfectly.

'But you'll hate me for dragging you out on a shit night like tonight. I bet you anything Eavan forced you to come out with me because I may have given her the impression that I fancied you and I do a bit, Claire, well, I always did . . . but I'm still not ready.'

'You know, Paul, that's . . . that's absolutely fine.' Claire hoped that the relief she felt that Paul wasn't actually interested in her wasn't reflected in her voice. 'I fancied you a little bit too. And you're right about me and Bill. I'm definitely not ready either. And I certainly didn't talk to Eavan about you.' She crossed her fingers.

'I never thought I'd get upset over a damn woman.' Paul took a hanky out of his pocket and blew his nose.

'You *will* get over her.' Claire found herself saying the words that people had said to her so many times before and which she'd never truly believed.

'Sure I will. But I thought that it was for ever, me and her. I can't believe I got it so wrong.'

Claire wracked her brain for sympathetic words. But she couldn't think of anything that didn't sound just as trite and clichéd as telling him he'd get over Bryony. So she sat in silence while he blew his nose again.

'I appreciate you listening to me,' said Paul. 'I've been looking forward all day to tonight because I knew that you'd listen. I couldn't tell anyone else in the club. They'd just blather on about plenty more fish in the sea but the point is that you think you've caught your fish – know what I mean?'

He looked pleadingly at her and Claire squeezed his shoulder. She

156

couldn't imagine how awful it must be to discover the person you loved had betrayed you. If Bill had cheated on her . . . she let her breath out very slowly. She couldn't even contemplate Bill cheating on her.

'You won't tell anyone, will you?' Paul looked anxious now.

'Tell them what?'

'About this? About me getting upset. I'm not the bloke who gets upset, you know that. Everyone thinks I get over stuff really quickly but I don't.'

'I won't say a word,' she promised. She took her arm away from him and smiled.

'Thanks.'

It was strange being the person who reassured instead of being reassured by someone else. And although Paul had said he didn't want people's sympathy she couldn't help wanting to comfort him.

'So, any advice?' he asked eventually.

'Paul, I'm the worst woman in the whole wide world to advise you!' cried Claire. 'Everyone thinks I've been a hopeless recluse since Bill died. I'm totally out of touch with what's going on in the world and . . .' she broke off suddenly and grinned at him. 'We're a pair of hopeless cases really.'

'They're getting married, you know. Bryony and Keith. Not only have I lost a girlfriend but I've lost a best mate too.'

'Oh, Paul.' She reached out and took his hand. 'I'm really sorry.'

He squeezed her hand and stared into space. Claire didn't know what to say so they sat in silence until he sniffed loudly, released her hand and then knocked back his drink quickly, ordering another for both of them before Claire could object.

'Um . . . that bit about fancying you?' He looked at her quizzically and Claire felt her heart flutter nervously in her chest.

'Yes,' she said cautiously.

'I didn't mean fancy in that I wanted to do anything about it. I meant – well, you were attractive.'

She smiled slightly.

'Still are,' he added hastily. 'I bet you'd have no problem finding a bloke.'

'When I said I wasn't ready I meant it,' Claire told him. 'Anyway,

I'm much happier just having male friends. I don't need complications. But thanks for finding me attractive. And like I said, I always thought you were a bit of all right on the court too. And . . .' she looked guiltily at him, 'I guess I came out with you to see what it would be like but . . . well . . .'

'That's OK,' he said. 'It's a but, well situation for me too.'

They finished their drinks. She looked at her watch.

'You want to go,' said Paul. 'I've really bugged you with all this feeling sorry for myself and being bitter and twisted.'

'You're not bitter and twisted,' said Claire softly. 'You're my friend.'

He put his arm around her shoulders and kissed her very gently on the lips. She pulled back from him, her eyes wide. She hadn't expected that, not after everything they'd said. And Paul Hanratty had kissed her many times before, though always after a match and always in a congratulatory way. This was different. This was a man kissing her. A man who wasn't Bill. And it didn't matter how casual the kiss was or how much he talked about not being ready, he'd still kissed her.

'I'm sorry.' There was a flash of hurt in Paul's eyes. 'I didn't mean . . .'

'No,' said Claire hastily. 'I'm sorry. Nobody has . . . I haven't . . .'

He looked at her curiously. 'Don't you miss it?'

'What?'

'Someone to kiss you. Someone to sleep with?'

She shook her head. 'No.'

'Will you ever?'

'To be honest, I doubt it.'

'You don't want to make a pact do you?'

'What sort of pact?'

'You know, that we can be each other's fallbacks. If we haven't found anyone in five years we marry each other.'

She laughed. 'I don't need a fallback. I'm happy.'

'I envy you,' he said.

She looked at him curiously.

'You've been through your bad time – and, Claire, I know it was truly terrible – but you've come out the other side and you're OK.'

'Lots of people don't think so,' she told him.

'Lots of people are wrong then.'

'You always did say the nicest things.' This time she kissed him. But it was a platonic kiss on his cheek.

'Come on,' she said. 'Let's go.'

He looked at his watch. 'It's only half-ten,' he told her.

'Yes, but I don't want to miss the last bus.'

'You want to catch a bus!' He looked aghast. 'Get a taxi.'

She shook her head. 'I don't.'

'What?'

'Do taxis.'

'Why ever not?'

'I don't like cars,' she said shortly.

'Oh,' he said. Eavan had told him that Claire had developed phobias since Bill's accident and had said that she didn't like cars. But Paul hadn't realised quite how deep the whole thing ran.

'I'll walk you as far as the bus stop,' he said.

'If you like. But it's miles out of your way, isn't it?'

'I'll get a taxi home,' he said. 'I'm OK with cars.'

It was still drizzling as they walked along Dame Street and up Westmoreland Street. Paul took Claire's dodgy umbrella and held it high over the two of them which meant that she had to cling on to his arm. As they arrived at the terminus a 44A pulled in.

'Excellent timing,' said Claire.

'Are you sure you wouldn't rather get a taxi with me?' asked Paul. 'I won't let anything awful happen to you.'

'This is just as quick,' she said.

'OK then.' He made a face at her. 'I can't think how long it is since I walked a girl to a bus stop.'

'I've never been walked to a bus stop before,' she said.

'I can't have been more than about fourteen or fifteen,' he told her. 'I rather thought I'd left that part of my life behind.'

She smiled, took her umbrella from him and let it down.

'Goodnight, Paul,' she said. 'And thanks for this evening.'

'Thank you,' he said. 'And if you ever do need a bloke to talk to – you have my number.'

'Sure,' she said.

'So, goodnight.' This time he didn't kiss her on the lips but pecked her briefly on the cheek.

'Goodnight,' she said. 'And thanks.'

'It was good to see you,' Paul said. 'Don't forget, call me if you need me.'

'Will do.'

She moved along the bus and sat down. The rain was still sliding down the windows, distorting her vision. But she saw Paul wave briefly at her before he thrust his hands into the pockets of his jacket and walked away from the bus stop. She sat back in her seat. It hadn't quite been the date she'd expected. But it had been worthwhile all the same.

Later that night she took her spiral-bound A4 notebook out of the pedestal beside her desk and opened it at the page she'd written on before.

6. *Men have feelings too.*

She sucked on her Biro. It wasn't as though she hadn't known that men had feelings. She'd seen Bill reduced to tears over the terminal illness of a four-year-old patient. She'd seen him enraged over spending cuts in the health service. She'd seen the joy in his eyes the day he'd first cradled the newborn Georgia in his arms. Of course men had feelings. But in the whole dating game most women were urged to forget that. She thought of the articles in the magazines which listed ways to get a man as though he was nothing more than a pet to be brought home and trained. She thought of the articles which told women how to dress and how to behave and how to make men fall in love with them. She thought of Paul's ex-girlfriend, Bryony, and wondered why she'd cheated on him with Keith Carty and how Bryony herself would have felt if Paul had cheated on her with Bryony's best friend. But if Bryony didn't really love Paul, Claire mused, then there wasn't any point in pretending. That thought hit her with startling clarity. She was planning to go out with men and pretend that she was interested in them. But how fair was that really?

7. *There isn't any point in pretending.*

Well, what the hell, she thought. There's no way I could fall for any of them, but maybe they could become friends. There's no rule that says I can't have friends even if I don't want lovers. She touched her lips where Paul had kissed her. That had been weird. Beyond weird, because it was Paul who'd done the kissing. And even though she hadn't wanted to kiss him, the touch of his lips had brought the sensations flooding back. She closed her eyes and let herself remember.

Then she opened them again, pulled the notebook towards her and made one more entry.

8.   *A kiss is just a kiss.*

Chapter 16

Jasminum (Jasmine) – Yellow or white flowers on weak stems which need support or twining stems for climbers.

The remnants of the storm blew themselves out that night. By midnight the last rumblings of thunder had passed over and the following morning the skies were clear again while the puddles which had accumulated over the last two days dried rapidly in the rising sun. Eileen Shanahan was sitting in her conservatory enjoying the morning rays when the doorbell rang. Alan Bellew, the senior estate agent in the firm of Bellew & Purcell, stood on the step accompanied by yet another couple who wanted to view the house. Alan smiled at her as she let them in but her return smile was half-hearted and full of resignation. Eileen knew that the estate agents were delighted with the interest being shown in Ambleside, but she was getting a bit fed up of people tramping through the house, undoubtedly peeking into her cupboards and commenting about the necessity for a complete interior makeover or the fact that there wasn't a downstairs loo.

She went out into the back garden and sat on the bench near the wall while he showed the house. Ideally, of course, she shouldn't have been there at all, but this was an unscheduled showing and Alan had called a little earlier to see if it would be OK. Eileen had agreed on the condition that she didn't have to leave the house. If only I had a job, she thought, or something else to do during the day. It had never bothered her before, but now she was restless in the house, feeling as trapped in it as she'd once felt in her marriage. She was glad that her split with Con was out in the open at last. It was

162

ridiculous to have kept the true state of their relationship a secret for so long. A secret from Claire, at least, if not from the more knowing neighbours who had long since realised that the Shanahans led more or less separate lives even though no one ever spoke about it. But Claire . . . Eileen shook her head. Claire had been so caught up in her own life and family that she never even noticed anyone else's.

She sighed as she thought of Claire but a faint hope flickered in her heart too. Even though she'd thought that her daughter had looked as washed out as ever (despite her faint tan) when she'd called to see her recently, she'd also detected a slight toughness coming back to her. Obviously she'd been upset about the news of the separation and ultimate divorce but she'd been quite sparky about the idea of Eileen living on her own and – even though she wouldn't in a million years live in the city – Eileen had been secretly pleased that Claire had cared enough to suggest that she should move to Dublin to be near her. I want things to be good for her again, she thought wistfully. I really do. My only child went through life so luckily until the accident that she never had to worry about anything. I don't like the fact that she does nothing but worry now.

She looked up as the possible purchasers stepped into the garden followed by Alan. She liked it when he was the agent bringing people around to the house – he was much older than the other guy they sometimes sent and she felt as though he understood her better. Plus (and she was surprised at herself for suddenly thinking this) Alan Bellew was attractive in an old-world kind of way. He had a mass of stone-grey hair with absolutely no sign of it thinning on top, a slightly weatherbeaten but kind face, and he wore impeccably cut suits and cufflinks in his shirts. She didn't find him attractive in a sexual kind of way. (She rather felt as though she'd never find a man attractive in a sexual way after Con. It was all very well to read the magazines which said that she should still be up for it in her sixties, but she hadn't ever truly been up for it at all once Claire had been born.) All the same, she liked Alan's manners and his genteel charm. And she liked the way he didn't appear to pressurise the potential purchasers but simply let them wander around and get the feel of the house. The other estate agent was pushier, constantly drawing attention to the size of the rooms ('you won't get these dimensions in any new development'); the potential to extend ('making it into a truly fabulous residence'); or the array of plants in the garden ('an amazing outdoor experience'). Alan pretty much told them that it was a wonderful house and garden and left them to it.

He walked over to her now as the couple chatted on the patio.

'They've put in an offer already,' he told her. 'That's five so far, Eileen.'

'A higher offer than the last?' she enquired.

'Two thousand more,' he confirmed. 'There's a lot of interest.'

'Are you telling me that I should have gone along with your advice and had it auctioned?'

He smiled at her. 'It's your choice.'

She nodded. 'I know. I don't know why I hated the idea of an auction. I suppose I just have this image of unscrupulous bidders and I know that's stupid! All the same, I'd like to think that the house will get nice people.'

'Everyone who views this house is a nice person,' he told her seriously. 'They all appreciate it and they'd all like to buy it. They just can't all afford it.'

'I never would have thought it when we moved in first,' said Eileen ruefully. 'Back then it was so bloody ordinary. Everyone had four bedrooms and a big back garden.'

'Times change,' said Alan.

'That's true.' She smiled at him. 'I guess I'd never have thought that I'd end up living in an apartment on my own.'

'Are you worried about it?' he asked.

'God, no.' This time she laughed. 'I'm looking forward to it, Alan. All my life I've lived with someone who basically just got in the way. Now I'm going to be able to do my own thing. And to tell you the truth, I can hardly wait.'

Claire was in her garden too. The heavy rain had beaten down on the flowers so that some of their stems were now bent sideways and their petals bruised. She walked barefoot through the damp grass, scissors in hand to cut them. Although Bill had never minded cutting the flowers (had, in fact, told her that it many cases it stimulated the growth of more blooms), she always felt bad about it. She'd once read that flowers feel pain and cry whenever they're picked. And even though she wasn't entirely certain whether this was truly the case, she always felt that they were screaming at her whenever she cut them. But there was no point in leaving bent and battered blossoms to be walked into the grass. Better that they fill up the crystal vase in the kitchen.

She knelt down beside the Indian Pink carnations and began snipping them, trying to convince herself that they weren't bleeding all over her hands. The bees were out in full force and she suddenly remembered that she hadn't rung anyone about the wasps' nest. She shuddered at the thought of the thousands of wasps that were undoubtedly partying in her roof and sighed because she was so bloody disorganised that she hadn't called either a garden centre about the garden or an exterminator about the wasps yet even though she'd told herself that they were urgent things to do.

Why can't I concentrate on things properly any more, she asked herself. When Georgia's here I'm twice as busy but I still get twice as much done! I need to do the wasps' nest thing. And I really must get in touch with Dad and tell him that I'm glad he's found a woman to love and that I hope he'll be happy with her.

She stood up and winced as the pain juddered through her knee. I can't get my head around bad relationships because of Bill, she thought ruefully. And it's even harder to get my head around a bad relationship when it was my parents who had it. But the bottom line is that I want them both to be happy. It's such a waste to be miserable!

As she carried the armful of flowers into the kitchen, the doorbell rang. She dropped the flowers on the table and walked through the hallway to open the door.

More flowers greeted her, this time a huge mixed bouquet of yellow roses and tiger lilies. Her eyes opened wide in surprise. And then even wider when she saw who was holding them.

'What do you want?' she asked.

'It's you.' Nate Taylor looked at her in surprise. 'With the dog. Knocking people over. I didn't know you lived here.'

'I wouldn't have expected you to,' she said. 'And you walked into me too, you know.'

He opened his mouth as though he was going to argue with her again, but sighed instead. 'Claire Hudson?'

She nodded.

'Then these are for you.'

'Who are they from?'

'I don't know,' he said irritably. 'Sarah makes them and I just deliver them. I don't ask about the person who ordered them or the person who's getting them or what they're for or why they've chosen roses instead of orchids. I deliver them. That's it.'

Claire looked at him, her head to one side. 'I don't know why you're involved in a customer-based industry,' she said. 'You hate people, you seem to hate flowers and you're the rudest person I ever met.'

He opened his mouth as though to argue with her and then closed it again. He stood in front of her, a wry expression on his face. Then he smiled. It was a genuine smile which transformed his dour appearance and lit up his odd-coloured eyes.

'I'm sorry,' he said. 'You're right. I'm the rudest person in the universe and I've been particularly rude to you and I apologise totally.'

She was taken aback by the apology and by the smile. And by the sudden bubbling of amusement in his voice. She looked at him doubtfully.

'No. I am,' he said, seeing her reservations. 'Sarah read me the riot act after you'd been in the shop and I guess you got me on a bad day.'

'So today's another bad day?'

'I've been having a few bad days recently,' he admitted. 'And I know I definitely shouldn't take them out on the paying customers but I suppose I've been letting stupid things get the better of me. And so I am, honestly, sorry for snapping at you.' He looked hopefully at her and Claire couldn't help smiling in return.

'Well, OK then,' she said. 'Since we all have bad days and I can be grumpy myself sometimes too, I accept your apology. Anyway I shouldn't really expect you to know who the hell sent me the flowers.'

'Obviously an admirer,' said Nate. 'This was a pretty expensive order.'

'Really?'

'Yes.' He looked at her. 'Do you want to take them from me or are you going to refuse them?'

'Of course not.' She took the bouquet. 'I'm just a bit overwhelmed with flowers at the moment. I cut some from the garden only a few minutes ago.'

'Feast or a famine,' he remarked.

'Oh well.' She pulled the envelope from the bunch and tried to open it with one hand.

'Let me,' said Nate. He opened it for her and then read the message aloud. 'Thanks for everything, Cinderella. I mean that. And don't forget you used to stay out past midnight. Love, Paul.'

Claire blushed.

'Like I said, an admirer.' Nate was grinning at her this time.

'Not really,' she said in embarrassment. 'An old friend.'

'Yeah, right.' He laughed while she stuffed the card back into the bouquet of flowers. 'So, this is the garden you wanted tidied up?' He gestured at the front lawn.

'More the back garden really,' said Claire. She hesitated. There might be no harm in asking him to look at it, but despite his apologies and his sudden efforts to be nice she wasn't prepared to automatically assume he'd be the right person to deal with Bill's garden. Still, it couldn't hurt to let him look, maybe give her a price for the work she needed done.

'D'you want me to check it over for you?' he asked as he turned back to her.

She nodded uncertainly. 'Come on through.'

She led him through the kitchen where she put Paul's extravagant bouquet alongside the carnations she'd brought in earlier. Phydough, who'd been asleep in his basket, got up and padded towards them. He stopped in front of Nate and looked at him curiously.

'He's a gorgeous dog,' said Nate.

'You said he was an elephant before,' Claire reminded him.

'Do you want more apologies from me?' asked Nate.

'No,' said Claire. 'But you can apologise to my dog.'

He laughed. 'Dog, I'm sorry.' He ruffled Phydough's fur in the way that the dog liked. Then he looked at Claire. 'OK? Am I now a fit person to look at your garden?'

She shrugged. 'I suppose so.' She opened the back door and they both stepped out on to the patio, followed by Phydough.

'Some size of garden for this close to town,' remarked Nate.

'It's why we chose the house,' she told him.

'Right.' He walked down the damp lawn and stopped under the first apple tree. Then he appraised the unkempt hedges, the parched flowers and the overgrown rockery before looking critically at the jumble of potted plants on the patio area.

'I didn't get round to doing them this year,' said Claire, embarrassed at their straggly nature. 'I've been very busy.'

'So you want it tidied up, the lawn mowed, the trees pruned – I might leave that till a bit later – all that sort of thing?'

She nodded.

'Would you like me to send you a quote?'

'Why not. If it's something you do.'

'I prefer design,' said Nate. 'I like doing gardens from scratch. But I can do this if you want, absolutely no problem. It's not complicated.'

Did she want him to though, wondered Claire. Did she want someone who obviously didn't think much of the layout and plants that Bill had spent so much time and effort on because it wasn't complicated enough? And who, despite turning on the charm now, might still be a grumpy old man? Well, not old. Probably around the same age as herself actually. And maybe not really grumpy either – but that wasn't the point was it? She'd seen him grumpy. And the garden needed loving care not grumpiness.

'By the way, d'you know you've got a wasps' nest in your roof?' he remarked.

She nodded. 'I keep meaning to get rid of it but I forget.'

'I know someone,' said Nate. 'He's good. I'll give you his card if you like.' He patted his pockets and eventually took out a dog-eared business card.

'Thanks,' said Claire as she took it from him.

'And if you're genuinely interested, I'll send you a quote for the garden as soon as possible.'

'OK,' she said. It couldn't do any harm to see the quote.

'Right,' said Nate. 'I'd better get back.' He turned towards the house and then glanced at the garden again. 'I love the jasmine,' he said.

Claire bit her lip. The jasmine had been Bill's favourite. She smiled slightly at Nate. 'I like it too.'

His eyes narrowed. 'Is everything OK?' he asked. 'You sure you want that quote?'

'Of course,' she answered robustly. 'It has to be done.'

'It's a shame you've let it get so overgrown,' said Nate. 'But it won't take much to get it back to its full glory. I could replace that rockery at the back for you too if you like.'

'You can include it in the quote.'

'Sure.' He cast a fleeting look at the bouquet on the table again before he left. 'That Paul bloke thinks a lot of you,' he said. 'It truly was one of our most expensive orders.'

Claire had run out of vases for her flowers and so put some of Bill's carnations into the glass jars she had lined up on the window ledge to take to the recycling depot. Paul's bouquet was really beautiful but she was embarrassed by its magnificence. She took out her mobile and sent a text message thanking him. Claire loved being able to send text messages. They freed her from having to talk to people.

Her phone buzzed in response and she smiled as she read Paul's reply telling her that she was welcome and that he'd see her soon but was off to Galway for a few days. She replied that she hoped he'd have a good time and perhaps meet new women. His response to that was a simple *Haha*.

She cleared away all the broken stems and the leaves that she'd stripped off the flowers and took them down to the compost heap at the end of the garden. On her way back up she stopped at the jasmine and rubbed one of the yellow flowers between her fingers. Life with Bill had been so bloody simple. It really had.

A wasp brushed by her and she walked determinedly back to the house. She'd left the card for the exterminator on the table. The company was called Stamp Out. She would ring them now.

'A wasps' nest?' he asked in response to her question. 'Sure. No problem. It'll be a couple of days because we're up to our necks. The country is overrun with them this year! Can I call you back

169

tomorrow and give you a definite time? I'm on my way to a house in Deansgrange at the moment and I can't access my diary.'

'Fine,' she said and gave him her number.

Right, she thought, as she hung up the phone. I'm getting organised at last. A quote for the garden. Someone to look at the nest. Not bad really!

She went back downstairs and picked up a magazine. 'How to Recognise the Man of your Dreams,' it said. She sat down and filled in the questionnaire at the end of the article. According to the results she was too demanding. A perfectionist. The magazine told her that she shouldn't set impossible targets for people.

'Rubbish,' she said, out loud, and pushed it to one side. 'Come on, Phy. Let's go for our walk.'

Chapter 17

Echinops (Globe Thistle) – Usually dark blue flower heads on fat stems. Wear gloves when handling.

On Friday morning Eavan's eyes flickered open and she looked at the red display of the clock beside her bed. It was a quarter to six. She turned over and realised that she was alone. She rubbed at her eyes. Glenn couldn't have got up already. It was far too early for that. She rolled over again and waited for him to come back to bed. But as she drifted between waking and sleep she realised that she could hear no sounds coming from the en-suite where she'd have expected him to be. Nor any sound of him pottering about in the kitchen downstairs.

She opened her eyes with a snap and sat upright in the bed. It was a roll of thunder that had woken her. Not again, she thought. Given that there'd been a storm the previous week, she'd hoped the weather would have cleared for good. But obviously not. She got out of bed and looked out of the window. Charcoal-grey clouds scudded across the morning sky. She reached for her pink and white dressing gown and pulled it tightly around her waist before walking out of the bedroom and then stopping outside the door of Saffy's room. She pushed it open gently.

Glenn was sitting in the wicker chair beside Saffy's bed, the little girl in his lap, her eyes closed. An almost finished glass of Coke was on the locker. He looked up at Eavan.

'Hi,' he said softly.

'Hi,' she returned. 'What's up?'

'Nothing,' he said. 'She woke up. I heard her. I didn't want her to disturb you so I came in here with her. I read her a story and she fell asleep again.'

'What time was this?' asked Eavan.

'Oh, about an hour ago.'

'An hour ago!' she squeaked. 'How come I didn't hear? How come you did? You never used to!'

'I was awake myself,' said Glenn. 'I went downstairs to get a drink. I heard her as I came up again.'

Eavan glanced at the Coke glass. 'Not very sleep-inducing,' she remarked.

Glenn shrugged and drained the glass while Eavan pressed her fingers to her temple. She'd woken with a slight headache thanks to the wet but muggy and humid weather.

'You could have put her back to bed,' she told him. 'Once she falls back asleep she's usually out for the count.'

'I know,' said Glenn. 'But she said she wasn't feeling well.'

'No?' Eavan walked over and placed the back of her hand gently on her daughter's forehead. She frowned slightly. 'She's a bit hot.'

'Yes,' said Glenn. 'That's why I stayed with her.'

'D'you want me to make breakfast?' asked Eavan. 'Now that I'm up?'

He didn't reply.

'Glenn?' she repeated. 'I'll make breakfast. Is there anything special you'd like?'

Glenn shook his head. He was gazing down at Saffy again. He was back in a world of his own.

Claire was up early too. She'd snapped into wakefulness, her heart thumping, her body sweating and her cheeks wet with tears, as always happened when she had the dream. It was of Jamaica, of course, and their holiday together, and though it came to her less frequently now it still had the power to reduce her to a quivering wreck. In her dream she stood beside Bill on the balcony of their hotel room looking out into the inky blackness of the balmy night. She could feel the warmth of his body and the steady beat of his heart beside her. And it was almost perfect. So much like being with him again, knowing that he was there, sensing him. And yet knowing that somehow none of it was real. She always knew, in the dream, that being with Bill wasn't quite real. Meanwhile a sense of foreboding grew within her so that she knew that something awful was going to happen. She knew, too, that there was nothing that she could do to stop it. Then, as she stood there with the feeling of dread mounting inside her, there would be a sudden flash and a sound and Claire would know that this was the horror but she still couldn't do anything; couldn't move, couldn't speak, couldn't cry out even though she knew that she had to warn Bill, who was still looking out at the dark sea as though he didn't have a care in the world. Then everything would suddenly go black and she'd feel the weight of water on her and hear the sound of people's voices saying that it was all her fault and that was when she would wake up, slicked with perspiration, the sheet twisted around her body and her cheeks wet with tears.

Usually, after the dream, she would go into Georgia's room and check that she was OK, to reassure herself that she hadn't lost her too. But today Georgia wasn't there and Claire had to make herself not pick up the phone and call her and ask her was she all right. Instead she went downstairs and into Bill's surgery and she stared at the walls and the sun-faded posters and wondered would there ever be a day when she could forget.

I don't want to forget, she muttered as she left the surgery and went into the kitchen where Phydough woofed gently in greeting and nuzzled her legs. I just don't want to remember it all in that damn dream any more!

She made herself a cup of coffee and watched the sunrise and then, at a more respectable hour, she sent Georgia a text just asking was everything all right. The reply 'of course' eased the knot of anxiety that had been in her stomach ever since wakening.

She couldn't settle in front of the ice-white computer. She felt restless and on edge. She needed to do something active. She went into her bedroom and took the badminton racquet from the wardrobe shelf again. She couldn't play badminton. Not early in the morning and not without someone to play against. And not against any of the people she normally played against either. She threw the racquet on the bed and then sat down beside it, staring unseeingly into the open wardrobe.

Suddenly her eyes focused on the clothes hanging from the rails and she was jerked into remembering the Dinner in the Dark event. E-mails had been flying between everyone about it, all talking about what to wear and how to behave and all sorts of silly gossipy stuff that was kind of fun but, Claire thought, pretty irrelevant too. But they were right about what to wear, she mused, as her gaze flickered over her clothes. She had nothing suitable. Nothing at all. She stood up. The magazines always said that shopping was good when you were feeling depressed though they warned about buying things you didn't really need. But she did need a new dress. She really did. And maybe going shopping would break the feeling of unease that always lingered after the dream but which she really didn't want to feel any more.

It had stopped raining in Galway and the sun had come out, glittering like hard diamonds on the shining black tarmacked surface of the yard outside the college. Georgia and Steve Ó Sé were sitting on the low wall that surrounded it. Georgia was listening to her iPod and Steve was reading a book about Irish folklore.

'This time next week we'll be on our way home,' remarked Steve as he closed the book.

'Hmm?' Georgia removed her earphones.

'We'll be on our way home this time next week,' he repeated. 'Seems hard to imagine.'

'You don't want to go home?' She looked at him shrewdly.

'Ah, no, I do,' he said. 'I'm bored here. If it wasn't for you I think I'd have legged it long before now.'

She grinned at him. 'If it wasn't for me?'

'You're the only interesting person here,' he told her.

'Don't be daft,' she said. 'I'm not interesting. I'm ordinary.'

'You're lovely,' said Steve. 'You're lovely to look at and you're lovely to know.'

Georgia blushed furiously and this time it was Steve who grinned.

'I like being with you,' he said. 'You're the first girl I've ever met who – who isn't like a girl.'

'Great,' said Georgia in mock horror. 'You see me as – what, exactly?'

'You know what I mean,' said Steve. 'You're not all giggly and silly and prattling on about boy-bands or girl-bands or so-called celebrities that I've never heard about.'

'I don't do that with you,' she acknowledged. 'But when I'm with my girlfriends my life is a whirl of silly gossip.'

'I bet it isn't,' said Steve.

'Not always,' she admitted. 'But I do like reading *Heat* and *Closer* and all those celeb-watch mags. How can you not? They're so awful really but it's great fun to see the hot chick of the moment with a horrible spot on her cheek or something. And I know it's shallow and that I should be more worried about my exams than Britney's skin, but I don't care.'

Steve laughed. 'And you're honest,' he said. 'I like that too.'

'I'm glad I pass all your tests,' she told him.

'It's not meant to be . . . I don't want you to think . . .' He looked at her awkwardly. 'It's not a test, Georgia. I just mean that I like you and I feel comfortable with you.'

'Good,' she said.

He looked around them. 'Can I kiss you?' he asked.

'Here, now?' She raised an eyebrow. 'I really don't think so, Steve Ó Sé. Mr Ó Murchu is coming in our direction and I don't think it would be a good idea. But maybe before we go home.' She slid from the wall as the teacher approached. '*Slán*,' she said to Steve, and winked.

After Glenn had gone to work Eavan took Saffy to the doctor's surgery. The little girl had been sick when she'd woken and was still feverish and cranky. Eavan thought about dosing her with Calpol but she was a little worried about Saffy's listlessness and so she braved the early-morning surgery, which was filled mainly with mothers and children. By the time Eavan and Saffy got in to see the doctor, Saffy was already looking and feeling much better.

'But better to be safe than sorry,' said Dr McCormack as she scribbled a few notes on Saffy's file. 'How are you, by the way?'

'Me?' asked Eavan. 'I'm fine.'

'You don't need me to look you over while you're here?' asked the doctor.

175

'No!' Eavan looked anxiously at her. 'I don't seem unwell, do I?'

Dr McCormack laughed. 'Of course not. I just thought you might like a two-for-the-price-of-one check-up.'

'I'm fine,' said Eavan. 'Honestly.'

'And your husband?' Dr McCormack asked. 'How's he?'

'He's fine too,' Eavan told her.

'Coping well?'

'Absolutely.'

'Great,' said the doctor. 'It's nice to have a family with a clean bill of health. Saffy's bug will soon clear up, if it hasn't done so already.'

'Thanks,' said Eavan.

She left the surgery with Saffy in tow and then strapped her daughter into the child-seat of the people-carrier. They drove back to the house with Saffy's chatter becoming more and more animated every second. I really should have heeded my own instinct that she was fine and not bothered with surgery, which always takes hours, though Eavan glumly. Now I'm way behind with the laundry and the ironing. Plus, she secretly admitted, she'd wanted to finish the big fat novel she'd bought in the supermarket the previous week and which was a total page-turner, all about a woman whose husband was cheating on her with her best friend. I'd kill Glenn, she'd thought as she flipped over the pages, I really and truly would.

When they got back to the house, Saffy started to play doctors and nurses with her favourite dolls, and Eavan went upstairs. She'd left Glenn's glass on Saffy's bedside locker, and now she went into the bedroom and picked it up. Then, feeling both incredibly silly and guilty, she sniffed it. All she could smell was the sweet aroma of Coke. And yet . . . there was a dribble of liquid at the bottom. She tipped the glass and allowed the drop to roll on to her tongue. It still only seemed like Coke to her.

She sighed deeply. It was ridiculous of her to harbour sudden suspicions about her husband. In the five years they'd been married he'd never given her the slightest reason to suggest that he hadn't given up alcohol completely. And those times that she wondered or worried about it – well, she didn't seriously worry. It was just a useful way of testing her feelings. But now her worry was different.

She was concerned because Glenn seemed to be acting erratically these days. His timekeeping was all over the place, sometimes leaving the house very early for work, sometimes seeming to be very late. His time for coming home had become equally erratic. He explained it all away by the business expansion drive and the meetings that had been set up, but it was still all over the place. As was his conversation. He argued with her about silly things. He contradicted himself. He sometimes seemed to forget he'd even told her something.

And they hadn't had sex since before Saffy's birthday. These days when Glenn got into bed he seemed to be asleep before his head hit the pillow. At first she'd put it down to extra work, but now she couldn't help wondering if drink had something to do with it.

He never actually appeared to be drunk. But didn't they say that this was something alcoholics were good at? Hiding the fact that they were sozzled out of their brains? Seeming to be perfectly normal while all the time they'd consumed a couple of bottles of spirits? Wasn't that how it went?

She sighed heavily. If he was drinking he was doing it outside the house. And if that was the case he was driving home pissed too. Would he really risk it?

She went downstairs and opened the drinks cabinet. They didn't keep alcoholic drink in here and as far as Eavan could see the cabinet still contained its usual quota of mixers and cartons of juice. She'd thought that if he had suddenly decided to start drinking again he might put the drink in the cupboard on the basis that it wasn't somewhere she'd actually look. But he was smarter than that. All alcoholics were smarter than that!

Suddenly she ran up the stairs again and into the bathroom. She lifted the lid of the toilet cistern and peered inside. You're such a fool, she told herself sheepishly as she lowered it. He wouldn't drink again, he isn't drinking again, and even if he was what on earth would make you think he'd hide a bottle in the toilet cistern? That's probably something that only TV lushes do.

Shaking her head at her silliness, she went back downstairs again.

Claire was having an unexpectedly great time in town. She'd forgotten how much fun it was to browse the rails in search of the perfect outfit, and she was also completely out of touch with what was in

177

fashion. She discovered that she liked the neckline currently in vogue and that it suited her. The slightly longer length of the summer's chiffon and voile skirts hid most of the scars on her legs. The vivid lime greens and bright oranges which seemed to have taken over the high streets worked with her colouring. She bought an assortment of coloured T-shirts and tops, one green and one orange skirt, and – for the Dinner in the Dark – a silk dress in a delicate mauve which she hadn't expected to suit her but which looked absolutely stunning. She blinked a couple of times at her reflection in the changing-room mirror. It was like looking at a different person. Whether it was her summer tan, the colour of the dress or simply the lightness of her mood reflected in her face, Claire admitted to herself that she suddenly looked younger and prettier and . . . less miserable. She hadn't realised that she looked miserable before. But it was the absence of it in her face that changed her completely.

The shop assistant who peeked in to see how she was getting on nodded approvingly at the dress and brought her a pair of elegant high-heeled sandals to try on with it. At first Claire had been about to refuse them, thinking that delicate wispy sandals with pretty purple flowers across the toes might look pretty but were totally impractical, but then she slid them on to her feet and was instantly enchanted. So she bought the sandals too.

It was a bit of a nightmare carrying her bags to the bus and finding space for all of them. I need to get over the car thing, she told herself as she held on to the rail with one hand and her selection of bags with the other. But that's for another day.

Chapter 18

Dodecatheon (Shooting Star) – Pink, white and purple blooms on upright stalks. Eye-catching in early summer.

As soon as she got home Claire tried on all her new purchases again before putting them away. Of course, she muttered as she closed the wardrobe door, I should've bought a bag to go with the new dress and sandals. That would've finished it all perfectly. But it was too late to go looking for handbags now; she'd spent ages in town and the wasps' nest man was due any minute.

She'd only just come downstairs again when the doorbell rang. David Beckham, the footballer who'd launched and shattered a thousand dreams, was standing on her doorstep.

Of course she knew it wasn't really Becks. There was no reason for him to be standing in front of her in a snow-white boiler suit, his straw-blond hair slightly tousled and a smile on his lips, but the guy opposite her was a complete body double for him, and Claire, who'd always fancied Beckham even when his fortunes had turned somewhat, stood still in amazement.

'I'm here about the wasps' nest.'

He had the voice that Becks should've been born with. Deep and sensual. It sent shivers down Claire's spine.

'Oliver Ramsey,' he told her. 'I rang you back a few days ago and we arranged it for now.'

'Oh, yes.' She couldn't take her eyes off him. 'Yes. The wasps' nest. Yes. That's me.'

'I *do* have an appointment for today,' said Oliver.

'Sure. Yes. Sure.' Claire hadn't felt so flustered in years. 'I know. I'm sorry. I was – busy. You caught me by surprise.'

'It's not inconvenient?'

'No. No. Not at all,' said Claire.

'Perhaps if I take a look at it and then I'll go out to the van and get my gear?' He nodded at the white minivan parked outside the house.

'Great,' said Claire. 'Yes. Good idea.'

She led him through the house into the back garden and pointed at the eaves, where both of them could see a steady stream of wasps exiting and entering. Oliver made a face. 'Yes, it's a nest all right.'

'I knew that,' she said a little impatiently. 'It's why I called.'

'Sometimes people think there's a nest because they see activity but the actual site is somewhere else,' he told her. 'I'll get the extension ladder. And my protective gear.'

Maybe people called pretending to have nests, she thought, as her eyes followed his progress back into the house. Maybe women called him out because they just wanted to look at him. She could understand that. She hadn't see a better-looking man in years – if, she conceded, you liked the Beckham look. But could millions of women the world over be wrong?

Bill used to tease her about her support for the ex-Manchester United footballer, telling her that he was highly over-rated, and she'd tease him back, saying that it was just a physical attraction and that Bill needn't worry, she wouldn't run off with Becks for his mind.

She couldn't believe that her heart was now racing in her chest at the thought of Oliver Ramsey walking back into the garden. She told herself to get a grip. He only looked like Beckham. Part of the man's appeal was his great six-pack abs and his skill as a footballer. Oliver Ramsey just killed wasps. She needed a sense of perspective, for heaven's sake!

He returned to the garden carrying the ladder, then went out again to get some more equipment.

'You'll probably want to stay inside while I spray this,' he advised Claire. 'They go a bit crazy.'

She watched as he put protective headgear over his head and face.

His hair, just below shoulder length, wasn't cut in a trademark Beckham style. It didn't matter.

Claire walked into the kitchen and sat on a high stool. She hadn't felt like this since she'd first seen a blond-streaked George Michael performing with Wham! (Bill had insisted that George had shoved a shuttlecock down his pants, though Claire had refused to believe him. Later, however, she conceded the possibility).

The darker clouds of earlier were rolling across the sky and suddenly the sun came out, washing the room with bright light. Claire opened the fridge and took out a smoothie. I can't believe I feel like this, she thought, as she unscrewed the cap. I actually fancy this bloke. And I don't even know a thing about him.

Which means, of course, that it's just his looks. And just because he resembles a man I like already. So it's pretty meaningless. But still . . . she swigged a mouthful of banana and passion fruit . . . it was very strange to know that any man was making her go weak at the knees.

He opened the kitchen door as he took off his headgear.

'That should do it,' he told her. 'You'll see activity around the nest for a while because all the wasps currently out and about will be coming back. But they won't go in. I'd say you had a big one there. Just as well you got me to do it for you now.'

'Um . . . yes . . . I'd been meaning to for a while,' said Claire as she opened her bag and took out her purse.

'I'll do you up an invoice,' he said. 'Just a second.' He took a receipt book from his pocket and starting writing. Claire noticed that he stuck his tongue out very slightly as he wrote. She thought it looked cute.

'There you go.' He handed her the invoice. 'If you have any problems give me a call. It's effective in ninety-nine per cent of cases but there can always be one stubborn nest. Not this time, I think, but we offer a full guarantee so it's no problem to call.'

'Great, thanks,' she said as she handed him the money. 'It's a relief to have it done.'

'Can I ask where you heard of us? Recommendation, Golden Pages, ad in the paper?' He looked at her enquiringly.

'A guy gave me your number,' said Claire. 'From the florist's shop down the road. Taylor's.'

'Oh, Nate, yeah – he's a good bloke.' Oliver grinned. 'Any time there's a nest where he's working he gives my number. I get a lot of business that way.' He glanced out at her garden. 'He could work wonders for you.'

'He's supposed to be sending me a quote,' said Claire. 'I haven't got it yet.'

'Not like him,' Oliver said. 'He's one of life's efficient men. Always on the go, always doing something. I keep telling him to slow down but it's not in his nature. It's no wonder—' He broke off and smiled, showing perfect white teeth. 'Sorry, I rant a bit.'

'That's OK.' Claire smiled too.

'Well, I'll be off then,' said Oliver. 'Hope I don't see you again!'

'Would you – would you like tea or anything before you go?'

Bloody hell, she thought. That's lame. He'll think I'm a complete idiot.

'You know, tea would be great,' said Oliver, 'but I'm up to my neck in work right now. It's why it took me so long to get around to your nest. So I have to pass. Sorry.'

'Never mind.' Claire had moved towards the kettle but now she turned back to him. 'Thanks again.'

'No bother,' he said. 'And, like I said, call if you have a problem.'

'OK,' she said.

He was carrying his ladder out of the house when Eavan's car pulled up at the kerb. She got out and helped Saffy from the baby seat. Oliver smiled at her and her eyes opened wide as she too took in the resemblance to Manchester's most famous footballer. Then she locked her car and walked up Claire's gravel path.

'Who was that?' she asked as the white minivan drove away.

'Becks,' said Claire dreamily. 'I'm having an affair with him.'

'Claire!'

'I wish you were exclaiming in an envious way and not a don't-be-so-ridiculous way,' remarked her friend.

'Well, I guess if you had to have an affair with anyone, Becks would be a reasonable start, but I somehow don't think he'd be at your house in overalls and driving a van,' said Eavan.

'Drink, Claire?' asked Saffy as she tugged at Claire's frayed jeans. 'I'm thirsty.'

'Sure thing, honey,' said Claire. 'Come on, we'll go into the kitchen.'

'Seven Up for her if you have it,' said Eavan. 'She was at the doc's earlier, bit of a feverish upset tummy. She's OK now but the Seven Up always seems to help.'

Claire took a bottle from the cupboard and poured a glass for Saffy.

'Garden?' asked the little girl.

'Actually not right now,' said Claire. 'A man was here killing wasps and there might be some out there which would sting you.'

'Oh!' Saffy's eyes widened.

'You're not telling me that the footie idol was a pest exterminator!' Eavan looked disappointed.

''Fraid so,' said Claire. 'But wasn't he a complete hunk?'

'If you're a Beckham fan.' Eavan smiled at Claire. 'Which was always your thing, wasn't it?'

'I liked him.' Claire blushed. 'Regardless of all that guff about affairs and stuff I always found him attractive.'

Eavan laughed. 'So what's the story with the exterminator?'

'None,' said Claire. 'I had a nest, I gave him a call, he came, he saw, he committed mass murder. Thankfully.'

'Married?' asked Eavan.

'Honest to God, Eavan Keating!' But Claire's tone was amused. 'I've no idea. Besides, he's a bit on the young side for me.'

'Oh, I wouldn't think like that.' Eavan was encouraged by the laughter in Claire's voice. 'Glenn told me he always thought Mrs Robinson was one of the sexiest women in a movie ever. He never understood why Dustin Hoffman ran off with Katharine Ross instead of sticking with Anne Bancroft.'

Claire laughed. 'If only real life was like that. Anyway, I rather think that our wasp exterminator is somewhat more experienced than the Graduate.'

'I'd imagine so,' agreed Eavan, 'with a body like that.'

'Indeed.' Claire looked quizzically at Eavan. 'Not that I'm not glad to see you or anything, but I didn't think you were going to drop by today. Your machine didn't confirm with mine.' She chuckled. She'd phoned Eavan on her way into town, wanting to let her friend know she'd gone shopping, but had got her machine instead and hadn't bothered to leave a message other than to say that she was now out but she'd call again later. On her return, her own machine had been blinking with Eavan's call back.

Suddenly the light went out of Eavan's eyes and Claire frowned.

'Is something the matter?' she asked.

'Oh, it's stupid,' said Eavan. 'But I'm kind of getting myself into a state over it. You – well, you're good at this sort of stuff, Claire. When . . .' She swallowed. 'Oh, you know. You can see things clearly. You always could.'

Claire looked at her friend in consternation. She realised now that Eavan's cheerfulness of earlier had seemed slightly forced. She turned to Saffy. 'I have a *Little Mermaid* video,' she said. 'Would you like to watch it?'

'Yes please,' said Saffy.

Claire settled her down on the sofa in the living room with some more Seven Up and a cookie. Then she came back to the kitchen, where Eavan was staring out of the back window at the tangled garden. She opened the fridge door and poured fruit juice into two glasses, then handed one to Eavan.

'I've asked someone for a quote,' she said. 'I'm getting it done.'

'Really?'

'Yes,' said Claire. 'Bill would be disgusted to see the state it's in, and so . . .' She shrugged. 'What's the problem, Eavan?'

'Actually, the real reason I planned to come today was nothing to do with any problem I might have.' Eavan's voice was determinedly light-hearted. 'It was to get the low-down on your date with Paul. I managed to speak to him for about half a minute earlier. He says he's heading to Galway. I wondered had you frightened him off?'

'I don't think so,' said Claire. 'But given my man-handling experience, you never know.' She smiled. 'Actually it wasn't a bad evening. But we'll always be just friends.'

'Was there talk of it being anything more?' asked Eavan hopefully.

'No,' said Claire. 'But I learned a lot.'

'You're not still going on about that, are you? Learning about men?'

Claire shrugged.

'You don't really need to anyway,' Eavan told her. 'You were always dishing out the advice when we were younger and sometimes it wasn't so bad.'

'Do you want advice about something now?' Claire heard the underlying tension in Eavan's voice. 'I might have come out with unasked-for stuff in the past but I'm not sure how good I'd be at it any more.'

'I . . .' Eavan's glance flickered to the living room but Saffy was engrossed in the video.

'What is it?' asked Claire. Her eyes widened suddenly. 'You're not pregnant again are you, is that it?'

'No,' said Eavan. 'And if I was it wouldn't be a problem this time.' She rubbed the bridge of her nose. 'God knows, Claire, one unplanned pregnancy was bad enough . . .'

'You dealt with it,' said Claire.

'I had an abortion,' Eavan reminded her tightly. 'And you're the only person who knows.'

'And since then you've met Glenn and had a lovely baby – don't beat yourself up over it, Eavan.'

'I'm not.' Eavan twisted her engagement ring around on her finger. 'I'm not. I don't. I – well – I suppose everyone wonders some-times . . .'

'It was your choice at the time,' said Claire. 'You didn't feel there was any alternative.'

'But maybe there was. Maybe I didn't try hard enough.'

'Oh, come on!' Claire put her arm around Eavan's shoulders. 'Think back, Evs. Remember how it was. Your mum was chronically sick, you'd only lost your dad a few years earlier. It was hard. You were doing everything at home. It just wasn't possible for you to have a baby.'

'Of course it was possible,' said Eavan. 'It just would have been very difficult.'

'So you made a choice,' said Claire.

'And you helped me.' Eavan sipped her fruit juice. 'You and Bill both. You were great.'

'So don't feel guilty now,' advised Claire.

'I never stop feeling guilty,' Eavan told her. 'But I don't think I made the wrong choice. Only sometimes . . . sometimes when things go wrong I wonder if I'm being punished for it.'

'You know how silly that is, don't you?'

Eavan nodded. 'Sure I do. But it doesn't stop me from thinking it anyway. And today . . .' She told Claire about Glenn getting up to see to Saffy and about finding him with the empty glass of Coke beside him. She told her about his erratic behaviour over the past couple of weeks and the fact that she was never sure where he was or what he was doing. She told her that they hadn't had sex in ages only she hadn't quite realised how long it had been. And then she admitted that she'd scoured the house for bottles of alcohol.

'Well, whatever you're thinking, this has nothing to do with you having had an abortion fifteen years ago,' said Claire firmly.

'But it's my life going wrong,' cried Eavan. 'All the things I have, I have because I had the abortion! You think that me and Glenn would've got together if I'd had a baby? I wouldn't even have met him! And I love him, Claire. You know how much I love him. But I can't help feeling that it's all under threat. And it's because of me. Because I'm being punished now for what I did then.'

'That's crazy, Evs.'

'I know. I know. But I can't help thinking it anyway.'

'Do you really believe he's drinking again?'

'It would explain a lot.' Eavan bit her lip. 'Oh, Claire, I hate to think the worst of him. I feel like I'm betraying him by even talking about it. And the fact is that I didn't find any drink in the house at all. But . . .'

'But once it's in your head you can't get it out,' said Claire.

'Exactly,' confirmed Eavan. 'I don't know what to do.'

Claire thought again about telling Eavan that she'd seen Glenn in a bar. But if Glenn and Eavan ended up arguing about drink and Eavan told him that Claire had spilled the beans, it might make things worse. Besides, it had been a hot day and he could just as easily have been drinking Ballygowan.

'I guess you need to talk to him,' she said finally.

'If I talk to him he'll just get all defensive,' said Eavan. 'He'll think I don't trust him.'

'But you don't,' Claire pointed out.

186

Eavan sighed miserably. 'I can't think of anything else that would make him act that way. I know it's been stressful at work for him, but he's dealt with that before—' Suddenly she looked at Claire, her eyes wide with horror. 'You don't think he's having an affair, do you?'

'Glenn? Having an affair!' Claire shook her head. 'Come on, Eavan, you know how much he loves you. He'd never have an affair.'

'You think that,' said Eavan. 'Every woman wants to think that. But in the end, who knows?'

Claire said nothing. She'd suddenly remembered her father and his affairs. More particularly the affair that had turned into a long-term relationship with Lacey Dillon.

'So it's possible, isn't it?' Eavan waited for Claire's reply, but Claire was still gazing into space. 'Claire? Isn't it?' she repeated.

'Sorry,' said Claire. She focused on Eavan again. 'If Glenn didn't have a problem with drink, would you think he could be having an affair?'

Eavan frowned. 'I don't know,' she said finally. 'But . . . well . . . maybe.' Her eyes were big and anxious in her face. 'Oh hell, Claire – yes! It fits, doesn't it? The erratic hours. The "only ring me on the mobile" instruction—'

'Only ring him on his mobile? What's that all about?'

'He says that he's out and about a lot with business,' said Eavan, 'and not to ring him at the office because he won't be there. Maybe he just wants a warning that I'm looking for him. Perhaps he's having the affair with someone at the office and he's locked in a room with her and doesn't want to be disturbed. And I bet I know who it is too! The engineer who works with them. She's the sluttiest woman you ever saw.'

'Eavan!'

'OK, OK, not slutty. But she has big boobs and she crams them into her overalls with the zip halfway down so that she looks like Pamela Anderson in a fucking catsuit . . . and they all fancy her, I know they do.'

'But why would Glenn suddenly be having an affair with her now?' asked Claire.

'Because . . . because – oh, I don't know.' Eavan covered her face with her hands. 'All I know is that something's wrong and it's either a woman or drink. Or both.' She looked miserably at Claire. 'And I don't know what to do.'

'You have to talk to him.'

'I can't,' whispered Eavan. 'Because either way I'm saying that there's something wrong.'

'But there *is* something wrong.'

'I know. I know. Thing is, Claire, I don't want there to be something wrong. Everything was fine till a couple of weeks ago. I don't know why it would suddenly change.'

'Bill used to say that it wasn't change you had to worry about, it was how you dealt with it,' said Claire wryly. 'I never listened of course! Look, Evs, if there's something going on you have to find out what it is and we can deal with it then. But while you're worrying and wondering and beating yourself up about it, there's nothing we can do.'

Eavan stared at her. 'You sound like the old Claire,' she said. 'The one who fixed things for me when we were younger.'

'I didn't fix things for you,' said Claire. 'You did it yourself.'

'You listened. You talked to me. You were like my older sister. Only my non-judgmental older sister.'

Claire smiled at her. 'We were friends, Eavan. That's what friends do. We still *are* friends. Even if I haven't made as much effort as I should over the last while.'

'Ah, don't worry about it,' said Eavan. 'You've gone through a lot. I worried about you. I suppose I still do.'

'There's no need.'

'Well, I know! You have Paul Hanratty asking you out for drinks even if it's just "as a friend" and gorgeous men calling round to your house on the pretext of killing wasps, don't you? Plus you've gone shopping for an exciting night out. Suddenly your life is on the up and up!'

'I told you, the Paul Hanratty thing is nothing,' said Claire. 'And the wasp guy is nothing too, just a shock because of his looks. A nice shock, I'll grant you. As for Dinner in the Dark . . .' She shuddered. 'Every time I think of it I want to back out.'

'If it all goes pear-shaped with me and Glenn I might be joining you,' said Eavan dismally.

'It'll work out,' Claire comforted her. 'Really it will.'

'I sure as hell hope so,' said Eavan, and went into the living room to prise Saffy off the sofa.

The little girl had fallen asleep watching the video. Eavan lifted her over her shoulder.

'She weighs a bloody ton!' muttered Eavan as she walked into the hallway. 'It's no wonder I have permanent backache.'

'Can you manage?' asked Claire as she opened the front door. 'D'you want me to – oh!'

This time the man standing on her doorstep, his finger poised over the bell, was Nate Taylor. His blue-black hair was as tousled as Oliver Ramsey's had been, but instead of looking boyish it simply looked as though it needed to be cut. He was wearing baggy cargo pants, a loose black T-shirt and ancient trainers. Claire realised suddenly that he was much taller and broader than she'd previously thought. Every other time she'd seen him he'd been carrying something or slouching so that she never noticed his height.

'Hi,' he said. 'I came with the quote. I wanted to apologise for it taking so long. We had some problems with our computer system and I thought it'd only take a couple of hours to fix, but it took a few days. I know I could've simply written out the quote and pushed it through your letterbox but I wanted you to see that we were an efficient organisation. Kinda backfired.'

'Right.' Claire took the envelope from him as Eavan, still carrying Saffy, stepped out of the front door. Eavan raised an eyebrow as she looked firstly at Nate and then at Claire.

'This is my friend.' Claire really didn't know why she was introducing them. 'Eavan Keating – Nate Taylor. Nate's the one who's quoting for the garden.'

'It used to be a wonderful garden,' Eavan told Nate. 'You could sit in it and be transported to another time. The scent of the flowers, the buzz of the bees . . . fantastic.'

'I can make it wonderful again,' said Nate. He nodded briefly at Claire. 'Let me know if the price works for you.' He hurried down the steps and out of the front gate.

'Claire Hudson!' Eavan shifted Saffy on her shoulder and looked at her friend. 'Another man about the house?'

'Don't be ridiculous,' said Claire. 'Like he said, he's quoting for the garden.'

'How is it that you managed to get the two handsomest men on the planet out to do your work?' demanded Eavan. 'The wasp guy was gorgeous, but so is the garden bloke.'

'Oh, I don't think so!' Claire shook her head. 'I'll admit Oliver is a walking dream. But Nate is just different.'

'I think he's a hunk,' said Eavan firmly. 'And much closer to your own age too.'

'For heaven's sake!' Claire looked at her in amusement. 'Even if he was it wouldn't make any difference. I first met him on the seafront and Phydough knocked him over and nearly killed him. Then I walked into him at his shop and broke a pot he was carrying.'

'And after all that he's still prepared to do your garden?' Eavan's eyes twinkled. 'Sounds promising to me.'

'He's married,' said Claire. 'To the girl that runs the new florist's down the road.'

'Oh well.' Eavan grinned. 'You'll have to stick with Becks junior after all.'

'I'm sticking with no one,' said Claire.

Eavan laughed. 'You know, you're happier all of a sudden, aren't you?'

'Sort of.' Claire bit her lip. 'I do feel different. But I don't know why.'

'Maybe it's all these sexy men wandering around.'

'Yeah, right.' She grinned.

'Perhaps you'll find one at that dinner thing. Perhaps you'll find someone who bowls you over.'

'No.' Claire looked at her very definitely. 'No. That won't happen. I can look at men and think they're attractive again. But to be honest, I could do that when Bill was alive. It's just that I can't . . . I can't connect with them. And I don't want to.'

'If you met the right man?'

Claire shook her head. 'There's no right man. I'd know if there was but there isn't.'

'You can't be sure of that.'

'You only have one soulmate,' said Claire.

'Maybe. Shouldn't stop you from taking a chance though.'

Claire shook her head again. 'Call me. Let me know what Glenn says. You're not alone in this, Eavan.'

'Thank you.' Eavan kissed her friend lightly on the cheek.

'Take care,' said Claire. 'D'you need a hand to get her into the car?'

Eavan shook her head. 'I'm used to it,' she said. 'But it's costing me a fortune in visits to the chiropractor!'

Chapter 19

Buddleia (Butterfly Bush) – Tiny flowers in a variety of colours which attract butterflies. Failure to prune results in gaunt bare branches.

Summer returned on the day of the Dinner in the Dark event. The sky was a cloudless cerulean blue and the temperature soared once more. Claire was tempted to call Rosie and tell her that she wasn't going to bother with the dinner at all because it was far too nice a day to head into the city and a pitch-dark hotel room. But she didn't have the nerve to back out now. Instead she sat in the hairdresser's salon (having suddenly decided that she should really get her hair done if she was serious about going out) and agreed with her stylist that maybe the time had come to tackle the threads of grey that were appearing in her cinnamon tresses.

'You're lucky,' Avril told her as she mixed a colour. 'You don't have many greys and they're hardly noticeable anyway. But this will give you a lift, I promise.'

Afterwards, Claire looked at herself in the mirror and smiled in delight at the soft colour which matched her own but which had added highlights and glints to make it look much healthier. Avril had trimmed her wayward fringe and thinned out some of the heavier parts of her hair so that her eyes were more visible and her face was framed by her softly falling curls.

She kept glancing at her reflection in the shop windows as she walked home, thrilled with the look but telling herself that she was being really silly in thinking that a new colour and a more stylish trim were important in the whole scheme of things.

She gave herself an hour to get ready, spending more time than usual

192

putting on her make-up. She'd never been very good at makeup, though, and she somehow felt that the ancient foundation and dash of eyeshadow, along with the (still bacteria-infested!) mascara wouldn't quite do justice to her lovely new dress and smarter hair-do. The weird thing was, she thought, as she sat on the bed in her M&S bra and knickers and struggled to varnish her toenails, she was starting to get a little bit excited about the thought of going out. It wasn't that she was expecting to find a man, of course. But there was a thrill there all the same, of doing something different, of being out with the girls and the potential of – well, she wasn't sure exactly what potential was there, but maybe something nice might happen. She tried to tell herself that that was nonsense, but the thought kept popping into her head that maybe there'd be someone at the dinner with whom she might click. A man who could become a friend. It was possible, wasn't it? Someone new. Someone who didn't look at her and always be reminded that she was Claire Hudson who'd gone through a terrible tragedy in her life.

And, of course . . . she nibbled at the corner of her lip . . . there was the competitive element too. Claire couldn't quite believe she was thinking like this, but she knew she'd be disappointed if the other Locum Libris girls met someone and she didn't. She put the fast-dry varnish on the bedside locker and shook her head. It wasn't a bloody badminton match! It was a night out, for heaven's sake! And she'd better get dressed or she'd be late.

The mauve dress was hanging in the wardrobe. She opened the door and pushed at her older clothes to take it out. And then she saw the other dress. The scorched ochre silk she'd worn on their last evening in Jamaica together. It had been her favourite, one she could only wear when she was feeling at her slimmest and most attractive, because it was tight-fitting and unforgiving. But she'd worn it that evening, even though it was a little uncomfortable because of her pregnancy, because it was Bill's favourite dress too. She slid her fingers along the smooth, flowing material, and it was as though she was back there again, standing on the balcony overlooking the sea, caressed by the warm Caribbean breeze, Bill's hand resting lightly on her shoulder. Damn it, she muttered as she felt tears prick the back of her eyes. I can't cry. Not now. My mascara will run.

*   *   *

At a quarter to seven that evening, when most people were still stuck in commuter traffic coming out of the city, Claire walked to the bus stop and caught the 44A. By the time she arrived at the hotel it was nearly a quarter past, and the Locum Libris crowd were clustered in the foyer.

'We thought you'd chickened out,' said Trinny, who spotted her first. 'But you look great, Claire! Come on, there's a champagne reception in the bar.'

The tiny bar was already crowded with people. The Locum Libris girls got their glasses filled and scanned the throng.

'I didn't think there'd be so many people,' commented Rosie. 'According to the thing I read over the net, one of these was held in New York recently and there were only about thirty.'

'How many would you say are here?' asked Joanna.

'Fifty? Sixty?'

'Enough for us all to snare someone, surely,' remarked Petra. 'Hey, look, there's a real hunk!' She nodded in the direction of a guy wearing a tux who was standing in the doorway.

'I think he's a waiter,' said Rosie.

'You're joking!'

'None of the men are wearing tuxes,' she pointed out.

'Bloody hell.' Petra sniggered. 'I'll just have to dive at him when the lights go out so!'

'You're supposed to be talking to people, finding out about their personalities,' Rosie told her. 'Not being shallow and going for looks.'

This time they all giggled.

'Hope they're thinking the same way,' said Joanna. 'After all, I'm the imposter who lied about her age to get here.'

According to the website, the upper age limit for women was thirty-five (forty-five for men, which Petra had muttered was ridiculously sexist). Joanna had decided that since she habitually knocked at least five years off her age there was no reason to change this time either. And Claire, who was also the wrong side of thirty-five but who hadn't noticed the age restriction at first, had then decided that since she wasn't really in the market for a man it didn't much matter how old she was.

'That age thing is so stupid,' said Trinny. 'You're by far the most glamorous of us, Jo, and I bet you'll have some guy eating out of your hand by the end of the night.'

'We'll all be eating out of our hands,' Claire pointed out. She sipped her wine and allowed her gaze to rove over the crowd. As she'd suspected, the women were young, thin and very, very attractive. Many of the men were attractive too, though there were a few who hadn't seemed to make much effort at all. Most of the women had pulled out all the stops. There were plunging necklines, high-cut dresses and footwear that appeared impossible to walk in. Not that her own light sandals were much better in the comfort department, she conceded. Her feet were already sore from the unaccustomed height.

A bell tinkled and the good-looking guy in the tux welcomed them all to the event, told them that he was Chris, the organiser, and announced that it was time to go in to dinner. He asked them to wait until they were escorted to their tables.

Maroon-coated waiters, wearing night-vision goggles, appeared from nowhere and began leading people into the blacked-out dining room.

'Christ,' muttered Celia. 'We're in a CIA movie! Tom Cruise or Ben Affleck will come abseiling down the walls toting AK47s any minute.'

'This way, madam,' said a waiter.

'See you later,' murmured Trinny as she was led away from them.

'I feel like I'm going to the guillotine or something,' remarked Petra as she followed.

Five minutes later, Claire was escorted into the room. It was pitch black with not the slightest chink of light entering. Somehow she hadn't expected it to be quite so dark. She put her hands out in front of her, terrified of tripping over a chair or walking into a table, and even more terrified of inadvertently touching someone. The waiter guided her into a seat and told people that this was Claire and to introduce themselves.

Claire couldn't see a thing. She felt completely alone as the darkness enveloped her. Even though she could hear the buzz of conversation around her, the loudest sound was her own heart hammering in her chest.

'Is anyone there?' she asked tentatively.

'I am,' said a female voice from the other side. 'My name is Tanya.'

'Claire,' said Claire.

'Amy,' another voice said.

'Are there any men?' asked Tanya.

There was complete silence.

'Ah, crap,' said Amy. 'We're at the only all-female table!'

'No.' A male voice came from Claire's left and she almost jumped six feet into the air. 'I'm here.'

'Well you'd better watch out,' said Tanya. ''Cos if you're the only bloke, you're in big trouble.'

There was another flurry around the table and Claire realised that more people had joined them.

'Let's introduce ourselves properly,' said Amy. 'I'll start and then I'll shake hands with the person on my right, and he can say his name and we'll go round the table like that.'

'Richard.'

'Stella.'

'Cormac.'

'Tanya.'

'Gary.' Claire felt a man reach for her hand and catch her by the elbow. She felt for his hand and shook it. His grip was firm and determined.

'Claire,' she said and turned to the person next to her. She missed his hand and poked him in the eye.

'Ouch,' he gasped. 'Ollie.'

'And now you're back to me again,' said Amy.

'Excuse me, madam.' The waiters had returned with their food. She put her hand out to the table and felt around for the plate.

'This is absolutely ridiculous,' said Gary. 'I can't believe I agreed to do it.'

'Ah, chill out!' cried Tanya. 'Sure, if you're really lucky, one of us girls might take all our clothes off!'

'Now you're talking!'

Claire wasn't sure which of the blokes had made the comment.

'Bit of a waste when you'll never even know,' said Stella.

'I've already taken mine off.' Claire ventured a joke.

'Really?' She could sense Ollie turning beside her and reaching out towards her. She moved slightly and he toppled off his chair, grabbing her arm as he fell. She helped him back into the seat.

'OK, undressing in the dark not quite such a good idea,' he said. 'Can lead to unexpected injuries. Sorry, Claire. I nearly killed you just then.'

'Hey, keep it easy over there!' called Stella.

'Sounds like the good fun might happen this side of the table,' Gary chuckled.

'What the hell is the food?' asked Amy.

'Prawns,' advised Cormac. 'There's a sauce to the side. I've already stuck my finger in it.'

Claire made another effort to find her food. Beside her, Ollie was keeping up a stream of talk about how unnatural the whole thing was and how he'd kill his sister because she was the one who'd arranged this for him as a birthday present and dared him to come along . . .

'Is she trying to set you up with someone?' Claire had finally managed to locate her prawns and popped one into her mouth. They weren't at all bad, she realised with pleasure. She'd somehow expected that the food would be inedible but actually, in the dark, the taste was even better than she'd anticipated. She licked at the spicy sauce which had dribbled down her arm.

'Always,' said Ollie. 'But what she doesn't realise is that I'm a sensitive soul and the women she tries to find for me are all much much tougher than me.'

'What a load of bullshit!' Stella laughed.

Claire was conscious of the different accents around the table. Amy, she decided, was from Cork, with her soft, languid tones. Richard was from the north of Ireland – she hazarded Belfast but she couldn't be certain. Tanya and Cormac were both definitely Dubs, and Stella had the much-maligned Dublin 4 accent – the one where people substituted the letter 'o' for the letter 'a' in speech so that they took the Dort instead of the Dart and their friends drove cors instead of cars. Mostly people who spoke of the Dort were in their early twenties or at college, so Claire built up a picture of Stella as being young and beautiful with caramel-streaked blonde hair. Amy sounded plump and friendly. Tanya, she thought, would have red hair and freckles. Her imagined pictures of the men were equally clear. Richard was thin, wore glasses and looked anaemic. Cormac would be big and burly. Gary – based on his handshake – would be tall and strong. And Ollie, on the other side of her – suddenly the niggling thoughts about Ollie exploded into clarity in her head. Ollie. Oliver. The wasp exterminator with the body of a god! Surely not, though. Not here. Beside her. In the dark.

The voice was right, wasn't it? Warm and sensual as she remembered. And there weren't that many people called Oliver in Dublin, were there? Could he possibly be the same guy? What were the chances? And if it was him, would he remember her and tell everyone that she was a total imposter because she couldn't possibly be under thirty-five; he'd seen her at home with no make-up to fill the cracks! She felt herself grow hot at the thought.

'So,' he said beside her. 'Tell me about yourself.'

I don't have to tell him anything, she realised. I can be whoever I want to be. Surprised by her own imagination, she spun him a tale about being a talent scout for a model agency and made up stories about tracking down gorgeous young men on the streets.

'I wouldn't have thought you'd need to come to a place like this,' he remarked. 'Your life must be full of gorgeous men already.'

'I'm not looking for gorgeous,' she said. 'I'm looking for someone interesting.'

'You see, that's just it.' His tone relaxed. 'I meet lots of women who think looks are everything. Their looks or my looks.'

'Are you good-looking?' Suddenly Claire couldn't help herself. She moved towards him and touched him softly on the face.

Was this what it was like to be blind? she wondered, as she traced her fingers lightly down the side of his cheeks, around the softness of his mouth and back up the other side of his face. I don't need eyes to see him. And it's definitely Oliver Ramsey. I know it is.

'You have an incredible touch,' he whispered.

'Hey, hey! What's going on over there?' called Tanya.

Claire took her hand away from his face and reached for her glass of wine, which she knocked over so that it soaked the tablecloth.

'Shit,' she muttered. 'I'm sorry, everyone.'

It only took a second for a waiter to arrive and begin to mop up the mess.

'Sorry,' she said again.

She sat in silence as the starters were cleared away and a palate-clearing sorbet was put in front of them. She realised that her heart was thumping in her chest. Touching Ollie's face had stirred up mixed emotions in her. It wasn't as though he could possibly fancy her, or that she could truly fancy him. But just touching someone like that again . . . She shivered suddenly despite the warmth of the room.

The general conversation around the table had splintered into smaller ones. To her right she could hear Gary and Stella chatting. Ollie seemed to be talking to Tanya. Claire felt very alone in the dark. But then she felt the touch of Ollie's hand on her leg. She almost shrieked out loud but she didn't want to make more of a fuss. She held her breath. His hand lifted. She exhaled again. Then he whispered, 'Sorry, I was looking for your arm,' and she began to shake with laughter.

'No, really,' he said anxiously. 'I don't want you to think I'm some kind of perv.'

She talked to Ollie again for a while, and then her attention shifted to Gary, who butted into the conversation. He worked in the construction industry and had been involved in the design of some of the city's best-known commercial developments. But, more importantly, he'd spent the last year in Kosovo helping with the rebuilding of the city there. Gary, in fact, was a much more interesting person than Ollie. It was a bit unfortunate, perhaps, that she was certain she knew what Ollie looked like and that, therefore, he was ahead in the desirability stakes. And then she shook her head at herself for even thinking like that.

By the time they were ready for dessert she felt as though she'd known both of them for years. She deliberately hadn't asked Ollie about his job because she knew that she wouldn't have been able to keep up the pretence of not knowing who he was. She realised that her heart was racing again because the lights were due to go on at any second. Even though she'd wished all through dinner that she could see the people she was talking to, she now felt that the darkness was her friend. In the dark she was Claire the glamorous talent scout. In the light she was Claire Hudson, Georgia's mum, over the age limit, who'd once been married to Bill.

When the chandeliers flooded the room with light, everyone blinked. Claire looked in astonished envy at Tanya, who was practically a body-double of Jennifer Lopez; in admiration at Amy, who wasn't dumpy at all but had the body of Kate Moss and the face of a *Vogue* cover; and in satisfaction at Stella, who exactly matched her imagined picture of her. Gary was slightly overweight but wasn't unattractive; Richard was thin with a cheerful grin and spiky haircut; Cormac had Viking good looks; and Ollie – Ollie was Oliver Ramsey, just as she'd thought.

He stared at her in utter amazement.

'I didn't know you were a talent scout,' he said accusingly. 'You said you worked from home!'

'Do you know each other?' asked Tanya, her huge brown eyes opened wide at them. 'I can't believe you know each other!'

'Is there any reason talent scouts can't work from home?' asked Claire, unwilling to admit to everyone that she'd lied about her job. 'Anyway, Oliver, I thought it was you.'

'You guessed who I was! How?'

She blushed. She didn't want to say that his sexy voice was what had given him away.

'Come on, Claire! How did you know it was me?'

Oh, what the hell, she thought.

'I recognised your voice.'

'Sexy,' Tanya told him. 'Very sexy.'

'Absolutely,' Amy added. 'The best voice in the place. And,' she added, looking at him wickedly, 'the best body too.'

Oliver looked pleased, while the other men looked grim and the girls giggled.

It was easier to chat in the light, thought Claire, but the conversation was lighter too, and somehow being able to see somebody made you less able to ask them questions about themselves. But she was still enjoying the company of everyone around the table and the sheer fun of being out with new people.

'Claire! Hiya, how're you getting on?' Trinny Armstrong walked by the table. 'Gosh, you managed to get some good-looking guys here. Ours were all terrible. Lovely people, definitely. But no lookers.' She looked archly at Oliver Ramsey. 'Good God, has anyone ever told you that you're the spit of David Beckham?'

'Lots of times,' said Oliver.

'Very appealing,' Trinny said. She turned back to Claire. 'Listen, Claire, there's a gang of us going for a drink and then clubbing later. Do you want to come? Bring Becks with you if you like!'

She shook her head. 'I don't think so, Trinny, thanks.'

'Oh, why not? Petra and Rosie are coming. Make a night of it with us.'

Oliver looked at her questioningly. 'It might be a bit of fun.'

It might, thought Claire. But it wouldn't be the same with the Locum Libris gang. It was much more liberating being with strangers. She looked at her watch. It was after eleven. She'd lasted the pace longer than she'd expected. But quite suddenly she was tired and she didn't want to go on a drinking binge.

'Honestly,' she told them. 'I've had a great time, but I'm heading off now.'

'OK, then,' said Trinny. 'Give us a call next week.' She beamed at Oliver. 'You don't have to stick with this lot, you know. You've obviously been landed at the boring table.'

Oliver smiled at her. 'We'll see.'

Claire got up. 'It was great meeting you guys,' she said. 'But I've got to go.'

'Claire!' Richard looked at her in disappointment. 'We were just talking about Table Seven going for a drink together. You must come.'

'Thanks,' she said. 'Another time maybe. But not tonight.'

'Why doesn't everyone give me their phone number?' said Tanya. 'We can arrange a get-together again sometime.'

Everyone except Claire had come with their numbers on little cards. She scribbled hers a few times on the back of the menu and tore it into strips, handing them around and apologising for being so unprepared. She glanced at the cards they'd given her in return.

'Amy Pointer,' read Claire. 'Clairvoyant.' She looked at Amy. 'Really?'

'Absolutely.'

201

'So did you know everything about everybody already?' demanded Claire. 'Could you see our auras or whatever?'

'Yes,' said Amy.

'So why are you here?' asked Tanya. 'Can't you just conjure up some bloke?'

'I wish,' said Amy. 'I thought this would be a great place to come. I could see what people were like without having to look at their faces.'

'And did you?' asked Tanya. 'What's my aura like?'

'Yours is warm and content,' said Amy. 'Claire's is a little sad. Richard's is vibrant.'

Claire blinked a few times. A sad aura. She didn't want to have a sad aura. She wanted a confident one.

They finished exchanging numbers and she picked up her bag.

'Are you sure you won't come for a drink with us?' asked Gary.

Claire looked doubtful. Should she go with them after turning Trinny and the girls down? After all, if she'd got through the whole dinner thing, surely she could manage to go for a drink too? What if they all got on tremendously well with each other and she was the only one left out?

'She's not ready,' Amy told him.

Claire looked at her, startled.

'You will be,' said Amy. 'But not tonight.'

Suddenly Claire didn't care whether her aura was sad or not, or whether everyone else had a rollicking good time and she was the only party-pooper. She wanted to go home. 'Great meeting you all,' she said. 'See you again sometime.'

She walked out of the dining room and looked at her watch again. She might just make the last bus, though she now felt that hopping on a bus was, as the other girls would have said, a complete let-down.

'Hey, Claire, wait a second!'

Oliver Ramsey stood beside her.

'You're going in my direction,' he said. 'I wondered if you'd like a lift home?'

'That's really nice of you,' she told him. 'But I'm fine.'

'How are you getting home then?' he asked.

'Bus, cab, walk . . .' She shrugged her shoulders. 'It's only a couple of miles.'

'I don't have the Killer Bug van with me,' he said. 'If that's what's bothering you. I have a car.'

She swallowed. The van would have been easier than a car, though Oliver wouldn't have known that.

'No, really,' she told him. 'I'll be OK.'

'I'd like to take you home,' he said.

'It's very nice of you to offer,' she told him. 'Really. But I . . . want to walk.'

'Look, if you can't stand me just say so.'

'It's not that,' she said. 'Honestly. I just . . . I don't know if . . .'

'So why did you come?' he asked. 'If you're going to turn down innocent offers of a lift home?' His eyes twinkled at her.

'It's not the lift home,' she said. 'Truly.'

'Come on,' said Oliver. 'I'll walk with you if that's what you want.'

Why not, she thought. Why the hell not? He's a nice guy, he's fabulous to look at . . . don't I deserve to have someone like him in my life?

But as they turned into Amiens Street, Claire saw the bus turning round the corner. 'Oh, look,' she said. 'I have to get it.' She kissed Oliver quickly on the side of his face. 'Thank you. Thank you for lots of things.'

She slipped off the dainty sandals which had become more and more uncomfortable with every step and sprinted across the road to the bus stop in her bare feet.

'Claire!' Oliver called after her.

'I know I said I wanted to walk,' she cried. 'But these sandals are highly uncomfortable. You'd have had to carry me.'

'Are you giving me the elbow before we've even started?' he demanded.

'No!' Suddenly she laughed. 'No, Oliver. I'm just playing hard to get.'

The bus pulled up in front of the stop and she hopped on before he had time to reply. But she could see him looking after it as it trundled her back towards home.

Chapter 20

Brachycome (Swan River Daisy) – Multicoloured daisies on feathery foliage which can resist drought.

Claire couldn't believe that an entire month had gone by and that it was time for Georgia to come home. Living on her own hadn't been as awful as she'd feared, although there had been days when the house had seemed unnaturally quiet and she'd missed Georgia's whirling in and out of rooms leaving a trail of debris behind her. Her daughter seemed totally incapable of being somewhere without leaving something behind – a scarf, a book, sweet wrappers, her iPod; once Georgia had been in a room it changed for ever! Claire hadn't quite got used to the idea of tidying up and not having all her handiwork undone a few minutes later.

But the main thing was that she had coped on her own. Whether it was by taking Phydough for longer walks than usual – especially on the sunniest days – or the fact that her life seemed to have got busier and more complicated, the time had simply flown by.

All the same, she couldn't wait to see Georgia again. She'd missed her laughter and her chatter and just knowing that she was there. The last month had seemed like stepping outside of her old life. Most of her was happy at the idea of stepping back in again.

So the morning that Georgia was due back, Claire rushed around the house in a frenzy of tidying, shaking out the cushions, wiping down work surfaces and cleaning up the bathroom while knowing that Georgia wouldn't notice whether the house was clean or not. She'd gone into Bill's surgery too, dusting it down and sweeping the wooden floor. She wanted to talk to Georgia about the surgery.

Leonie O'Malley had offered to drive Claire to the station once more and Claire had accepted, although every time she thought about getting into the 4x4 she felt her heart beat faster and her legs tremble. She knew that sooner or later she'd have to get help about the car phobia. Even though she'd coped over the past couple of years without one, her reaction to cars was interfering with her life. Oliver Ramsey hadn't called her since she'd rushed away from him after the Dinner in the Dark (not that she'd expected him to really). She knew that she must have seemed terribly offhand with him and she couldn't blame him for not contacting her. However, for her future life, even though she had no intention of having a car of her own, she needed to be able to sit as a passenger without going crazy with fear. So she accepted Leonie's offer even though she wasn't looking forward to the trip to the station.

There was another half-hour to go before Robyn's mother would arrive. Claire glanced out of the kitchen window at Nate Taylor and chewed the inside of her lip. Not that she was worried about leaving him here, she thought. She knew where he worked, after all. But Bill had been fanatical about having people unsupervised in the house. It put everyone in a difficult position, he'd once told her. If something went missing then the finger of suspicion would naturally fall on whoever had been there on their own. Even though the likelihood was that nothing would go missing, or if it did it was because Claire or Georgia had lost it. Actually Bill's concern was really because of his medical equipment and the drugs that he kept in the surgery.

Things were different now, thought Claire, as she watched Nate dig out the flowerbeds along the west-facing wall. There wasn't anything worth stealing in their house any more. Nate stretched his arms over his head and once again Claire couldn't help noticing how strong his body looked. It was his first day of work in the garden. She'd accepted his very reasonable quote despite still harbouring misgivings about him. But, she told herself, Bill would have preferred anyone at all to do the work rather than let the garden grow ever wilder. She opened the kitchen door and walked outside.

The sun was warm and getting warmer. It seemed as though this blast of hot weather was even more scorching than the heatwave prior to the storms.

Nate turned to look at her as she stepped on to the patio. She was wearing the lime-green skirt and one of her new tops, and her clusters of cinnamon curls were teased back into a lazy ponytail. Her eyes sparkled and her rosebud mouth smiled. Nate knew, because she'd spoken about her fourteen-year-old daughter when she'd called him to accept his quote for the garden, that Claire Hudson must be in her late thirties. But right now, with the sun glinting off her curls, and wearing the happy-go-lucky skirt and flat sandals, she looked at least ten years younger. He stuck the spade into the earth and smiled at her.

'How's it going?' she asked, stepping on to the lawn.

'Pretty good,' he told her. 'None of this will take very long. Like I said when you phoned, if you wanted a big design change I'd have people to help me and we'd speed things up. But right now we're doing OK as it is.'

Claire looked at the pile of weeds in the wheelbarrow beside him. 'It had got really messy, hadn't it?'

He shrugged. 'These things happen when you don't have time.'

'I'm glad you were able to fit it in.'

This time he grinned at her. 'Didn't want you to change your mind. This is a lovely garden and I wanted to get it up to its full potential again.'

He was so different when he smiled, she thought. His face lost that harried, resentful look that he habitually wore and he seemed almost pleasant.

'I've got to go out,' she told him. 'I'm picking up my daughter from the station. It'll take about an hour or so.'

'Fine,' he said. 'I'll get on with things here.'

'I – um – well, I'll leave the kitchen door open,' she told him, 'if you want to make yourself tea or anything.'

'You can lock up the house if you like,' he said.

'No.' Claire pulled at her ponytail. 'No, it's fine. You might need to use the bathroom . . .'

Nate grinned at her. 'I have great self-control.'

'I'm sure you have,' she told him. 'But I'd rather you had options.'

'Don't worry.' His voice was suddenly very reassuring. 'I won't.'

206

He picked up the spade again and thrust it deep into the earth.

'Good soil,' he said.

'So my husband used to tell me,' said Claire. 'He was a doctor, gardening was his hobby.'

Nate grunted as he pulled an enormous dandelion and then tossed the weed into the barrow. 'Did you split up?'

'He died,' said Claire shortly.

'I'm sorry.' Nate thrust the spade into the earth again. 'That must have been difficult for you.'

'Oh, I'm OK.'

'Were you married long?'

'Years,' said Claire. 'We married young.'

'So did I,' Nate told her. 'Glad it worked out for you.'

Claire frowned. If Nate was in his late thirties, or at most his early forties, as she was pretty sure he was, Sarah must have been in her teens when he married her.

'Not Sarah,' he added, noticing the expression on her face. 'My first wife. Felicity. It didn't last.'

'Oh.'

'I'm not actually very good with women.' He smiled wryly.

The sound of the front door bell broke through the air.

'That's my lift,' said Claire, partly relieved because she wasn't sure about hearing Nate's confidences, yet still curious to know more about him. 'I'll see you later.'

'See you,' said Nate. He watched her for a moment as she walked back to the house. Then he started digging again.

She sat in the passenger seat of Leonie's SUV, high up above the snarling, snaking traffic. As soon as Leonie slid the automatic gear into the drive position, Claire felt her heart begin to race and her hands tremble. She closed her eyes.

Leonie didn't look at her but concentrated on the road ahead, keeping up a constant stream of conversation about what a good time Robyn seemed to have had in the west of Ireland and how great it was that she and Georgia hadn't fallen out or squabbled during the entire month.

'I'm sure they fought about something,' said Claire, one hand grasping the arm-rest on the passenger door, the other holding tight to the rim of her seat while she kept her eyes clamped closed. 'Girls do, don't they?'

'Oh, Robs is very easy-going,' said Leonie.

'So's Georgey, I suppose,' said Claire.

'She's great, your Georgia.' Leonie stopped at a set of traffic lights and glanced at Claire. 'You've done a really good job with her.'

'Not just me,' said Claire. 'Bill was a fantastic dad and my parents have always been very supportive. So are his, though they're in New Zealand for the summer with his brother. They keep in touch, though. Georgey e-mails Jessie quite a lot.'

'I know Bill was great, but it's mostly down to you, Claire.' Leonie eased the car away from the lights again. 'Let's face it, he was a busy, busy man. A great doctor, everyone said so, but totally absorbed in it. And you were working with him and looking after Georgia . . .' She flicked a very quick glance at Claire again. Her eyes were still closed and she was still gripping tightly to the arm-rest and seat. 'Then, after the accident – you know, you were fantastic, Claire. You really were.'

'Don't talk nonsense,' said Claire shortly.

'You *were* fantastic,' repeated Leonie. 'You never once complained about how unfair everything was and you were brilliant during all that time when she didn't speak – if it'd been me and Robyn I know I would've cracked up.'

'You wouldn't,' said Claire. 'You'd have dealt with it too, Leonie. Because you don't have a choice. You're a mother and you've got someone depending on you and you can't . . . you can't give in and become a quivering wreck.' She opened one eye for half a second. 'Which I know sounds daft right now.'

'Well, I just want you to know that I admire you in spades,' said Leonie as she drove into the car park at Heuston station.

When Leonie had parked the car, Claire opened her eyes properly and smiled faintly at her.

'You admire me?' she said. 'The woman who has to keep her eyes closed on a simple car journey?'

'Yes,' said Leonie. 'And God knows, if that's the worst thing you do, then I admire you even more.'

Claire laughed, relieved to be out of the car at last.

'C'mon,' she said. 'Let's go and get our daughters.'

The train was pulling in as they walked into the station. Suddenly the platform was full of squealing, shrieking teenagers, spilling from the carriages, pushing and shoving and generally larking about. Claire scanned the crowd for Georgia but at first couldn't spot her among the crowds. And then she saw her walking towards the barriers and she caught her breath.

'Mum! Mum!' Georgia saw her too and waved. Robyn O'Malley beamed widely as she caught sight of Leonie.

Claire couldn't quite believe it as Georgia walked towards her. It had only been a month and yet it seemed to her that her daughter had practically grown up overnight. The long red-gold curls that she'd left Dublin with were gone, replaced instead by a shorter, straighter haircut which emphasised Georgia's long, slender neck. Her jeans were hacked off at the bottom in what Claire realised was the current in-fashion look, and she couldn't help feeling that Georgia had probably grown a couple of inches too, because despite the fact that she was wearing vibrant-yellow flip-flops (new, Claire noted), she seemed to tower above Robyn.

'Would you look at the hair,' muttered Leonie. At first Claire thought she meant Georgia's, but then she realised that Robyn had had hers cut too. And that Robyn's was coloured with purple streaks.

'Hi, Mum!' Georgia flung her arms around her. 'It's good to see you again.'

'You too,' said Claire. 'You're looking great. I've missed you.'

'I was looking forward to coming home at last,' said Georgia. 'Though to be honest I had a brill time. Made lots of friends and . . . oh, hang on!' Her phone beeped with a text alert and Claire watched as a slow smile spread over her face. Her fingers tapped out a reply.

'New friend?' asked Claire.

'Loads of new friends,' said Georgia.

'Come on, girls,' said Leonie. 'Let's try and get out of here before the car park gets too busy.'

They hurried to the parked car and loaded their bags. This time Claire got into the back seat beside Georgia. She pulled her seatbelt across her chest.

'You OK?' whispered Georgia.

Claire nodded and closed her eyes.

Robyn and Georgia talked nonstop all the way home. They raved about the house where they'd stayed, moaned about the amount of work they'd had to do, laughed at some of their memories, complained about the teachers and broke into fits of unexplained laughter every so often. Then, after Leonie had commented about their hair-dos, they told her that they'd had them done for half-nothing by a student hairdresser in Spiddal.

'I like it,' said Claire, opening and closing her eyes very quickly to look at Georgia. 'Though it makes you look amazingly grown-up.'

'That's why I got it done!' cried Georgia. 'Those waves and curls were very passé. And you got yours cut too.'

'Not quite as dramatically.'

Georgia laughed.

'I got the streaks 'cos my hair is so boring,' said Robyn.

'So a good time was had by all,' said Claire when Leonie finally pulled up outside the house.

'Definitely, Mrs H,' said Robyn.

'Thanks for the lift, Leonie.' Claire grunted as she hauled Georgia's case from the car. 'God help us, Georgey, this is even heavier than when you went.'

'I dunno why,' said Georgia. 'There isn't much more in it.'

'I'll see you soon,' said Leonie as she got back into the car. Robyn rolled down the window and waved frantically at her friend.

When Claire had unlocked the front door, Georgia hurried into the house. 'I missed Phydough a lot,' she called over her shoulder to Claire. 'I know that he'll remember me 'cos dogs do, but still . . . Oh my God!'

'What?' Claire followed her into the kitchen and then stopped. Georgia had wrenched open the kitchen door and was staring into the back garden, where Nate Taylor was still digging the flowerbeds. Because it had grown even warmer, Nate had taken off the black

210

T-shirt he'd been wearing earlier and was now clad in only his loose cargo pants and heavy-duty garden boots.

'Who the fuck is that?' asked Georgia.

'Georgia Hudson!' Claire looked at her daughter angrily. 'I don't know what language you thought was OK to use while you were away, but if that's a sample of it you can forget it right now.'

'I'm sorry,' said Georgia, annoyed with herself for swearing in front of her mother. Parents were so pathological when it came to swearing, she thought. It was only a word, after all. And she didn't use it that often really.

'Hi there.' Nate dug the spade deep into the earth and turned towards them.

His torso glistened with sweat. Claire could see beads of it on the hair on his chest. Slightly grey hair, she noticed, in tufts around his pecs. Strong-looking pecs too. She breathed out. He wasn't absolutely gorgeous. He wasn't a hunk. He wasn't as beautifully Beckham as Oliver Ramsey. He wasn't like Beckham at all. But quite suddenly she found him undeniably attractive. Attractive in a way she hadn't felt for a man, ever. Because it was different when you fell for someone aged five. With Bill she'd simply grown into feeling sexual attraction. This had hit her like a thunderbolt. She didn't know why it should be. It wasn't his looks. It wasn't his physique (though he seemed even stronger and more powerful without the T-shirt). It wasn't his personality – least of all his personality! But there was something about the way he was standing there, one foot on the blade of the garden spade, his head slightly to one side and a drop of perspiration rolling down his face (there was a scar on his cheek, she noticed, deeper even than her own); there was something there which made her mouth go dry and her mind go blank.

'Who the hell are you?' asked Georgia. 'Mum, who is this?' She looked accusingly at Claire, who swallowed hard and moistened her lips with the tip of her tongue.

'This is Nate Taylor,' she said huskily. 'He's doing the garden.'

'Dad's garden,' said Georgia abruptly. 'He's digging up Dad's stuff.'

'I'm clearing it out,' said Nate carefully. 'Not getting rid of anything. Helping it to grow again really.'

'Why are you here?' asked Georgia.

'Why d'you think?' Claire was beginning to regain her lost composure, though her heart was hammering in her chest. 'I hired him to do the garden. Heaven knows we've talked about it for ages.'

'Why did you wait till I was away?' demanded Georgia. 'I'd have liked to have a say in what goes on in my garden.'

'There was an opportunity for Mr Taylor to do it and I took it,' said Claire.

They were interrupted by a grey and white whirlwind which whooshed up the garden and threw itself at Georgia, almost knocking her off her feet.

'Phy!' she cried in delight. 'Where were you? How're you doing, boy? Who's my favourite doggy then?' She sank to her knees and buried her head in the dog's fur.

Nate and Claire exchanged glances. Claire looked away as quickly as possible, back to Georgia.

'You should apologise to Mr Taylor,' she said. 'You were rude, Georgey.'

'Well, I arrive home and there's a strange half-naked man in the garden. I'm entitled to be a bit rude,' said Georgia as she stood up again.

Nate laughed. Shit, thought Claire. I even like his laugh now! What the hell is going on here?

'You're dead right,' said Nate. 'I'd be put out if there were half-naked men wandering round my garden too.' He reached for his T-shirt and pulled it over his head.

'No need on my account,' said Georgia.

'Georgia!' Claire stared at her.

'Well, I've seen loads of half-naked blokes over the past month,' she told Claire calmly. 'I mean, the first couple of weeks were scorching so none of them wore any T-shirts or anything. It's not fair really that blokes can wander round with no tops. I have strap marks all over me!'

'Right,' said Claire faintly.

'Are you going to make it OK again?' Georgia looked directly at Nate. 'Are you going to get rid of the weeds and the overgrown stuff?'

'Of course,' he said. 'It's my job.'

'You won't cut down anything?'

'Only to cut it back,' he told her. 'Nothing will go. I promise you it'll be exactly like you want it when I've finished.'

She studied him for a moment and then nodded. 'OK then.'

'Well, I'm glad that's sorted,' said Claire. 'Mr Taylor, Nate, I'm sorry that Georgia was so abrupt. I didn't have time to tell her you were here and I guess she was a bit surprised.'

'No problem,' said Nate.

'Well then, I'll let you get back to it,' said Claire briskly. 'Come on, Georgey. You've unpacking to do.'

'I don't have to do it right now,' complained Georgia. 'Quit fussing, Mum. I'll be in in a minute.'

'Fine,' said Claire. 'I'll put the kettle on. I'm sure Mr Taylor would like a cup of tea.'

'Actually, no,' said Nate. 'Water will do me just fine.' He nodded at the litre bottle on the garden table. 'If you could fill that up for me again I'd appreciate it.'

Claire took the bottle and filled it from the jug of filtered water in the fridge. Her hands were shaking. *What the hell is this all about?* she asked herself. *Why on earth am I suddenly feeling . . . feeling . . .* She had no real idea what she *was* feeling. She sat down abruptly on the kitchen stool.

Georgia walked into the kitchen a moment later and saw Claire at the counter, her forehead resting on the tips of her fingers.

'Are you all right, Mum?' Her voice was anxious.

'Oh, sure, yes.' Claire looked up and smiled. 'Just hot all of a sudden.'

Georgia smiled too. 'I know. It's lovely, isn't it? D'you think it'll stay nice again?'

'I hope so,' said Claire.

'Only problem is, it's so hard to sleep at night when it's hot.'

Claire nodded.

'Plus, Robyn snores.' Georgia made a face. 'I couldn't cope with that, you know. Noise at night. I'm not used to it.'

'How did you manage?'

'Well, once I phoned you.' Georgia grinned. 'And a lot of the

213

time I put on my earphones and listened to music to drown her out.'

'Good thinking.'

'That's why I'm looking forward to going to bed tonight,' confessed Georgia. 'I'm a bit tired but not that knackered. I just want a quiet night.'

Claire nodded.

'Will I take that out to him?' asked Georgia.

'Huh?'

'The water. Will I take it out to the gardener?'

'Sure.'

'I got a shock,' said Georgia, 'when I saw him there. I knew it wasn't Dad of course but I couldn't get my head around a bloke digging the garden. It threw me a bit.'

'I understand,' said Claire. 'I should've told you.'

'He's kinda cute.' Georgia's eyes sparkled.

'No he's not!'

'Ah, Mum, of course he is. For an old man anyway.'

'Georgia Hudson! He's not an old man. He's around the same age as me.'

'As I said.' Georgia grinned. 'Ancient.'

Claire made a face at her.

'Do you like him?' asked Georgia.

'For heaven's sake, Georgey, he's doing a job for us, that's all. And he's OK, but a bit abrupt.'

'I thought that he looked at you funny,' said Georgia.

'What?'

'You know. Like he fancied you.'

'Right, Georgia.' Claire stood up. 'I don't know what kind of hormonal world you've been living in while you've been away, but Mr Taylor certainly doesn't fancy me. And I don't fancy him either. As a matter of fact he's married. So even if we fancied the socks off each other, it would be irrelevant.'

'Oh, I dunno.' Georgia shrugged. 'People have affairs.'

'Georgia!'

Georgia laughed. 'Chill out,' she told Claire. 'I was just winding you up.'

'Well don't,' said Claire. 'I've had a hard day.'

'No you haven't.'

'Every day with you is a hard day.' But she smiled to let Georgia know she was joking.

Chapter 21

Anaphalis (Pearl Everlasting) – Rapidly spreading silvery leaves and large clusters of small white starry flowers. Can be dried.

Later that evening, after Nate had gone and both of them had wandered round the garden to check out his handiwork, Claire broached the subject of Bill's surgery with Georgia.

'I wondered,' she said slowly as they sat at the patio table, 'whether you might like to have it as your own space.'

Georgia stared at her.

'Your bedroom is small,' continued Claire. 'You have a lot of stuff in it. You could probably do with a bit more room.'

'But – downstairs?' Georgia said slowly. 'The surgery and the waiting room? There's a separate entrance. It'd be like a flat of my own.'

'I wasn't quite thinking like that,' admitted Claire. 'I thought maybe you might like the surgery part as a den, you know. You could keep your own bedroom as it is or move downstairs, whichever you like. We could convert the waiting room into a bedroom, no problem. You'd be a little cut off from me, that's all.'

'I love the idea of my own space,' Georgia told her. 'I really do. And I think you should convert the waiting room too. But . . .' She peeped at Claire from under the newly cut fringe, which still fell into her eyes. 'But I'm not sure about sleeping down there. You're right. I'd be a bit cut off.' Suddenly her eyes brightened. 'I know, Mum! We could make it into a guest bedroom with two beds and then if Robs or someone came for a sleepover we could be there. Otherwise I could be in my own room.'

'OK,' said Claire. 'If that's what you'd like.'

'Of course it's what I'd like.' Georgia beamed at her. 'I bet it's really naff to think your own mother is cool, but – well, you are.'

Claire smiled. 'I'm glad you think so.'

'One of the guys at college was telling me about his family.' Georgia blushed slightly as she spoke. 'His name's Steve. His parents went backpacking or something this year. They sent him to summer camp to get rid of him. They sound awful. I told him about you. He said you sounded great.'

'Georgey-girl . . .' Claire stopped. 'Georgia – thank you,' she said finally. 'I do my best. It's not always great, but it's still my best.'

'I know that.' Georgia smiled at her. 'And I know that by next week we'll probably be fighting about something. But tonight you're great.'

Claire laughed. 'Good.' She stared out over the garden. 'I have something else to tell you.'

'What?' Georgia looked anxiously at her.

'It's about Gran and Gramps.'

'What about them?'

Claire told Georgia about Con and Eileen's decision to part. She also told her about Con's relationship with Lacey Dillon, although she didn't say that her father had had affairs with other women before her. Georgia said nothing while Claire explained that both Con and Eileen felt this was the right thing for them to do.

'Poor Gran,' said Georgia when she'd finished speaking. 'Poor Gramps too. It can't have been much fun being together all that time when they didn't love each other.'

'No,' agreed Claire. 'Though it seems a bit crazy to me for them to split now. But I understand it.'

'Well, there's no point in them staying with each other just for the sake of it,' Georgia said practically. 'I mean, they might as well have a bit of happiness, don't you think?'

'Oh, sure,' said Claire. 'I guess I was taken by surprise when your gran told me.' She looked curiously at her daughter. 'I thought you'd be upset.'

'Why?' asked Georgia. She sighed. 'Well I guess I am a bit. But I'm upset for me, that things are not going to be the same. I'm not

217

upset for them. They want to do it. I'm sad that Gran is selling the house in Dundalk. I loved going there.'

'I'm sad about that too,' said Claire.

'I'm a bit dazed by Gramps having a new woman,' admitted Georgia. 'I mean – how old is he, Mum? It's a bit gross, isn't it?'

'He's in his sixties,' said Claire. 'But that isn't so old these days.' Georgia snorted.

'Though I suppose for someone who thinks forty is old, sixty is decrepit!' Claire grinned at her.

'Well if it's not old then he's entitled to have someone,' Georgia said. 'But sixty-something sounds pretty ancient to me. You'd think he'd be a bit beyond it, wouldn't you?'

'Georgia Hudson!' But Claire suddenly found herself gripped by a fit of giggling.

'What?' Georgia giggled too.

'You're – you're – irrepressible.'

'Thanks,' said Georgia. 'I don't know what that means, but thanks.'

'Look it up in the dictionary,' said Claire as she got to her feet. 'Now come on, honey. It's getting late. I'm being savaged by the midges. Time to go in.'

Neither Claire nor Georgia was awake early the following morning. In fact it was the sound of the front door bell that dragged Claire out of a deep and dreamless sleep. She stumbled out of bed and pulled her long T-shirt over her head before going downstairs to answer it. She opened it a crack and peeped out.

Nate Taylor was standing there, dressed in a white T-shirt and long shorts. The sky was clear blue and the temperature already rising.

'I'm sorry,' said Nate. 'Am I too early? I wanted to get started as soon as possible. I didn't realise . . .' He looked at Claire's sleep-filled eyes and tousled hair. 'D'you want me to come back later?'

'What time is it?' she asked.

'Half-eight.'

She blinked in astonishment. She couldn't remember the last time she'd slept past six-thirty in the morning. She yawned and rubbed her eyes.

'I'm terribly sorry,' she said. 'I thought it was about seven! I guess

I just flaked out. Come in.' She stood back and let him walk through the hall to the kitchen. 'Would you like a cup of tea or anything?' she asked as she unlocked the kitchen doors.

'No thanks,' he told her. 'I've had breakfast. I've been up for ages.'

Claire suddenly remembered that she was wearing nothing but a T-shirt, even if it did reach her knees.

'I'd better get dressed properly,' she said. Her heart had started to beat faster again and she felt the colour rise in her cheeks.

'Well don't mind me,' Nate told her. 'I'll get to work.' He walked into the garden. She went upstairs.

How come she was finding this man so attractive? What the hell was it about him – or about her? She hadn't liked him the first time she met him; she'd felt obliged to allow him to quote for the garden and then was unable to turn down what was a very reasonable price; but she hadn't wanted him here really. Now that he was here, though, she couldn't keep her eyes off him. She swallowed hard. Was this what they meant when they talked about lust? She knew that she was lusting after him. Already she was imagining him without his T-shirt again, body glistening with sweat. And she wasn't into hot and sweaty, for heaven's sake! She didn't like her sex to be rough and ready. She liked the whole sensual thing with candles and soft lighting and cool fresh sheets.

She shivered. Three years. Three years and she hadn't felt the slightest desire to have sex with anyone. And now she was thinking about it with a bloke she didn't like, and what was worse, a bloke who was married to someone else. There must be some kind of neurosis there, she told herself as she walked into her bedroom. Definitely.

She sat on the edge of the king-sized bed and looked at the picture of Bill on her bedside locker. It was her favourite picture of him, taken on the beach in Dollymount the year before the accident. They'd gone for a walk one evening in early autumn. It had been glorious when they'd set out but the clouds had suddenly rolled in across the bay and the wind had whipped up so that the waves were white-tipped and frothy behind him. The sea was spectacular and Claire had taken out the camera-phone that Bill had bought her for her birthday and snapped him with the sea behind him in a casual, unposed photograph. He was smiling at her in the photo, but not the smile of someone who knows they're being snapped, the smile of someone who's sharing a joke. She reached out and picked up the photo in its silver frame. Suddenly she wasn't lusting after Nate Taylor any more.

'There'll never be anyone else,' she whispered softly as she held it to her cheek. 'Ever.'

It was nearly three hours later when Georgia emerged from her bedroom and padded downstairs. She glanced out of the kitchen window at Nate Taylor and then frowned as she wondered where Claire was. Sounds from the surgery made her walk back through the hall and down the stairs to the basement area.

Claire was peeling old notices off the walls of the waiting room.

'Need a hand?' asked Georgia.

'Oh. So you've finally got out of bed.'

'I told you,' said Georgia. 'I got no sleep in Galway.'

Claire grinned. 'I looked in on you an hour ago. You were totally out for the count.'

'I know,' said Georgia. 'But I'm up now.'

'I was thinking that we could walk down to Edge's Corner and get some paint,' said Claire. 'The walls need painting both here and in the surgery.'

'D'you mean we have to do all that before I can bring stuff down?' Georgia sounded disappointed.

'Not if you don't want to,' said Claire. 'But if you're going to have a den it might as well be a nice one. And if the other room is going to be a sleepover room you'll want that to be nice too, won't you?'

Georgia nodded. 'Can I choose the colours?'

'Of course,' said Claire. Then she looked sternly at her daughter. 'More or less. No black or violent purples or anything.'

'You're no fun,' said Georgia, but she winked at Claire all the same.

The hardware and paint shop was a fifteen-minute walk away. After Georgia had washed and dressed they left Nate Taylor working in the garden and set out to get the paint. The sun scorched down from the cloudless sky and Claire wished she'd slapped some sunscreen on to the back of her neck. As they walked past her favourite coffee shop, where the tables on the pavement outside were taken with people enjoying the warmth, she suggested to Georgia that they get an all-day breakfast on the way back.

Georgia nodded happily. ''Cos a can of paint will weigh a ton,' she pointed out. 'We'll have to stop on the way back for a rest.'

Claire nodded in agreement. This was the one time that not having a car was a real nuisance, she thought. For most things it didn't matter much any more. She did her on-line shopping at Tesco and there were plenty of convenience stores nearby where she could pick up bits and pieces; furniture or appliance stores always delivered; and she lived close enough to the city centre to be happy to use the bus or the Dart. But lugging home five-litre tins of paint was a bit of a chore.

'That's the florist's where our gardener works,' she told Georgia as they passed Taylor's. Claire could see Sarah inside, threading stems into a green oasis for a display. She felt a tug of guilt at the know-ledge that she'd had a fantasy about the other woman's husband. But there was no harm done, she thought, as they walked briskly by. Sarah would never know. Neither would Nate. And she was over that mad fit of passion now anyway.

Georgia chose a vivid yellow paint for the surgery walls and Claire, despite thinking that it would dazzle her every time she walked into the room, went along with her daughter's selection. They paid for the paint and for new brushes and then set out for home again.

As they arrived at the café, a couple of girls got up from one of the outside tables, so Claire and Georgia nabbed it quickly. Georgia ordered the full Irish breakfast of bacon, sausage, egg and tomato, while Claire chose a toasted bagel with cream cheese and salmon. Georgia looked at her with interest.

'I haven't seen you tuck into anything like that in ages,' she said. 'I thought you'd become a fruit freak.'

'I'm starving,' Claire told her. 'And we need something to keep our strength up. That paint is even heavier than I thought.'

Georgia's mobile beeped and she checked her message. She smiled and replied. The phone beeped again. She replied again. It beeped once more.

'Oh for heaven's sake!' cried Claire. 'Talk to the person!'

'We're done now.' Georgia closed the flip top and smiled at her mother.

'Who was it?'

'A friend.'

'What friend?'

'I don't ask *you* those sort of questions,' said Georgia.

Claire shrugged and turned her attention to her bagel. She'd been telling Georgia the truth when she said she was hungry. She could actually feel her mouth water as she lifted the food to her lips.

Although Georgia had said that she'd help with the painting, she got bored after about half an hour and decided to take Phydough for a walk instead, leaving Claire to continue on her own. The surgery wasn't a big room – in fact Claire was beginning to think that even with doing both the surgery and the waiting room they'd bought far too much paint. Decorating had been Bill's thing, not hers. She sneezed as a drop landed on the end of her nose and decided to take a break. Ideally she would have loved to go out into the garden, but Nate was still digging and clearing up and she didn't want to disturb him. Nor did she want to feel disturbed by him. Instead she climbed the stairs to Georgia's room to appraise how much stuff her daughter had accumulated and how it would fit into the surgery space.

Georgia's small wooden desk, which Claire and Bill had bought her for her tenth birthday, was piled high with books and papers. Her clothes, which she was meant to have unpacked and put away, were scattered around the room. The chest of drawers was crammed full of tops and blouses and underwear while Georgia's Clearasil creams and Boots 17 make-up littered the top of it. Claire sighed deeply. She'd tidied the room when Georgia had gone to summer camp but now it looked as though her daughter had never been away at all.

Which, she told herself as she went to leave again, was not entirely a bad thing. It was nice to have her back. Then she swore shortly as she knocked against one of the books on the desk and brought a variety of them tumbling to the floor, including Georgia's diary. Claire found it extremely difficult not to flick through the pages, especially when a folded piece of paper fell out.

'I won't read the diary,' she said out loud. 'I absolutely won't.' But she couldn't help unfolding the paper and glancing at it.

REQUIREMENTS FOR MUM'S BOYFRIEND
1. *Reasonably good-looking (no facial hair/back hair/not too much chest hair).*
2. *Clean (fingernails especially/also ears).*
3. *Not patronising (no heavy sighs when I say something).*
4. *Money (not rich but well off enough not to freak about price of CDs/DVDs/phone cards).*
5. *Kids (this is difficult. Good-looking son might be interesting tho).*
6. *Interests – music/history/sports (but not bloody football)/fashion (but not pervy).*
7. *Car – something flashy.*

Claire stared at the list. Did Georgia think she had a boyfriend? Did she want her to have a boyfriend? Was she worried that Claire would start looking for someone new to disrupt their lives? She read it through again and smiled slightly. Perhaps it was a joke. But it wasn't a bad list all the same.

Chapter 22

Pyracantha (Firethorn) – Tough and hardy, masses of small flowers. Red, white or yellow berries. Wear gloves when pruning.

Eavan still hadn't had her serious talk with Glenn. She hadn't been able to work herself up to it over the weekend. Glenn had suggested a barbecue on Saturday afternoon and had invited the neighbours from either side. It had been fun and Eavan had noticed that Glenn drank nothing but chilled mineral water all day. In fact if anyone had overindulged in alcohol it had been herself and Ruth Gorman from next door, who'd demolished a couple of bottles of Chardonnay between them. Which was the main reason why she hadn't managed to talk to Glenn on the Sunday – she was the one with the hangover.

On Monday morning, feeling more alert, she went to the supermarket and pushed her trolley around the aisles. When she returned to the car with Saffy she shrieked in annoyance at the sight of the fresh scrape along the passenger door. This was the second time someone had damaged their car in the supermarket car park and hadn't had the decency to own up.

The scrape was superficial. She checked it again when she got home. It could've been worse. She wondered whether Glenn would rather she booked it in to the garage for a touch-up or whether it would be just as quick and easy to get it done by a bodywork specialist. She furrowed her brow as she tried to recall whether Jim Trench, a friend of Glenn's, did paint jobs or engine jobs. She picked up the phone and pressed speed-dial for Glenn.

'Trontec, Mary speaking, how can I help you?'

Eavan grimaced. She'd dialled the company rather than his mobile as Glenn now preferred. If Trontec's phone system had been automated like so many were these days (and which drove her insane) Eavan would've hung up. But since a real person had answered she didn't. She asked for Glenn instead.

'Glenn Keating,' said the receptionist in the singsong voice that so many of them used. 'Which department?'

'Sales.' Eavan decided not to point out that Glenn was a senior sales executive. The girl on the phone was clearly new to the company and wasn't familiar with all the staff yet.

'I'm sorry, I don't have that name in front of me.'

'He works with Jarlath O'Connor and Stephen Liddel,' said Eavan.

'I'll put you through to Jarlath,' said the receptionist, clicking a button. Eavan had been about to tell her not to bother, that she'd get Glenn on the mobile, but now it was too late.

'Jarlath O'Connor.'

'Hi, Jarlath, it's Eavan Keating,' she said. 'I'm sorry to bother you. The receptionist put me through to your number. She's obviously new.'

'Um – yes, right. How are you, Eavan? How are things going?'

'Oh, fine,' she said lightly. 'Listen, is Glenn there?'

'Um – Glenn? Here?'

'Yes,' said Eavan. 'I wanted to check something with him. It isn't important really. I know he's out and about a lot and I should've called the mobile, but I hit the Trontec number by mistake.'

Jarlath was silent.

'Jar? You there?'

'I . . . yes, Eavan. But why are you ringing here for Glenn?'

'Why not?' asked Eavan. 'Doesn't he come into the office at all these days?'

There was another silence.

'Jar? Is something wrong?' Suddenly Eavan felt anxious.

'Well, look, Eavan . . .' His voice trailed off.

'What?' she demanded.

'I don't think it's up to me to—'

'What?' she demanded again, more fiercely. 'What's going on, Jarlath?'

'Well, Eavan, it's just that – I can't believe you don't know already.'

'Know what?'

'Ah . . . it's . . . Glenn doesn't work here any more.'

'What?' This time she spoke the word with bewilderment. 'What are you talking about?'

'I thought . . . I didn't think . . . I expected . . .'

'Jarlath!'

'Look, Eavan, Glenn was let go,' said Jarlath rapidly. 'There was an issue about sales targets. He's left.'

'You mean he was fired?' she asked incredulously.

'Not fired. Just – well, let go.' Jarlath sounded very uncomfortable. 'Eavan, I'm sorry. I really am. I didn't know that he hadn't told you.'

'But he's going to work,' she said. 'Every day.'

'Maybe he's got another job,' suggested Jarlath.

'So why wouldn't he tell me?'

'I don't know.'

Suddenly Eavan wanted to be sick. She gripped the receiver tightly in her hand as she felt herself sway.

'I've got to go,' she said abruptly and hung up.

She staggered into the kitchen, followed by Saffy.

'I want ice-cream!' cried the little girl.

'In a minute.' Eavan sat down at the table.

'Now.' Saffy tugged at her skirt.

'I said in a minute.'

'I want ice-cream!'

'For crying out loud, Saffy, didn't you hear me!' shouted Eavan. 'I said in a minute and that's what I meant. Now sit down and be quiet.'

Saffy's blue eyes opened wide at the harshness of her mother's voice. Then they filled with tears.

'And don't bloody bother crying,' said Eavan. 'You're spoiled, you know that. Just sit down and shut up.'

Saffy's bottom lip wobbled. She walked slowly away from the table and sat in a corner of the room, her blue teddy bear in her arms.

Eavan rubbed her forehead. The feeling of nausea had almost passed, but now an icy fear gripped her. What the hell did Jarlath

226

mean when he said that Glenn had been let go? Why hadn't Glenn said anything? What was he doing all day? She rubbed her face over and over again. It couldn't be true. Glenn couldn't have lost his job. They looked up to him in Trontec. He was a senior person. They didn't just let people go like that.

Although, she admitted to herself, they did. She remembered a couple of years earlier when the entire customer services function had been transferred to a call centre in India. Twenty people had lost their jobs. And the research division, which had relocated to Dublin, had been relocated back to California before that. Trontec could quite easily have decided that the sales division could be moved too. Only that didn't really make sense. Because you had to have sales people on the ground, visiting clients. You couldn't do sales from India or California.

Why hadn't he said anything? Why hadn't he told her about this body blow? She bit her lip. Maybe he was numbing it all with drink. She'd thought that he was drinking again and hoped that he wasn't but now she could understand why he might be. She moaned softly.

'I'm sorry.' Saffy came over to her and put her hand on Eavan's arm. 'I didn't mean to be bold.'

'Oh, honeybunch, that's OK.' Eavan put her arms around her daughter and lifted her on to her lap. 'I'm sorry for shouting at you.'

'Are you all right?' asked Saffy.

'Of course.'

'So can I have ice-cream now?' Her blue eyes looked trustingly into Eavan's.

'Sure,' said Eavan. 'Sure you can.'

'So, Eileen.' Alan Bellew looked at the silver-haired woman in front of him. 'This is the best offer yet. Are you going to accept it or do you want to wait a little longer.'

'I've spoken to my husband about it,' said Eileen. Then she smiled ruefully at Alan. 'My ex-husband, I guess. He thinks we should accept this one.'

'But I thought the decision was yours,' said Alan.

'It is,' Eileen told him. 'But I still talk things over with Con. I can't help it.'

'And he's recommending acceptance?'

She nodded. 'He wants the money.'

'And you?'

'I want the money too,' she said honestly. 'And I want to be out of here. But there's been a delay in finishing the apartments and so . . .'

'It could probably be negotiated,' said Alan. 'People often want a quick sale or purchase but it doesn't always work out like that. Your solicitor should be able to help you out on that one.'

'My solicitor's probably sick of the sight of me,' said Eileen cheerfully. 'When Con and I decided to file for divorce I was a bit of a wreck, to tell you the truth.'

Alan looked at her curiously. 'Didn't you want the divorce?'

'It wasn't that,' replied Eileen. 'It was just that I couldn't get my head around the fact that I had to make decisions of my own. I was so used to Con making them for me that it was almost beyond me. I know that makes me sound very pathetic, but it's true.'

'I don't think you sound pathetic at all,' said Alan. 'In fact I think you're a very determined lady who knows exactly what she wants.'

Eileen smiled. 'I do now,' she said. 'I didn't always.'

'So do you want me to go back and accept this offer?'

Eileen got up from the table where they'd been talking and looked out of the back window while Alan Bellew busied himself with brochures about the house.

Eileen was remembering. As clearly as though it was happening in front of her again, she was remembering a day when Con and Claire had been playing hide and seek in the back garden. Claire had been very young at the time and had hidden behind the shrubby honeysuckle bush near the end of the garden. She'd been easily visible but Con had spent ages looking behind other flowers and shrubs, wondering aloud where she could be. And eventually he'd given up and shouted, 'Come out, come out, wherever you are,' at which Claire had rushed out from behind the bush, shrieking with joy that her father had been deceived. She could easily hide behind it now, thought Eileen. It had grown to its full height of three metres and was packed with golden leaves. Eileen wondered what memories the young couple who were borrowing a huge amount of money to buy her house would have in thirty or forty years' time.

'Eileen?' Alan's words broke into her thoughts.

'Oh, I'm doing my old woman thing,' she said lightly. 'I'm thinking of how things were.'

He nodded.

'I suppose you get a lot of that.'

'Sometimes,' he agreed. 'Though these days so many people just think of their homes as a financial move. They buy in their kitchens and their bathrooms and their gardens and they don't have the same emotional investment in them.'

Eileen nodded. 'I think my emotional investment has paid off now,' she said. 'Go ahead and tell them we accept the offer. I'll contact my solicitor today.'

'Great.' Alan stood up and held out his hand. 'Thank you for the business.'

'You're welcome,' said Eileen. 'You really are.'

Georgia and Robyn were sunbathing at the seafront. Robyn was wearing a pastel-pink cropped top and a pair of incredibly skimpy white shorts. Georgia was wearing a similar top in sea-green and one of the short skirts that Claire had bought her before going away.

'So have you heard from Peadar today?' asked Georgia as she lay on her back and watched a seagull whirl overhead.

'He texted me this morning,' said Robyn. 'He's going to try and get his folks to come up to town for a weekend. How about Steve?'

'Poor Steve.' Georgia sighed. 'His parents are back from their trip and he says that they're making his life hell. They want him to go to some other camp even though he's not booked in. Something to do with inner development.'

'They're bats,' said Robyn.

'They don't care about him,' agreed Georgia. 'I feel really sorry for him. Especially since I've come home and Mum has been so great about converting the surgery for me and everything. I realise how decent she is compared to some other parents.'

'Yeah, the surgery sounds great!' said Robyn enthusiastically. 'I can't wait for it all to be done.'

'We went into town yesterday and picked out new beds,' said

Georgia. 'I got to choose. I'm going to use Dad's desk in the den part, though. I thought it would be nice to do that.'

'And how did your mum feel about that?'

'She was OK,' said Georgia. 'You know, Robs, she seems a lot better since I got home.'

'Missed you, obviously,' said Robyn.

'No, better than before I went,' Georgia clarified. 'Sort of more light-hearted or something.'

'Has she got a boyfriend?'

'Oh, don't be ridiculous,' said Georgia scathingly. Then she wrinkled up her nose. 'Though she did go out with an old badminton friend of hers while we were away. And to some dinner with the people from work.'

'So maybe it's something to do with the old friend.'

'She hasn't gone out with him since,' said Georgia.

'We've only been back a couple of days.'

'She hasn't even mentioned him.'

'Oh well, even if she's only going out a bit more that's a good thing, isn't it?'

'Yes.' Georgia nodded. 'And if going out makes her buy me new stuff then that's absolutely brilliant!'

Chapter 23

Canna (Canna Lily) – Bright flowers and coloured leaves make this very eye-catching. Needs sheltered spot in full sun.

Eavan put Saffy into the child seat in the car and drove to Claire's house. She needed to talk to someone about Glenn's situation and the only someone she had confidence in was Claire. She parked behind the green van which was half on the pavement and half on the road outside Claire's house. As she got out of the car she saw Georgia walking up the street. She didn't recognise her at first because of her changed hairstyle, but when Georgia called Saffy's name she realised who the tall and elegant teenager was.

Saffy shrieked with delight at seeing Georgia, who picked her up and whirled her around in the air. Then she made a face at Saffy and told her that she was getting far too big and heavy to be lifted up like that. Saffy giggled as Georgia ruffled her dark hair.

'Is your mum in?' asked Eavan.

'Sure,' said Georgia. 'She was working when I left her this morning.'

'You look great,' said Eavan. 'Did you enjoy your time away?'

Georgia nodded. 'It's really weird not having every second of every day mapped out for me now,' she confessed. 'But I've stuff to do. We're redecorating Dad's surgery and turning it into a den for me.'

'Are you?' Eavan was surprised.

'Yes,' said Georgia. 'But Mum has to do the painting. I can't bear the smell.'

'Slacker.' Eavan smiled.

'Don't tell her I'm faking it.' Georgia laughed. 'I'm looking forward to getting things right but the painting is just too much like hard work.'

'Well would you like to amuse Saffy for me while I call in to see your mum?' asked Eavan hopefully.

'Sure,' replied Georgia. 'I was just coming home to grab a sandwich. I'll put one together and then Saffy and I can wander across to the park.'

'She'd like that,' said Eavan.

She waited while Georgia let herself into the house and yelled out to Claire that she was home and that she had company. A couple of seconds later Claire herself came running lightly down the stairs.

She looked different though Eavan wasn't exactly sure how. Her hair was pinned up in a soft knot on top of her head which meant that her face wasn't hidden by her cascading curls as usual. Her eyes were brighter and sparkled more, and the colour in her cheeks was more evident. But she looked a little harried all the same.

'Hi,' she said noticing the troubled expression on Eavan's face straight away. 'Let's go into the kitchen.'

Claire and Eavan sat at the kitchen table while Georgia made up an unnecessarily large batch of sandwiches, handing one to Saffy and taking one herself before telling Claire that she'd put the rest in the fridge to keep them fresh and that she was taking Saffy out for a while. Claire nodded in agreement.

'Would you like something?' she asked Eavan. 'Tea, coffee, juice?'

'Tea,' said Eavan.

Claire filled the kettle, switched it on and took a couple of mugs from the cupboard. Eavan didn't speak while she was doing this and Claire knew that there was something badly wrong. When the kettle had boiled and she'd made the tea she sat down beside her friend.

'Well?' she asked.

Eavan told her about her phone call to Trontec and her discovery that Glenn no longer worked there. 'I don't know when it happened,' she wailed, 'but I'm guessing it was that weekend where he had to go in on Saturday. His behaviour's been weird ever since.'

'Oh, Eavan.' Claire reached out and took her friend's hand. 'I'm sorry. This must be awful for you.'

'He didn't tell me.' Eavan's voice wobbled. 'I'm his wife, Claire.

I'm supposed to be the person he shares everything with, but he didn't tell me.' She exchanged a sudden guilty look with her friend. 'I know. I know. We don't always share everything, but . . .'

'Maybe he was hoping that something else would turn up,' said Claire gently.

'Like what?' demanded Eavan. 'How could he imagine that I wouldn't find out eventually? What sort of craziness is that? And what's he been doing every day for the last couple of weeks? He goes out as though he's heading to work. Sometimes he's out until late in the evening. He told me that he was at meetings. What kind of meetings?' A tear trickled down her cheek. 'You know I thought he was drinking. And I'm so afraid . . .' She bit her lip. 'Oh, Claire, I'm so afraid that he is. But if he's drinking then he's driving home pissed. He'll kill himself. Or someone else.' She buried her head in her hands and began to cry steadily. 'I love him. I want to help him. But he won't let me.'

'Of course he'll let you,' said Claire. 'Look, this must have been a real shock for him, Eavan. I can understand that he found it difficult to admit it to you. He was probably afraid of your reaction.'

'He shouldn't need to be afraid,' cried Eavan. Her shoulders shook with the ferocity of her sobs.

Claire sat beside her and uneasily recalled seeing Glenn alone outside Bruxelle's bar. But she said nothing about this to her friend. Eventually Eavan lifted her head and looked tearily at her.

'I'm sorry,' she said. 'I always seem to come to you with my stupid problems.'

'They're not stupid,' said Claire. 'And I'm glad you've come. But you'll have to talk to him about it. Maybe it'll be a relief to him that you know.'

'He'll just get pissed off at me for ringing the company.' Eavan sniffed. 'I don't blame him for that.'

'He won't get pissed off at you,' said Claire. 'He'll be embarrassed probably. But that's all. And you have to tell him everything too.'

'I can't!' cried Eavan.

Claire looked at her silently. Eavan buried her face in her hands again.

'I know, I know!' she mumbled. 'I know what you're getting at, Claire, but it's different.'

'How is it different?'

Eavan said nothing, but continued to sob. Claire put her arm around her friend's shoulders again and held her until her tears subsided.

'I know this is the conversation we had last time.' Eavan sniffed and looked up at her. 'But what if he is drinking to deal with it?'

'That's something you'll have to work out,' said Claire. 'Doesn't he have a support group?'

'Yes.'

'Then they'll help, surely?'

'I guess so.'

'Eavan, we can't do anything until you and he talk.'

'I know,' she said. 'It's just that I'm dreading it.'

She wiped her eyes with a tissue from the box Claire had put on the table alongside the cups of tea. Then her eye was caught by movement in the garden. Thankful to change the subject, even if only for a moment, she looked at her friend in surprise.

'I never noticed before,' she said. 'You've got someone in.'

Claire nodded. 'He's doing a good job.'

'It's looking miles better already,' said Eavan.

'It's nearly finished,' said Claire. 'He's dug out all the flowerbeds and replaced some of the plants. Plus he's building up that little wall at the side and adding a few more outside lights.'

'Was it expensive?' asked Eavan.

'Not too bad,' said Claire.

'I'm glad you finally got someone in,' said Eavan. 'This was always a lovely garden.'

Claire nodded. 'I was so . . . against someone else coming in to do things after Bill,' she said. 'But I was being silly.'

'Oh, I can understand it,' said Eavan. She sniffed. She didn't want to return to the subject of Glenn just yet. 'Hey, didn't you go to the dinner thing last week?'

Claire nodded. 'And it was fun. I'll tell you about it another time.'

'Did you meet anyone?'

'Yes and no.' Claire told her about Oliver Ramsey.

'But you should have let him come home with you!' cried Eavan. 'He was so gorgeous!'

'Yeah, but I told him I was a talent scout.'

'Claire Hudson!'

'I didn't want people knowing about me,' she told Eavan. 'And it was great. But I haven't heard from anyone and don't expect to. It was a good night out, that's all. Look, you and Glenn are more important right now than the stupid dinner.'

'I don't want to talk about Glenn any more.' Eavan sniffed and took another tissue from the pack. 'I have to bring it up with him tonight. Now that I know what's happened it's easier. But, you know, the real worry is money.'

'Money? I thought you were OK.'

'We gave up a lot when I stopped working. It put a lot of pressure . . .' She looked at Claire, her face stricken. 'It's my fault,' she said. 'Because I stopped working he went for different jobs. Stuff that he didn't really like. I made him do it because I wanted the house in Howth and because I wanted to stay at home with Saffy!'

'Don't be stupid, Eavan.'

'It's true.' Eavan blew her nose. 'He preferred research but I made him go into sales. I should have known. I really should.'

'It's not your fault,' said Claire.

'He probably didn't tell me because he thought I'd freak out about the house,' said Eavan. 'As if I would.' Suddenly her eyes hardened. 'He's such a fool.'

'All men are,' said Claire. 'It's up to us to keep them on the straight and narrow.'

'I'll have to get a job,' said Eavan. 'I'm sure that's what he's been doing. Job-hunting. Only he hasn't got one yet. You know how it is, Claire. When you're working it's easy to find something new. When you're not . . .' She twisted a strand of her hair anxiously. 'What if they got rid of him for drinking?'

'Stop torturing yourself,' commanded Claire. 'Go home, have a soak in a bath and then talk to him about it.'

Eavan nodded. 'But there's no chance of the soak in the bath,' she said. 'Saffy'll see to that.'

Claire had meant to get back to work after Eavan had gone, but she couldn't settle down to it. Georgia popped her head around the office door to say that she was going to the video store to get something for later in the evening. She also suggested hopefully that as part of the den refurbishment project Claire might see her way to buying a DVD player for Georgia's own television.

'We'll see,' said Claire as she put the computer to sleep, knowing that any more work was impossible. She looked out of the window. Nate Taylor was tying up plants at the end of the garden. He was bare-chested again, his skin already bronzed and weathered. As she observed him, he straightened up and looked at his watch. He stretched his arms over his head, then rubbed his back and walked to the patio. She couldn't see him at that point but almost immediately he walked down the garden again and plonked himself under the apple tree, a bottle of juice in his hand. Claire wondered if he'd eaten. She hadn't noticed him stop for a lunch break earlier.

She went downstairs and opened the kitchen door.

'Are you hungry?' she called.

He shrugged in response. Claire considered for a moment and then remembered the sandwiches Georgia had made earlier.

'I have some sandwiches made,' she told him. 'You're welcome to one if you like.'

Nate got up from beneath the tree and pulled his T-shirt over his head. He ambled towards her.

'Thanks,' he said. 'I *was* getting a bit peckish. I didn't bring anything today.'

Claire took the plate of sandwiches from the fridge and put them down on the patio table.

'Georgia always goes crazy when she makes food,' she said. 'She does far too much. I think they're mainly salad.'

'Great.' Nate picked one from the pile and bit into it while Claire went back into the kitchen to get some more juice.

'Oh, shit.'

She heard his words as she opened the fridge door again.

'Sh-it. Claire!'

'What? What's the matter?' She hurried outside.

Nate was still sitting at the table, his hand to his throat. His face was red.

'Are you choking?' she asked.

236

He shook his head.

'What then?'

'Nuts,' he gasped. 'There must be nuts. I – nut allergy.'

'Oh no.' Claire looked at him in horror. 'Peanut butter spread. She must've put some on them. She's crazy about it.'

'Got to call . . . someone,' he said shakily. 'I – react – really – badly.' He wheezed loudly with every breath.

'Wait,' she told him. 'Wait.'

She went back into the kitchen and took out the big green first-aid box. She removed a cylindrical object which she unwrapped quickly, taking off the grey safety cap as she walked outside. Nate's face was even redder. When he saw what she had in her hand he loosened his jeans and slid them down. Claire held the EpiPen to his thigh and pressed it hard. The auto-injector clicked. She watched Nate carefully.

'I'll call an ambulance,' she said. 'You rub the area, OK?'

As she dialled the emergency services she kept watching him closely, relieved that his breathing seemed slightly less ragged than before.

'I can't believe you had this,' he wheezed. 'Lucky – old – me . . .'

'They'll be here very soon,' she told him as she looked at her watch. 'Don't talk.'

He nodded weakly. She continued to watch him.

'You feeling better?' she asked after a couple of minutes.

His smile was fleeting. 'I think so. I'm usually . . . so careful. I didn't think . . .' He exhaled slowly. Although his breathing was still laboured, Claire thought it was beginning to ease.

'I'm sorry,' he said after another minute or so, when his breathing had definitely improved and his colour had begun to return to normal. 'This is ridiculous. Look, I don't need an ambulance. I'll be fine.'

'Probably,' said Claire briskly. 'But you need to be monitored in case you start to react again.'

'How do you know all this?' Nate's voice was growing stronger.

'I'm a doctor's wife,' said Claire. 'Had you forgotten?'

'I'm glad.' Nate grinned feebly. 'It wouldn't have been great business for me to . . . die . . . on your doorstep.'

Claire smiled back at him but she was concentrating on listening to the sound of his breath and checking to see that he wasn't developing a further wheeze or breaking out into a rash. Feeling more confident that he was beginning to recover, she went to the front door. The ambulance had just pulled up outside the gate and two paramedics hurried up the steps.

'Anaphylactic shock?' said one.

'He's in the back garden,' Claire told them. 'He's had one dose of an EpiPen and I think he's recovering.'

The paramedics went through to the kitchen and Claire was about to follow them when she saw Georgia running at full tilt down the road.

'It's OK, it's OK,' said Claire as the girl raced up the steps and almost collided with her. 'Everything's fine.'

Georgia's face was ashen beneath her summer sprinkling of freckles. 'I saw the ambulance,' she panted. 'I thought . . . I thought . . .'

'It's OK,' repeated Claire. She put her arms around Georgia and pulled her towards her. 'There's nothing the matter. Nate had a bad reaction to something and went into shock. But he's fine now, I promise you.'

Georgia stayed immobile in her mother's hug until Claire prised her away from the door to allow the paramedics to carry Nate Taylor to the ambulance.

'He'll be grand,' one of them told her. 'We're taking him to Beaumont. Do you want to come?'

'No. No,' said Claire hastily. 'We're not . . . I'm not . . .' She looked at Nate. 'Do you want me to call Sarah?'

He shook his head gingerly. 'No, I'll do it from the hospital,' he told her.

'Are you sure?' asked Claire.

'Yes.' Nate was adamant. 'I don't want to scare her. I'm fine now.'

'He certainly seems to be,' said the paramedic. 'But we're taking you to the hospital now, mate, and they'll keep an eye on you for a while.'

'Thank you.' Nate's words encompassed both Claire and the paramedics. As he was loaded into the back of the ambulance Georgia squeezed Claire's hand.

'Can we go in?' Georgia's voice was still shaky, and Claire looked down at her anxiously.

'Are you all right?' she asked as she closed the front door and led her into the kitchen.

'Now I am,' said Georgia. 'I got a fright, Mum. When I saw the ambulance I thought . . . I didn't know what to think.' She rubbed at her eyes with the back of her hand. 'I . . .'

'It's OK,' said Claire. She put her arms around Georgia again. 'I would've got a fright too.'

'It was like the accident,' said Georgia, her voice trembling. 'Although it couldn't really have been like it because I don't remember it. But when I saw the flashing blue light it was like . . . I did remember it . . . I remembered something.' A tear rolled down her cheek. 'I was frightened.'

Claire hugged her closer still. 'There's no need to be frightened,' she said. 'I'm here. I'll look after you.'

Georgia said nothing but Claire could feel her body shaking with sobs. After a moment or two she lifted her head and sniffed loudly. 'I'm sorry,' she said. 'I'm being a baby.'

'No you're not,' Claire assured her.

'I can't be a baby,' said Georgia. 'I can't cry.'

'For heaven's sake!' Claire looked at her in concern. 'Of course you can cry. Anyone who gets a fright can cry. It's a perfectly normal reaction.'

'But . . . but . . .'

'But what?'

'I have to be strong,' said Georgia.

'No you don't,' said Claire firmly. 'You can be a big softy if that's what you want.'

A glimmer of a smile played around Georgia's mouth and she wiped away the tears again. 'I was never a softy.'

'Perhaps not.' Claire kissed her on her forehead. 'Why do you have to be strong?' she asked.

Georgia swallowed. 'For you,' she said eventually. 'You need me to be strong.'

'Georgia!' Claire looked at her in astonishment. 'Why do you think that?'

'Because of Dad,' cried Georgia. 'Because you're broken-hearted. Because you lost the one person you loved. You need me to be strong.

239

I wasn't at the start. I was feeble and silly with all the not-talking nonsense. I didn't mean to be but I was. And then I heard them talking about you and how hard it was for you and how you were so worried about me . . . I felt awful about it. Awful.'

'Oh, Georgey-girl!' Claire hugged her daughter even more tightly. 'Don't for one second think like that. Don't. Of course I lost somebody. We both did. But I didn't lose the one person I loved. I still have one person I love more than anything. I still have you, Georgey.'

'But it's not the same.' Georgia sniffed. 'It isn't. You love me because I'm your daughter. That's all.'

'Georgia Hudson.' Claire felt more shocked than she'd ever been in her life before. 'You can't possibly think that I only love you out of a sense of duty. How could you even imagine that?' She looked at her daughter, a worried frown furrowing her brow. 'Darling, you're the most important, precious thing in the world to me. And I love you more than anything.'

'Not more than Dad, though,' said Georgia simply.

Claire was silent. Her heart was pounding in her chest. She was devastated at the thought that her only child could possibly think that in some way she wasn't loved for herself, wasn't loved with the same depth of feeling as Bill had been.

She spoke slowly. 'Obviously I loved your dad very much, and loving someone you're married to is very deep and very emotional. But haven't you ever heard about how mothers love their children? How they run into burning buildings to save them? How they starve themselves to feed them? How they'll do anything, absolutely anything for them?'

Georgia nodded. 'Sure, you hear about that sort of stuff. But it's not real.'

'It is,' said Claire fiercely. 'It is, Georgey-girl. I would walk into any burning building if I thought you were in it. If anyone was to touch a hair of your head in harm I'd kill them without a second thought. I love you, Georgia Hudson. You're the most important person in the world to me. And I'd be nothing without you.'

Georgia bit her lip. 'But you miss him, Mum. And I can't help you.'

'Of course I miss him,' said Claire. 'I knew him for a long time.

You miss him too. But we do have each other. And we love each other. We're a family, you and me. It's very, very important to me that you understand that.'

'I do understand that,' said Georgia. 'I just thought that . . . well . . .' She sighed.

'Maybe I haven't been very good at getting over things,' admitted Claire. 'And I'm not sure that I'm as over it as I need to be just yet. But one thing that's never going to change is how much a part of my life you are, Georgia. I love you absolutely and unconditionally, and whether Bill was here in the room or not my love for you would be exactly the same.'

Georgia's smile was a little wobbly. 'Am I being really silly?' she asked.

'Utterly,' agreed Claire. 'But that's all right because I'm pretty silly too. And I'll tell you something else, Miss Hudson, I wouldn't have been able to get out of bed every day for the past three years if it wasn't for you.'

'Really?'

'Of course.' Claire grinned broadly at her. 'Let's face it, you need someone to haul you out of yours. If I didn't do it, you'd spend all day burrowed beneath those covers.'

Georgia made a face at her and Claire kissed her again. They sat together in silence for a while.

'So – so what happened to Mr Taylor? What made him go into shock?' asked Georgia eventually. She giggled. 'You didn't wiggle your bum at him, did you?'

'Clown!' Claire was relieved to hear Georgia make even the smallest of jokes. 'Of course not. He ate one of your sandwiches, Georgey.'

'Oh!' Georgia's eyes darkened in understanding. 'Peanut butter.'

Claire nodded.

'So it was me,' said Georgia. 'I nearly killed him.'

'Well I offered him the sandwich, honey. So if it was anyone it was me.'

'Both of us could've killed him!' Georgia's eyes were wide saucers in a face that was beginning to regain its colour. 'Gosh, Mum, we could have been prosecuted as murderers.'

'OK, OK, now you're being daft,' said Claire. 'But I felt bloody guilty when I saw what had happened. And when I realised he was going into shock . . .'

'Did he have one of those needle things?' asked Georgia. 'If he's allergic to nuts does he carry one around?'

'No,' said Claire. 'This is the lucky bit. I got one from the first-aid cabinet. Remember, your dad always had some. There were half a dozen, three for adults and three for kids.'

Georgia nodded. 'Would he have died?'

'I don't think so,' said Claire. 'It wasn't the worst reaction I've seen. But better to be safe than sorry, don't you think?'

'Still, you might have saved his life.'

'A minute ago I was a murderess.'

'Better to be a lifesaver, I think,' said Georgia. She smiled at Claire. 'Dad would've been impressed with you.'

'D'you think so?'

'Absolutely.'

'I'll tell you something, Georgey. I was impressed with myself.'

Georgia giggled. 'D'you think he'll finish the work in the garden? Or will he be afraid to come back?'

'I hope he'll come back.' Claire looked out of the window. 'It's looking a lot better, isn't it?'

Georgia nodded. Her mobile beeped and she took it out of her pocket. And Claire was relieved to see that she seemed to have recovered her composure enough to smile broadly before she sent a text in reply.

Chapter 24

Polygonatum (Solomon's Seal) – Bell-like flowers usually white or cream. The leaves are clasped by arching stems. Thrives in deep shadow of trees or shrubs.

Eavan was sitting in the conservatory when she heard the sound of the car pulling into the driveway. She took another sip from her glass of water. She was nervous. She didn't know exactly what she was going to say to Glenn. She'd rehearsed different scenarios over and over in her head but she had the feeling that as soon as he walked through the door she'd forget all of them. She wanted to be calm and under-standing but inside her stomach was churning. She'd always thought that she'd had the only difficult conversation she'd ever need with Glenn when he'd admitted his alcoholism to her. But now she knew that there were even more difficult things to talk about. And she was afraid.

She heard the front door opening and the sound of his footsteps in the hallway. Through the glass doors that led from the conservatory to the kitchen she saw him putting his briefcase on the kitchen counter and she bit her lip. How awful must it be for him to pretend every day, she thought unhappily. And so terrible for him to feel that he had to carry this burden on his own.

'Honey, I'm home!'

It was a joke between them that sometimes he said this. And those times she would rush to meet him and kiss him and ask him how his day was in the sugary tones of a 1950s housewife in a saccharine Hollywood movie.

She got up from the deeply cushioned bamboo chair and walked into the kitchen.

'Hi,' she said.

'How're you?' Glenn smiled at her but she could see the anxious look in his eyes. How the hell hadn't she spotted it before?

'I'm great,' she said carefully. 'And you?'

'Oh, busy busy,' he said.

She kept her eyes fixed on his face. 'Busy but not at Trontec.'

'Huh?' He stared at her.

'I didn't mean to,' she told him, 'but I rang the office today.'

'Eavan! I told you not to ring me there! I told you—'

'I know what you told me, and why you told me,' she said. 'When you're not working for the company it doesn't make a lot of sense for me to call you there, does it?'

'Eavan, let me explain—'

'I'm listening.'

So he told her about his meeting with the top brass of the company, and how they'd decided that the overall sales strategy could be better worked on from their US office, and that, yes, local sales people were necessary but not really someone of Glenn's calibre. Although, they said, he probably preferred the research side of things, which was what he'd started out doing. Unfortunately research was being handled in California now.

'Those bastards!' Eavan looked at him in fury.

'What could I say to them?' Glenn shrugged. 'We've gained market share but not at the rate they wanted. They were putting some new worldwide strategy in place. It wasn't just me that was let go; John Mara, Ken Farrell and Sean Carew went too.'

'Bastards,' said Eavan again. 'How can they be like that?'

'You know what it's like these days,' said Glenn. 'You're just a commodity to them.'

'You're not just a commodity!'

'I feel like it,' he said wryly.

'Why didn't you tell me?' Suddenly she began to cry. 'A horrible thing happened to you and you didn't tell me.'

'I knew you'd cry,' he said.

'Of course I'm crying,' she said. 'But I'm crying because I feel useless to you. If you couldn't share this with me then what's the point of anything?'

Glenn's jaw twitched as he watched his wife scrub her eyes with a piece of kitchen towel.

'Look, it's difficult enough for me without having to deal with you too,' he said.

'Glenn!' She crumpled the kitchen towel into a ball.

'I wanted to look after things in my own way.'

'By pretending it hasn't happened?' Eavan looked at him incredulously. 'You must have known I'd find out sooner or later.'

'I thought I might get a job first. Then you'd never need to know.'

'You'd no right to do that,' she told him. 'I'm your wife. I'm entitled to know.'

His jaw twitched again.

'There are decisions that have to be made,' said Eavan. 'Decisions that affect you and me and Saffy. You can't keep it all to yourself.'

'I'm supposed to be the breadwinner,' said Glenn. 'I'm supposed to deal with it all myself.'

'You know that's utter bullshit,' cried Eavan. 'We're married. You're supposed to share!'

'I wasn't ready to share,' he told her.

'But for heaven's sake, Glenn, you can't do everything on your own.'

'You wanted me to,' he pointed out. 'When you asked me if you could give up your job to be with Saffy. I knew how important that was to you, so I agreed. But it meant that I was the one responsible for bringing in the money. And it's my responsibility to sort it out now.'

'Don't be so daft!' she exclaimed. 'We've always been a partnership. We sort things out between us.'

He looked at her mutinously and she wanted to cry with frustration. How had it happened, she asked herself, that they'd arrived at a point in their marriage where he was unwilling to tell her something so very important? And how had the conversation slipped into a kind of argument when all she'd wanted was to be understanding and sympathetic? She'd visualised him being relieved to finally share the burden with her and she'd imagined comforting him over the loss of his job. But he was standing there rigidly in front of her, talking to her but not really letting her in.

'So . . . have you been out looking for something else?' she asked finally.

'What the hell do you think I've been doing for the past couple of weeks?' He stared at her. 'Of course I've been looking for a job. I've been doing nothing else but looking for jobs. I've e-mailed my CV to every damn business in the country. I've applied for jobs I'm way overqualified for. You don't think I've been sitting on my arse all day doing nothing, do you?'

Eavan told herself that he was stressed and upset. He'd tried to hide this from her and she'd found out so he was probably feeling guilty too. So it shouldn't be surprising that he was lashing out.

'I'm sure you have being applying for jobs, of course you have,' she said hastily. 'I just wondered how it was going.'

'How the fuck do you think?' he asked. 'I'm not working, am I?'

'But you've had interviews?'

'I'm the wrong age,' said Glenn harshly. 'I'm forty-one. If I was thirty-nine I might have a better chance. But they look at my CV and they see forty-something and they think that I'm too old and too stupid to know what I'm doing. I've had one interview and the child conducting it was about twenty. I'm on the bloody scrapheap already.'

'Oh, come on,' she said encouragingly. 'It's early days. And the age thing is nothing.'

'It's not nothing,' said Glenn. 'All they want is youth. And I don't have the right kind of management experience for other jobs.'

'But you did consultancy before.'

'That was crap,' said Glenn. 'It wasn't like I was coming up with great strategies. Besides . . .'

Eavan knew what the besides was. Glenn's drinking problem had been at its height during his consultancy years. He'd lost that job too.

She didn't want to ask but he was looking hard at her, daring her to. So she did.

'Are you drinking now?'

'That's what it all comes down to in the end, isn't it?' he asked. 'A little bit of bother and everyone starts worrying. Will Glenn crack? Will it all be too much for him? Will he slide down the slippery slope and not be able to pull himself up again?'

The element of hysteria in his voice made Eavan flinch.

'Of course I'm not drinking,' he continued harshly. 'Don't you think things are bloody well bad enough without that?'

'You've been acting weird,' she said. 'I know that it must be because of losing your job but I thought . . . I was afraid . . .'

'I thought you'd know me better than that. I thought you trusted me.'

'I do trust you!' she cried. 'But God knows, Glenn, maybe if it was me who lost my job I'd turn to the bottle myself.'

'Yeah, well, I haven't. So you don't have to worry. I might be a loser but I'm not a drunk loser.'

'You are *not* a loser,' she said fiercely.

'What else would you call me?' he asked. 'I've been let go from two companies. I have a drink problem. Sounds like loser material to me.'

'You're a good husband and a good father,' said Eavan. 'You've tried really hard to give me everything I want. And maybe I've asked for too much. I pushed and pushed for us to get this house even though I knew it was a huge stretch. Remember when we bought it? You said that we'd both be working for ever to pay off the mortgage. And what happens? I get pregnant and I want to give up work. So you agree. And I should have known that it would be too much. You allowed yourself to move departments so that you had the chance to earn more money even though it was an area you weren't interested in. Perhaps if you'd stayed where you were this would never have happened!'

'It would've happened earlier,' he told her sourly. 'Research was moved back to California, remember? But you were working then. Earning good money too.'

Eavan sighed. 'We can deal with this together. You know we can. What's the story on our finances?'

'I spoke to the bank. It's not as bad as all that because we have mortgage protection insurance and that'll cover the repayments for a few months. The bank will extend the life of the mortgage too, so that after the insurance money runs out we can pay back at a lower level.'

'That's OK then, isn't it?'

247

'It's only a short-term solution. We don't have any savings.'

'That's my fault too.' Eavan raised her china-blue eyes to him. 'I'm the one who insisted on borrowing money to get the garden done. I'm the one who likes to shop in expensive stores. I'm the one who says that we should get the best of everything. I'm the one who puts on the pressure to get new stuff all the time. It's me, not you.'

'Everybody wants the best,' said Glenn. 'We're entitled to it.'

'Not if we can't afford it,' said Eavan simply. 'I don't need to have my hair done every week. I don't need to buy the most expensive brands of everything. I like it, but I don't need it.'

'Well if I don't get something soon you'll be buying the cheapest brands of everything,' Glenn told her.

'We could sell the house.'

He looked at her in disbelief. 'Sell the house! After all we went through to get it? After all the money we've spent on it already? Are you out of your mind?'

'Darling, it's just a house.'

This time his stare was even more disbelieving. 'Just a house! Eavan, that's not what you said when we first looked at it. You said it was your perfect home. You said you had to have it. You said that once you'd seen it you couldn't possibly be happy anywhere else. It's not just a house. It's everything.'

'Glenn, it's a house.'

'We're not selling the house,' he told her.

'Listen to me,' she said urgently. 'House prices in Howth have skyrocketed since we bought this place. We could sell it and buy something smaller. Out of town maybe. Then we'd have spare cash in the bank and we wouldn't have to worry.'

'Don't be utterly ridiculous,' he said. 'We've worked hard for this house and we're keeping it. It's our best asset. We can borrow more against it if we have to.'

'And then maybe one day it'll be repossessed and we're out of it anyway!' cried Eavan.

'I won't let that happen.' Glenn's tone was grim.

They stood in silence.

'OK,' said Eavan eventually. 'We don't have to sell it yet anyway. But I think the best thing is if I start to look for work myself.'

'No.'

'Why not?' she demanded. 'You know that women are much more mobile when it comes to the workplace. I can use a keyboard, answer the phones, whatever.'

'I'll get a job,' he said. 'It's taking time but I will get one. And I'm not having you rushing out to get work as if I'm a useless moron.'

'Oh, Glenn, you know I don't think that!' Eavan moved to put her arms around him but he stepped back from her and she stopped, arms in mid-air.

'I suppose you have a better chance,' he said. 'You're younger.'

'I'm thirty-eight,' she said. 'I'll be competing with kids out of school for crappy office jobs. But I'll do it if I need to.'

'And what will happen to Saffy while you're doing this job?' he asked.

She shrugged. 'If you haven't got anything then you can look after her.'

'You have it all planned out, haven't you?'

'Of course I haven't!' She looked pleadingly at him. 'Come on, Glenn. Stop being so defensive about it all. These things happen. Those guys in Trontec are complete bastards. But they don't have to ruin our lives.'

'They don't need to,' said Glenn sourly. 'I'm managing to do that all by myself.'

Eavan bit her lip. A tear rolled down her cheek but she didn't bother to wipe it away. It plopped on to the highly polished granite tiles. She wanted to help him, she wanted to be positive. She wanted to reach out and hold him and reassure him that nothing mattered other than the fact that they had each other (and that he wasn't drinking or having an affair – although, of course, she couldn't ever, ever let him know that she'd allowed herself to think he might be having an affair). But she had a horrible feeling that trying to be positive wasn't actually helping at all. And that somehow, despite her best efforts, she was only making things worse. More tears tumbled down her face and this time she did wipe them away.

'Oh, hell, Evs – I'm sorry!'

Suddenly Glenn was the one who reached out. He put his arms

around Eavan and held her close to him. 'I'm being a complete shit but I can't help it.'

'That's all right.' Her voice was muffled in the crook of his arm. 'I understand.'

She relaxed into his arms, thankful that he was holding her, trying to make him realise that she needed him as much as he needed her. She put her arms around him too, pulling him towards her, hugging him fiercely.

Glenn felt the force of her embrace as he inhaled the scent of the shampoo she used to wash her hair. He allowed himself to relax a little. She was right. He should have told her before now. And sharing his worries with her meant that the band of tension that had held him in a vice-like grip for the past few weeks had finally loosened. He released his breath. It seemed to him that he'd been holding his breath ever since Jim Smith had called the meeting at Trontec's offices and told him there wasn't a place for him any more.

But knowing that it wasn't a secret between them still didn't make things right. He was still the breadwinner in the family. And he wasn't going to have Eavan rushing out to work to support him. It wasn't on. So he'd have to do something about it. Fast.

He felt the band of tension wrap itself around him again.

Chapter 25

Ranunculus (Persian Buttercup) – Colourful ball-shaped double blooms. Thrives best in full sun.

Claire finished painting both Georgia's den and the new guest room the following morning. The bright yellow was a definite hit in the sun-starved basement rooms and Claire had to admit that Georgia's choice had been perfect. Now, with the narrow shaft of late-morning light slanting through the windows, the surgery had suddenly become part of the house again.

Georgia was thrilled with her new-look den. Even before moving her stuff it now felt like her space and not the empty and unused surgery it had been before. She didn't mind that it had been where Bill had worked. In fact, she quite liked the idea that she was going to use it. She knew (or at least she thought she knew) that her mother hadn't seen things the same way when she started working from home. Claire hadn't used the surgery as her office, not because it was dark (anyone could have seen that a lick of paint would brighten it!) but because she'd been unwilling to change anything of Bill's. Georgia felt that Claire believed it was in some way disrespectful for her to use his place.

She felt differently. She didn't need things the way they were. It was time for them to change. It didn't mean that she'd forgotten her father or that she loved him any less. If anything, using his surgery and turning it into her den brought him closer to her now. It wasn't that she'd be thinking of him every time she sat at the desk and did her homework, but she knew that his presence was there all the same. It had to be, whether she felt it or not. And it comforted her to know that maybe some of his thoughts or dreams or hopes were still in the room, still swirling around her, part of her.

She laughed at herself when she thought of this. She hadn't been part of him in the same way as Claire, of course, and so losing him had been very different for her. But in some ways she was closer to him than Claire would ever be because she was actually, genetically part of him. And what Claire didn't understand, what Georgia hadn't been able to explain to her during her three months of silence or even afterwards, was that Bill had been part of her for all of her life. Sure, he and Claire had met up when they were both kids and so they'd been part of each other's lives for a long, long time. But there had been a time when they didn't know each other. There had never been a time when he hadn't been Georgia's father.

She sat cross-legged on the yellow and green bean-cushion that she'd brought down from her bedroom and stared at the freshly painted wall in front of her. There was no sign now of the long oblong mark where one of Bill's posters of the human body had been until a couple of days ago. She'd been amazed that Claire had been able to tear it off the wall in the first place. But now things had changed. Claire had taken down the posters, got stuck into the painting and removed the white surgery light from outside the door – and she hadn't cried at all when she'd thrown it in the bin.

In fact lots of things were changing and Georgia was happy about it. She'd been totally astonished the previous day when (after the shock of Nate Taylor being carted off in an ambulance) Claire had suggested that the two of them go into town together for something to eat. To steady our nerves, Claire had said, and so they'd taken the bus into Temple Bar and gone into the Elephant & Castle, where they'd demolished a huge bowl of spicy chicken wings followed by a burger for Georgia and a massive Caesar salad for Claire. Then Claire had told her all about the night of the Dinner in the Dark and Georgia had stared at her in amazement at the thought of Claire sitting at a table with a complete bunch of strangers and eating unidentified food with her fingers.

'What did you wear?' she'd demanded, and had been astonished when Claire told her about her shopping trip and the new silk dress and totally impractical sandals.

'I haven't seen much of the new stuff,' she complained, and Claire said that it was because she'd been living in jeans and shorts since Georgia had come home because they were easiest for doing up the den.

Georgia asked for more details on Claire's date with Paul Hanratty too. She liked Paul, who'd called around to the house some nights to pick Claire up for matches. She felt that if Claire was going to start going out with a man again the chances were that he'd be someone she already knew. And she herself would prefer the idea of her mother going out with someone even vaguely familiar. The idea of a man she didn't know suddenly coming into their lives was difficult to deal with, no matter how much she encouraged her mother to go out a bit more. So maybe Paul was a good possibility even though Claire had said there was no chance.

And, thought Georgia, it was a damn sight better than the idea of Claire ending up with an internet boyfriend! She'd thought that her mother had sprung all her surprises on her when Claire, rather shamefacedly, admitted to registering with HowWillIKnow.com. She'd stressed that the main reason was because it was the only way she could go to the Dinner in the Dark, but she'd also confessed to having sent an e-mail message to one of the people on their books. Georgia had been horrified and told Claire that for all she knew people who advertised on the net could be complete psychopaths and she could end up murdered in an alleyway somewhere. She'd become so upset that Claire had told her, very hastily, that she'd no intention of contacting anyone else from HowWillIknow and that she hadn't put up her own details and Georgia truly wasn't to worry.

Easier said than done, thought Georgia. It had been bad enough worrying about Claire when she was so deeply unhappy about the accident. Worrying about her picking up totally unsuitable boyfriends was even worse!

Her phone vibrated, interrupting her reverie, and she took it out of the pocket of her jeans. The text message was from Steve Ó Sé. Since coming back from the summer camp he'd got a job in a local leisure centre, helping behind the reception desk. He loved the job, he told her; it got him out of the house and away from his parents. Steve didn't get on with his folks. Georgia couldn't imagine what that would be like. She knew that she didn't tell Claire every little thing about how she felt or how her life was going. But she knew beyond anything that she could trust her and that Claire only ever wanted the best for her. She couldn't understand how Steve's parents didn't feel the same way about their only child too. But from what Steve told her, they considered him to be a nuisance. They liked doing their own thing. He was always in the way. That was why they sent him off to camps or to stay with relatives while they got on with their own lives. They were both academic people who studied Celtic history and lectured on various aspects of it all over the world. Steve told her that he was proud of his heritage too but he was fed up with having it rammed down his throat all the time. That was when she'd stopped calling him Stiofán and called him Steve instead. Besides, she'd told him, it's easier to key into my phone.

Now she replied to his message asking how she was by telling him that her den was great, that there'd be a guest room soon and that she hoped one day he'd come to visit her. She couldn't help blushing when she read his reply, which said that wild horses wouldn't stop him. And he'd ended it *luv S*. Which gave her a warm feeling inside.

The two new single beds arrived later that afternoon and Georgia and Claire set about making them up so that the waiting room was now a fully fledged guest room. Then they brought Georgia's school stuff from her old bedroom to the den. By the time they'd finished, Claire was hot and sweaty and wanted to soak in the bath while Georgia flopped back on to the bean-bag and asked if it would be OK to invite Robyn over to see how it all looked.

'Sure,' said Claire as she went upstairs.

She ran the bath, crumbled her rose-scented cubes into the water, and slid thankfully into it. She heard Georgia run up the stairs and bang on the door to say that Robyn couldn't come over because Leonie was having a family dinner that evening and she didn't trust Robyn not to come home. But it was OK if she called round there, so did Claire mind?

'Not at all,' Claire called through the closed door. She smiled as Georgia clattered down the stairs again and slammed the front door behind her. The house was suddenly still. It was a welcome stillness, thought Claire. Even though it was absolutely wonderful to have Georgia back, it was actually quite nice to have some time to herself again!

She dozed in the lukewarm water of the bath, letting her mind drift in and out of the various issues that nagged at her. Eileen selling the house. Con and Lacey. Eavan and Glenn . . . Eavan had called the previous night to say that she'd talked to Glenn and that they'd sorted things out between them, although sorting things out in an overall sense would be more difficult. Claire was glad the couple seemed to be dealing with the problem together. No matter what, she thought, things are always easier when you've got someone to share the load.

She heard the phone ring downstairs but she ignored it. Her mobile was perched on the windowsill. If it was Georgia she'd call the mobile. If it was anyone else – well, she didn't feel like talking to anyone else. She was in a relaxed zone right now and she wouldn't be in the slightest bit relaxed if she tried to wrap herself in a towel and race to the phone before it stopped ringing. It stopped. She relaxed some more. Then she took the tub of body scrub that Georgia had bought her the previous Christmas and rubbed it all over her skin.

The hairs on her legs, which she'd shaved the night of the Dinner in the Dark, had grown back again. Before the accident she used to wax her legs but afterwards, because of her scars, she'd been afraid. Shaving wasn't as good as waxing though. And her scars had healed. They were marks, nothing more. She got out of the bath, wrapped herself in a towel, and opened the cabinet. There were still cold wax strips in it. She grimaced and looked at them for a sell-by date. She couldn't see one. What the hell, she muttered, and opened the packs.

Her eyes watered as she whipped the first strip from her leg. She'd forgotten how bloody painful this could be! But she persevered, ruthlessly sticking and unsticking the strips even while the tears streamed down her face. As far as she remembered, the first time was the worst. And it hurt more if you'd shaved in between waxes. But still . . . She hopped around the bathroom, her legs tingling. There was a soothing cream in the cabinet too. She scooped a handful out of the tub and smeared it over her smarting skin and wondered why she'd ever thought this was worth doing again.

*   *   *

Georgia arrived home at six and joined Claire and Phydough (whom Claire had taken for a walk after her bath) in the back garden. The dog woofed in greeting, while Claire put down the magazine she was reading and perched her sunglasses on top of her head.

'There's trouble in Robs' house,' said Georgia as she flopped down into a garden chair. 'Slimeball Pete wants to cut her mum's maintenance.'

'Don't use that expression about Robyn's father,' said Claire.

'*She* does.'

'Even so.'

'It's not right, though, is it?' demanded Georgia. 'I mean, Robs is his daughter and you'd think he'd want to make sure that she was OK, but he doesn't.'

'No.' Claire remembered Pete Grainger, who'd walked out on Leonie on Robyn's sixth birthday. She'd been at the party with Georgia that afternoon and the house had been invaded by hordes of screaming children. Leonie and her two sisters had been supervising everything, and in the mêlée nobody had actually noticed that Pete wasn't there. In fact it wasn't until the party was over and most of the children had gone home that Leonie realised her husband wasn't around; she'd gone upstairs and opened his wardrobe and seen that most of his clothes were missing. So was all of the money from their joint bank account. And his passport. Pete had disappeared for six months before resurfacing with a new, pregnant girlfriend and a demand for half the value of the house.

Claire sighed. How was it that some men were so awful when there were other, wonderful guys out there? And how did you know which was which? In the end, she remembered, Leonie had managed to borrow the money to pay Pete but had also extracted monthly maintenance payments for Robyn from him. Now he didn't even want to give her that much.

'Robs says she'd rather not have the money at all,' confided Georgia. 'But that her mum thinks it's a point of principle.'

Claire nodded.

'Her mum thinks she'll have to take him to court, though, and that could cost her more than it's worth. And apparently Mike is in a real temper about it 'cos Pete said that since Robyn took his name he can pay for the privilege.'

'Yeuch,' said Claire.

'Why do people mess it up so much?' asked Georgia.

'I was wondering the very same thing myself,' Claire told her. 'And I haven't got a clue.'

Georgia sighed. Then she picked up the magazine that Claire had been reading.

'What's this?' she demanded. '"Fifty Ways to Leave Your Lover". Do you have a lover? Is that why you're reading it?'

'Don't be silly,' said Claire. 'I'm just . . . well . . . reading it.'

'If you haven't got a lover then why?'

'For information,' said Claire.

'What sort of information?'

Claire sighed. 'Well, it seemed to me that when you phoned me from the Gaeltacht and asked me about love and life and all that sort of stuff I wasn't very helpful. So I thought I'd try and find out a bit more.'

'Really?'

She nodded and Georgia giggled. 'Is that why you joined the internet agency and went to the dinner thing?'

'Yes,' said Claire.

'Oh, Mum!' Georgia looked at her in disbelief. 'You've got to be kidding me.'

'No,' said Claire. 'It seemed like a good idea.'

Georgia burst into a fit of laughter. 'Mum, you're meeting . . . older people,' she said. 'It's not the same.'

'I know it's not the same,' said Claire defensively. 'I just thought it might help.'

Georgia tried to keep a straight face but she started to laugh again. 'You're priceless,' she said. 'But I do love you.'

'Gosh, thanks.'

'No, really,' said Georgia. 'I do. But you don't have to go out with a string of men because of me.'

'Would you prefer that I didn't go out with anyone at all?' asked Claire.

This time Georgia had no difficulty in keeping her face straight. 'I don't know,' she said.

'Well, I have to tell you that I enjoyed the night out and, well, there was a guy who was kinda nice . . .'

'Mum!'

'. . . but I haven't heard from him since so I think we can safely cross him off the list.'

'There's a list?'

'Not exactly,' admitted Claire. 'And speaking of lists . . . I have a confession to make.'

'Oh?'

'I read *your* list.'

'My list?'

'Of guidelines for my boyfriends.'

'Mum! That was private! In my diary!' Georgia's face flushed with anger.

'It fell out,' said Claire. 'Honestly. I didn't look at your diary. I wouldn't. But I just read this thing.'

Georgia stared at the ground.

'It was interesting,' said Claire.

'Yeah, well, it was just a bit of fun. Me and Robs were talking about it when we were away and I just came up with that stuff. It's nothing serious.'

'I could see that,' said Claire.

'And you're not really ever going to have a boyfriend no matter what you say. 'Cos you're still in love with Dad.'

'Do you actually want me to have a boyfriend?' asked Claire.

'I dunno.' Georgia stared at the ground again. 'Sometimes I think maybe it would be good for you. But not maybe for me. So I don't know really.'

Claire hugged her. 'I'm honestly not looking for a boyfriend,' she said. 'But I will go out a bit more with my friends because I think that's a good idea. I know I've spent too much time at home and maybe that can be a bit suffocating for you. But you're right. I still love your dad. And no one can replace him.'

'I know that.' Georgia smiled at her. 'Can I order a pizza for tonight? I'm starving.'

'Sure,' said Claire.

She sat back on her lounger and flicked through the magazine again while Georgia went to phone the pizza delivery.

'Hey, Mum.' Georgia came back into the room, a shocked expression on her face.

'What?'

'There's a message on the phone for you. It's from some guy called Gary. He wants to know if you'd like to go and see *My Fair Lady* with him in the Point Depot on Wednesday night.'

Chapter 26

Poncirus (Japanese Bitter Orange) – A tangled mass of twisted stems. Fragrant flowers in late spring following a warm autumn.

It was not until later that night, after Georgia had gone to bed, that Claire phoned the number Gary had left on her machine. She couldn't believe he'd called. She hadn't believed that any of them would call despite the handing round of various numbers on the Dinner in the Dark night. In fact she'd thrown all the business cards and scraps of paper in the bin, pretty sure that she'd never see any of them again. And now Gary, the tall man with the extra-firm handshake, had asked her out on a date. She didn't know what to say.

She hadn't been particularly attracted to him on the night of the dinner but she had been intrigued by the fact that he'd worked on rebuilding projects in Kosovo and South Africa and so was obviously a decent person. But to go out with him? Why would she?

Georgia teased her unmercifully. She asked Claire to go over the Dinner in the Dark event again in minute detail. She wanted to know everything about Gary Collins, nodded approvingly when Claire told her about he was in construction (everyone knows that builders are loaded, she told her mother), nodded even more approvingly when she heard about his work in Kosovo and then told Claire that she should definitely go for it – especially, she reminded Claire, since *My Fair Lady* was one of her favourite musicals.

Claire knew she wouldn't be able to talk coherently to Gary with Georgia still around, which was why she waited until her daughter had finally gone to bed before nervously picking up the phone. And then she worried that eleven o'clock was far too late to be ringing someone who'd called so much earlier in the day. If he doesn't answer after three rings I'll hang up, she promised herself as she dialled the number.

But he answered after the second ring. Claire remembered his voice clearly. In fact she remembered his voice much more distinctly than how he looked, which, she supposed, had been the object of the exercise in the first place.

'Claire! How lovely to hear from you.'

'And you,' she said. 'Thanks so much for the invitation.'

'Can you make it?'

She could hear a touch of anxiety in his voice. What did he have to be anxious about? she wondered. After all, there were plenty more women from that night that he could ask! Suddenly she remembered how nervous she'd felt about calling Paul Hanratty, even though he was a friend. And how she'd hoped he wouldn't say no to the drink despite the fact that she'd been scared stiff of the idea herself.

'Of course I can make it,' she said. 'I love that musical.'

'You said so,' Gary reminded her. 'When we were chatting.'

'Oh.' She felt herself blush. It had been a throwaway comment when they'd been talking about their likes and dislikes. She hadn't expected anyone to remember it.

'So, would you like me to pick you up?'

'You live in Dundrum, don't you?' she remembered.

'Yes.'

'Well then there's no reason for you to come all the way over here just to backtrack again. I'll meet you there.'

'Are you sure?'

'Absolutely,' she said. 'Outside the gates.'

'Grand,' said Gary, and Claire thought she could detect another note of relief in his voice. 'I'm looking forward to it.'

'So am I,' said Claire. And she thought she might actually have meant it.

At eight-thirty on Monday morning she opened the front door and was confronted, once again, by an enormous bouquet of flowers.

Nate Taylor lowered the bouquet and smiled at her. 'Hi,' he said.

'Oh, Nate, hello.' She opened the door wider. 'I didn't really expect you today.'

'Why not?' he asked as he stepped inside. 'I'm fine now.'

'It was still a shock to your system,' she told him.

'Ah, nonsense!' He grinned. 'These are for you.'

She looked for a card inside the bouquet.

'From me,' he added. 'As a thank-you.'

'Oh.' She shrugged. 'You shouldn't have.'

'I could've died without you,' he told her.

'I doubt it,' she said. 'And given that it was my fault, the least I could do was to get help!'

'You were amazing,' he said. 'So decisive. Definitely hospital matron material.'

Claire chuckled. 'I don't think so. I hate hospitals, to tell you the truth.' She carried the flowers into the kitchen, followed by Nate. 'Did Sarah pick up the van?' she asked as she began to snip the stems. 'I saw it had gone when Georgia and I came home later that evening and I thought about phoning the guards because the first thing I thought was that it had been stolen. Then I copped on to myself.'

He nodded. 'She did try your door to tell you but she said you were out.'

'Me and Georgey went for something to eat,' Claire told him.

'More peanut butter sandwiches?'

'Chicken wings,' said Claire. She placed the pink and purple blooms into a vase. 'These are lovely.'

'They are, aren't they?' He smiled. 'Anyway, I'm back to work. I'll be finished this week. There isn't much more to do.'

'It looks great,' said Claire. 'It really does.'

'It's a lovely garden.' He looked at her carefully. 'Your husband must have spent a lot of time working on it.'

'Never enough,' she told him. 'At least that's what he used to say. He really enjoyed being here. Anyway,' she smiled brightly, 'I'd better get on with the day. I've got to go out at lunchtime and I need to get myself organised.'

'Sure,' said Nate. 'I'll get organised too.'

Claire went upstairs again, getting back to the task she'd set herself of clearing out her wardrobe. She'd unearthed all the clothes that had been too tight for her prior to the accident and was gratified to find that they all fitted perfectly now, even if some of them were a little dated. She should go shopping again soon, she thought. Liven things up a bit, because despite the new skirts and the mauve dress she still didn't have a very extensive wardrobe. Maybe Eavan could come with her. She always looked fantastic, had a real eye for clothes. They could have a girly day out. Cheer Eavan up a bit. Claire nodded to herself with satisfaction at the thought.

Georgia had gone shopping with Robyn, Sive and Emma. The day had been fun, trying on clothes, experimenting for ages with the make-up testers in Boots until the assistant told them either to buy something or leave the shop and then wandering around Virgin Megastore where Sive spent ages deciding which PlayStation game to buy for her younger brother's birthday. Things hadn't been so good, though, when they went to McDonald's, where a gang of teenage boys had bumped into Georgia as she carried a tray full of Coke back to the table. The sticky liquid from the supersized drinks had gone everywhere and one of the blokes had made an offensive remark about Georgia's hand which had turned Emma into a spitting fury, telling them where to get off with themselves, until a supervisor had come along to calm things down.

It had taken the gloss off the day and even though the girls had insisted that Georgia just shut up apologising because it wasn't her fault the tray had fallen, she still felt uncomfortable about it. It didn't really matter whether it was her fault or not. She was still the one who'd dropped it.

When she got home she sat in the garden for a while, her arms wrapped around Phydough's neck, her head buried in his soft fur. Then her mobile beeped with a message from Robyn. It told her that she must never forget that even if she was missing one irrelevant finger it didn't matter because she still had great tits and fellas would always be seduced by big tits. Georgia smiled wryly. Then she hugged Phydough once more, went indoors and tried to shave a few more seconds off her best Gran Turismo lap time.

Claire was talking to Trinny Armstrong in her small office which just about afforded a glimpse of Dublin Bay. They were planning Claire's work schedule for the next few weeks. As always, there was plenty

263

for her to do and she was looking forward to getting stuck in to something new. Then Trinny asked her if she'd been talking to Eavan Keating lately, because Eavan had been in touch about the possibility of coming back to Locum Libris.

Claire had no intention of sharing confidences with Trinny. She'd no idea what her friend might have told her.

'Thing is,' Trinny said, 'we don't have anything in accounts right now and that's really Eavan's area of expertise. But she was always a good worker. You and her both.' She grinned at Claire.

'I think things are a bit tight financially for her at the moment.' That was as much information as Claire was prepared to give. 'So if there's anything at all, I'm sure she'd be interested.'

Trinny nodded. 'I'll look out for her,' she said.

'That'd be great.' Claire got up to go and Trinny waved at her to sit down again. 'Did you enjoy the Dinner in the Dark evening?' she asked.

'It was OK,' replied Claire cautiously. 'I'm not sure about doing it again, though.'

'I went out a few nights ago with a bloke from our table,' Trinny told her.

'How was it?' asked Claire.

'I don't know why I did it,' admitted Trinny, 'though he was a nice guy. Not really for me, but a nice guy. Only Josh found out.'

'Oh.'

'And he went ballistic,' said Trinny.

Claire listened sympathetically as Trinny described just how ballistic Josh had gone, culminating in him walking out on her.

'And the thing is,' said Trinny miserably, 'I always goaded him about leaving me if he didn't like the way our relationship was. But now that he has . . . well, I wish he hadn't.'

'You'd better call him then,' said Claire.

'I did,' said Trinny. 'He told me to get lost.'

'If he loves you he'll forgive you,' said Claire.

Trinny laughed shortly. 'You're a romantic at heart, aren't you?'

'Me? Romantic? I don't think so!'

'Of course you are,' said Trinny. 'You honestly believe that love comes to you in a blinding flash and it's starry-eyed and wonderful for ever.'

'I don't,' said Claire.

'You believe in for ever. You believe in love.'

'Doesn't everyone?'

'Grow up, Claire,' said Trinny. 'Not these days. These days it's all about finding someone you can put up with.' She looked down at the paperwork on her desk. 'How about your love life?' she asked abruptly. 'The Dinner in the Dark? Any luck?'

Claire blushed. 'Well, actually I'm going out with one of them soon.'

'Claire Hudson!'

She told Trinny about the invitation from Gary Collins.

'Which one was he?' asked Trinny. 'Not that gorgeous bloke who looked like Becks, by any chance? Say yes and I'll cry.'

'No, sadly.' Claire grinned.

'Still, Claire. At least you've got a date.'

'Dates aren't important,' said Claire. 'Not when you have someone already, Trinny. Call Josh. Tell him you love him. You've got to sort out what you want in your life.'

Trinny looked at her wryly. 'Crazy isn't it? I help run a company with fifty employees but I can't run my own life. How sad is that!'

Georgia was already home. Claire could hear the sound of her PlayStation car-racing game as she put her key in the lock. Georgia was an absolute whizz at the game, which Bill had bought for her the Christmas before the accident. Both Bill and Claire had watched in astonishment as their daughter whirled digital racing cars, rally cars and concept cars around a variety of tracks, setting lap records over and over again. Neither of them had been the least bit competent at the game, which had amused Georgia no end. She'd curled up in fits of laughter as first Bill and then Claire would round a corner at speed and send the car into a spin, wasting valuable lap time. The only thing was, Claire had muttered to Bill one evening, when Georgia eventually started to drive herself, she'd be a bloody maniac on the roads!

Claire knocked on the door of Georgia's den and walked inside. The room was now utterly transformed. The walls were covered in framed pictures of Phydough and posters of Georgia's favourite boy-band, while the delicate glass and shell chimes which Bill had bought for her in Jamaica, and which she treasured, hung from the ceiling. Every other available surface of her room was covered with her collection of stuffed toys, CDs, PlayStation games, books and magazines.

Georgia looked up from the game and smiled briefly at her mother. Then she turned her attention back to the track. But in that instant Claire knew something was wrong.

'What happened?' she said.

'Huh?' Georgia winced as she misjudged the racing line and the car she was controlling cut over the grass.

'Something's wrong,' said Claire.

'Nothing's wrong.'

'C'mon, Georgey. It's me you're talking to.'

Georgia sighed and paused the game. She stretched her arms out in front of her and cracked her fingers, keeping her arms extended as she told her mother about the incident in the burger bar.

'. . . and it wasn't anything terrible, but I felt so – stupid,' she finished.

'Anyone could've dropped the tray,' Claire pointed out.

'I know,' said Georgia. 'But it was me. So people could blame it on my hand and not the fact that those blokes banged into me.'

'Did the girls blame it on your hand?'

'Well, no,' admitted Georgia. 'They kept saying it wasn't my fault. They always stick up for me.' She bit her lip. 'Not everyone does. Karen Devlin is a complete bitch. She's always making snide comments.'

Claire looked at Georgia thoughtfully. 'Does it bother you?'

'Of course it bothers me,' admitted Georgia. 'But everyone knows Karen is nothing but a slapper anyway.'

'She's probably insecure,' said Claire.

Georgia snorted. 'Don't be so feeble, Mum. She's far too secure for her own flippin' good. She's gorgeous and she knows it and everyone wants to be friends with her.'

'But her popularity is only based on how she looks,' said Claire.

'Oh, I know that!' Georgia looked disdainfully at Claire. 'Knowing it doesn't make it different, though, does it?'

'I guess not.'

They sat in silence beside each other.

'I don't want people making allowances,' said Georgia eventually. 'I don't want them to say, "Poor Georgia Hudson, no dad, no finger, no chance."'

'Oh, honey, they won't!'

'You'd be surprised,' said Georgia grimly.

Claire didn't know what to say.

'I'll be all right.' Georgia could see the concerned expression on her mother's face. 'I just don't want to be different. And if I mess up because of my hand I want them to say so!'

'But you said that dropping the tray had nothing to do with your hand.'

'I know.'

'Then are you being a complete goose?' asked Claire.

'Probably,' said Georgia. She sighed. 'Oh Mum, you know I don't really mind the finger and the scars and all those things any more. They're kind of part of me now. It's just – we talk about blokes and stuff and we meet fellas and mostly they're great, but sometimes . . .' She picked up the game control and looked at it. 'Sometimes I wonder if I'll ever meet someone who really doesn't notice my hand. I mean – well – like – there's blokes who say it doesn't matter, but that means they've thought about it and decided it doesn't matter. I'd like to meet someone who doesn't even think about it.'

'You will,' promised Claire.

'Maybe.'

'I thought you were doing all right,' said Claire. 'What about the boy you keep texting?'

Georgia blushed. 'He doesn't count,' she said. 'He's nice. He's a friend. But he lives in Navan. It's not like we can meet up that often.' She peeped at Claire from beneath her fringe. 'Not like we can meet up at all unless he comes into town. And that's not easy for him 'cos he has a summer job and it has mad hours. So we just text.'

'You'll find the right person eventually,' said Claire. 'But you've loads of time, Georgey. Loads.'

'Ah, I know.' Georgia shrugged. 'Don't mind me. I'm blathering.'

Claire ruffled her hair and Georgia looked at her severely.

'And don't mess with the hair,' she told her mother. 'You'll ruin my look!'

Chapter 27

Gladiolus (Sword Lily) – Variety of colours with wide flowers which can vary enormously in height. Water in dry weather.

By the middle of the week, Nate had finished in the garden, including getting someone in to wire up the soft green lights which were now sunk into the rockery area at the back wall. Both Georgia and Claire agreed that he'd done a great job and that the garden was absolutely wonderful.

'You need to hold a barbecue or something,' said Nate. 'Celebrate its return to its former glory.'

'Great idea!' cried Georgia. 'But you should've built in a barbie for us.'

'I did ask,' said Nate mildly.

'Did you? Oh Mum, don't tell me you said no!' wailed Georgia.

'Of course I said no.' Claire made a face. 'It might be the most glorious summer of the decade, but how many times do we ever have a barbecue? Even when your dad was alive we probably only did it once. And that was only 'cos he wanted to do macho things with hot coals and steaks.'

'I think it's a shame,' said Georgia. 'This garden is just crying out for one.'

'I'll think about it,' said Claire.

'But it's too late now,' Georgia told her. 'Honestly, Mum, you could've consulted me about it.'

Claire laughed. 'I'll buy a gas one,' she said.

'It's not the same.'

'It'll have to do.'

She went into the kitchen and wrote a cheque for Nate, thanking him again for all the effort and assuring him that she couldn't have been happier about how things had turned out.

'I enjoyed it,' he said. 'It's a while since I've done something like this on my own. It was very therapeutic.'

'For me too,' said Claire softly. She looked out of the windows at the neatly trimmed lawn, the restored rockery, the shaped and tapered hedges and the patchwork of dazzling colour that was her flowerbeds. 'I used to feel sad when I looked at it. Now it lifts my spirits.'

'That's what all good gardens should do.' Nate smiled.

She turned to him. 'Thank you,' she said.

His blue and green eyes caught her look. She'd grown used to their odd colours and now, instead of feeling uncomfortable with them, she was mesmerised by the depth of the blue and the brilliance of the green. And she couldn't help thinking that his face was strong and determined rather than dour and angry as she'd once thought. She was conscious of his closeness to her and the warmth of his body – the scent of his body. Not sweaty from the heat of the sun and the work he'd done earlier, but musky, tinged with newly mown grass and warm earth. She wondered how he'd got the scar on his cheek. She wanted to touch it, trace it across his cheekbone and down to his jaw. She had to clench her fists together to stop herself reaching out to him.

She handed him the cheque wordlessly, wondering if his fingers would brush hers as he took it from her, totally at a loss to understand her feelings. Lust, she'd thought before, and yes, there was still lust. But an ache too. An ache of wanting someone, wanting something and not knowing exactly what it was. And knowing that Nate Taylor couldn't give it to her anyway.

He was still watching her as he folded the cheque and put it into the back pocket of his cargo pants. Her mouth was dry.

'Hey, Mum!' Georgia spun into the kitchen. 'Is it OK if Robs and I go to UCI this afternoon? She texted me to see if I can. But we'll come back here so's I can get my stuff together and her mum will pick us up for tonight.'

Claire felt the bubble in which she'd been suspended explode around her. She blinked and looked at her daughter.

'Huh?'

'Tonight. Me having a sleepover with Robs? So's you can stay out late for your big date! You hadn't actually forgotten, had you?' She rolled her eyes heavenwards.

'Of course I hadn't forgotten,' said Claire. 'And yes, you can go the cinema if you want to.'

'Great!' said Georgia, already rapidly sending a message back to her friend.

Claire cleared her throat. 'Are you sure you don't want to take your stuff with you and go directly to Robyn's?'

'Are you mad?' demanded Georgia. 'I'm not carting all that into the cinema with me. Besides . . .' she looked wickedly at Claire, 'I want to be here to see how you look.'

'Oh, for heaven's sake!' Claire knew she was snapping at Georgia but she couldn't help herself. 'I'm perfectly capable of getting dressed myself.'

Nate looked from one to the other.

'My mum is going on a date tonight,' Georgia confided. 'With a bloke she met at a party!'

'Lucky you,' said Nate. 'I'm sitting in with a bottle of beer and a pizza.'

'Sounds good to me,' said Claire tautly. She smiled briefly at him. 'Anyway, thanks again for everything.'

'Don't forget I'll be back to deal with your trees,' he said. 'It was already included in the price.'

'You'll have to come back all the time,' said Georgia. 'We've got used to you round the place. You can be our gardener.'

'Georgia! Really. That's not how Mr Taylor works.'

'I could,' said Nate, 'if you wanted. Come every two weeks or so?'

'We'll see.' Claire was flustered.

'Anyway, I'll go now.'

'Yes. Thanks.'

He went out to the garden again and gathered up his belongings then put them into a wheelbarrow and brought it to the front of the house.

'Be seeing you,' he said as he loaded it into the back of the green van.

'Be seeing you,' said Claire, and walked back into the house.

*　　*　　*

271

After Georgia had gone too, Claire sat in the garden, enjoying the scents of the flowers and the brightness of the colours but feeling forlorn at the thought that Nate Taylor wouldn't be back again at eight o'clock the following morning. I'm being ridiculous, she told herself. Utterly, stupidly, childishly ridiculous. And I don't know why, because I might have these lust-filled moments when I see him, but I really don't know him at all.

She closed her eyes and fell asleep. At first the dream was of Jamaica again and a part of her knew that this would be the horrible dream and didn't want to have it now. But instead of fading into the dread-filled moment where she stood on the balcony with Bill, she was suddenly walking along the twisting pathway through the hotel garden. And the gardener who was hacking at the enormous fronds of the coconut tree outside their room was Nate Taylor. As they walked by him, he handed her an orchid which Bill then tucked behind her ear.

A tiny fly landed on her cheek. She brushed it away and woke herself up. Her heart was thumping again, but not with the terror that the usual Jamaica dream brought. It was thumping with not knowing what would have happened next. And how the hell did Nate have an orchid in his hand, she muttered to herself as she rubbed her eyes, when he was supposed to be cutting a coconut tree?

It was five o'clock. She went into the kitchen and made herself a cup of pear tea. Then she sat down at the table and opened the newspaper. She'd barely read the first page when she heard Georgia's key in the lock and the two girls burst into the kitchen.

'Hi, Mum, it was a great movie!' cried Georgia enthusiastically.

'Really excellent, Mrs H,' agreed Robyn.

'Glad you enjoyed it. Would you two like anything to drink? Or are you maxed out on Coke and popcorn or some other rubbish?' she asked as she folded the paper.

'Any juice in the fridge?' Georgia was already opening it. She took two cartons from the shelf and handed one to Robyn. 'What time's your mum getting here?'

'Six,' said Robyn.

Georgia looked at her watch, and then at Claire. 'What time are you going out?' she asked.

'I'm meeting Gary at seven,' replied Claire.

'You'd better get your skates on,' said Robyn.

'Plenty of time,' Claire told her.

'What are you going to wear?' asked Georgia.

'I haven't decided yet.'

'Oh, Mum!' Georgia looked anxious. 'You'll be late, you know you will. How're you getting to the Point?'

'The bus to Amiens Street and then walk,' said Claire.

'It's a long walk!' cried Georgia. 'If you don't go soon you'll never make it.'

'I'm not going until Leonie calls for you.'

'I'll text her,' said Robyn. 'Make sure she gets here in plenty of time.'

'Meantime, you'd better change,' said Georgia.

'OK, OK.' Claire drained her tea and went upstairs.

Honestly, she thought, Georgia was getting far too bossy for her own good! She took her recently unearthed blue floral skirt (it wasn't one she'd worn much because it had always seemed a bit tight but was now perfect), white top and blue jacket out of the wardrobe and laid them on the bed. Then she went into the bathroom, washed her face, cleaned her teeth and dabbed on some tinted moisturiser. She changed into the skirt and jacket, sprayed herself with Kenzo and went downstairs again.

'OK?' she said.

Georgia looked at her gloomily. 'That's what you're wearing?'

'What's wrong with it?' asked Claire defensively.

'Well, you look like you're going to a meeting!' cried Georgia.

'I am,' said Claire. 'I'm meeting a man.'

'She means a business meeting, Mrs H,' said Robyn. 'It's a bit dull. And the colour isn't great.'

Claire frowned. 'This is a perfectly nice skirt,' she said. 'You bought me the top, Georgey, so you can't complain about that.'

'It's fine,' said Georgia, 'just not very sexy and hopelessly out of fashion.'

'I don't want to be sexy!' cried her mother.

'Of course you do,' objected Georgia. 'You're on a date.'

'I'm seriously worried about what you girls think constitutes the right get-up for a date,' said Claire dryly. 'And it's not that kind of date.'

'Well, what kind of date is it?' demanded Georgia. 'You're meeting a bloke, Mum. A bloke you don't really know. He's invited you out.'

'Yes, but that doesn't mean I have to dress like Christina Aguilera, for heaven's sake!'

Georgia and Robyn burst into a fit of giggles.

'OK, bad example,' conceded Claire. 'Nobody goes out dressed like Christina for any reason.'

'I know that it's not the same as normal people going for a date,' said Georgia seriously. 'All I'm saying, Mum, is that you should look as though you've made an effort.'

Claire remembered her night out with Paul and all the men and women on the bus who'd appeared to have made an effort. And that Paul had made an effort for her. She supposed that wearing a five-year-old skirt and jacket, even if she hadn't worn them for at least three, wasn't exactly a real effort.

'And what would making an effort entail?' she asked.

'Something livelier,' said Robyn. 'You know, something that says "I'm free and single and up for it".'

'Robyn O'Malley!'

Robyn and Georgia started to laugh again.

'It's not funny,' said Claire, although her mouth was beginning to twitch.

'All we're saying,' Georgia told her, 'is that you don't have to look like a nun who's been let out of the convent for the day.'

'I don't!' protested Claire.

'Maybe if you slapped on a bit more lippy, Mrs H . . .' suggested Robyn.

'That's it,' agreed Georgia. 'That blue makes you look really pale and uninteresting. Extra blusher and lippy would sort you out.'

'I don't need sorting out.' Claire was firm. 'I'm fine.'

The two girls looked unconvinced.

'What about your new skirts?' demanded Georgia.

'They're too casual,' protested Claire.

'OK, whatever,' said Georgia. She shrugged and then winked at

Robyn. 'Come on, Robs. Let's go to my den and watch TV until your mum gets here.'

'Right-ho.' Robyn nodded and the two girls trotted out of the kitchen.

Claire unfolded the paper again.

Leonie O'Malley picked them up on time and caused shrieks of joy by telling them that they'd be stopping off at their favourite Chinese on the way home because she didn't feel like cooking. She waved at Claire and told her to have a good time and then took off into the evening.

After they'd gone, Claire went up to her bedroom and stared at herself in the mirror. She didn't look pale and uninteresting. She looked like a normal woman going out for an evening. Not a thirty-something woman trying to look twenty-something. Just . . . well . . . normal. But maybe, she conceded, maybe a fraction dull. Perhaps that was why she'd shoved the skirt and jacket to the back of the wardrobe. Not because they were too small for her, just because they were too dull for her!

She sat down on the edge of the bed and thought for a moment. When she'd gone out with Bill (not bloody often enough, of course, because he was always knackered at the end of a day's surgery) she'd usually worn jeans and a T-shirt. Or jeans and a pretty top. If she was getting dressed up she'd wear one of her floral printed skirts instead of the jeans or, depending on how much effort she wanted to make, one of her tight-fitting dresses. When she did that she'd wear her hair up, which Bill always liked. The dresses, of course, also depended on how fat she was feeling at the time. Sometimes she felt like a version of the Michelin man with wodges of fat that would ripple down the side of the fabric and so they were impossible to wear. If she'd been on a crazy diet she might feel skinny enough to give them a go. She usually bought a dress whenever she was starting a diet to encourage her to keep going. They weren't really much of an encouragement, of course; more often they drove her to despair. But then on the occasions she could fit into them she felt wonderful.

She chewed on the inside of her lip as she looked through her clothes. She didn't have anything that was both dressy and casual at the same time. The closest was the scorched ochre silk with its tiny pattern in sapphire beading that she'd worn in Jamaica and any other time she felt skinny enough to squeeze into it. It was ancient but very beautiful and could be either dressed up or down depending on her accessories.

She slipped out of her skirt and top and slid the dress over her head. It fitted perfectly now, of course. Her hip bones stuck out from beneath the silk.

The memory came back to her like an arrow. Anniversary dinner. Cork. Incheydony. Bill had surprised her by taking her to the renowned spa, where she'd been massaged and kneaded and wrapped and scrubbed until she glowed. They'd had dinner in the restaurant overlooking the Atlantic Ocean and she'd worn the scorched ochre dress.

She wriggled out of it and hung it up. Then she took her favourite jeans out of the wardrobe and put them on along with a white T-shirt and a black leather jacket. She looked at herself again. Not entirely sexy, she thought. But thank God for jeans and T-shirts, which never went out of style.

Chapter 28

Cheiranthus (Wallflower) – Usually yellow, orange and red flowers on erect spikes. Plant firmly.

Crowds of people swirled around the Point and at first Claire was afraid she wouldn't be able to see Gary. In fact she was concerned that she wouldn't recognise him – after all, she knew his voice better than his face! But then she saw him, standing just inside the gates, dressed in casual trousers and a sea island cotton shirt, a navy blue jumper draped over his shoulders. He'd worked hard to look so casual, thought Claire. Suddenly she felt bad about choosing the jeans and T-shirt, even though she knew she looked OK in them. Maybe she should've worn the scorched ochre silk after all! God, she thought, this dressing up for going out is a complete nightmare.

Gary smiled in recognition as he caught sight of her, then kissed her lightly on the cheek and put his hand on her back to shepherd her through the queue. She felt positively grown-up as she stood beside him, in a way that she'd never felt with Bill. When she'd gone out with her husband they'd always been equals, friends of course, lovers certainly, but neither one of them dominating the other. Gary, on the other hand, took complete charge of the evening, ushering her into her seat, fussing over her and making sure that she was perfectly comfortable. It's nice to be looked after, thought Claire, although I'm not sure I could put up with someone being this attentive all the time. But, she told herself, that's only because it's our first date. She supposed that if she went out regularly with Gary he'd probably make her be the one to go back to the foyer for the programme or buy the drinks! She smiled inwardly as she made another mental note to keep for Georgia. They can be really, really charming but you have to ask yourself, will it last? Is it real?

Gary chatted to her as they waited for the show to start, talking about a project his firm was involved in and the problems they were having sourcing labour and materials. She listened attentively, feeling that it was important to him that she took an interest in his work. But she was glad when the music finally started – there was only so much she needed to know about pre-fabricated walls and the depth of foundations.

The production was superb. She cried at the end when Eliza went back to Professor Higgins, even though she knew that the George Bernard Shaw play on which it was based had ended differently – and probably more realistically, she thought wryly as she sniffed. Gary smiled at her and offered her a tissue.

'I have my own,' she said, rummaging in her bag.

'Just as well,' he told her. 'Because I only have a silk hanky and it's never actually been used.'

They laughed. She was enjoying herself. They moved outside with the rest of the crowds.

'Thank you,' she said as they stepped into the balmy evening air. 'That was really great.'

'Oh, there's more to come.'

She looked at him questioningly.

'Champagne,' he told her. 'And strawberries. Back in my apartment.'

This time she stared at him.

'It's a top-floor apartment,' he told her. 'The best in Dublin. We were the builders of the block. I have wonderful views over the city.'

'Sounds lovely,' she said. 'Your apartment, I mean. But I can't possibly go there.'

'Why not?' he asked.

She didn't know which reason to give him. That she thought the sound of chilling champagne already waiting for them was completely over the top; that it implied them sleeping together, which wasn't going to happen, because even if she wanted it – and she didn't – she'd still have to be home for Georgia the next morning; that there

278

was no way she could get to Dundrum anyway because it would mean being driven by someone there and back . . .

'It's really sweet of you,' she told him. 'But I'm not . . . not ready to go to your apartment.'

'Oh, come on, Claire!' He laughed. 'Of course you want to come back.'

'No,' she said. 'I don't.'

This time he stared at her. 'We're both adults,' he said. 'There's no big moral issue here.'

'It's nothing to do with morals,' said Claire. 'It's simply that I don't want to go to your place tonight.'

'Claire, I think you're a really attractive woman. I'd like you to come back with me.'

'I think you're very attractive too,' she told him. 'But there's no way.'

'No way!' He looked at her in amazement. 'We've had this great evening together and you're telling me no way?'

'Am I obliged to come back with you because of it?' She frowned. 'Am I? Is that one of the rules?'

'I seem to have got this all wrong,' said Gary. 'You were at the Dinner in the Dark. We held hands around the table. You talked about getting naked! And now – now you won't come home with me?'

'I didn't come home with you then either!' she cried spiritedly.

'I bought the best tickets in the house,' said Gary.

'Yes, well, you didn't buy me.' Claire turned away from him and began to walk quickly towards the gates.

'Claire! Claire!' He caught up with her. 'Wait.'

She turned to him.

'I'm sorry. Maybe I was a bit crass. I didn't mean to imply that you had to come home with me. I just thought – you'd want to.'

'No,' she said. 'I don't. I had a good time with you, but . . .' She bit her lip. 'I'm sorry, Gary. I really am. Maybe it's my fault. If I'm not prepared to quaff champagne and hop into bed with people then I shouldn't accept their invitations.'

'You're making me sound like a goddamn pimp,' he said angrily. 'I don't think there's anything wrong with assuming that a woman will want . . . will decide . . . for crying out loud, Claire, it's just sex!'

A group of people, hearing his raised voice, turned to look at them. Claire felt her face flush.

'Maybe it is,' she said. 'But it's not for me. I don't want to have sex with you, Gary. I do like you. I did have a great time tonight. But I'm not getting into bed with you.'

'I don't believe there are still women like you around the place,' he said. 'It wasn't a problem with Amy!'

Claire's hand flew to her mouth. She looked at him through wide eyes. 'You slept with Amy?'

'Sure I did,' he said. 'And we had a great time. She loved the champagne. She loved the strawberries. And she loved my apartment.'

'Well why the hell didn't you bring her out tonight?' demanded Claire.

'Because I like you too,' said Gary. 'I thought it would be fun. You were fun at the dinner.'

'Oh my God.' Times had changed, she thought. People didn't have exclusive relationships any more. There was nothing wrong with Gary wanting to go out with Amy and Claire and anyone else he chose. Though the idea of him sleeping with all of them bothered her. Maybe I'm just too old-fashioned, she thought wryly.

'You think there's something wrong with that?'

She shook her head. 'Actually, I suppose not. Grown-ups and all that sort of thing. I'm sorry, Gary. I'm obviously not that grown-up.'

'No wonder your husband headed off,' he said tersely.

Claire said nothing. She'd told them at the Dinner in the Dark that she had been married and had dismissed a comment from Cormac about the fact that she still wore a wedding ring. She hadn't told them about Bill's accident. So when they'd assumed she was divorced or separated she hadn't enlightened them. But now she wished she'd told the truth, so that Gary couldn't possibly think that Bill had left her.

'I'm going now,' she told him as she opened her bag and took out some money. 'Here's my share for tonight.'

'Oh, don't be silly.' He looked at her in resignation.

'No, really,' she said, holding the notes out to him. 'I hate to think that you're out of pocket.'

'Forget it,' he said. 'I misread the situation. I thought you'd be up for it, Claire. It's fine. No problem.' He turned from her and walked to the rows of parked cars.

Claire slid the money back into her purse. She'd misread the situation too. She'd agreed to the date partly because, having learned how difficult it was to actually ask someone out, she didn't feel able to refuse; partly because she thought she might find out more stuff for Georgia; and partly because she wanted her daughter to see her as a strong person who could go out with new people. She'd been shaken by Georgia's admission that she believed she had to show strength for Claire's sake. If she went out with other men, Claire thought, Georgia would surely think she was over Bill and wouldn't feel as though she had to watch over her.

She sighed deeply. It seemed to her that she did things with the best of intentions but somehow they never turned out quite as she expected. And whoever would've thought that Gary – possibly the least attractive of the men round the table – had already bedded Amy! Claire wondered whether or not he was working his way through all the girls he'd met that night. She giggled. It was funny when she thought about it in the abstract, even though not quite so amusing when you were the next on his list.

It seemed a longer walk back to the bus stop than from it. Fortunately there were a lot of people heading in the same direction, as Claire suddenly realised that this area of the city was quiet after dark. She walked along the quayside, watching the reflection of the old-fashioned streetlights ripple in the murky waters of the Liffey.

God, she thought, I'm such a fool. And Eavan was right. I can't go out with men just because I want to see what it's like! Or just because I want to appear strong and resilient to my daughter. They *do* want more. And even if not all of them would want me to hop into bed with them like Gary, it isn't fair to go out with them under false pretences.

She bit her lip. Had going out with Gary been going out with someone under false pretences? Had she done it to find out about men for Georgia, like she'd promised herself, or because she'd been flattered and secretly pleased that he'd asked her? Of course he'd

281

asked someone else too! He'd asked Amy. And Amy had slept with him, which was what he'd really wanted all along.

Maybe she would have felt differently if Oliver had done the asking out. She couldn't help wanting to know Oliver better because he was so damn good-looking, even if she had chickened out by leaping on to the bus after the dinner. But it seemed to Claire that she really wasn't in control of how she felt about anything any more. On the one hand she couldn't bear the idea of anyone but Bill having a place in her life. On the other . . . on the other, her body seemed to be telling her that it wasn't a crime to want someone else.

Maybe it was just some kind of physical need inside of her that had been dormant for the last three years. Perhaps, unknown to herself, she was turning into a sex-starved nymphomanic.

Her body or her mind? She wished she damn well knew which was right!

Oh get a grip, she muttered under her breath. You weren't a nympho with Bill. You had a good sex-life. A fulfilling one. But you didn't need to jump his bones every day! You don't need to do it now to complete strangers either. For any damn reason.

There was nobody at the bus stop. She glanced at her watch and wondered whether she had missed the last one. It was after half past eleven. She couldn't remember what time the last bus left. She looked around her uncertainly. The idea of walking home didn't really bother her, but she was tired.

A taxi drove by, its yellow sign bright on the roof. She swallowed hard. Could she do it? Could she get a taxi on her own? If she was feeling more light-hearted about life, if things didn't seem too awful any more, surely she'd be able to get into a taxi? But the first panic attack had happened in a taxi. They still happened in cars. So what would she do if she was gripped with panic again? All the same, the journey was less than ten minutes at this hour of the night. She'd be home before she knew it.

Another taxi drove by. And another.

Come on, Claire, she urged herself. If Georgia can put up with horrible boys calling her names, you can get into a goddamn taxi! She raised her arm and the next cab pulled in beside her. She opened the door. The whiff of a pine-scented air-freshener assailed her. There had been a pine-scented air-freshener in the Jamaican taxi. She felt prickles of sweat on the back of her neck. Less than ten minutes, she told herself. Maybe only five. Five minutes was nothing.

She got into the back seat and gave her address to the driver. She closed the door. The smell was overwhelming. It seemed to wrap itself around her, clinging to her. She felt her heart beat faster. She closed her eyes and gripped tight to the arm-rest.

She could hear the taxi-driver saying something to her but she had no idea what it was. She thought she might have grunted an answer at him but she wasn't sure. The sweat was rolling down her back now and into the V between her breasts. Her palms were wet against the arm-rest. I can't stay in here, she thought wildly. I just can't!

'Here you are.'

She realised that they'd stopped. She opened her eyes. They were outside her house.

'Thanks.' She pushed open the car door and stood outside on the pavement as she fumbled with her purse.

'I'd have killed you if you'd been sick in my cab,' the driver told her. 'Honest to God, woman, you'd think you'd have more sense.'

He thought she was drunk. She almost laughed at the idea.

'All this binge bloody drinking,' said the taxi-driver. He took the notes from her and rummaged in the coin tray for change.

'It's OK,' she said. 'That's fine.'

'Thanks.'

She knew she'd overtipped him but she didn't care. She hurried up the garden path and let herself into the house. She wished that Georgia wasn't sleeping over at Robyn's tonight. She wished that there was someone with her now, someone to tell her she wasn't a stupid woman who hadn't a clue about life.

She went into the kitchen and made herself a cup of tea. Phydough, who was sleeping in his basket, opened one eye and then closed it again. Poor old Gary, she thought, as her heartbeat slowed down and the feeling of dizziness passed. A bottle of champagne waiting at home and no one to drink it with! Not really poor old Gary, of course. He'd probably just call Amy. Or Stella.

She emptied the dregs of the tea into the sink and rinsed the cup

283

before leaving it on the drainer. She went into the hall and set the alarm. As she keyed in the numbers she noticed that the red light of her answering machine was flashing.

Hell, she thought, I hope Georgey wasn't looking for me. But Georgia would've called on the mobile, and although she'd set it to silent in the theatre she would have known if it was ringing.

She pressed Play on the answering machine.

'Hi, Claire,' said the voice. 'This is Oliver Ramsey. I was wondering if . . . if you'd care to come to the theatre with me? I've tickets for *My Fair Lady* next week. You mentioned that you liked musicals. Let me know. Thanks. Goodbye.'

Chapter 29

Cerastium (Snow-in-Summer) – A carpet of white flowers that can spread quickly and choke out nearby plants.

The following Tuesday Glenn and Saffy were curled up on the sofa watching cartoons when Eavan walked in the door. Glenn looked up at her and Eavan smiled uncertainly.

'How'd it go?' he asked.

'Well . . . sort of good,' she replied.

'Oh?'

'They offered me a job.' Eavan's tone was apologetic. 'I mean, it's not a great job or anything, Glenn, it's mainly book-keeping stuff and the salary isn't anything to write home about, but it's a start.'

Glenn said nothing. Eavan held her breath.

She'd received a phone call that morning in response to a e-mailed CV she'd sent to a DIY store on the industrial estate a few miles away. She'd spotted the ad on an internet jobs page and reckoned that it would be worth her while replying. She'd been hoping that the news from Locum Libris would be positive, but Claire had phoned at the weekend to tell her that at the moment it didn't look like there was anything doing in her old company. Eavan kept her disappointment to herself – doing work for Locum Libris at home would've been ideal.

Hearing that they didn't have anything had shaken her, because from the moment Glenn had told her of his departure from Trontec she'd held on to the belief that she could make everything all right by simply working for Trinny and Joe again. After all, it had happened for Claire. Realising that she couldn't just step back into the job had been disconcerting. And so she'd looked up other jobs on the internet, telling herself that anything would do. At the same time she was hoping that something would come up for Glenn – he'd shown her the list of places that had his CV and she was even more shocked (though she tried to hide it) at how many companies he'd contacted and how many didn't have anything for him.

The DIY store had been the first interview she'd done. Looking at the expression on Glenn's face now, she felt guilty that they'd offered her the job.

'Full time?' he asked.

She nodded. 'Ordinary office hours.'

'And what about Saffy?' he asked.

'What about me?' Saffy stood up on the sofa and beamed at Eavan.

Eavan handed her the lollipop she'd bought on her way out of the store (she really disliked the way they put sweets at the checkouts; such a nightmare for parents) and Saffy took it in delight.

'While you're at home you can look after her,' said Eavan. 'Once you get something else, we'll see.'

'When do you start?'

'Next week,' said Eavan.

'What's the salary?'

Eavan told him and he looked at her thoughtfully. 'That's not too bad, is it?'

'Well, I guess they needed someone quickly and they were prepared to pay a bit more . . .'

'You were quite senior when you chucked in your job before,' he said. 'You were well paid.'

'Oh, it was easy to become senior in Locum Libris,' said Eavan dismissively. 'I was there for years!'

'You *wanted* to give it up, though, didn't you? You were the one who asked, even though you always said you had an interesting job.'

Eavan sighed. 'This is a completely different job. Not as senior. Not as interesting. And I'm sure it's only temporary.'

'But you're stuck doing it because of me.'

'Oh, for God's sake!' She tried to keep the exasperation out of her voice. 'Glenn, these things happen. They really do. To everyone.

So please, please, please stop being so miserable about it. You will get another job. You know you will.'

She sat down in the armchair opposite. 'In the meantime . . .' She moistened her lips, '. . . in the meantime there's an estate agent coming to look at the house tomorrow.'

Glenn looked at her speechlessly while Eavan told him once again that as far as she was concerned she couldn't feel the same about the house ever again and that it was much better to take the money for it and run than try to kill themselves by keeping it. And she told him that as far as she was concerned they were partners, not rivals, so she didn't want him obsessing about the fact that she'd got a job and he hadn't because he was a specialist whereas she just turned her hand to any old thing. It was, she said, one of the great benefits of being a female. People offered you jobs and didn't expect you to try and rob theirs once you got into the place. When she finished talking she looked defiantly at him.

'You're right,' he said eventually. 'Right about everything. Which is a real pain, because you always want to be right.'

She said nothing.

'And if you're the one who has to get up at the crack of dawn and go to work for a few months while I spend some quality time with my daughter, that's fine by me. It really is.'

'I know it's not easy,' she said.

'It's not easy because my ego is in bits,' he admitted. 'But you're right. I can't just think of me. I have to think of all of us. And if this works for all of us . . .' He shrugged.

'Great.' She got up from the armchair and kissed him. Then she went upstairs and took off her jacket. She leaned her head against the bedroom wall. Please, she prayed silently. Please let him get something soon.

Georgia and Claire had gone to visit Eileen in Dundalk. Because she was getting ready to move, even though it would be a few more weeks before the contracts were finalised, the house already had an air of neglect about it.

'I'm not neglecting it!' cried Eileen in response to Claire's comment. 'It's just that I'm not killing myself keeping it up to scratch.

It's strange, but it doesn't feel like my house any more, and it's actually quite odd still being here when I know there are other people plotting and planning to change things in it.'

Claire nodded in understanding.

'Why don't you move out now?' asked Georgia.

'Because the apartment isn't ready yet,' Eileen told her. 'Actually the whole thing is being precision-timed – they're due to move in almost the day I'm due to move out.' She made a face. 'Only thing is, they keep calling round to take measurements and stuff like that. It's driving me crazy.'

'Well why don't you stay with us for a while?' asked Georgia.

Eileen glanced at Claire. 'I really don't think your mum and I could live in the same house for any length of time.'

'Why not?' demanded Georgia. 'It's not like you hate each other, is it?'

'No,' said Eileen. 'But it's different when two adults are living under the same roof. Your mum has her way of doing things and I have mine, and we might get on each other's nerves.'

'You wouldn't get on anyone's nerves,' declared Georgia.

Eileen laughed.

'She has a point,' said Claire. 'Come and visit for a while. You don't have to stay until everything is completed if you don't want to. In any event we're only talking about a few weeks at the most. What makes you think I can't put up with you for a few weeks?'

'Yeah, Gran, you could stay in my room and I can move down to the den,' said Georgia. 'I don't sleep in it on my own usually 'cos it's in the basement and Mum sleeps near the top of the house and it feels like miles away even though it isn't really – but if you're staying, that's different.'

'We'll see,' said Eileen. 'Thank you, Claire. And Georgia.'

'Anyway, I can have Robyn over for a few more sleepovers if I'm downstairs,' said Georgia. 'We had great fun last Saturday night. We watched movies for ages.'

'I know,' said Claire drily. 'You were supposed to be in bed.'

'Yeah, right.' Georgia giggled. Claire laughed too.

Eileen looked at her daughter and her granddaughter with affection. Both of them were looking well, she thought. Georgia, especially, with the new haircut and summer tan, appeared both healthy and attractive. Claire also looked a good deal healthier than the last time she'd seen her. And less stressed. Though there was still a reflection of pain in her eyes. Eileen wondered whether it would ever leave her.

'Did Mum tell you about her date?' asked Georgia mischievously.

'Oh, did you go?' Eileen looked at Claire. 'An old friend, you told me.'

'Ah, Gran, you're way behind the times,' said Georgia. 'You're thinking about Paul, aren't you?'

'There's more?'

'Way more!' Georgia's eyes gleamed. 'You've no idea!'

'Claire?'

'Honestly, Georgey, you're such a stirrer.' Claire tucked a curl behind her ear and made a face at her. 'I went out with the girls from work, Mum. And then a guy asked me out and I went.'

'Claire!'

'She hasn't told you what it was all about,' said Georgia. 'Go on, Mum.'

So Claire told Eileen about the Dinner in the Dark and her subsequent date with Gary. She didn't, however, mention the champagne and strawberries, merely telling her mother (as she'd already told Georgia) that she'd had a good time but that she doubted she'd see Gary again because he just wasn't her kind of guy.

'And have you heard from any of the others?' Eileen was absolutely astounded that Claire had gone to the dinner in the first place. She would never have imagined it as anything her daughter would do.

'This is what's so amazing,' Georgia said before Claire could speak. 'She's going out with another one tomorrow night! Can you believe it, Gran? I mean, I'm the one who should really be having loads of blokes, but Mum is attracting them like bees to honey.'

'Georgia!' Claire flushed a deep crimson.

'So do you think this man is more your type of guy?' asked Eileen. 'What's his name?'

'Oliver,' said Claire.

'She met him before,' explained Georgia. 'He came to get rid of a wasps' nest when I was in Galway. Mum says he's gorgeous!'

'Is he?'

Claire squirmed. 'He's very attractive,' she admitted. 'But honestly, you guys, it's just a coincidence that he asked me out.'

'Coincidence my eye!' exclaimed Georgia. 'I think she's working her way through them all.'

Just like Gary, thought Claire.

'And how about you?' asked Eileen, looking at Georgia. 'How's your love-life?'

Georgia blushed and Claire laughed. 'Her text-life, more like. Though who were those boys I saw you and Robyn walking down the road with on Sunday afternoon?'

'They're in her music class,' said Georgia. 'They're just guys.' She blushed again. She hadn't realised that Claire had seen them on Sunday. Sam and Denzil were nice blokes but they were just friends. Not like Steve. Steve. She closed her eyes and conjured up his face.

His last text had been full of how shitty life was at home. His father had gone to England for a couple of weeks and his mother was busy writing her book about Celtic mythology. She didn't even notice that he was working the graveyard shift at the leisure centre. She didn't actually notice him at all. He couldn't wait to get back to school. He was fed up with the long holidays. Two months was ridiculous. Nobody else in the world got two months' holidays.

Georgia had texted him back to beg him to come up to town on his next day off. They could meet for coffee, she told him. Spend a day together. He'd texted back to say that he didn't actually have a day off for a while. But that he'd seriously consider it. Which had made Georgia feel warm inside.

Chapter 30

Alchemilla (Lady's Mantle) – Branching sprays of tiny flowers, commonly yellow-green. Self-sown seedlings can be troublesome.

Georgia sat on the double bed and watched as Claire made up her face for her second trip to see *My Fair Lady*. She'd cracked up with laughter when Claire told her where she was going, telling her that she was plain silly for not admitting to Oliver that she'd seen it already. And then she'd made wide eyes at Claire and wondered aloud whether it wasn't because Oliver was so totally hunky that she didn't mind where she went with him.

'It's not like that at all,' said Claire as she brushed her hair. 'I didn't want to embarrass him by saying that I'd seen it. I was afraid he'd think I was just making excuses.'

'I always thought you were meant to be honest with blokes,' said Georgia.

'Honesty *is* best,' admitted Claire, 'but . . .'

'Were you always honest with Dad?'

Claire put her brush on the dressing table and considered Georgia's question.

'I was honest with him about the major things,' she said after a moment. 'I was always honest about how I felt, or what I thought was best for us as a family.'

'But you weren't about everything?'

'Well . . .'

'What?' Georgia's eyes gleamed. 'C'mon, Mum. What did you tell him whopping great fibs about?'

'Minor little white lies,' amended Claire. 'About . . . well, remember how he loved wearing baseball caps? Backwards? He thought it was so cool. But he looked really daft. And I always said that I loved the liqueur chocs he used to buy for my birthday – actually I hated them, but we were once given some by one of his medical mates and I said they were really gorgeous and then, months later, Bill produced them for my birthday as an extra present and I couldn't say that I hated them because he'd gone to so much trouble.' She paused for a moment, then continued. 'I pretended that I liked sci-fi movies because he loved going to them so much but wouldn't go on his own but how many times can you watch someone save the planet from total destruction? *And* I allowed him to keep buying me all those Dior scented bath things which he thought went with my Chanel perfume – he didn't know that I'd switched from Dior and I didn't bother telling him.'

'Mum!' Georgia looked at her in astonishment. 'You were supposed to be soulmates! You were supposed to know everything about each other.'

'We did, in things that mattered,' said Claire. 'We knew what made each other happy or sad; we knew when to talk and when to keep quiet; we knew how to enjoy each other's company. Those were the soulmate things. The other stuff was incidental.'

'I dunno.' Georgia sounded sceptical. 'I think that blokes should definitely know what perfume you wear.'

Claire laughed. 'I did wear the Dior for ages. But men are creatures of habit, Georgey. They discover something you like and they keep on and on giving it to you. They discover something they like and they go on and on about it until you want to hit them! It doesn't make you love them any less.'

'You sound like you had to put up with him!' cried Georgia.

'I loved putting up with him.' Claire grinned at her in the mirror. 'And those things are so minor that they don't really matter. You adapt with someone else too, I suppose. I love cucumber but Bill hated it so I never put it in salads. He liked food a bit spicier than I do but he accepted that if I made a curry it wasn't going to have him dousing out the flames in his mouth. That's what happens when you marry someone.'

'So what about this Oliver bloke?' demanded Georgia. 'What do you think about him?'

292

Claire looked shamefacedly at her daughter.

'I want to go out with him,' she admitted, 'because he's a good-looking bloke and because he was sort of sweet at the dinner thingy.'

Georgia stared at the floor.

'It's all very casual.' Claire sensed that her daughter wasn't entirely happy with her answer.

'What if you fall in love with him?'

'Would you mind?'

'I don't know.' Georgia twisted a strand of hair furiously between her fingers. 'I don't know him.'

'It'd be ages before I fell in love with him,' said Claire. 'And he'd have to fall in love with me too, which I honestly think is very unlikely.' She fastened her chain around her neck. 'Oh, Georgey, I don't know! What I do know is that no one will ever replace your dad. But I can see that people have a point when they say that I'm not going out enough. So I suppose if I've got to go out it might as well be with someone gorgeous.'

Georgia took a piece of paper out of her pocket. 'How does he rate on my boyfriend list?' she asked.

'He's not a boyfriend!'

Georgia looked at her pityingly.

'Read me the qualifications again,' said Claire.

'Reasonably good-looking – no facial hair or hair on his back and not too much hair on his chest.'

'You have a thing about hairy men?' asked Claire.

'I don't like blokes with hair on their back.' Georgia shivered. 'Looks gross. But you've already said that Oliver is attractive, so that bit's OK.'

'I said he looked like Becks,' Claire said. 'He doesn't have a beard.'

'Becks has a bit of face fluff from time to time.'

'Oliver definitely hasn't,' Claire said.

'Clean,' read Georgia. 'Fingernails especially. And ears.'

'I don't know,' said Claire. 'He seemed to have cleaned up pretty well to me.'

'Not patronising.' Georgia looked up. 'You can't deal with this one 'cos I haven't met him yet. But if he's one of those blokes who

293

heaves a sigh every time someone younger than him makes a point, then forget it.'

'I've taken note of that,' said Claire seriously.

'Money?' Georgia looked hopeful.

'It was a busy year for wasps' nests,' Claire told her. 'It took ages before he could get to the house because he had so many to do. But I can't honestly see it being a huge fortune-builder somehow.'

'OK,' said Georgia. 'We'll put the money thing to one side.' She frowned, then looked at Claire again. 'Kids?'

'I don't know,' said Claire. 'It wasn't a conversation we had.'

'I suppose not,' Georgia acknowledged. 'Would you like more kids, Mum?'

Claire blinked a couple of times. Georgia didn't know that she'd lost a brother or sister in the accident. Claire hadn't thought that it was something she could cope with. She still didn't think it was something Georgia could cope with. She knew that keeping things from her wasn't ideal, but Georgia had muttered about everything being all her fault before and Claire definitely didn't want her thinking that losing the baby had been her fault too.

'Your father and I did want more kids,' she said eventually.

'But would you go out with a bloke who had them?' asked Georgia. 'Would you want to marry a bloke who had them?'

'Georgey, honey, I don't want to marry anyone!' exclaimed Claire. 'I'm going out for a spot of socialising but that's all. I'm not looking to marry and set up a whole new family.'

'I dunno about the kids,' said Georgia. 'I mean, let's say you got married and he had two or three – I'd be outnumbered then, wouldn't I? So I'd always be stuck on my own.'

Claire looked at her daughter's anxious face. She came over and sat on the bed beside her, then put her arms around her and hugged her.

'Goose,' she said.

'I know,' mumbled Georgia as she leaned against Claire's shoulder.

'Anyway,' said Claire, 'I doubt if Oliver has any kids.'

'Interests.' Georgia pulled away from Claire and looked at her list again.

'Food,' said Claire. 'He talked a lot about the meal that night.

294

Music, obviously, if he's taking me to a musical. And theatre too, I suppose.'

'Boring,' said Georgia. 'He's not a bit gay, is he?'

'A bit gay?' Claire laughed. 'How can you be a bit gay?'

'You know, sort of theatre-ish and over the top.'

'I don't think so.' Claire chuckled.

'Does he like sport?'

'Dunno.'

'He'd have to, for you to like him,' said Georgia. 'You watch more sport than anything else on telly. Robs says that's weird for a mother, it's usually the fathers who're glued to *Grandstand* or whatever.'

'I like sport,' said Claire. 'I like competition.'

'Hmm.' Georgia looked at the list and then at her mother again. 'Car?' She said this very doubtfully.

'He has one but I don't know what make.'

'But you'll never get into it,' said Georgia.

'I'm trying about that,' said Claire. 'I really am. I got a taxi home the night I went out with Gary.'

'Did you?' Georgia looked at her in astonishment. 'I didn't realise. I thought you must've got the last bus.'

Claire shook her head.

'So is Oliver picking you up?'

'No,' said Claire. 'I told him I'd meet him there. I didn't want to arrive like a wreck.'

'Poor Mum.' This time it was Georgia who hugged Claire.

'Ah, I'm fine,' said Claire. 'And I'd better get a move on. What time is Robyn coming?'

Georgia glanced at her watch. 'She should be here any minute.'

'Well, I want you two to behave yourselves,' said Claire. 'I'll be home by midnight at the absolute latest.'

'We'll be good,' promised Georgia. 'I won't raid your stash of illegal substances or anything.'

'Very funny,' said Claire. 'C'mon, Ms Hudson, I'd better finish fixing my face.'

'You should wear a darker lipstick,' Georgia told her as she watched.

'I always wear pink,' said Claire.

'But it's drab. Hang on a minute.'

295

She got up from the bed, went into her own room and returned with a lipstick which she handed to her mother.

'Try this.'

Claire applied it and looked at herself in the mirror.

'Much better,' Georgia assured her. 'Definitely.'

The door bell rang.

'Robs!' Georgia clattered down the stairs.

Claire looked at her reflection in the mirror again. Then she added another coat of Georgia's lipstick to her lips.

Oliver Ramsey looked after her every bit as well as Gary had done. And the show was equally good, if less enthralling second time around. But she still sniffed at Eliza's return, even though Oliver didn't appear to notice. People noticed him, though. Claire watched as people saw him and did a double-take as they realised his likeness to the football star. She decided that it must be very hard work being a famous person and always having to look good. It would be impossible for anyone in the public eye to date a person who wasn't equally gorgeous, she thought, because otherwise they'd crack up under the strain.

Oliver asked her if she'd like to stroll down to the hotel for a drink after the performance. They'd hardly had time to talk before the show because Claire had managed to miss the bus and had arrived with only minutes to spare, so that she was flushed and panting from having run along the street.

'It'll have to be quick,' she told him as she glanced at her watch. 'I promised my daughter and her friend that I'd be home before midnight.'

'No problem,' said Oliver.

He linked his arm with hers. Better than holding hands, she thought. But weird all the same. It suggested a closeness that wasn't there. Yet it was comforting to be walking along the quays with someone. And nice to be part of a couple instead of a woman hurrying home on her own. The only thing was that she felt that she wasn't glamorous enough for someone like Oliver – despite her efforts with the lipstick. He really could've done with a supermodel on his arm.

They walked into the hotel bar and she sat down in one of the trendy but not very comfortable armchairs. She ordered a white wine, while Oliver had a beer.

'Thanks again for tonight,' she said. 'I really enjoyed it.'

He flicked his hair behind his ear. 'Me too,' he told her.

They sat in silence. Funny, she thought. The silence at the Dinner in the Dark had been mildly erotic. The silence between them now was strained.

'How're the wasps?' she asked.

'Still there,' he said. 'Lots of big nests.'

'How did you get into it as a business?' she asked.

'Family,' he said succinctly. 'I studied horticulture at college and worked at it for a while, but the business was there and so . . .'

She nodded.

'Of course I have thought about the celebrity-lookalike scene,' he told her, his voice brightening. 'Maybe move to the UK and earn a few bob opening supermarkets and things like that.'

She looked at him sceptically. 'You wouldn't, would you?'

'If the money was right. The pest extermination business will always be there. My brother is involved too.'

'And does he look like a footie star too?'

Oliver shook his head. 'But he's reasonably good-looking. When he was a kid he was used in an advertising campaign for one of the chain stores. Everywhere you looked there were pictures of him wearing a green fleece and jumping into a pile of autumn leaves.'

'And did you do any child modelling?' asked Claire.

'No,' said Oliver. 'They thought my face wasn't strong enough.'

'Huh!'

'I don't think Becks has a particularly strong face either,' he said.

'Maybe not. But he makes the most of what he's got.' She grinned. 'So do you. I like that wavy hairdo.'

'I take pride in my appearance,' said Oliver. 'Lots of guys don't. I think it's important to look good.'

She nodded.

'So do you think I'd make it?'

She stared at him. 'Make what?'

'The world of modelling?'

'Sorry?'

'You said you were a talent scout.' He looked at her accusingly. 'Were you really spoofing everyone?'

'Oh God, Oliver – I didn't think anyone took that seriously!'

'I was told not to take it seriously. But I couldn't help wondering . . .'

'I'm sorry,' she said. 'I didn't mean to mislead you.'

'I'd love a crack at it.' His voice was wistful. 'Just to see what it'd be like. Make a change from having to dress up in a damn spacesuit and squirt chemicals around the place.'

'I'm sorry,' said Claire again.

'You don't know anyone in the industry?' He looked at her hopefully.

She shook her head. 'I was joking,' she told him. 'Honestly.'

'Oh well.' He sighed. 'Nate told me that I was barking up the wrong tree, but I said that I had to be sure.'

Claire stared at him. 'You asked Nate Taylor about me? Why?'

'It was because of him you rang me,' Oliver reminded her. 'So I thought he might know more about you. And he was doing your garden. I asked him whether it was possible.'

'And he said?' Claire's voice was incredulous.

'He said that you worked from home but that he didn't know doing what. You spent a lot of time locked in your office. You walked the dog every day and that was pretty much that. You could, he said, be a scout but he really didn't think so. He said you had been married to a doctor and it seemed highly unlikely that the media world and the medical world would come together like that.'

'I can't believe you were discussing me with Nate.' Claire flushed at the thought.

'Look, if it makes you feel uncomfortable, I apologise. It was an opportunity to find out about you, that's all. You intrigued me at the dinner.'

'Because you thought I was a talent scout?'

'Yes.' He looked sheepish.

'And tonight was to find out for sure?'

'Well . . .' He looked even more sheepish. 'I guess so.'

'Why the hell didn't you just ask me on the phone?'

'Because you might have lied to me. You might have actually been a scout only not thought I had the right look. And you'd think that I'd keep harassing you.'

'Oliver, you know that you're being totally ridiculous, don't you?' Claire drained her wine. 'If I was a scout searching for new faces – or even faces that look like current or past-it football stars – I wouldn't have pretended. I'd have given you a card and told you to get some photos taken.'

'You might have wanted to suss me out,' he explained.

'Maybe that really is how things work out in LaLa land,' she told him. 'I've no bloody idea.' She stood up. 'I'd better go.'

'Hang on, Claire,' he said. 'Don't rush off in a rage or anything.'

'I'm not raging,' she said. 'I'm amused. A bit peeved, I guess. But it's fine. Don't worry.'

'I'll drive you home,' he said.

'It's OK,' she said. 'I'll get home myself.'

'Oh, Claire, I didn't mean to upset you.'

'I'm not upset,' she said. 'Truly. Honestly. Not one bit. I hope that you manage to find fame and fortune, if that's what you're looking for. And if not that the pest extermination business goes from strength to strength.'

She walked out of the hotel and into the cooler night air. Despite her protestations to Oliver she *was* a little upset. Eavan had warned her against using men but hadn't warned her against them using her. And, in the end, out of two dates from Dinner in the Dark that was pretty much what had happened. One guy had just wanted sex. Another just wanted to be famous. Neither of them really wanted her. Or maybe, she thought ruefully, maybe they knew that I didn't really want them either, no matter how much I might have pretended to myself.

Chapter 31

Helianthus (Annual Sunflower) – Yellow, orange or red blooms. Can grow up to 3m. Feed weekly.

Two weeks later, and a few days before Georgia went back to school, Eileen moved in to Claire's house.

'It's only for a fortnight or so,' she assured Claire, 'and then I'll be out of your hair.'

'Stay as long as you need,' said Claire, although she wasn't entirely sure how the arrangement would work out. Suddenly, with her mother living in her house, she felt like a daughter again, as though Eileen was the person to whom she should defer before making any decisions. She felt as though her mother was watching her all the time, seeing how she did things and assessing how good she was at running her house and being a parent. She knew that this wasn't really the case, but she couldn't help feeling as though she were sitting a motherhood exam with Eileen as the examiner.

On the third day she was tackling another one of her Everest-style piles of ironing (how, she wondered, did it all keep piling up like this?) when the doorbell rang. Eileen, who'd been sitting in the back garden enjoying the weather, which was still incredibly mild, got up to answer it.

'I was going to,' objected Claire.

'Nonsense,' said Eileen. 'You're busy.'

That was another thing, Claire thought. Eileen obviously felt as though she had to keeping doing things, like stacking the dishwasher or offering to nip down to the shops for the papers (not realising that Claire had hers delivered every morning) or emptying the rubbish bins. Claire wished that her mother would just sit down and relax, but she supposed that the older woman found it difficult. After all, she'd run her own house for most of her adult life. Maybe relaxing didn't come easy.

'A visitor for you.' Eileen looked at Claire with interest as Nate Taylor followed her into the kitchen. Phydough, who'd been asleep in his basket, woofed in greeting and Nate tickled him under the chin.

'Oh, Nate, hello.' Claire felt her colour rise. 'Nice to see you. What can I do for you?'

'I brought you a present,' said Nate.

'A present?' She looked at him in confusion. 'What sort of present?'

'Remember you were looking for a thermometer for the wall?' he said. 'But you didn't like the wrought-iron ones?'

She remembered, though it hadn't been a major issue. She'd spoken of it in passing as something she'd get sometime. She nodded.

'These came in the other day and I thought you'd like one.' He handed her a box. The thermometer was in the shape of a large sunflower, the mercury rising through the stem.

'It's lovely,' she said. 'Really gorgeous. How much do I owe you?'

'It's a present,' Nate reminded her. 'You don't owe me anything.'

'I can't take gifts from you,' said Claire. 'It wouldn't be right.'

'You paid me a lot of money for doing the garden,' Nate said. 'It's the least I can do.'

'Oh, but—'

'Claire!' He interrupted her gently. 'Stop! It's a present. From Sarah and from me. For saving my life!'

'Oh, well . . .' Claire shrugged. 'I suppose – well, thanks.'

'Do you want me to fit it for you now?'

'If you like,' she said.

'You go out and watch him fit it,' said Eileen. 'I'll finish the ironing.'

'Don't be silly, Mum,' said Claire. 'I can do it.'

'Oh, go on.' Eileen sounded impatient. 'I'm bored anyway.'

Claire frowned and looked at her mother, who shrugged and smiled amiably.

'Come on then,' she said to Nate. 'Let's find a spot.'

'This is still a sun-trap,' he said as he walked out on to the patio. 'It's been such a wonderful summer it's a shame to think it's beginning to slip away.'

'Might make me work a bit harder,' observed Claire. 'I find it really difficult to be indoors when the sun is shining. Um – I think here would be just right.' She pointed at a spot on the wall.

'OK.' Nate took a power-drill from the box he was carrying. 'So how have you been?'

'Fine,' said Claire. She was conscious that her heart was beating faster again. And that Nate Taylor, dressed today in a green polo shirt with 'Taylor's Flowers & Gardens' neatly embossed on the front, was looking as attractive as ever. Why? she wondered. Why do I feel like this about him? Why do I just want to have sex with him?

As the thought hit her, she felt dizzy. She didn't want to have sex with him! How could she even think such a thing? She didn't want to have sex with anyone! She couldn't possibly, when the only thing she really wanted was to be able to make love to Bill Hudson one last time. Having sex was a completely different thing. And it wasn't on her agenda. At all. Least of all with someone else's husband.

'How's Sarah?' Her voice was croaky.

'Not bad.' Nate drilled two holes into the wall with easy precision. 'Very busy, which is great.'

'And you?' she asked. 'No more anaphylactic shocks?'

He grinned. 'Thankfully not. I'm steering well clear of peanut butter.'

Claire smiled too. The thing is, she thought, he's easy to know. She wondered how that could be when he'd been so difficult at first. Rude and nasty and not very pleasant. Yet ever since he'd started working for her he'd been nothing but pleasant. Of course, she realised, she'd been paying him to work for her. Maybe that was it. Maybe the fact that he was taking money from her was forcing him to be nice.

'I was talking to Ollie the other day,' he said conversationally.

'Ollie?' Claire had spoken before she realised who he meant, and then her face flushed again.

'Yes, the wasp guy.'

302

'Oliver. Yes. Well . . .' She knew that her voice was even croakier now. 'He seemed to think that I was some kind of talent scout.'

'He said he'd met you at a singles dating thing and that you told him that's what you did. But then you said you didn't. So he wasn't sure.'

'I know,' said Claire. 'We talked it through. And apparently you and he talked it through too.' She narrowed her eyes. 'I'm not sure how I feel about being an object of discussion between the two of you.'

'I did tell him.' Nate pushed a plug deep into the wall. 'I said he was barking up the wrong tree.'

Claire didn't say anything. The moment when Nate had pushed the plug into the wall had brought a memory flooding back to her. Of Bill, doing exactly the same thing. Only it had been indoors, he'd been fixing a shelf and she'd been sitting on the edge of the table talking to him. The image, buried deep in her memory, was as clear as though it had just happened. And she was racked with a sudden sense of loss, so deep and so painful that it was all she could do not to cry out loud. It had been so different then, when she knew exactly where she stood, when she didn't have to worry about who was using who, when it didn't matter what other men looked like because they didn't even register with her.

'Claire?' Nate's voice seemed to come from a different existence. 'Claire, are you OK?'

She blinked a couple of times and dragged herself back to the present.

'Sure. Yes. Sorry.'

He looked at her, his expression concerned. 'Did I say something? Do something? You're awfully pale.'

'No,' she said. 'No. I just – remembered – I have to . . .'

She walked abruptly away from him and towards the house. She pushed open the kitchen door, took a glass from the drainer and filled it with water straight from the tap. It was warm and tasteless but she swallowed it back in two gulps.

'Are you all right?' Eileen looked up from the ironing.

'Of course I am,' said Claire sharply. She stood beside the sink for a moment, looking out to the garden where Nate was finishing the job. Her eyes followed his movements. Nothing like Bill at all, she thought, as she watched him. Not even remotely. He was a completely different person with a completely different way of life and a completely different personality. He was as unlike Bill Hudson as it was possible for anyone to be. So how could it be that for one split second he'd made her remember what it had been like before?

She heard the front door open and Georgia burst into the kitchen.

'Hi, Mum, anything to eat? I'm starving.'

'It's nowhere near time to eat,' said Claire.

'Can I make a sandwich?'

'Sure.'

Georgia opened the fridge door and took out some tomatoes. She straightened up and glanced out of the window.

'Hey!' she cried. 'He's back. What for?'

'Putting up a thermometer.'

'Did he find one? A good one?' Georgia didn't wait for her reply but went outside and stood beside Nate.

'Hiya,' she said. 'How's it going?'

'Nearly finished,' he told her.

'Is it hot?' she asked, squinting to see the line of mercury.

'Not as hot as it was.'

'I'm back to school soon,' she told him, 'so I don't really care.'

'Selfish thing.' He laughed.

'Did you persuade Mum to get the barbie yet?' she asked.

'I didn't try,' said Nate. He picked up the plastic bag that had contained the thermometer and bundled it into his pocket.

'I've begged her and begged her but she says that the weather has broken and there's no point.'

Nate raised his eyebrows at Claire, who'd followed Georgia outside again. 'Not quite broken yet. And don't forget we always have a few gorgeous days in September.'

'If only we knew in advance when they'd be.'

'According to the weather forecast we can expect another week or so of this,' said Nate.

'You see!' Georgia looked passionately at Claire. 'Only another week. And then I'm back to school anyway. Oh, Mum, come on! It'd be great fun, especially 'cos Gran is here too. I could ask all my friends. You know I'm always going to things that their folks have organised. I practically live at Robyn's some of the time! And Sive's mother had that great birthday party for her last year – remember? It was so cool. You could ask Eavan and Glenn – you know how they're always asking you places . . .'

'Georgey, it's a lovely idea, but—'

'But why not?' interrupted Georgia. 'We could ask *everyone*. We could have *fun*.'

Nate put his electric drill in its case.

'I'd better be going,' he told Claire. 'But I agree with Georgia. You've got such a lovely garden again, you should show it off.'

'You see!' Georgia beamed at Nate and then at Claire. 'Our gardener thinks it's a good idea. And why shouldn't he? Hasn't he made it look fantastic?'

'Oh for heaven's sake!' Claire looked at Nate. 'Why are you egging her on?'

'I'm not, I'm not.' He held up his hands. 'I'm sorry, it's none of my business.'

'You could come too,' Georgia told him. 'Oh, Mum, pleeeeaaaase.'

Suddenly Claire laughed. 'You're impossible, you do know that, don't you? You want me to do everything straight away, and if it's a barbecue then I'll have to invite people really soon because the weather might break and then what'll we do? But if we try to have it by next weekend it's such short notice for everyone and maybe they won't be able to come . . .'

'Ah, come on.' Georgia's tone was wheedling now. 'It doesn't have to be huge. Just a few people we know. If they don't come, so what?'

'I'll come,' said Nate.

'You see!' Georgia looked at Claire triumphantly. 'At the very worst it's you, me, Gran and Nate.'

Claire sighed. 'Nate and Sarah. And we couldn't not ask your grandad. But if we ask him we have to ask Lacey.'

Georgia's eyes widened. 'Oh, but *yes*. I have to meet her. D'you think she'd come?'

'Perhaps Gran wouldn't want her there.'

'Mum, you're so not with it about Gran and Lacey. She doesn't care.'

Nate looked from one to the other. 'The guest list sounds intriguing,' he said. 'But I'd better be going.'

Both Claire and Georgia followed him to the front of the house.

'Thanks again for the thermometer,' said Claire. 'It's really lovely.'

'You're welcome,' said Nate.

'We'll be in touch about the barbecue,' Georgia told him.

He grinned at her and nodded.

Claire turned to Georgia. 'Come on, miss. You promised to do some housework for me today. Let's get on with it.'

'Sorry if I've delayed you,' said Nate.

'Not me!' cried Georgia. 'She wants me to clean windows!'

Nate laughed. 'Slave-driver.'

'I'll let you know if we go ahead it with,' said Claire suddenly.

'Is that a promise?' Nate's eyes held hers for a moment.

'Sure,' she said lightly. 'Absolutely. Now, come on, Georgey, we've things to do.'

She ushered Georgia inside and closed the front door.

'Honestly, Mum,' said Georgia, 'you'd swear you were trying to get rid of him. And I like him.'

'You nearly killed him, as I recall,' said Claire as they walked into the kitchen, where Eileen was still ironing.

'Nearly killed who?' she asked.

Georgia explained about Nate and the peanut butter sandwich and Claire's intervention with the EpiPen.

'Which is why he's been so nice to us since,' said Georgia. 'Although he was always nice. Personally, I think he fancies Mum but unfortunately he's married.'

'Georgia Hudson!' Claire looked at her angrily. 'Stop talking nonsense and get on with your chores.'

'I was only . . .'

'Now!' said Claire in a voice that allowed no possibilty of dissent.

Later that evening, when she and Claire were sitting watching the television, Eileen casually asked her daughter about Nate Taylor. But Claire carefully deflected the subject by simply saying that his idea of a barbecue was a good one and asking Eileen what she thought about it. Eileen was so surprised that Claire might even consider inviting people to the house for a party – even something as casual as a barbecue – that she forgot that her primary purpose had been to find out whether Claire was harbouring feelings for the attractive (but unfortunately married) gardener.

'Would you really have one?' she asked.

'For Georgia,' said Claire. 'She made the very valid point that she's always being looked after socially by her friends' parents and that we do nothing. It'd be nice for her to be able to invite them to something.'

'It sounds like a good idea,' said Eileen. 'Would you mind if I asked some people too?'

'Of course not.'

'Because I thought Alan Bellew might like to come.'

'Who?'

'The estate agent who looked after the house.'

Claire glanced at her quizzically.

'Your dad's not the only one who has friends of the opposite sex,' said Eileen as a pink blush spread across her cheeks.

In fact, after Claire, Eileen and Georgia had sat down together and run through the names of the people each of them wanted to invite, the guest list was bigger than Claire had first imagined. Georgia, of course, wanted to ask all of her friends, despite Claire pointing out that there'd be lots of boring adults around and surely a gang of teenagers would rather be doing something else?

'Don't you want me to have friends?' demanded Georgia.

'Of course I do. And of course I'd rather they were here with you than that you were off terrorising shopkeepers or whatever it is you get up to when you turn into delinquents,' said Claire. 'But I'm just afraid you'll all be bored!'

'No we won't,' said Georgia. 'Can I ask one of my friends from Galway?'

'Galway!' Claire looked at her in astonishment. 'I don't really think anyone would come from Galway for the day! How would they get back?'

'Oh, Mum, you are being pathetic!' cried Georgia. 'Not coming from Galway. One of the people I met at the camp, of course.'

'Well of course you can,' said Claire.

Georgia beamed at her. 'Thanks.'

'I hope it'll be fun.' Claire looked worried. 'We have three generations of Shanahan women here, so it's asking a lot for everyone to enjoy themselves when we probably all want different things.'

'I never thought of that before,' said Eileen. 'But of course we can enjoy ourselves! Anyway, we're not really Shanahan women. That's your dad's side of the family. We're Nelligan women, and we come from a long line of party-goers.'

Claire chuckled.

'Do we?' asked Georgia. 'Were you a party-goer in your day, Gran?'

'I was the odd one out,' admitted Eileen. 'I was the one who liked sitting home with my knitting, which I know sounds a bit pathetic. But my mother, your great-grandmother, Kate, she was considered to be quite a beauty in her day. And she loved going out. Apparently when she was about sixteen she climbed out of her bedroom window to go to a party when her father had expressly forbidden it.'

'Gosh,' said Georgia. 'Good for her.'

'Not really good for her,' said Claire sternly. 'Her father probably had a really good reason for telling her not to go.'

'Had he?' Georgia looked enquiringly at Eileen.

'Oh, absolutely,' her grandmother assured her. 'The party was in the house of his bitter enemy, James Murphy. The Nelligans and the Murphys didn't get on but Kate and James's daughter Peig were secret friends. There was uproar, apparently, when her father found out but she said she didn't care. She'd made herself a dress in secret too, a beautiful orange silk – rather like that lovely one of yours, Claire, though God knows where she managed to find the material . . . anyway the whole thing was a bit of a scandal as far as our family was concerned and poor Kate was locked away for weeks!'

'So you see,' Claire told Georgia. 'You have it far too easy!'

Georgia made a face at her. 'You'll have to tell me more sometime, Gran,' she said to Eileen. 'When Mum isn't around.'

'Certainly.'

'Still, three generations of Nelligans getting jiggy with it now is a good thing,' said Georgia.

Claire looked at her. She wasn't sure exactly what the expression

308

meant. But she didn't have the strength to ask. Not when her mother and her daughter were both looking at her with bright, excited eyes at the idea of being the party Nelligans.

After everyone had gone to bed, Georgia sent a text to Steve Ó Sé telling him about the possibility of a barbecue at her house. He'd be welcome to come, she said, even though there'd be lots of adults around. But it wouldn't be too boring. The girls would be there too, and some of her other friends. Always providing that it actually happened and that her mother didn't chicken out.

It was one of the longest text messages she'd ever sent, and almost as soon as it had gone she wished she hadn't sent it. She sounded pathetic and sad, she thought, telling him about something that wasn't even definite. Asking him to come to a barbecue that was really for her mother and her mother's friends. Maybe none of the girls would bother coming either and she'd be left wandering around the garden like a lost soul before finally managing to make her escape. It was all very well talking about generations of party Nelligans getting it together, but how possible was it that they'd all have a good time? Maybe her mother was right about that. And asking Steve – well, that was plain stupid. If he had the slightest desire to see her it wouldn't be at her house in front of her mother! Shit, she thought. I'm so not cool about stuff. Fourteen-year-old girls aren't meant to get on with their parents. Mum was right, I should be wandering around with a sulky face and telling everyone how dense she is. Not encouraging her to hold stupid barbecues! Her phone beeped.

Lt me no whn. Wll try.

She looked at it and excitement fizzed up inside her. It might be a stupid barbecue. But if he came – if he came, then it wouldn't be stupid at all.

Chapter 32

Sempervivum (Houseleek) – Yellow red and purple flowers in rosettes. Mother rosette dies when flowering is over.

Eavan finished printing off the sales reports and bundled them together before bringing them into her boss's office.

Ken Casey – or Ken Crazy, as the rest of the office called him – was sitting back in his leather chair (an assembled version of the flat-pack product for sale in the store below) with his feet on the desk (also available in the store, and discounted that week in one of their Crazy Cash Value days).

'Thanks,' he said. 'Everything going all right for you?'

'Fine,' she said.

'You learning the ropes?'

'Absolutely.'

'Graham says that you're very bright. Quick. Ready to learn.' His grey eyes looked at her appraisingly.

'It's not rocket science,' she told him. 'Anyone could do it.'

He raised an eyebrow and took his feet from the desk, sitting up straight in the chair as he continued to watch her.

'Everything's coded, it all makes sense, not quite foolproof but not difficult.'

'You know, everyone else here tells me how bloody difficult their job is and what stress they're under,' he remarked.

'Ah well, everyone would say that.' She smiled, slightly. 'And it's not that we're not stressed out, Ken, because it's very busy out there. But once you have a system it's not so bad.'

'And you have a system?'

'Of course.'

This time his look was more quizzical. 'I thought you'd come back to work after taking a few years off,' he said. 'I didn't realise that you were so up-to-the-minute about things.'

'I'm not,' she said. 'The programs have changed a bit since I was last in an office but the basics are still the same. And yes, I was out of the paid workforce for a while, but I was running a house. You definitely have to have a system when you're running a house.'

He laughed. 'Mary told me that you were sparky at the interview,' he said.

'I'm not sparky,' said Eavan.

'Oh yes you are.'

'No,' she said. 'I'm knackered. It's been a long day and I need to get home.'

'Would you like to come for a drink with me?' He looked at his watch. 'I'm just finished up here.'

She shook her head. 'I have a husband and a three-year-old daughter waiting for me to get home. I'm not available to go out for drinks.'

He shrugged. 'I'm not hitting on you,' he said. 'I just thought that, well, you're new and you might like to socialise with us a little.'

'Thanks for the thought, but I can't,' said Eavan.

'Another time perhaps,' said Ken.

'Perhaps.' Eavan turned and walked out of the office.

No perhaps, she muttered under her breath. No way! She couldn't begin to think of how Glenn would react if she went out for a drink, however innocent, with her new boss.

She went to her desk and took her jacket from the back of her chair. Then she hurried down the stairs and out to the car park.

The traffic from Baldoyle to Howth was appalling. Twenty minutes after leaving the DIY store, Eavan was sandwiched in a slow-moving convoy between an articulated lorry and a huge delivery van. That was the problem about working in an industrial estate, she thought, every other vehicle was so much bigger than yours, even when you were driving a decent car.

She eased her foot off the clutch and the Audi slid forward a few feet. They'd talked about selling it before she got this job. When Trontec had let him go Glenn had bought it from them, but only to keep her from finding out that he was out of work. They'd agreed that it didn't make much sense to be a two-car family when one of those cars cost a heap of money to maintain, but once Eavan was offered the position in the DIY store it made more sense for her to drive than try to catch the inconveniently routed buses, and so it became a question of needing both cars again. Besides, as Glenn had pointed out, the Audi was taxed and insured until the end of the year anyway. So now he was the one driving the Micra, which had all of Saffy's bits and pieces already installed, while Eavan cruised to and from work in the Audi. She sighed sympathetically as she thought of Glenn squeezing his long frame into the small car while she sat in comparative luxury. Even though she'd rather be anywhere else than in this frustratingly slow-moving trail of interminable traffic.

But the work wasn't bad. The people in the office were nice – as well as Caroline and Delia there was Graham, the accounts manager; Mary, the office manager, who had interviewed her; and, of course, Ken Crazy himself and his assistant Lucinda.

Caroline and Delia spent endless hours discussing Ken and his relationships as well as their own tangled and involved love-lives (Caroline had split up with a boyfriend because she fancied his best friend; Delia had just started going out with someone new though her ex-boyfriend continued to ring her every day) and though Eavan had stayed apart from the conversations at first she was as caught up in them as anyone by the end of her first week. Caroline and Delia had managed to elicit the information that she was back to work because her husband had lost his job, even though she'd tried not to talk about Glenn very much. They'd been sympathetic and supportive and told her that all those big corporations were shits and that nobody could ever feel secure working for them. You were just a cog in the machine, said Caroline, who'd worked as a receptionist for a high-tech firm which had gone spectacularly bankrupt a few weeks after she'd joined. They'd wanted to know all about Saffy, and Eavan had taken the photo out of her bag to show them. Delia then nipped down to the store and bought a novelty picture frame so that Saffy's face now beamed out from a miniature television screen on Eavan's desk. Eavan promised herself that she'd bring in a photo of Glenn to have on the desk too.

The traffic eased forward again and she yawned. She was exhausted. But it was a different sort of exhaustion to being with Saffy. It was the exhaustion of doing new things, of having to think in a different way, of interacting with adults the whole time. It had been fun, more or less, but she was glad to have finished for the week.

She'd listened to almost her entire Dido CD by the time she pulled into the driveway. The big For Sale sign at the front of the house made her flinch. When they'd moved in, she'd expected to be there for ever. Maybe it had been a stupid expectation, she told herself, as she switched off the ignition. But it had coloured how she felt about her whole life. And now . . . she'd been telling the truth when she'd told Glenn that it didn't mean the same to her any more, that in many ways it had become a symbol of wanting too much. But she knew that it would break her heart the day they walked out of the front door for the last time.

The television was on in the living room. Eavan heard the familiar sounds of *Toy Story* being played for the millionth time. She pushed open the door.

'You're home!' Saffy leaped up from the sofa and flung herself at Eavan's legs. 'Read Cinderella. Daddy doesn't do it right.'

'I'm sure Daddy does it perfectly well,' said Eavan as she lifted her up. 'Do you know that you weigh a ton?'

'Yes,' said Saffy cheerfully. 'Daddy told me that.'

'Then we must be right.' Eavan kissed her on her soft pink cheek. 'How was your day?'

'We went for a walk along the pier.' Glenn came into the room. 'It was lovely. We looked at the boats in the harbour and we counted – how many, Saffy, how many with red sails?'

'Ten,' she said proudly. 'Ten red sails.'

'How clever of you,' said Eavan admiringly as Saffy rushed through the count to ten to prove her point.

She set the little girl on the floor and smiled at Glenn.

'How're you?'

'Great,' he said. 'There's a lasagne in the oven and some red wine breathing on the counter for you.'

'Celebrating?' She tried to keep the hope out of her voice.

'Not a job.' His own tone was carefully neutral. 'But we had a nice day, Saffy and me, and I know it's been a long week for you. So . . . celebration.'

'Great,' she said. She took off her lightweight jacket and hung it over the back of the chair. Then she walked into the kitchen and opened the oven door. The smell of basil, oregano and melted cheese wafted out.

'Not so bad, huh?' Glenn stood at the counter. 'It'll be ready in five minutes.'

'Garlic bread?' she asked.

'Shit.' He frowned. 'I forgot about garlic bread.'

'There's some in the freezer.' She moved towards it.

'I'll do it,' he said. 'You sit down.'

'But—'

'I'm making dinner,' he said sharply.

'The garlic bread will take about fifteen minutes.'

'Well then, the lasagne can stay in the oven a bit longer.'

'The cheese will burn.'

'For Christ's sake, Eavan!' He looked angrily at her. 'Stop picking on me. I've managed perfectly well without you so far.'

'I was only trying to help!' She walked out of the kitchen, through the conservatory and into the back garden. Tears pricked at the back of her eyes. He didn't have to snap at her. She was tired. It had been a hard week. And all she'd done was give him some advice. It wasn't as though she particularly wanted the damn garlic bread anyway, he was the one who really liked it.

She walked through the garden, picking up the debris from Saffy's playtime – abandoned dolls, brightly coloured balls, play bricks, cuddly toys. She carried them back into the house, through the kitchen where Glenn was unwrapping the frozen garlic bread, and up the stairs to Saffy's room. She placed the cuddly toys and dolls on her Little Princess quilted bed and put the bricks and balls into the red and yellow toy box in the corner of the room.

Actually, it was incredibly tidy. There were often times when she'd walk into Saffy's room and think of it as an abandoned toy store. But today everything was already neatly in its place. Probably because Glenn had taken her to the pier, Eavan thought. She hadn't had time to wreck her room.

She went next door to their own bedroom. It, too, was neat and tidy, her bottles and creams lined up in ordered ranks on the wrong side of the modern dressing table and her jewellery painstakingly arranged on the other. It was clear to her that the dressing table had been dusted that day. She bit her lip and pinched the bridge of her nose. She changed from her tailored suit into a pair of loose-fitting trousers and a T-shirt and went downstairs again.

'Five minutes,' said Glenn briefly.

She was about to speak when the phone rang. He picked it up.

'Oh, hi, yes. She's here.' He handed the receiver to her. 'Claire,' he said.

'Hello, Claire.' Eavan kept her voice bright.

'Hi. Are you all right?' asked Claire.

'Of course.'

'Have I rung at a bad time?'

'We're about to have dinner,' said Eavan.

Claire could hear tension in Eavan's voice. 'It's not urgent,' she said quickly. 'Call me later.'

Eavan replaced the phone while Glenn took the lasagne and garlic bread out of the oven. The top of the lasagne was a little scorched. Glenn ladled some on to plates and put the garlic bread into a long basket.

'D'you want to eat in here?' he asked.

'Yes. It's fine.'

'Saffy!' he called. 'Are you going to have some of this with us?'

'Hasn't she eaten already?' Eavan wished she hadn't spoken. Glenn's face was rigid.

'Yes,' he said. 'But she told me she'd like some lasagne.'

Saffy bounded into the room and scrambled up to the table.

'No cheese,' she told Glenn. 'Specially not black!'

He spooned some meat and sauce on to her Winnie-the-Pooh plate and put it in front of her.

'It's hot,' warned Eavan. 'Blow hard on it before you eat it.'

'I know.' Saffy looked at her in disgust. 'I'm not a baby.'

'Mum thinks we're both babies,' said Glenn as he brought the other two steaming plates to the table.

'No I don't.'

'She thinks we can't manage without her.'

'No I don't.'

'She thinks she's the only one who knows anything.'

Eavan popped a forkful of hot lasagne into her mouth and her eyes watered.

'Wine?' asked Glenn.

'Thank you.' She dabbed at her eyes with a paper napkin as he filled her glass.

'Can we do the boats again tomorrow?' Saffy asked Glenn.

'We can't go tomorrow,' said Eavan. 'Dad and I are going out to see Auntie Claire.'

Saffy's mouth puckered.

'Your mum will organise us,' said Glenn. 'I'm sure she'll plan it all out for us, Saffy.'

'For God's sake!' Eavan put her fork beside her plate. 'Give me a break.'

'What are you talking about?' He looked at her coolly.

'I don't organise you. I won't organise you.'

'But it's the weekend,' he pointed out. 'You're back at home, back in charge. We're doing what you want tomorrow, going to Claire's. We'll do whatever you want on Sunday too.'

'It's what *we* want. Not what *I* want.'

'You're the breadwinner now,' said Glenn. 'You've got the biggest clout.'

'And you're being incredibly stupid.' Eavan pushed her chair away from the table and walked out of the kitchen and into the garden again. Saffy watched her with wide eyes.

'Is Mum upset?' Her own voice wobbled as she looked at Glenn.

'She's just being silly.' Glenn stabbed his fork into his lasagne.

'Will I make her better?' Saffy scrambled down from her chair and ran into the back garden. Glenn watched as she tugged at Eavan's trousers and was lifted into his wife's arms. He pushed his own barely tasted lasagne away from him.

Eavan held Saffy close, burying her head in her daughter's dark curls. Like a Madonna and child photograph, he thought savagely. The two of them united while he sat here on his own. Not really needed.

He got up from the table and scraped the lasagne from the plates into the waste disposal. He looked longingly at Eavan's full glass of red wine. The evening sun, slanting through the kitchen window, made it glow gently and enticingly. He could almost taste it again. Rich with exploding fruits against his palate. Warm as it made its way through his system. Comforting. He reached out to the glass and picked it up. He looked out of the conservatory window again. Eavan was still holding Saffy, still had her back to him.

'Goddamn it.' His voice was a strangled cry in his throat. 'God fucking damn it to hell.' He dropped the glass on the floor. The wine splashed his loafers and spread into a mulberry-red puddle at his feet. He stood at the edge of the puddle and cried.

Con and Lacey were finishing their evening meal when Claire called them. Claire would have been astonished to know that Con (who'd never lifted a finger in the house when she was small, regarding anything domestic as Eileen's territory) had roasted the chicken and potatoes and had timed things to perfection so that the meal was almost ready when Lacey came home from work; he'd allowed them time for a glass of wine together before eating so that Lacey could sit with her feet in his lap and allow him to massage her ankles while she told him with satisfaction of the new contract that the company had landed and the relief of having placed a very difficult client with an equally difficult company that day.

'Hi, Dad,' said Claire. 'Is this a good time to talk?'

'Of course,' he said. 'Everything OK?'

'Sure. I just wanted to check that you and Lacey were still all right for tomorrow.'

'I said we were.' Con had been absolutely astonished earlier in the week to get the posted card, clearly a product of Claire's computer, inviting him and Lacey to a barbecue at his daughter's house. He'd

317

been so surprised that he'd waited a day before ringing her to say that they'd be delighted to come, just in case she'd already posted another card telling him that it was all a mistake.

'I'm just doing a ring-around tonight,' she explained. 'I want to get a good handle on the numbers.'

'We'll be there,' promised Con. 'You know we're looking forward to it immensely. And I'm very glad that you felt able to invite both of us along.'

'Yes, well.' Claire's tone was dry. 'It's probably not my ideal situation but I do know that it's yours and – and I want you to be happy, Dad.'

'Thank you,' he said. 'I want you to be happy too. I'm hoping that deciding to have the barbecue is a sign that maybe you're getting there.'

'It's a sign that Georgia and Mum have ganged up on me,' said Claire ruefully. 'They wouldn't let me say no.'

'That's your mother all right,' said Con.

'Dad?'

'Yes?'

'You're sure that you and Mum are OK about all this?'

'What does your mum say?'

'Naturally she says it's no problem. And she's invited friends of her own! But I wanted to be certain. I . . . well . . . this is something I haven't done before and I don't want it to go wrong. I don't want some big family bust-up in the back garden!'

'It won't go wrong,' promised Con. 'Your mum and I are fine. And Lacey is really looking forward to it.'

'Good,' said Claire.

'So we'll see you tomorrow,' said Con. 'Is there anything you want me to bring?'

'No thanks,' replied Claire. 'I think I've got it all under control.'

She replaced the receiver in its cradle and rubbed the back of her neck. She still couldn't quite believe that she'd gone along with the barbecue plan and that it was all happening so quickly. Eileen and Georgia (behaving rather like children, she thought) had swept her along, urging her not to wait because otherwise the weather would break. Now she was surprised that so many people had responded to her e-mailed, texted and posted invitations. The barbecue, instead of being a low-key affair, had turned into a major event! Included in her pile of replies to invitations had been a lovely card from Sarah Taylor with a picture of a bright red dahlia on the front, telling her that both Sarah and Nate would be delighted to come and saying that she couldn't wait to see how the garden looked because she'd heard so much about it from Nate.

Maybe it would be easier with Sarah there, thought Claire as she stared, unseeingly, into the distance. Maybe she allowed herself to feel the way she felt when Nate was around simply because it was safe and easy to fantasise about a man who was committed to someone else. And maybe when that someone else was actually with him those feelings would evaporate as though they'd never existed in the first place. She hoped so. She didn't want them any more.

She rested her chin on her hands as she explored her emotions again. Whenever she thought about Nate Taylor she felt a tightening in the pit of her stomach followed by a flurry of a thousand butterflies. And her heart would beat faster at the memories of him digging the garden, carrying rocks to the rockery, cutting back bushes or simply sitting tall and strong and bare-chested beneath the apple tree. It was a pleasurable experience but tinged with a sense of despair that in spite of how much she enjoyed thinking about him, he belonged to someone else. And in the end it left an ache that laid itself over the ache she felt for Bill and made her wonder whether she actually enjoyed being miserable, whether there was something about her that simply prevented her from wanting to be happy.

Perhaps, she mused as she struggled to get to grips with her wayward feelings, she could tell Georgia about the hurt of un-requited love, because even though she didn't love Nate Taylor, she wanted something from him that he couldn't give her. And the weird thing about that was that for the first time in years her feeling of wretchedness wasn't entirely due to the fact that Bill was no longer there.

She walked upstairs to her bedroom. Eileen was in the living room watching TV. Georgia was secreted in her den playing Grand Theft Auto. Phydough was asleep in his basket beside the back door.

319

She sat on the edge of the bed and picked up the picture of Bill again. 'I don't love Nate,' she whispered, as she looked at Bill's photograph. 'I fancy him, which is different. But I feel a bit guilty about that too. Because you were always the only person I ever fancied. Well, except for George Michael. And Becks, of course!' She closed her eyes. She remembered dancing with Bill, at a party – but she couldn't recall where or why – and George singing 'Careless Whisper' while she rested her head on Bill's shoulder. And Bill telling her that he'd never, ever betray her with anyone. Because she was, and always would be, the only woman in his life.

I don't want anyone else. She opened her eyes and looked at Bill's smiling, windswept face. I don't even fancy anybody else. Not really. I'm only pretending. Just so's I can feel something different again. Something other than missing you. Something other than feeling guilty that I'm here and you're not.

It was nearly half past nine when Eavan phoned her back.

'Of course we're coming,' she told Claire tightly. 'Didn't you get my e-mail earlier? Well, *I'm* definitely coming. Candida had agreed to babysit Saffy tomorrow but I'm not sure if that's exactly on now so there might be a problem with Glenn.'

'I got the e-mail all right,' admitted Claire. 'I'm just doing a check-around. I do hope Glenn can make it.'

'I hope so too,' said Eavan.

'Is everything all right?' asked Claire.

'Of course.'

'You sound a bit . . . odd.'

'Just tired,' said Eavan. 'It was a long week.'

'I know. That's why I didn't ring you before today,' said Claire. 'I reckoned that you'd be knackered from work. And I'm sorry for calling at dinner time. That was stupid. So how's it going?'

'Oh, it's OK,' said Eavan cautiously. 'Nothing special.'

'Are the people nice?'

'You know yourself!' Eavan laughed drily. 'It's an office. I'm sure there are all sorts of politics going on that I haven't quite worked out yet. The boss asked me for a drink tonight but apparently that's par for the course with new employees.'

Claire laughed too. 'Jeez, Evs, you're only just back and you're right in there!'

'I'd rather not be.'

'I'm sure you slapped him down wonderfully well. More to the point, are you shattered after your first full week?'

'Utterly,' admitted Eavan. 'It's having to haul myself out of bed and make myself presentable that's so bloody difficult. And, of course, the traffic. I've become all road-ragey again.'

'How's Glenn getting on?'

Eavan said nothing.

'Nothing yet?'

'No.'

'How's he coping with you working?'

Eavan was silent again.

'Eavan? Is it a problem?'

'I – well – sort of.'

'He'll get over it,' said Claire. 'And I'm sure something will turn up for him.'

'I hope so.'

'Can't you get him to look on it as a bit of time to spend with Saffy?'

'I wish I could.' Eavan's voice cracked a little.

'Is it bad?' asked Claire. 'If there's a problem don't make yourself come tomorrow if you need to stay home.'

'I want to come,' said Eavan fiercely. 'I want to get out and just be a normal person for a while.'

'I wish there was something I could do,' said Claire.

'Don't worry about me,' Eavan told her. 'I'll see you tomorrow. Everything will turn out OK in the end.'

'Of course it will,' said Claire confidently. 'Any news on the house?'

'It's on the market now,' said Eavan. 'We had two people come to see it during the week but nobody has made an offer yet.'

'They will.'

'I know.' She sighed. 'Part of me wants them to but part of me doesn't. I mean, I've said that I want out of it and mostly I do, but . . .'

'It's only a house,' said Claire.

'I know. I know.'

'Anyway, don't think about it now. Just remember to be in good form tomorrow. I'm really looking forward to seeing you.'

'I hear you've asked other people from the club,' said Eavan. 'I got a text from Amanda asking me about it. You're really pushing the boat out.'

'Oh, I guess if I'm doing it I might as well do it properly.'

'I'm sure you will,' said Eavan.

'Eavan?' Claire's voice was uncertain.

'What?'

'You don't think – oh, look, I kind of know this is silly, but . . . you don't think it's being a bit disrespectful of Bill to have it here, do you?'

'Claire! Of course not. It's your home, where else would you have it?'

'I know. I know. The whole idea came about because Georgia wanted to celebrate the garden getting back to its former glory, so obviously it has to be here. Only . . . only I feel a bit . . . weird about it.'

'Don't feel weird,' ordered Eavan. 'Feel good.' Her voice softened. 'And I'm really glad you got the garden done. It always was a lovely place to be.'

'I know.'

'So I'll see you tomorrow.'

'Only if it's OK for you,' said Claire. 'Don't feel that you have to turn up if you don't want to. Please.'

'I do want to,' said Eavan firmly. 'No matter what.'

After she'd finished speaking to Eavan, Claire stretched out on the big bed and closed her eyes. She was tired from the sudden rush of organisation, of ordering mountains of food and drink on-line, of talking to people she hadn't spoken to in months. Of being nice to everyone. She let her thoughts drift and slide until, suddenly, she was asleep. She was still sleeping when Eileen came up the stairs nearly two hours later and draped a sheet over her shoulders.

Chapter 33

Impatiens (Busy Lizzie) – Many and varied colours and can be long-lasting in right conditions. But difficult to raise from seed.

The only cloud in the sky by lunchtime on Saturday was a vapour trail from a jet high above them. Claire stood in the garden, a glass of orange juice in her hand, as she tried to imagine how it would be in a few hours' time. It was so long since she'd had any kind of party or event at her home that she couldn't quite visualise it now.

Phydough trotted beside her as she walked across the patio and looked at the sunflower thermometer. Twenty-one degrees in the shade and it was still before noon. *Maybe I should've got sunshades.* She looked again at the gas barbecue which Mike O'Malley had dropped off earlier that morning. One of his many toys for boys, Leonie had said when she called to say he was on the way. And, she'd warned, they were going to be absolutely on time later on because Mike was absolutely insisting that he flip burgers and char sausages himself. He'd pretend, Leonie said, that he was helping out but he'd go berserk if anyone else went near it.

Claire smiled to herself as she thought about it.

'What are you grinning at?' Georgia joined her outside.

'Men and barbecues,' replied Claire.

'Dad used to love it,' recalled Georgia. 'I remember he was always going to buy a big one, wasn't he?'

'He wanted to,' agreed Claire. 'I just thought it was a waste of time.'

'But fun.'

'Hmm.' Claire smiled again. 'We had one, you know.'

'A barbecue?'

'Yes. But like now. As a party. Much smaller, though.'

'Did you? I don't remember.'

'You were only about three or four.' Claire frowned. 'And your dad bought this absolutely useless kettle barbie from one of the DIY places. He was dying to try it out. So the next half-decent day he invited a few people round and he did his best to give them food poisoning by burning the outside of everything and leaving it raw inside.'

'Yeuch.'

Claire laughed. 'I'd forgotten about it until today. I think I'd deliberately pushed it out of my mind.' She thought for a moment. 'People came quite late and Bill put up a string of lights in the garden.'

'Oh, yes!' Georgia widened her eyes. 'We should do that, Mum. It'd be lovely.'

'We don't have any lights,' said Claire.

'What happened to the ones you used then?'

'Honey, they could be anywhere. And I'm sure that they're broken by now anyway.'

'We could look,' said Georgia. 'Maybe they're in the attic.'

Claire made a face. 'I don't do the attic,' she told her. 'Too dark, too dusty.'

'Can I?' begged Georgia.

Claire looked uncertain.

'Please?'

'Oh, all right,' said Claire. 'But be careful with the stepladder and don't . . .' But she was speaking to thin air. Georgia had disappeared already.

'The Tesco delivery is here!' Eileen called to her from the kitchen, and Claire went back into the house to unpack the bags and load up the fridge with burgers, sausages, chicken wings and salads.

'Actually this is quite exciting,' said Eileen as she surveyed the packed shelves. 'I haven't been to a party in years.'

'It's not a party,' said Claire.

'It is,' Eileen told her. 'And I'm really looking forward to it. So's Josie. She's keen to see you again, Claire. She hasn't since Bill's funeral.'

'I never saw Josie regularly in any case.' Claire kept her own voice as matter-of-fact as her mother's. 'Are you sure she's going to come?'

'Yes, absolutely.'

'And how about this Alan Bellew bloke?' asked Claire. 'Your arm-candy estate agent to make Dad feel jealous? Is there more to this than meets the eye?'

'I'm not trying to make your dad jealous,' said Eileen defensively. 'I just don't want to look like an old hag when he has a new woman.'

'You look great,' Claire told her warmly.

'Ah, no.' Eileen shook her head. 'I look what I am. A granny.'

'Do you want to look different?'

Eileen sighed. 'I can't look different.'

'Of course you can,' cried Claire. 'If that's what you want.'

'I'm too old to give a damn,' said Eileen.

'Nobody is too old to give a damn,' Claire retorted.

'I don't want to compete with Lacey,' admitted Eileen. 'She always looks so chic and sophisticated. If I started dyeing my hair and getting my face done people would say that it's because of her.'

'No they wouldn't!'

'They would.'

'Mum, if you'd done all those things while you and Dad were still together they might think that. But you're getting divorced. Think of all those women who have a makeover once they're divorced and how great they look.'

'I always thought it was a little pathetic,' said Eileen.

'Rubbish!' cried Claire. 'They're saying that they're entering a new period in their lives and they're ready to face it. And there's nothing wrong with slapping on a bit of foundation and a new lippy while you're doing it.'

Eileen laughed. 'Maybe. But it's not exactly something you're doing yourself, is it?'

Claire made a face at her. 'I'm in a different place with my life,' she said.

'But are you ready to move on?' asked Eileen.

'I'm having this damn barbecue,' retorted Claire. 'If that's not moving on, I don't know what the hell is.'

Georgia sat in the dim attic and pulled at old cardboard boxes. She knew better than to expect to unearth musty keepsakes or ancient treasures – Claire was a relentless thrower-out of things. She didn't keep back issues of newspapers or unwanted gifts or toys – the papers went into the recycling bin and Georgia's old toys had regularly been donated to charity shops. All of their important family documents were kept in the filing cabinet in Claire's office, along with the less important but more sentimental ones (like all of Georgia's school reports, which were carefully filed away). The only items that were stored in the attic were the Christmas decorations. Which was why Georgia thought she might find the garden lights there too.

She was poking around under a beam when her mobile beeped and startled her so much that she thwacked her head on the roof. Her eyes were watering as she took the phone out of the pocket of her shorts and looked at the message.

Wll b der 2day. Cnt w8. Luv S.

She felt her heart race in her chest. Steve was coming! She couldn't quite believe it. She'd texted him with the date, saying it was OK if he couldn't make it because of his job. But he was going to come. Sive, Emma and Robyn would all see that he liked her enough to take a day off work, and she would be there, among her friends, with a guy who'd bothered to come all the way from Navan to be with her despite the fact that she wasn't the prettiest, or the coolest, or any of those things. Despite the fact that she had scars on her legs and arms. Despite the fact that she was missing a finger. He was still coming to see her.

Of course she'd invited a few other blokes to the barbecue too – after all, Denzil and Sam, who went to the same school, were both friends. To them she was just another person. But they weren't boyfriends. Steve was.

She texted back to say how great it was that he could come, and then rummaged some more in the cardboard boxes until she found a plastic bag with a label attached written in Bill Hudson's illegible doctor's scrawl. She peered inside and saw the lights. She gave a triumphant whoop as she grabbed them and then switched off the attic bulb before swinging herself out of the trap door and on to the stepladder below.

Phydough was being driven demented by the competing scents of burgers, sausages and chicken. He was also aware that the house was in a state of frenzied activity and that things were being dragged out of their normal places, which he didn't like. He sat under the kitchen table, looking hopefully at the fridge every time Claire, Georgia or Eileen walked by. But it remained resolutely closed, and now they'd all gone outside with the bag that Georgia had brought down from the attic. He sighed deeply and followed them into the garden.

'People won't be here late enough for the lights to make any difference,' remarked Claire as she laid the string out on the grass and looked at it.

'Of course they will,' protested Georgia. 'They won't be coming until about five, for heaven's sake.'

'Yes, and they'll probably all be gone by nine.'

'It's dark enough by then,' said Eileen. 'I like the idea of the lights, Claire.'

'I know, I know. You two do nothing but outvote me on things.' Claire tightened the screws on the plug which she was checking before shoving it into the outside socket. Immediately the string lit up and Georgia clapped her hands with pleasure.

'It'll be like a fairy grotto,' she said.

Claire looked sceptical. 'Where will I put them?'

'Where did Dad put them?' asked Georgia.

'At the time there were a couple of skinny bushes at the side wall,' remembered Claire. 'But he cut them down.'

'How about through the first apple tree?' suggested Eileen. 'Will they reach?'

'Sure they will,' said Georgia. 'The flex goes on for ever. Will I do it, Mum?'

'If you like.'

Claire and Eileen watched as Georgia shinned up the tree, taking the lights with her. Claire tried not to appear anxious as her daughter hung out of the branches with scant regard for safety and the laws of gravity while she twisted the lights among the leaves.

'Try them now,' she called when she'd finished.

It was difficult to see the coloured fairy lights in the bright sunshine but they all agreed they would look lovely by the late evening.

'Provided they don't blow the entire fuses for the house,' said Claire. 'I'm sure there must be some kind of shelf life for them.'

'Yeah, but you hardly ever used them,' Georgia pointed out. 'They're probably still like brand new.'

'What would be really good would be those insect repellent torches you light and stick in the ground.' Eileen waved at a fly which had landed on her arm. 'You know what it's like in the evening when all those midges come out.'

'We should have thought of that!' Georgia looked anguished. 'I'm sure I saw them on the Tesco website.'

'Too late now,' said Claire.

'Maybe the hardware shop has some,' suggested Georgia. 'Will I go and check?'

'If you like.' Claire was quite relived at the idea of Georgia getting out of the house for a while. She was exhausted by her daughter's efforts at ensuring that the barbecue was the most successful social event ever to have happened in their lives.

'Have you got any money?' demanded Georgia.

'My bag is on the kitchen table,' said Claire. 'Try not to spend it all!'

'Don't worry. I'm limited by what I can carry,' said Georgia cheerfully and trotted off.

Claire and Eileen exchanged glances. Both of them smiled.

'How about a cup of tea?' suggested Eileen.

'Wonderful,' said Claire.

They'd just finished their second cup and Claire was wondering how long it would take Georgia to get to the hardware store and back when she returned, staggering through the house with half a dozen six-foot-high torches.

'You must be knackered!' Claire took them from under her arm. 'How on earth did you manage to get that lot back?'

'Easier than you think.' Georgia flopped on to a chair. 'I got a lift home.'

'Huh?'

'On the way to the hardware shop I called into Taylor's,' she explained. 'I thought that maybe they did them.'

'Georgia, it's a florist's, for heaven's sake.'

'They're a gardener's as well,' Georgia pointed out. 'And it would have saved me a lot of effort. But they don't. Nate explained to me that they can get stuff for gardens – like the thermometer – but they don't carry much stock. Certainly nothing very big because the shop is really quite small.'

'So you ended up going to the hardware store?'

'Yes, but Nate drove me.'

'He what?' Claire's voice was filled with consternation.

'I don't mind being in a car,' said Georgia easily. 'And when I told him what I was doing he offered to drive me up to Tesco because he knew that they were doing a special offer on them.'

'Honestly, Georgia!' Claire looked at her angrily. 'You shouldn't have allowed him to do that.'

'He offered,' repeated Georgia.

'I know. But he's still a stranger and I've told you a thousand times about getting into cars with strange men.'

'Oh for heaven's sake, Mum!' Georgia's eyes flashed with annoyance. 'It's Nate we're talking about. He was here every day for ages. He's nice. I know he is.'

'It doesn't matter how nice he seems,' said Claire. 'You don't know him or anything about him.'

'I know he's nice,' protested Georgia. 'He gave us the thermometer, didn't he? And he never did anything to make you think that he wasn't . . . You're just being cranky. And mean. I know there are weird, pervy blokes out there – we did a thing about it in school last year – but Nate definitely isn't one of them.'

'Maybe you're overreacting a little, Claire,' said Eileen gently.

'Maybe.' Claire exhaled loudly. 'But still. I'm sure he had better things to do than take you to Tesco.'

'It only took him a few minutes,' said Georgia. 'And they were doing a two-for-the-price-of-one on the torches. I wouldn't have been able to carry six back from the hardware. You know I wouldn't.'

Eileen looked from her daughter to her granddaughter and then suggested that maybe it was about time she got ready and that perhaps Georgia could help.

'Absolutely.' Georgia looked pleased. 'I can do your hair for you.'

'Sure.' Eileen tried to keep the trepidation out of her voice.

'Don't worry, I'll turn you into a sex symbol,' Georgia assured her. 'So that you look sensational in front of the new woman.'

'Well . . .'

'I'd want to,' said Georgia firmly.

'Would you?' Claire looked at her curiously.

'Well of course I would!' cried Georgia. 'Let's face it, Mum, no matter what, you always want to appear desirable to blokes you've once gone out with.'

'How do you know that?' demanded Claire. 'I wasn't aware that there was such a big supply of ex-boyfriends in your armoury.'

'There isn't,' agreed Georgia. 'But it's common sense, isn't it?'

'Yes.' Eileen nodded. 'It is. And OK, Georgey, you can do my hair.'

'I'll do yours too if you like, Mum?' She looked enquiringly at Claire.

'Thanks but I can manage,' said Claire.

'Well don't forget to make yourself look gorgeous anyway,' Georgia told her.

'I'll do my best,' replied Claire drily. 'I really will.'

Fifteen minutes before the first guests were due to arrive, Eileen, Claire and Georgia stood in the kitchen. Claire was uncorking a bottle of white wine. She eased the cork gently from the neck of the bottle and filled two glasses, half filling a third, which she handed to Georgia.

'No sneaking drink when you think I'm not looking,' she warned.

'You're no fun.' But Georgia's eyes twinkled.

'Cheers.' Eileen held out her glass. Claire and Georgia clinked theirs against it.

'Bottoms up for the party Nelligans,' said Georgia. 'And Gran, even though I say so myself, you look absolutely fabulous!'

'She's right,' agreed Claire.

'Thank you.' Eileen blushed slightly as she checked her appearance (for the twentieth time) in the small kitchen mirror. 'You did a great job, Georgia.'

'I know.' Georgia looked smug as she regarded her grandmother.

Eileen's normally wavy and unkempt salt-and-pepper hair had been tamed into a sleek bob, held in place by Georgia's favourite fixing gel. The change in style knocked about ten years from her age, and despite the fact that she was still wearing her glasses (she couldn't, she told Georgia, leave them off, she'd keep walking into things), her entire face was more open without hair tumbling waywardly about it. Georgia had been surprised to realise that Eileen also had amber flecks in her slightly darker eyes and that, with the aid of some foundation which Claire had given her, she had an almost continental complexion.

'You look chic,' she told Eileen. 'Kind of middle-aged Parisienne.'

Eileen laughed. 'Ancient Parisienne, maybe.'

'No, truly.' Georgia was quite serious. 'The make-up suits you. You should wear it more often.'

'I don't normally bother,' admitted Eileen.

'You and Mum both.' Georgia sighed theatrically. 'I do my best, but what good is it if you both let me down!'

'At least I'm wearing make-up,' said Eileen as she looked accusingly at Claire.

'I'm wearing tinted moisturiser!' cried Claire. 'And blusher!'

'Mum doesn't really do the make-up thing,' Georgia told Eileen. 'Even though I'm always telling her that darker lippy would be good.'

'Oh, shut up!' But Claire smiled.

She looked at herself in the mirror too. Although she'd gone light on the make-up she knew that the summer's sun had given her face and body a healthy glow. She was wearing the leaf-green cotton dress she'd worn for her lunch date with Con and Lacey because she knew that it suited her colouring. She'd pulled her cinnamon hair into a very loose ponytail, held in place by a vivid green scrunchie. She thought she looked OK. Maybe a little more than OK, because even though there was a part of her that was apprehensive about today, there was another part of her that was just a bit excited. And that part brought a sparkle to her eyes.

She looked away from her own reflection and at her daughter instead. She'd had to clamp down very hard on her initial reaction when she'd seen Georgia's outfit of an impossibly short tangerine skirt and a figure-hugging sunflower-yellow belly-top. There was no doubt that Georgia had the build to carry off the totally unforgiving look. In fact, Claire had thought in horrified amazement, Georgia looked incredibly sexy and grown-up in it, with her hair gelled and spiked and an incredibly deft application of make-up which gave her smoky, rock-chick eyes and pouting, kissable lips. How the hell did she turn into a creature like this before my very eyes? wondered Claire. What happened to my baby daughter? And how the hell am I going to keep her away from predatory blokes for another few years when she looks so damn wonderful?

'I'm not really sure I like wine.' Georgia put the glass on the table. 'According to Sive's sister, alcopops are miles better.'

Claire felt a dagger of fear in her heart. 'I really don't want you drinking that stuff,' she said as mildly as she could.

'I dunno.' Georgia shrugged.

'Please, please don't go out and drink alcopops,' begged Claire. 'If you want to try them, maybe we could do it at home.'

'Claire! Georgia's only a child!' Eileen was scandalised at the thought of her daughter and granddaughter sitting at home slugging alcopops.

'I'm not a child,' said Georgia sharply. 'I'm not an adult but I'm not a child.'

The sound of a car door slamming was a welcome one. Georgia rushed to the door and opened it. She waved excitedly at Robyn, who'd got out of the SUV, Leonie and Mike following her. Leonie was wearing a similar skirt to Georgia, in shocking pink.

'Come round the side!' called Georgia. 'Everything's set up.'

Eileen and Claire exchanged glances.

'Here goes,' said Claire, as she stepped outside.

Chapter 34

Dictamnus (Burning Bush) – Pale pink or white, the surface oils are an irritant and will ignite if a match is struck beside them on a warm sunny day.

Eavan Keating walked out of the en-suite bathroom and back into the bedroom. Glenn's jeans and casual shirt were still on the bed. She opened the wardrobe door and slipped on her royal-blue sun-dress before clipping a pair of gold ear-rings on to her ears and fastening her gold locket around her neck.

She heard the sound of the front door bell and Saffy's welcoming cry as Glenn opened it and Candida walked in. Their voices were muffled as they went through into the living room. Eavan looked at her watch. It was after five. She walked down the stairs.

Glenn glanced at her as she entered the room and then turned his attention back to Saffy.

'Hi, Candida,' she said brightly. 'How're you?'

'Great thanks, Eavan.'

'We're not expecting to be too late,' Eavan told her. 'We'll go as soon as Glenn's ready.'

He got up and walked wordlessly out of the room. Eavan looked after him while Candida frowned slightly.

'It's a lovely day for a barbecue,' the babysitter said eventually.

Eavan nodded.

'When I told my dad where you guys were going he got all enthusiastic about having a barbecue himself,' Candida told her. 'So he nipped out to B and Q and bought one of those disposable ones.'

'Want a barbecue with you.' Saffy pouted.

'We'll have one of our own,' promised Candida. 'Just you and me.' She smiled at Eavan. 'Any news on your house sale?'

'Not yet,' said Eavan tightly. 'But it's early days.' She heard Glenn's footsteps on the stairs and he reappeared in the doorway wearing his jeans and shirt, his hair ruffled and uncombed. It looked cute that way, thought Eavan, unlike his normally neat style. But she didn't think, somehow, that he meant to look cute.

'Ready?' he asked shortly.

'Sure.' She smiled at Saffy and dropped a kiss on her head. 'Be good,' she said.

'Always am.'

'See you later.' Eavan's words encompassed both Saffy and Candida as she followed Glenn out of the house.

He walked around to the passenger side of the car.

'You want me to drive?' She looked at him uncertainly.

'It's set up for you, isn't it?' he asked.

'Sure, but . . .'

'Then you can drive.'

She pressed the central locking key and opened the driver's door. Glenn got in beside her. She started the car and edged out of the house and on to the main road. They drove in a silence that was becoming more uneasy with every passing second. Though how things could be getting worse was a mystery to Eavan. After all, she thought miserably, they'd spent the last twenty-four hours locked in silence. And she wondered whether that was ever going to change. Because there was more to it now than Glenn losing his job. There was more to it than her working part time. Since last night, things between them had changed irrevocably.

She'd stayed out in the garden with her back to the house, hoping that he'd come after her and put his arms around her like he'd always done before when they'd argued. But he hadn't and then she'd heard the sound of breaking glass. Her heart had skidded in her chest and she was filled with the unaccountable fear that maybe he was smashing up the house in his frustration. Part of her would have understood that. She'd hesitated and then walked back inside, to find him mopping the wine from the kitchen floor. She looked at him, aghast at the sight of the spilled alcohol, unsure of what had happened.

'I knocked it over,' he said abruptly. 'Don't panic. I didn't drink it. I didn't dare. It would have been more of an admission, wouldn't it?'

'An admission of what?' Her voice shook.

'An admission that I can't keep up with your demands for perfection,' he snapped. 'An admission that I'm a lousy father and a lousy husband and an all-round lousy drunk.'

'But you're none of those things,' she said quietly.

'I'm all of those things,' he retorted. 'I should never have married you, Eavan. I can't give you what you want.'

'You've always given me what I wanted!' she cried.

'Then you've set your sights too low,' he said. 'I can't keep up with your ideals.'

'For Christ's sake!' She stared at him, her eyes scalding with unshed tears. 'I don't have ideals! I don't deserve you either.'

'No, you don't,' he agreed. 'You deserve someone without a past like mine. Someone you can depend on. Someone you're not expecting to fall off the wagon at the slightest provocation!'

'I don't!' she cried. 'I need someone like you.'

He turned away from her and she stood watching him helplessly, clenching and unclenching her fists as conflicting thoughts tumbled through her mind. It was important, she knew, to say the right thing now. Not to make him feel worse than he did already.

'Glenn, come on!' she said, trying to keep her voice relaxed. 'We were always a good partnership. We've been happy together. We can't let this come between us. It's nothing in the whole scheme of things.'

'We might have been a partnership but now it's all weighted in one direction,' said Glenn, his back still to her. 'And if you think that this is nothing, then you really don't understand me at all.'

'Of course I do!' she cried. 'Glenn . . .'

'It might be stupid and immature of me to resent the fact that you're the one who's doing everything now,' he told her tightly. 'But I can't help it. And I can't help resenting that you're the one with the blameless past yet you're still the one who's had to make sacrifices now and who's simply rolled up her sleeves and got on with it.'

Eavan swallowed. 'I don't have a blameless past,' she said.

'No dark secrets, though,' he said harshly. 'No personal problems that colour everything thing that happens to you. People don't look at you and define you because of something unsavoury in your life.'

'Alcoholism isn't something unsavoury,' she said. 'It's a disease.'

'Yeah, yeah. I know the shit they make us say.'

'Glenn . . .' She bit her lip. 'I . . . there's more to it . . .'

'Oh, let's not continue talking about this!' He looked round at her. 'I'm tired of it.'

'Listen to me,' she said urgently, glancing out to the garden where Saffy was sitting unconcernedly in her sandpit. 'It's not only you who has problems or gets things wrong. Honestly it isn't.'

He snorted while this time she clenched her fists so tightly that she could feel her nails cut into her palms.

'I'm not the person you think I am,' she continued breathlessly. 'You've built me up into some kind of wonder woman and I'm absolutely not. I . . .' She looked at him and swallowed hard. 'I've made mistakes too. Terrible mistakes.'

'Like what?' he demanded roughly. 'Buying the wrong shade of blue for the curtains in the living-room?'

She had to tell him. But it was really hard. She didn't want to tell him. But if she didn't do it now . . . and he deserved to know. Maybe, though, this wasn't the right time. Oh hell, she thought, no time would be the right time. She swallowed hard and pressed her fingers to her temples.

'I had an abortion,' she told him starkly. 'Before I met you.'

Glenn stared at her in silent disbelief. The tears which she'd kept in check suddenly spilled from her eyes and down her cheeks.

She choked out the story to him. Of the one-night stand with a guy whose name she didn't know. Of the impossibility of having a baby when her mother had been so ill. Of the fact that Bill and Claire Hudson had been the only non-judgemental people in her life right then and of how they'd helped her.

'Claire Hudson,' said Glenn. 'I might have guessed. That's why you've stayed so friendly with her even though she's driven you mad ever since Bill died.'

'She was good to me when I needed someone,' said Eavan. 'You've no idea what it was like.'

'Seems not,' said Glenn sourly. 'Seems I didn't know as much about the person I married as I thought. Seems like all of the being honest with each other was one-sided. Seems like I was taken for a fool.'

'Oh, Glenn!' Eavan looked miserably at him.

'I need to be on my own for a while,' he said.

He'd walked out of the kitchen and up the stairs. He'd stayed upstairs all evening, and when Eavan eventually went to bed, she'd realised that he was sleeping in the spare room.

Since then it had been a cat-and-mouse game. Whenever she'd gone into a room, Glenn had left it. She'd been determined not to be the one to crack and speak first even though she really just wanted Glenn to understand why she'd kept it a secret from him and beg him to forgive her. But she was afraid. She knew she should talk to him again. Yet for the first time in their married life, she really had no idea what to say.

She didn't really want to go to Claire's barbecue either, but nor did she want to stay in the house. And so eventually she was the one who broke the silence and asked him whether they were going.

'I said I'd come.' His voice was taut. 'I can't let her think she's the only one who's been caring and understanding towards my wife.'

Now Eavan choked back the urge to cry again and gripped the steering wheel of the car more tightly. She wanted to be anywhere but in the car with him, with anything else planned rather than a social gathering where she was supposed to be animated and fun. The truth was, she hadn't expected that they'd be going. But she didn't know what else to do.

'Shit!' She braked hard as a car cut in front of her.

'You were going too slowly,' said Glenn. 'That's why he overtook you like that.'

'No I wasn't.'

'Oh, sorry, forgot.' He glanced at her. 'You're perfect. You can do no wrong. Oh, sorry, forgot again. There was that little episode of the abortion I knew nothing about.'

'For crying out loud!' This time she slammed on the brakes and the cars behind her hooted in annoyance. She pulled over to the side of the road and switched on the hazard warning lights. Then she turned to Glenn. 'I can't take this any more. I really can't. I had a

337

terrible, terrible choice to make when I had the abortion and there's a part of me that still isn't sure whether it was the right damn choice. And I kept it secret from you because I thought that you'd despise me for it. And you do, don't you?'

'I don't know how I feel about you,' said Glenn. 'I don't know how I feel about you or me or anything any more. Because I thought we were living one life and it turns out it was all based on lies.'

'No it damn well wasn't! OK, I admit I kept something from you. But I didn't lie to you. In the end you kept something from me too. Let's call it quits.'

'It's hardly the same thing, is it? I don't tell you about losing my job. You don't tell me about—'

'Glenn, please,' begged Eavan as she rested her head on the steering wheel. 'Please, please understand.'

Glenn opened the car door. She looked up anxiously.

'Where are you going?'

'I need to walk,' he said.

'But what about Claire?'

'You go to Claire's,' he said. 'I'll see you there.'

She bit her lip. 'It's still miles away.'

'So?'

'But . . .' She hesitated. 'Look, why don't I park the car some-where and walk with you?'

'Because I want to be on my own.'

'Glenn . . .'

'I want to be on my own,' he repeated firmly.

'I love you,' she said. 'This is messing with my head.'

He leaned into the car. 'It's messing with my head too.'

He closed the car door and walked towards the seafront. Eavan watched his tall figure as he strode away from her. Then she started the engine and pulled away.

Georgia was looking out for Steve Ó Sé. He still hadn't arrived and now she was beginning to wonder whether he ever would. She hadn't said anything to the girls, wanting it to be a big surprise for them when he showed up, wanting to appear aloof and casual about it.

338

But she was getting edgier and edgier until Robyn asked her what the hell was the matter.

'Nothing,' she said, glancing towards the knot of people at the side of the house and willing Steve to suddenly appear among them. But the latest arrivals were a group of women who she guessed were from Locum Libris. They shrieked with enthusiasm when they saw Claire and made their way over to her, laughing and embracing her.

Georgia watched them with narrowed eyes. Somehow she'd always thought that the people her mother worked with would be more like Claire herself. Or at least how Claire had become. Quiet and serious. But the Locum Libris women were bright and bubbly and in their company Claire seemed bright and bubbly too. Georgia looked on in astonishment as Claire high-fived Trinny Armstrong. Maybe it's her mother persona when she's around me, thought Georgia. Maybe she thinks she has to be serious and quiet. She smiled as Claire laughed at something Trinny said. Georgia knew that she needed Claire to be serious sometimes. That she depended on knowing that her mother would always do the right thing. But it was nice to see her laugh so unselfconsciously too.

'It's not a bad bit of fun, is it?' Robyn nibbled at a chicken wing, oblivious to Georgia's thoughts. 'Though I wish your mum hadn't got in quite so much food. I'm going to have to go on a diet.' She pinched a bit of flesh around her waist. 'Gross, isn't it?'

'You don't need to diet,' said Georgia loyally, though she knew that Robyn had put on loads of weight during the summer thanks to the tons of food available at the Irish College. She would've put on weight herself, she thought, if it hadn't been for the fact that she'd obviously inherited her grandfather's genes. He'd always been lean. She was too.

'You look so much better in that top than me,' added Robyn. 'Plus, your tits are even bigger now.'

'D'you think so?' Georgia looked anxiously at her boobs. 'I was hoping that it was my imagination.'

'Nope.' Robyn wiped barbecue sauce from her chin. 'I'm telling you, Georgia Hudson, you could make it big in lingerie modelling!'

'Get lost!' Georgia dug her friend in the ribs and then caught her breath. 'Oh.'

'Oh what?'

'Oh,' said Georgia again. 'He came. He actually came.' A wide beam broke across her face as she saw Steve Ó Sé walk into the garden.

Eileen Shanahan was discussing rising house prices with Alan Bellew, who had (somewhat to her surprise) arrived at five o'clock exactly and was, therefore, one of the first guests to show up. Despite the sun and the casual nature of the barbecue, Alan was once again dressed in an elegantly tailored suit, with a crisp white shirt and dark red tie. His white hair was neatly styled and his shoes gleamed. (Eileen always noticed a man's shoes. Well-polished shoes had been one of Kate Nelligan's standards for men to live up to.)

He's attractive, thought Eileen. He really is. And I'm glad that I did something a bit racy for me and asked him to come along. It was worth it. It's not like I'm expecting very much out of this but it's nice to have someone good-looking beside me. Someone who seems to want to be beside me. She smiled at him and tucked a wisp of hair behind her ear.

'I like it,' he said.

She looked at him in puzzlement.

'What you did to your hair. It's different. It suits you.'

'Thank you.' She realised that she was blushing. 'My granddaughter styled it for me. She's the young thing in the short skirt. At least, she's calling it a skirt. To me it's more like a hairband around her waist!'

Alan followed her gaze to where Georgia and Robyn were standing, looking in Steve's direction.

'She's very pretty,' he said.

'Isn't she?' Eileen's tone was wry. 'She's going to give her mother a ton of trouble in a year or two.'

'Maybe not.' But Alan sounded doubtful.

'Not intentionally,' Eileen amended. 'She's a good girl really. She just doesn't realise how pretty she is.'

'I thought beautiful women always knew.'

'To be honest, it's only in the last couple of months that she's blossomed,' said Eileen. 'And, of course, there are the injuries.'

Alan frowned and Eileen explained about the accident in Jamaica.

'How awful,' he said. 'It must be really hard to get over something like that.'

'I'm hoping that they're managing,' said Eileen.

'If they're anything like you, they'll manage just fine.'

She realised that his blue eyes were looking affectionately at her. She blushed again. Alan smiled and squeezed her arm. It seemed natural to her to rest her head on his shoulder for a second before looking up at him again. And then she saw Con and Lacey making their way over.

Con's eyes widened as he saw Eileen look up at the man beside her. There was an expression on her face that he hadn't seen in a very long time. A way she'd once looked at him. He stared at both of them, lagging behind Lacey, who walked straight over to them.

'Hi, Eileen,' she said. 'You're looking well.'

'Thanks,' said Eileen. 'So are you.' She took in Lacey's expensive cerise dress, multicoloured shoes, and matching bag. Her trademark chunky jewellery was silver and her golden hair gleamed in the evening sunlight. 'I like the shoes.'

Lacey smiled. 'Lovely to look at, crucifying to wear, you'd think I'd have more sense.' She glanced at Alan and held out her hand. 'Lacey Dillon.'

'Alan Bellew,' he said.

Eileen felt her heart race as she noticed how Alan's glance flickered over Lacey's trim, toned body. She was horrified to realised that she resented his evident approval of how the other woman looked.

'Hello, pet.' Con almost, but not quite, kissed Eileen on the cheek. 'You look amazing.'

'And you're keeping well, I hope?' Eileen always found it strange to have casual conversations with Con. She didn't love him any more. She was perfectly happy to have him living his life with Lacey. But she couldn't ever truly feel at ease in his company. And she couldn't stand beside him and not remember that one night of abandoned passion which had resulted in Claire and in a marriage that she'd never really wanted.

'Fine,' he said. He adjusted the waistband of his trousers. They were biscuit-coloured casuals. Slacks, Eileen would once have called them, but she was pretty sure there was a different term for them now. His shirt was striped and loose. He looked OK, she thought, but not half as groomed as Alan. Although, in all fairness, Alan was dressed for a Dublin 4 garden party rather than a Saturday barbecue. But she couldn't help feeling a flash of satisfaction that she was standing beside such an attractive man right now. And a slight frisson because she knew he was attracted to her. The subdued excitement made her eyes sparkle and her skin glow.

'Alan, this is my ex-husband, Con,' she said.

'Pleased to meet you,' said Alan. 'I'm delighted to have been able to work on Eileen's behalf.'

Con looked surprised.

'Alan was the main negotiator on the sale of Ambleside,' Eileen explained.

'Oh.'

'He was extremely helpful.'

'I see.'

'There's Claire!' Lacey suddenly spotted her in the crowd of people. 'I should say hello.'

'And I'm just going to get another drink,' said Eileen. She smiled at Alan and at Con.

'Can I get you guys anything?' They both shook their heads and she walked away, leaving them together.

'Lacey Dillon? Is that the recruitment crowd?' asked Alan.

Con nodded.

'Amazingly successful.'

'Yes,' said Con.

'Worth a lot of money.'

Con shrugged. 'I don't know about that. I suppose she's well off, but we haven't discussed it very much. What's hers is hers and what's mine is mine.'

'You're getting half the proceeds of Eileen's house?'

'It was the family home,' said Con edgily. 'And it's none of your damn business.'

'Of course not,' agreed Alan.

Con looked at him speculatively. 'You're not thinking of moving in on her, are you?' he asked sharply.

Alan laughed. 'Moving in on her?'

'Eileen. She's a very sensitive woman, you know. I don't want you messing with her feelings.'

'I rather think she knows how to look after her own feelings,' said Alan.

'You needn't think that just because she has some money from the house you can romance it away from under her nose.'

Alan laughed again. 'You're getting the wrong end of the stick,' he said. 'I've no intention of doing any such thing. But I like Eileen. She's a good woman. And attractive too.'

'Attractive . . . well . . .'

'You don't think so?' Alan looked over to where Eileen had stopped to talk to another woman. 'I think she's very attractive. Especially so today.'

'She does look well today,' agreed Con. He looked at Eileen. Certainly the new hairstyle took years off her. But she was still a plump, motherly woman in a flowery skirt and plain top, even if she was smiling more than he'd ever seen her smile before and even though her eyes sparkled in the afternoon sun. Then he looked over towards Lacey, who was talking to Leonie O'Malley. As he watched, Lacey slid her foot out of one of her high-heeled shoes and rubbed her ankle.

'She's very attractive too,' said Alan, following his glance. 'In a different way.'

'I think I'll get a drink after all,' Con said. 'Excuse me a minute, will you.' He walked towards the bar. And stopped to speak to Eileen again as he went.

'You never said he was coming!' cried Robyn accusingly to Georgia. 'You didn't say you'd invited him.'

'I wasn't sure he could make it.' Georgia's eyes gleamed with excitement.

'I didn't realise you fancied him quite so much.'

Georgia looked at her friend and giggled. 'Neither did I,' she said.

Claire had seen Con and Lacey arrive but had been diverted by Joanna Gregory, who'd stopped her to ask who the attractive man in the suit was. Claire, rather distractedly, told her that Alan was a friend of her mother's, at which Joanna's face dropped.

'Are there any single men at all?' she demanded just as Frank Maddox, from the Smash & Grab club, walked by.

'Actually, yes,' said Claire firmly. 'Frank – Joanna. Joanna – Frank. Both of you are single. Chat to each other for a minute.'

She left the two of them together in startled silence while she bore down on Con.

'Dad!'

'Darling.' He hugged her and kissed her on the cheek. 'This is wonderful. I never thought I'd see anything like this happening here again.'

'It's a bit of a nightmare,' she said. 'I seem to have a lot of single female friends looking for men and not enough of them to go round!'

'I see you've managed to find one for your mother.'

'Not me.' Claire looked appraisingly at her father. 'She found him all by herself. Nice, isn't he?'

'If you like that sort of man,' said Con. 'Bit strait-laced, don't you think?'

'At first,' said Claire blithely. 'But once you get to know him he's really lovely. I think he likes Mum a lot.'

'Do you now?'

'Absolutely,' said Claire. 'She says there's nothing between them, but . . .'

'Surely not,' said Con. 'He's totally wrong for her.'

'Excuse me?' Claire looked at her father in wry amusement. 'You're the man who was totally wrong for her, don't you think?'

'Oh, but for heaven's sake!' Con nodded in Alan's direction. 'Look at him. Suit and tie and shiny shoes. That's not the sort of man Eileen needs.'

'I don't think it's up to you any more, Dad,' said Claire. 'Besides, you have Lacey, don't you? And she's hardly the sort of woman I pictured for you either. Don't forget, I was the one who thought you and Mum were a perfect couple.'

'It's just . . .' Con scratched the back of his head. 'I didn't see your mother as being the sort of woman who'd find someone else.'

'Well, she has,' said Claire pertly. 'And I'm delighted for her.'

344

'You still blame me,' said Con.

'Ah, Dad, no.' Suddenly Claire put her arm around him. 'I don't. And I know I was a bit childish about it but I think you were right to call it a day. And I honestly hope that you and Lacey are very happy together.'

'Thank you,' said Con. 'I want to introduce her to Georgia. If that's all right with you?'

'Sure . . . and Georgey is . . .' Claire looked around. 'I've no idea where Georgey is. She was here a minute ago . . . there's a little gang of her friends at the back of the garden, obviously not wanting to mix with the old fogeys up here. But I don't see Georgia herself . . .'

Georgia and Steve were sitting on the grass at the back of the garden, half hidden from view by the apple tree and the huge escallonia bush. Georgia was surprised at how much skinnier Steve seemed compared with the guy she remembered from Galway, and how many spots had suddenly appeared on his face. (Not, she told herself hastily, that spots were a problem, wasn't she always getting them herself, but still, his poor skin seemed to have erupted all over the place!) It was nice to see him, but in her head she'd built up a picture of him as a taller, more athletic bloke. The actual Steve somehow wasn't as gorgeous as she remembered.

'I can't believe you came,' said Georgia.

'You invited me,' he pointed out.

'I know.'

'It was nice to have something else to do on a Saturday for a change.'

'Thanks for all the texts,' she said.

'I enjoy them,' Steve told her. 'Keeps me sane sometimes.'

'How's things at home?' she asked.

'The same as usual.'

They sat in silence as bursts of chatter and laughter from the other people at the barbecue floated down the garden towards them. How was it, wondered Georgia, that they'd been able to keep up text conversations that had blasted through her phone credits in a single afternoon but that it was so much harder to talk to him face

345

to face? She didn't want to say anything stupid, anything that would make him regret coming. And yet he wasn't helping, sitting here beside her and not saying anything unless she spoke first. She'd imagined that when they finally met there'd be a spark between them again. She'd thought, somehow, that things would click into place and he'd realise how much he cared about her. And that she'd know how much she cared about him too. She'd thought that they would find out they were meant for each other. Soulmates. She picked at a blade of grass and rubbed it between her fingers. How stupid could that be? They weren't soulmates. They were just ordinary mates.

'You OK?' he asked suddenly.

'Sure, yes.'

'I thought you might be regretting asking me.'

'I thought you might be regretting coming.'

He smiled. It was his smile, she remembered, that she'd found so attractive in Galway. It crinkled up his face and his eyes and it made him look suddenly attractive again. Despite the spots.

'I'm not good on girl stuff,' he said. 'It's easier by text.'

She nodded in heartfelt agreement. And then they started to talk again, the words bubbling between them so that they interrupted each other as they filled in the gaps that the texts had left out.

When they finally paused for a moment Georgia glanced around the garden. Robyn, Sive and Emma were standing beside the jasmine bush looking in her direction. Denzil and Sam were helping Mike O'Malley with the barbecue.

'I think I'd better get back to my friends,' she told Steve.

'I'm not a friend?'

She made a face at him. 'You know you are. But I can't leave the girls stranded among the parents! Besides, I'm sure they want to talk to you too.'

'Maybe. But I need to do this first. I didn't do it very well in Galway and I've been thinking about it ever since.'

He put his arm around her shoulder and drew her closer to him. She could smell his aftershave (or perhaps not aftershave, she thought, as he moved his face closer to her and she realised that his stubble was still downy-soft. Perhaps just scent. It was nice, though. A musky, woody smell. An outdoors kind of smell.). She closed her eyes and felt his lips on hers.

It was so different to Galway. There it had been rushed and furtive, behind the sports pavilion on the day that they were going home. Their teeth had clattered against each other and Steve had been so embarrassed that he'd pulled away from her and made a joke about it. And, as she'd thought about giving it another go but was uncertain as to how Steve would react, Mr Ó Cinnéide had rounded the building, taken one look at them and ordered them back to the main hall where hordes of students were milling around waiting for the coaches to take them to the station.

This time they got it right. Georgia lost herself in the pleasure of his kiss, aware of a whole new range of sensations coursing through her. I'm doing it properly, she thought. Me, Georgia Hudson, the girl with the dodgy hand and the scars. A bloke is kissing me and my mates can see it and I like it. She slid her arms around his body and held him tightly. She remembered, suddenly, a phrase in one of the magazines she'd read. Kissing hungrily. She thought that she was probably kissing Steve Ó Sé hungrily. But it was like her body was detached from her mind. It was doing things of its own accord. Her lips were working on their own!

'Hello, Georgia.'

The sound of her grandfather's voice brought her back to reality. She pulled away from Steve and looked up at Con. She didn't like the dark expression on his face one little bit.

There was still no sign of Nate and Sarah Taylor. Claire was annoyed with herself for constantly looking around to see if they'd arrived. Everyone else seemed to be here – the entire Locum Libris crew; the Smash & Grab club people (including Paul who was back from his Galway trip and who'd spent most of his time so far in the company of Petra – they were now sitting on the garden bench and he was feeding her chicken wings); the neighbours (with whom she'd only exchanged a few words, but who seemed nice and friendly and made her feel guilty about her neglect of them . . . Eavan, she realised suddenly. Eavan and Glenn weren't here either. But as the thought

347

came into her mind she saw Eavan walk around the side of the house and look uncertainly in her direction.

'Hi there!' Claire made her way over to her. 'I thought you weren't going to make it.'

'I thought the same.'

'Are you all right?' Claire looked at her in concern. 'Where's Glenn.'

'Walking,' said Eavan. 'Can I get a drink?'

'Of course.' Claire grabbed a bottle of white wine from the cooler and poured a glass for her friend. To Claire's complete astonishment Eavan knocked it back in a couple of gulps. She refilled the glass wordlessly.

'I never knew why people drank like that before,' said Eavan. 'I've always enjoyed my alcohol at the end of the day. Socially. Not as a crutch. But I can see how it can be like that.'

'What's the matter?' asked Claire.

Eavan told her that she'd confessed to Glenn about the abortion and that he didn't seem to be handling it very well.

'I shouldn't have told him. Not now. He can't bear the sight of me but because I'm the one earning money he can't let me know how much he despises me.' She swallowed hard. 'I think it's going wrong between us,' she said shakily. 'I don't know if it can be fixed.'

'Oh, Eavan.' Claire put her arm around her friend. 'Don't think like that. You two love each other. You have a good marriage.'

Eavan shook her head. 'We loved each other when everything was going right.' The words jerked out of her mouth. 'Now that things are going wrong . . .'

'Do you still love him?' asked Claire.

'I said so today.' Eavan blinked a couple of times. 'And then afterwards I wondered about it. I love him but I don't know if I love him enough to live like this any more.'

'It's a bad patch,' said Claire. 'Everyone has a bad patch.'

'You and Bill?' asked Eavan wryly.

'Of course.'

'When?'

Claire considered. There'd been the time shortly after Georgia was born, when Bill was working ridiculous hours and seemed to be going out every night on house calls, and neither of them was getting any sleep . . . they'd gone through a period of snapping at each other and generally being short-tempered and there had been a few days when Claire had wondered whether they would manage to last the course. It had been the only time she'd doubted their love for each other. But they'd come through it. She'd apologised to him for yelling at him that he was the most selfish man on the planet, that all he cared about was other damn people and not those closest to him. And he'd apologised for the fact that he'd let it become that way because he'd automatically assumed that she'd love him no matter what.

'I do love you no matter what,' she'd said that night as they lay in bed together.

'You shouldn't have to,' he replied. And he'd teamed up with another doctor to share house calls in the future.

'Claire?' Eavan's voice broke into her thoughts.

'We apologised to each other,' said Claire. 'Any time there was something wrong. One or the other of us would say sorry.'

'Even if you weren't?'

'I guess that part didn't matter. It was making the effort that counted.'

'I feel like I'm the one making most of the effort,' said Eavan as she drained the second glass of wine. 'And I'm still not sure that it's worth it.'

Claire watched her friend, her eyes clouded with worry.

'Oh, look,' Eavan said suddenly, with studied brightness. 'Your hunky gardener is here.'

'What the hell do you think you're doing!' Con Shanahan looked angrily at Georgia and Steve as Georgia hastily pulled her tiny skirt lower and rearranged her top. She'd never felt more embarrassed in her life. Being caught in a clinch by her grandfather was mortifying, and she had a horrible feeling that he'd think more was going on than had really happened. She cleared her throat and bit her lip.

'This is Steve,' she said. 'Steve – this is my grandad.'

'Pleased to meet you,' said Steve as he got to his feet.

Georgia giggled. She couldn't help it. Steve sounded so serious and grown-up and not at all intimidated by the angry figure towering over him.

349

'I don't see what you have to laugh at,' snapped Con. 'Behaving like a common tart!'

This time Georgia felt the tears prickle at the back of her eyes. She felt herself grow hot, then cold, as her grandfather radiated fury.

'She most certainly was not,' said Steve indignantly. 'We were kissing, that's all.'

'Your hands were all over my granddaughter! And in her home too!'

'Gramps, please.' Georgia looked at him pleadingly. 'Don't create a scene.'

'Me!' Con snorted. 'I'm creating nothing. It's you. And you were creating more than a scene! I don't know what your mother will have to say about this.'

'Oh, Gramps!'

'Look Mr . . . Shanahan, is it?' Steve's voice was steady. 'I know Georgia well. We're good friends. I care about her.' He reached out and took her by the hand, closing his grip over the scarred part where her little finger used to be. 'I wouldn't do anything wrong with her.'

'You don't think rolling about under the escallonia is wrong?' demanded Con.

'Maybe with all these people around,' admitted Steve.

The two of them stared at each other, Steve young and defiant, Con older and angry. Georgia felt the beat of her heart in the base of her throat. She wondered if she'd be sick.

'I should talk to your mother, young lady.' The fury had gone out of Con's voice.

'I hadn't seen him in ages,' said Georgia. 'We met in Galway. We were catching up.'

'I hope you didn't get up to that sort of thing in Galway!'

'Of course not.' Georgia bit her lip. 'Gramps, you must know what it's like to be young and stuff. I mean, you and Gran and . . . and now you and Lacey . . .' Her voice trailed off.

'We're adults,' said Con.

'Yes, but I bet you kiss!' This time Georgia's voice was defiant.

Suddenly Con laughed. 'Yes, we do.'

'Well then,' said Georgia.

'You're fourteen years old,' said Con. 'I really don't think—'

'We were only kissing,' repeated Steve.

'OK, OK.' Con shook his head. 'You've kissed. Now come back to the barbecue with me. Georgia, I want to introduce you to Lacey. She's dying to meet you.'

'Sure, Gramps.' And this time it was Con who was the recipient of a kiss from Georgia, a light peck on the cheek before she hurried back up the lawn with him, Steve following behind.

'Hi, Claire.' Nate was standing on the patio, a plate laden with food in his hand. 'Fantastic party. And the garden looks wonderful.'

'Really great,' agreed Sarah beside him. 'Hello again.' She smiled at Claire as she pinched a sausage from Nate's plate. 'He did a good job, didn't he?'

'Yes,' said Claire. 'Of course the layout was done by my husband.'

'Nate told me,' said Sarah. 'He had a good eye for a garden.'

'It was his hobby.'

'Am I right in believing that he died?' Sarah's blue eyes were sympathetic.

'Yes,' said Claire shortly. 'An accident. When we were on holiday.'

Nate and Sarah exchanged glances.

'I'm sorry,' said Sarah.

'Life goes on.' Claire was aware that her voice was unnaturally bright. And that she'd never spoken in such a flippant way about the accident before. Not that she felt flippant. She felt as though she was going to faint. She still fancied him. She really did. Even with his beautiful wife beside him. And this was so wrong. She shouldn't have asked them.

'Hey, Claire – you haven't tried any of my food yet!' Mike O'Malley called at her from behind the barbecue. 'It'll all be gone soon.'

She'd never felt less like eating in her life but she turned gratefully towards him.

'He's right,' she told the Taylors. 'Excuse me while I grab a burger.'

Alan Bellew looked at his watch and then, apologetically, at Eileen.

'I have to go,' he told her.

'I know,' she said. 'The anniversary dinner. The one you can't get out of.'

'My twin sister and her husband,' said Alan. 'Forty years together. I can't get my head around that, to be honest.'

'Why didn't you ever get married?' asked Eileen. 'I could understand you getting married and it not working out, or perhaps if you lost your wife . . . but you're a nice bloke, Alan, and I'm surprised you escaped unhitched!'

He laughed. A hearty, generous laugh. She'd never heard him laugh like that before.

'My heart was broken,' he told her. 'When I was twenty-one. The girl I loved, the girl I expected to marry, dumped me for someone else.'

'And you were scarred for life?' Eileen looked at him sceptically.

'I decided there were other things in life,' he told her.

'You're right about that.'

'But maybe they're not always as important as we think.' He smiled at her. 'Thank you for inviting me. I see that your daughter is caught up in conversation and I don't want to disturb her, but thank her for me too.'

'You're welcome,' said Eileen. 'And my thanks for the house stuff again.'

'Maybe you'll invite me to the apartment sometime?'

'Maybe,' she said.

'I want to see you again,' he said.

Eileen felt herself blush. 'I'd like that very much,' she told him.

He kissed her on the cheek and walked away.

'I'm utterly scarlet!' hissed Georgia to Robyn after she had met Lacey and told her that she hoped she and Con would be very happy together. 'My grandfather went berserk!'

'What were you doing when he caught you?'

'Just kissing,' said Georgia nonchalantly.

'Was it wonderful?'

Georgia considered Robyn's question as she relived the kiss over again in her mind.

'I wonder what it's like kissing different blokes,' she mused as Robyn looked enquiringly at her. 'It was great.' She paused as she tried to explain to her friend.

'It was wonderful but not because I'm in love with him. I was in love with the idea of him but now that he's here and now that I've kissed him properly . . . it's different. He's a mate. He'll always be a mate. And I guess he's a good kisser too, though the only other bloke I've kissed was that tosspot Jamesie O'Sullivan. It was nice with Steve but maybe it'd be even more spectacular if you were truly madly deeply in love.'

'I don't understand you,' said Robyn. 'Everyone knows you've been besotted with him since we came back from Galway.'

'No they don't.'

'Oh, come on!' Robyn laughed. 'You're always talking about him. If you're not texting him.'

'Am I?'

'Yes.'

'I like him a lot,' said Georgia. 'I want to kiss him again. But he's not my soulmate.'

Claire took more beers out of her fridge and put them into the big blue coolers on the patio. The party had taken on a life of its own now, with people wandering through the garden and mingling with each other. Rosie and Celia were talking to a couple of the girls from the Smash & Grab club while Petra and Paul were still together, now sharing a bottle of wine.

Georgia and her friends, including the boy Claire didn't recognise but who was obviously interested in her daughter (every so often he'd catch Georgia by the hand), had formed a circle on the grass and were eating burgers. Phydough had joined them, his brown eyes looking mournfully at the disappearing food.

Con was talking to her next-door neighbour. Eileen and her friends had taken over the patio table. Joanna was still talking to Frank Maddox. Lacey was standing barefoot in the grass chatting to Trinny Armstrong. Lacey and Trinny were alike, realised Claire. Both of them were strong, confident women, both good at business. But both bad at men. The thought came to her suddenly. Trinny didn't know how good she had it with Josh, always looking for someone or something else, never satisfied. And Lacey – well, Lacey had found Con but only after disastrous relationships with the fathers of her children. Maybe it wasn't possible to be good at everything, thought Claire. Though that was a dispiriting notion.

Eavan Keating and Nate Taylor were standing side by side. Claire wondered uneasily what they were discussing. Nate said something to Eavan, who smiled faintly. Then he turned away from her and walked across the garden. There was still no sign of Glenn, who should have arrived by now. Claire knew that Eavan was worrying about him because she could see the frown on her friend's normally smooth forehead and the way she kept looking towards the gate. She hoped against hope that things would work out for her friend. Eavan had been through a lot already. She tried to be tough, Claire knew, but she wasn't really. She'd been devastated all those years ago when she'd made the choice to have an abortion. But afterwards she'd insisted that there was no point in wondering what if. It hadn't been possible to carry the baby at that time. She'd made the right decision for her. But maybe pushing it to the back of her mind hadn't been the right thing to do. Maybe she should've told Glenn about it earlier and then he wouldn't have put her on the pedestal she now claimed he'd elevated her to.

Why are men so stupid? Claire asked herself as she closed the lids on the coolers. Why don't they understand things better?

'It's going well.' Nate's voice startled her out of her thoughts.

'Thanks.' How had he managed to sneak up on her like that? She'd thought that when he left Eavan he was going to get something to eat.

'This garden likes people,' he told her. 'It likes life in it.'

'I thought of a Zen garden,' she said. 'When I realised how badly it needed to be seen to. I thought perhaps white sand and a few rocks would do the trick.'

He smiled. 'Too much sand and too many rocks.'

'Perhaps.'

'And no place to bring people.'

'I didn't really want to bring people here,' she said. 'Even today.'

'Why not?'

She didn't want this conversation with him. The casual questions. The feeling that it would be easy to be with him. She didn't want it. And she couldn't have it.

354

'I'm sorry,' she said abruptly. 'I have to get more drink from the fridge.'

She smiled briefly and walked away from him. But she didn't bother going to the fridge. She went upstairs and into her bedroom.

She opened the drawer in the locker at what had been Bill's side of the bed. She took out the video. She hadn't looked at it in three years. She'd only looked at it once before.

The compact TV and video was on a tall chest of drawers in the corner of the room. She slid the tape into the slot and pressed Play.

The blue Jamaican skies filled the screen. Then a shriek from Georgia and the camera panned to her, standing on the balcony of their hotel room. A much younger Georgia, Claire realised. A childish, carefree Georgia who waved her undamaged hands in front of her and made faces at the camera. Her red-gold hair reached almost to her waist. Claire had forgotten how long it had once been. Then Bill focused the camera at Claire herself, zooming in on her pale face with the dark circles under her eyes. She begged him to stop, to wait until she had a bit of sun on her body before he took any more shots.

The next frames were of the beach. Herself and Georgia lying on sun beds. Sitting on chairs at the water's edge sipping extravagant cocktails. Both the same, Claire remembered. Non-alcoholic because of her unborn baby. She pressed her fingers against her stomach and bit her lip until it was bruised.

Then came the part she remembered the clearest, the part she'd replayed over and over again the only other time she'd watched the video. She'd decided to put the tape away, believing that reliving the past wasn't helpful, but now she needed to see it again. Georgia had taken the camera that night. She'd captured Claire and Bill on the dance floor of the hotel. Holding each other tightly. Smiling at each other. Bill looking down at her, joking, though she couldn't hear what he was saying over the recorded buzz of conversation and music.

She'd been wearing the scorched ochre silk that night and she'd laughed with Bill that he'd better not spin her around too much because she might burst out of it. She'd blamed the tightness of the dress on her pregnancy, not on the fact that she'd spent the best part of the week eating everything in sight.

'I . . . will always love you.' She saw him mouth the words, knew it was because he was singing along with the music. And then she kissed him. She heard Georgia's voice muttering, 'Cringe, cringe,' and her daughter turned away from them and began shooting footage of the statuesque Jamaican singer instead.

She stopped the video. There was no more film of herself and Bill together. That was the only bit. Everything else was of her or of Georgia.

She sat in front of the blank screen for a moment. She rewound the tape until the dance sequence began again.

'I . . . will always love you.' She hit Pause and stared at the moment, frozen in time, not hearing the sound of laughter in the garden as it floated through her open window.

Chapter 35

Prunella (Self-Heal) – Mauve, pink or white flowers. Water in dry weather.

When she eventually came downstairs again she found Lacey Dillon in the kitchen, sitting in the old-fashioned rocking chair. Claire looked at her in surprise.

'I'm sorry,' said Lacey. 'But I had to sit down. My feet were killing me.' She looked ruefully at the high-heeled shoes on the floor beside her. 'My ankles are in shreds!'

Claire lifted down the first-aid box and took out a couple of blister plasters which she handed to Lacey.

'I always keep lots in stock,' she said. 'I usually slope around in trainers, so every time I wear proper shoes I seem to get blisters.'

'Thank you.' Lacey peeled away the paper and stuck the plasters to her ankles. 'You'd imagine we'd get more sensible as we get older.'

'Oh, I don't know.' Claire gazed out of the window at Paul and Petra, who were now sitting so close together on the wooden seat that Petra was practically on his lap. And, as she watched, they kissed.

Looks like you won't need me to be your fallback woman after all, she thought in amusement. She felt a sudden tug of envy for Paul and for the fact that he had finally moved on and wondered, for a split second, what would have happened if she'd returned the kiss he'd given her in the pub with the passion that Petra was now using! She shook her head, surprised that she'd even had the thought.

'I'd better find your father,' said Lacey as she got up out of the chair.

'I'm happy for you.' Claire blurted out the words and Lacey's eyes widened.

'Really,' added Claire. 'I know I wasn't exactly friendly at lunch but I suppose I was still surprised about the whole thing. If you can find someone who loves you and who you love that's a good thing. So I'm happy for you.'

'And not resentful because of your mother?'

Claire smiled slowly. 'I rather think my mother is moving on.'

'With the man in the suit?'

Claire nodded.

'It's quite surprised Con,' said Lacey wryly. 'He's been muttering about him all evening. He all but asked him whether his intentions were honorable.'

'You're joking!' Claire laughed.

Lacey laughed too. 'I guess he'll always look out for your mother,' she told Claire. 'But he does love me. I know that. And I love him. And Claire, I adore your daughter,' she added. 'She's so sweet and incredibly pretty.'

'She looks great today,' agreed Claire. 'And I'm terrified because I never realised before how stunning she can look. Plus, there's a guy I don't know who keeps grabbing her by the hand . . .'

'Steve,' Lacey told her. She filled Claire in on the details of Con's encounter with the two of them.

'Oh, hell!' Claire's voice was full of concern.

'I wouldn't worry,' advised Lacey. 'She told Con later that he was totally wonderful and that she liked him a lot but that he wasn't her soulmate.'

Claire bit her lip at the term. Georgia shouldn't be looking for soulmates. Not at fourteen years old. If her daughter was looking for Mr Right so early in her life she'd be doomed to disappointment. There must be some advice Claire could give her, something clever and profound so that she'd know when the time was right for having fun and when it was time for falling in love.

At that moment Georgia, a half-open rosebud from the red bush tucked into her hair, bounded into the kitchen and demanded that they light the garden torches, offering to do it herself if Claire liked.

'Be careful,' warned Claire, and Georgia rewarded her with a pitying look.

Lacey grinned. 'Just like Solange,' she said. She began to talk about her daughter, but Claire was only half listening. She knew that the stories weren't important. What was important was that Lacey was clearly devoted to her. She spoke of Solange with the same proud tone as Claire used when she talked about Georgia.

They were interrupted by Eavan, who looked anxiously round the door.

'Oh, sorry,' she said as she saw both of them. 'I didn't mean to interrupt.'

'You're not.' Claire took a bottle of wine from the fridge. 'Do you want a glass?'

Eavan shook her head. 'I'm driving,' she said. 'I've already had my limit. I wasn't expecting to be driving, of course. Glenn does that. But Glenn still hasn't arrived.'

'I'm sure . . .' Claire faltered. There was no way she could be sure of anything. If Eavan had dropped Glenn off as she'd said earlier, he should be here by now. In fact he'd almost have had time to walk the entire way from Howth by this stage!

'I don't know what to do.' Eavan's voice was full of misery. 'Oh, I fucking hate those bastards at Trontec!'

'Trontec? Trontec the telecoms company?' Lacey looked at her curiously.

'Yes.' Eavan sniffed. 'My husband used to work there but he was let go.'

'I used to have their account but I stopped,' said Lacey. 'Lots of the people I placed with them left. They found it a very difficult working environment.'

'Really?' A look of hope passed fleetingly across Eavan's face. 'It wasn't a good place to work? He's better off out of it?'

Lacey nodded. 'Impossible targets, incompetent management,' she said.

'Maybe Lacey has something on her books that might be suitable for Glenn?' Claire looked tentatively between Eavan and Lacey.

'I'm sure Glenn has sent his CV in to you already,' said Eavan dismally. 'He's sent it almost everywhere.'

'I'll check,' said Lacey. 'If he hasn't, then please do ask him to send it in. We do a lot of work in the sector but we wouldn't be one of the main companies that people think of.'

'Glenn Keating.' Eavan spelled out his name and gave Lacey their address too.

'I'll check,' repeated Lacey. 'Now, I'd better get back to Con.' She eased her feet into her shoes and winced. 'The plasters help,' she said. 'But one day I'll remember that I have to walk in shoes.'

She went back out to the garden while Claire tried to persuade Eavan that having Lacey on-side was a good thing, and that it would only be a matter of time before something came up.

'Maybe you're right.' Eavan sighed deeply. 'Look, do you mind if I go home? I can't be late because Candida has to go. If Glenn shows up . . .' She swallowed. 'He won't. But if he does, tell him I'll see him back there.'

Claire nodded and let her friend out of the house. She wished there was something she could do for Eavan but she really didn't know how to help. It was hopeless to keep telling her that everything would work out fine. How the hell did anyone know whether it would work out fine or not? But the idea that Glenn and Eavan, who had been so happy together, could somehow lose it all was simply terrible.

She walked around to the back garden. The flames of the torches lit up the evening gloom and the fairy lights which Georgia had strung through the tree sparkled with a rainbow of colours. The garden lights around the rockery glowed green and white. An aroma of charcoal and smoky meat hung in the air, but it was a good, outdoors kind of smell. Phydough lay on the patio, his tail thumping gently, satisfied because Georgia's friends had finally taken pity on him and fed him a plate of sausages. They were now sitting beneath the apple tree. As far as Claire could see, they all seemed to be in good spirits. Georgia was at the centre of the group, talking animatedly and drinking bottled water.

'It looks even better at night,' remarked Sarah Taylor, who stood beside her.

'Yes,' agreed Claire uncomfortably. She didn't want to talk to Sarah. There was no way the other woman could possibly know that

360

she had fantasised about her husband, but Claire somehow felt as though Sarah would be able to find this out if she was near her for long enough.

'Nate enjoyed doing it,' said Sarah. 'I haven't seen him so enthusiastic about a job in ages.'

'He worked hard.'

'He used to whistle on the way out in the mornings.' Sarah smiled at Claire in the half-light. 'I haven't heard him whistle since before Felicity.'

Claire tensed.

'She broke his heart, you know,' said Sarah. 'He used to be such a great guy, so outgoing and enthusiastic about life. Then he married her and – bang – it all went so horribly wrong.'

'You knew him before his first marriage?'

'Of course,' said Sarah. 'I've known him since I was a kid. We're cousins. Not direct, actually. Once removed, I think the term is. But our families were quite close. And so I always knew him. Hero-worshipped him from afar because, of course, he was older than me and so much cooler. They used to laugh at me, the way I would follow him around. I used to call him my soulmate.'

Claire wondered if her body could get any more tense as she imagined a small, equally pretty version of Sarah following a younger Nate around the place.

'I told everyone that I was going to marry him one day,' said Sarah. 'For ages I believed it. And then he went to the States and met Felicity.'

'He mentioned her to me once,' said Claire casually.

'I suppose he didn't tell you what a bitch she is,' said Sarah, and Claire couldn't help hearing the bitterness in her voice.

'Bitch?'

'She's life's original power-woman and gorgeous with it. Tall, thin, blonde – naturally blonde, of course – chic, stylish . . . all the things that Nate isn't really. He's chilled and relaxed even though he's so passionate about his gardens, but she was always out and about networking, you know the sort! I'd never have imagined for a second that he'd fall for someone like her, but she dazzled him. He did a makeover of the courtyard garden at the legal company where she was a partner. He met her while she was out having a cigarette break. He doesn't even approve of smoking! Anyway it was love, lust, whatever you like, at first sight. They were married. Sometimes I still ask him why he had to be so stupid as to marry her! He doesn't know. It was a complete disaster from the start. He didn't want to become a hotshot garden designer and do chi-chi numbers for her friends in Seattle or LA but she wanted to turn him into a kind of celebrity gardener. She said that his designs were great and that he looked cool. He was marketable, she said. When he told her she was nuts she called him unambitious and lacking in the will to provide for his family. So he gave in and made a stupid DVD about how to garden which actually sold in shedloads. As if anyone in LA actually does their own garden! But he refused do it again and they fought about it all the time and so she divorced him.'

'Not very nice,' agreed Claire.

'He still loved her,' said Sarah. 'He told me that she was trying to do her best for them as a family. And he's a stupid softy. So he let her take him for every last cent – every last cent that he'd worked really hard for because he hated doing the video and that was the only thing he'd made decent money out of! And not that she needed it anyway with her being a blood-sucking lawyer! But of course there was Hoshi, their daughter, to consider too. Felicity made all of her demands on Hoshi's behalf. Made herself out to be a devastated mom raising her daughter single-handedly. Gave all single mothers a bad name if you ask me!'

'He has a daughter!' Claire was stunned.

Sarah nodded. 'She's sixteen now. An amazingly nice kid, though he hardly gets to see her these days what with them being in the States. He wanted custody. He practically raised her, of course, because Felicity was always off at some lawyerly convention or other. Cue hysterical laughter from all and sundry at the idea, though. He had no hope. How could he? She made out that he was a brute of a husband and a shit father even though everyone knew it wasn't true! Eventually he couldn't take it any more and he came home. He keeps in touch with Hoshi, although when she was smaller she wouldn't speak to him. But things have changed in the last few years and they do speak now. He's been going through a hard time lately, though, because Hoshi wants to become a gardener too – she has some notion of creating inner city gardens for underprivileged children – and as you can imagine Felicity thinks that's a complete waste of her talents . . . Apparently she's got some phenomenal IQ and so of course Felicity wants Hoshi to study law. She keeps calling Nate in the middle of the night to get him to "talk to her" which, naturally, he won't. He thinks that Hoshi should do what she wants. He's hoping that they're finally coming to an agreement where Hoshi takes a year off and does what she wants before making a final decision. So maybe it'll all sort itself out.'

'Sounds grim all the same.'

'Well, stressful, I guess,' agreed Sarah. 'Because he wants what's right for Hoshi although he's a bit concerned that she only wants to do the gardening thing to piss Felicity off. And it's hard when she's so far away from him. Poor Nate! He's too intense for his own good really even though deep down he's a pushover. He was a mess after he divorced Felicity, you know.'

'I suppose everyone's a mess when things go wrong,' said Claire.

'So he came to me.' Sarah stared out over the garden, towards where Nate and Mike O'Malley were chatting animatedly.

Claire said nothing.

'And I married him. Like I said I would.'

Nate and Mike were laughing. Mike put his arm on Nate's shoulder and the two of them walked to one of the coolers and took out a couple of tins of beer. Claire watched as Nate pulled the ring tab and raised the tin to his mouth, arching back his neck. He looked even better than usual tonight in his blue denim shirt and a pair of sand-coloured chinos. He seemed relaxed and casual. And why wouldn't he? she asked herself. He'd gone through a messy relationship but had ended up with his childhood sweetheart.

'Of course that was a big mistake.'

Sarah's words took a moment to sink in. When she realised what the other woman had said, Claire turned to her and frowned.

'Mistake?'

'Oh, come on!' Sarah sounded impatient. 'He was my hero. You should never marry your heroes. Keep the dream alive, that's what I say.'

'So . . . so things aren't working out?' Claire didn't know why she felt a tremor of terror in the base of her stomach.

'They never did,' said Sarah in resignation. 'Funny, you know. Before we got married Nate and I slept together and it wasn't a problem. But as soon as we had rings on our fingers . . . well, it was like sleeping with my own brother. I don't know why that happened. But it did. And to him too. It was awful.'

'But . . . but you get on well together?' Claire was surprised at the depth of Sarah's confidences.

'Oh, sure,' she replied. 'We're good friends. Really.' She smiled faintly. 'Not soulmates after all, of course. But good mates still.'

'So what are you going to do? Will things change between you?'

'I hope not,' said Sarah. 'He's good to work with and the divorce had nothing to do with the business.' She grinned. 'Actually, I suppose the business was Nate's divorce present to me! I wanted to try my hand at my own florist's – that's what I trained in; the whole gardening thing is in the Taylor family blood, I guess – and Nate agreed to join me on the gardening side. It works quite well.'

'You're divorced!' Claire's voice was almost a squeak.

'Well of course we are!' Sarah looked at her in astonishment. 'You didn't think we were still married, did you?'

'I – you wear a ring. You were jogging together. I saw you hugging in the shop one day! I assumed . . .'

Sarah glanced down at her left hand. 'I suppose I should stop wearing it,' she agreed. 'But it's a great defence mechanism. And I'm not in the mood for blokes to start hitting on me just yet. Daft as it sounds, I'm much happier working with Nate than living with him. And I want to work right now. One day the right bloke might come along.'

Claire nodded wordlessly.

'He didn't tell you?' Sarah looked surprised.

Claire shook her head.

'I don't know why he didn't tell you,' said Sarah. She frowned. 'I thought . . . I really thought that . . . well . . . he whistled, you see.'

'Huh?'

'Like I said. I haven't heard him whistle for years. Not even when he was with me, although it didn't really bother me at the time. But when he started again . . .'

'I don't see why him whistling before he came to work here should mean anything,' said Claire.

'Whistling is his thing,' said Sarah. 'When he's happy.'

'I – I – but it's nothing to do with me,' said Claire.

'Of course it is,' said Sarah. 'He came here to you and even though the whole Hoshi thing is bugging him like crazy and even though he gets really tense about Felicity, he still whistled. He was happy, and it's ages since he's been happy.'

'Sarah, you're being daft.'

'Don't you think you could give him a chance?'

'A chance at what?'

'He was gutted when he heard you'd gone out with Oliver Ramsey,' said Sarah. 'He talked to me about it. He said Oliver was all wrong for you. And that he was asking you out under false pretences only it probably didn't matter because you could charm him anyway.'

'Huh?'

'That's what he said. And I asked him if he didn't like you a bit himself, and instead of snapping my head off he just smiled. Knowingly.'

'Sarah, you're getting this all wrong. I'm sure he has no interest in me whatsoever. This is all nonsense.' Claire could feel her heart racing at a hundred miles an hour in her chest. Nate and Sarah weren't married. She didn't have to feel guilty about her fantasies. In fact, if she wanted, she could go out with him. Sarah was practically throwing her at him. He was a perfectly available man.

A chill crept around her. Go out with him? If all that Sarah was saying was true, if he wanted to go out with her, it would be a real date. Not a date because of Georgia. Not a date with an old friend like Paul. Not a date because the bloke who'd asked her out thought she could help his career. Not a date because the person concerned wanted to add her to a list of people he'd slept with (at least, she didn't think so). If she went out with Nate, it would simply be because both of them wanted to be in each other's company.

The fantasies were guilty fun. But the reality – even a non-guilt-ridden reality – wasn't something she could face right now. Stunned, she realised that she'd been OK about going out with Paul and Oliver and Gary because she didn't really care. But with Nate . . . she had a horrible feeling that she could care. And she didn't want to. Because at some point it could all go wrong. And she couldn't bear the thought of falling for someone and losing him again. It hurt too damn much.

'I like Nate,' she said eventually. 'And I'm really sorry that he appears to have had such a difficult time. But I couldn't possibly go out with him.'

She walked away from Sarah, back towards the now cooling barbecue. And almost collided with Glenn Keating, who was coming in the opposite direction.

'Where's Eavan?' he asked.

Claire frowned. The abrupt way he'd spoken to her was so unlike the Glenn she knew that she understood instantly why Eavan was so worried. And Glenn himself appeared disoriented. Shit, she muttered under her breath as she tried to gather her whirling thoughts. Eavan was right. It's all going wrong for them.

'She went home,' she said. 'She thought you weren't coming.'

'She doesn't fucking trust me any more.' Glenn's words were bitter. 'I'm useless to her now. The man with no job.'

'Oh, for heaven's sake, Glenn!' She couldn't help snapping at him even though she'd wanted to be sympathetic. 'Get real, would you? People lose their jobs. That's the way of things. You're not useless, you know you're not. And you know Eavan doesn't think you are either.'

'You're all the same,' said Glenn in disgust. 'You say it but you don't really mean it.'

'I never say things I don't mean,' cried Claire. 'Eavan went home because it was getting late and because she didn't want to keep Candida over time. That's all.'

Glenn sighed deeply. 'I'm losing her.'

'If you carry on like this, yes, you are,' agreed Claire. 'It's difficult for both of you.' She bit her lip. 'She told you stuff yesterday and it was really hard for her, and all you did was give her the cold shoulder.'

'You knew about it,' said Glenn coolly. 'You knew about it but you never said anything. God knows what else she's kept hidden from me.'

'Nothing,' said Claire. 'And you know that perfectly well. But now she thinks you despise her.'

'*She* despises *me*!'

'No she doesn't.'

'She should.'

'If you despise yourself then maybe she won't be able to help it,' said Claire. 'She was very upset earlier. But she still told me she loved you.' She didn't add that Eavan wasn't sure whether she loved him enough any more.

He stood silently in front of her. Claire was struck by how small he looked, even though he was a tall man. He seemed to have folded in on himself, hunching his shoulders and keeping his hands in his pockets so that it was impossible to see the breadth of his frame.

'Glenn . . .' She hesitated, unsure of how to ask him, but then blurted it out anyway. 'Are you drinking again?'

He stared at her, his jaw working angrily. 'Why does everyone have to think that?' he demanded. 'Eavan is the same. That's all she cares about. That's all anyone cares about. That they'll have to worry about me drinking again.'

'That's not true,' retorted Claire. 'We worry about you. Not about your drinking.'

'Yeah, right.' Glenn hunched his shoulders again and walked away from her.

'Where are you going?' called Claire.

But he didn't answer.

She phoned Eavan to tell her that he'd shown up but had gone again, and her friend, too, asked about his drinking. Suddenly Claire understood what bothered Glenn so much about it. It was as though it was the defining thing about him, the only thing that people cared about. She tried to convey this to Eavan but all Eavan could do was repeat that she hoped he wasn't drinking and that she didn't know how she'd cope if he was. After she'd hung up, Claire stood in the hallway with her hand on the receiver, uncertain about what she should do next.

She was still standing there, lost in thought, when Nate Taylor walked into the hall.

'I'm sorry if I'm interrupting you,' he said. 'I was looking for the loo.'

'You know where it is.' She waved him in the general direction, for once not even noticing him. She leaned against the wall and wondered what on earth she could do to help Glenn and Eavan while knowing that it wasn't anything to do with her, it was their own problem. But when people you cared about had problems, she thought unhappily, you wanted to help. It was an inbuilt desire. She wasn't sure there was anything she could do for the Keatings, though, except hope that they could help each other.

'Still here?' Nate asked as he returned from the bathroom. 'Everything OK?'

He wasn't anything like Bill to look at. He was taller, broader, darker . . . and those green and blue eyes were still the most unusual thing she'd ever seen. He didn't look as easy-going as Bill either, although there was something strong and dependable about him. Maybe it was that illusion of strength and dependability that she found so attractive. The idea, perhaps, that he was someone who could look after her.

Only he hadn't managed to look after his two wives very well, had he? Even if it hadn't been his fault, he'd told her the truth that day when he said he wasn't very good with women. So why would he be any good with her? He could love her and leave her and then she'd be on her own again. So what was the damn point?

'You OK?' he asked again. His voice was softer than she remembered from when he'd worked in the garden.

'Sure,' she said.

'Only you look a little upset.'

She shook her head. 'Dealing with other people's problems,' she told him. 'It's fine now.'

'People are dancing in the garden,' he told her. 'Someone put a Norah Jones CD in the deck. It's lovely out there in the torchlight beneath the stars. Want to dance?'

She shook her head. 'I'm hopeless.'

'Georgia says you're good.'

'Georgia does?'

'I danced with her,' said Nate. 'She told me that it would be good for her street cred. Though personally I think it was to make her boyfriend jealous. Not that he'd need to be jealous of an old crock like me, but still . . .'

He smiled.

That was different to Bill too. Bill's smile was wide and generous. Nate's was easy and relaxed. Which was strange, she mused, because he wasn't an easy or relaxed person really. She recalled her first encounter with him again. Rude and obnoxious. She should keep that in mind. He'd probably been rude and obnoxious to Felicity. She couldn't have been such a complete bitch. And maybe he'd been horrible to Sarah too at some point.

'I thought you and Sarah were still married.' The words were out of her mouth before she could stop them. 'She doesn't understand why you didn't tell me that you're not.'

'The opportunity didn't arise,' he said. 'We didn't have those kind of conversations over the flowerbeds.'

'You were childhood sweethearts.'

Nate shook his head. 'She used to follow me around. A kind of hero-worship thing that was irritating at the time. But then after I split with Felicity – who certainly didn't hero-worship me – I needed a bit of attention from the sort of person who thought the sun shone out of my arse.'

'You have a daughter,' said Claire.

'Hoshi.' Nate took his wallet from the back pocket of his chinos and extracted a photograph. He passed it to Claire. The girl in the photo was sitting on a rock, staring at the camera. There was no mistaking her for anyone other than a child of Nate's. Her face was strong, like his, and there was a hint of defiance in her eyes, half-hidden by a strand of long dark hair which blew in front of her face.

'She's pretty.'

'Attractive rather than pretty, I always think,' said Nate. 'Which is preferable, I hope. She wants to study horticulture too.' He chuckled. 'It's driving Felicity crazy. She wanted her to be a lawyer. We fight

369

over it. I kind of hoped our fighting days were over but you'd do anything for your kid. Well, you know that yourself. I've seen you with Georgia. You're great with her.'

'Your daughter's not a bit like Georgia,' said Claire.

'I wouldn't expect her to be,' said Nate. 'Felicity isn't a bit like you.'

'You know what I mean,' said Claire. 'Georgey isn't some substitute daughter for you.'

Nate frowned. 'Whoever said she was? She's a great kid but she's her own person.' Then he smiled. 'So, how about it? A dance with the guy who's managed to get divorced twice in a lifetime?'

She didn't want to. And yet she did. Her mind was a whirl of conflicting emotions.

'Come on,' he urged gently. 'Just the one.'

'Maybe. Let's go outside anyway.'

He reached for her hand but she raised it out of his grasp and checked the back of her hair instead. Then she followed him outside and into the night.

Chapter 36

Indigofera (Indigo) – Graceful, tall purple flowers from midsummer to autumn. Stems may be killed by winter frost but regrow.

They were still playing Norah Jones. Claire recognised the easy beat of 'Shoot the Moon' as she stepped on to the patio where most of her guests, including Georgia and Steve, were moving slowly in rhythm to the music.

'Well?' asked Nate. He held out his hand to her and she took it. Her heart was hammering even faster now as he drew her closer to him. She held her body stiffly beside him, not moulding in to his, keeping her face within conversational distance.

'You did a great job in the garden,' she said stiltedly.

'You've told me that a million times.'

'I was afraid,' she said, 'that it would be wrong when you finished. That I'd have lost it.'

'I wouldn't have let that happen.' His fingers closed more tightly around hers.

Georgia, her own head resting on Steve's shoulder, raised her eyes to look at her mother and Nate. She looks as though she's balancing a block of ice on her head, thought Georgia. She doesn't want to be doing this with him. She sighed and Steve held her closer.

'You're suffocating me,' Georgia muttered and she felt Steve laugh. She lifted her head from his shoulder. 'What's so funny?'

'This is nice music for dancing,' he said. 'And you're worried about suffocating.'

'Guess I'm not a dancing kind of girl.'

'Guess you're not.' He kissed her on the lips.

'My mother will see,' she hissed. 'And I don't love you, you know.'

'Who says you have to?'

Claire saw the fleeting kiss and, impossible though it seemed, her body stiffened still further.

'What's the matter?' asked Nate.

'Georgia,' she whispered. 'And that boy. Kissing. Again.'

'It's what they do.'

I know it's what they do, thought Claire. But I can't get my head around the fact that she's the one doing it. She hasn't even introduced him properly to me! And what do I do if he becomes her boyfriend? According to Dad, she doesn't think he's her soulmate. So why is she kissing him?

She closed her eyes. She's going to be hurt by him. And I hope I'm able to help her when she is.

The music slid gently into 'Come Away With Me'.

'Sounds enticing,' said Nate.

'Huh?'

'Walking through yellow grass with you.'

'I'm surprised you approve of yellow grass,' she told him. 'Obviously not watered enough!'

He laughed and hugged her. She gasped in surprise.

'You know I want to go out with you, don't you?' he asked.

She said nothing.

'You must know that!'

'Why would I?' she asked.

'I thought I was making it obvious,' he said.

She shook her head again.

'I know that you had a really bad time,' he said softly. 'With your husband's accident and all.'

She stiffened again. 'I don't want to talk about it.'

He said nothing. They danced a little more.

'Come Away With Me.' He whispered the lyrics of the song.

'I certainly will not.'

'Come out with me then,' he said.

'Oh, Nate, I don't know.'

'Why not?'

'I . . . just don't know.'

'Is it because of the two divorces?' He laughed shortly as he spoke. 'I realise that it makes me seem a bit – unreliable.'

'I didn't know about the two divorces,' she said flatly. 'I thought you were still married to Sarah.'

'Oh.' He tried to hold the look of her amber eyes. 'I guess I never realised that you might think . . . I see now, of course. But . . .' He smiled. 'It makes it possible for you to go out with me, doesn't it?'

'Why do you want to go out with me?' she asked.

'I like you,' he said. The music changed again. 'It's the Nearness of You,' he told her.

'Stop talking to me in song titles.'

'You're so unromantic!'

'Yes,' she said shortly. 'I'm unromantic. You get that way when your husband has been decapitated.'

'Oh, Jesus.' He looked at her in horror.

'He was killed in an accident. At first they told me he'd broken his neck.' She swallowed hard. 'I thought that was bad enough. But they were just sparing my feelings at the time. They didn't think I could cope.'

'I'm so sorry,' he said.

'Georgia doesn't know that,' she said rapidly. 'I can't . . . I won't tell her.'

'Claire . . .' He held her closer.

'It's OK.' Her voice was muffled against his shoulder. 'I'm OK now.'

'I know. You went out with Oliver.'

'That was different.'

'Why?'

She said nothing.

'You're too good for Oliver.'

'I'm not really in the market for going out with men at all,' she said. 'Besides, there's Georgia to consider.'

'Georgia seems to be doing pretty well on her own account.' Nate glanced towards Georgia and Steve, who were now sitting side by side on the step outside the kitchen door.

'Perhaps. But I – well, I don't know.'

'Dinner?' suggested Nate. 'I scrub up well, you know.'

'I'll think about it.' The music ended and Claire moved out of his reach again. 'But right now I'm fine the way I am, thanks all the same.'

The guests began leaving at around ten o'clock. Paul Hanratty came up to Claire and told her that he and Petra were going to the pub for a quiet drink together. Claire looked at him quizzically and he smiled and told her that Petra was a really nice girl and that they'd clicked somehow, and that perhaps she was The One.

'You're making that decision tonight?' asked Claire sceptically.

He shook his head. 'But I'm ready to give her the opportunity. She's the first woman since . . .' He shrugged and smiled. 'Thanks for asking me, Claire. I wouldn't have expected you to.'

'Hey, just because you and I were never going to be an item doesn't mean that I can't allow you to date my friends,' she told him playfully.

'You seemed to be becoming an item with that guy Nate,' said Paul.

'Not really.' Claire's tone was dismissive.

On the way past, Petra whispered the same thanks to Claire. 'We clicked,' she murmured as she kissed her friend on the cheek. 'We absolutely clicked.'

Mike and Leonie left next, promising to collect the barbecue again in a couple of days. Both of them told Claire that it had been a wonderful evening and wasn't she so lucky that it had stayed warm and dry? Perfect barbecuing weather, Mike said. Pity it never stayed like that when he wanted to char a few burgers! Robyn, Sive and Emma left with them, yawning widely and winking profusely at Georgia, whispering at her as they went.

'Come on, you girls,' said Leonie. 'If you want us to give you a lift home you'd better hurry.'

'Where are your other friends?' asked Claire as she watched them leave.

'Sam and Denzil wandered off a while back,' said Georgia. 'Maeve and Lilith's parents collected them about ten minutes ago. You didn't notice.'

'And Steve?' asked Claire.

'They're all accounted for,' Georgia told her dismissively. 'Oh look, here's Trinny.'

She drifted away while Claire continued to say goodbye to people. Nate and Sarah were among the last to leave.

'Thanks for a wonderful evening,' said Sarah as she pecked Claire on the cheek. 'See you again sometime.'

'Sure,' said Claire.

'See you again,' said Nate. 'Soon, I hope. I'll call.'

Claire nodded imperceptibly.

'Are you going?' Suddenly Georgia rushed up to them. 'Thanks for coming, Nate and Sarah. And thanks for taking me to Tesco earlier, Nate. The torches were great.'

'My pleasure,' said Nate.

'I like the way you talk to me.' Georgia giggled. 'Like a real grown-up. Doesn't he, Mum?'

'I treat you like a grown-up too,' said Claire tersely. 'Now come on, I'm sure Nate and Sarah want to go. It's late.'

'At least we can lie in the morning,' remarked Sarah. 'I'm not a morning person.'

'Neither is Mum,' confided Georgia. 'But she used to pretend for Dad's sake.'

'Shut up, Georgey,' said Claire. 'Honestly, Nate and Sarah don't need to know everything about us.'

'They're interested,' said Georgia. She looked at Nate. 'Aren't you?'

'Very.' He grinned at her.

'Goodnight.' Claire held out her hand to him. He looked at her in amusement and took it. His own hand was warm and dry.

'I'll call,' he said.

The creamy nightlight at the side of Saffy's bed glowed gently. Saffy herself was sleeping spread-eagled across her bed, both arms and one leg thrown outside the pretty pink and blue covers. Her face was in the shadow but Eavan could see her dark lashes against her soft, slightly flushed cheeks. She was already asleep by the time Eavan got home and so Candida had said not to bother driving her back to her own house, that she'd walk. The baby-sitter hadn't made any comment about Glenn's absence and Eavan hadn't been able to think up anything sensible to say. So she'd simply told Candida that Glenn had elected to walk too.

'It's the warm weather,' Candida had said cheerfully. 'Nice to be outdoors. Bet the barbecue was wonderful.'

She'd headed off home then and Eavan had walked around the house, tidying up things that were already tidy, plumping up cushions and unloading the dishwasher, a job she loathed.

Then she'd curled up in the chair beside Saffy's bed and watched her daughter sleeping. What will happen to you? she wondered, as she gazed at the rise and fall of Saffy's breathing. Will you meet someone who sweeps you off your feet and who'll make you happy? Will you manage not to make terrible mistakes with your life? Will everything be right for you or will it all go wrong? She felt a surge of protective energy towards her daughter. She didn't want things to go wrong for her. She wanted everything to be perfect. But life wasn't like that. Eavan was sure that her own mother had wanted nothing but perfection for her too but she hadn't been able to stop Eavan getting stupidly pregnant at a time when she herself had been going through a period of deep depression and needed special care. Eavan had never told her about the abortion. She didn't want her to feel in some way responsible. It had been her own choice in the end.

Sometimes she wondered what life would have been like if she'd had the baby. But she couldn't imagine it. Because her life had changed so completely from the day that she'd met Glenn Keating and fallen so madly in love with him.

Where was he now? She let out the breath that she realised she'd been holding. Where was he, what was he doing, when would he be home? Claire had phoned earlier to say that he'd turned up at the barbecue and that he'd seemed upset. But, she'd said, she didn't think he was drunk.

Eavan wrapped her arms around her body and pulled her knees up under her chin. She recalled her first date with Glenn, in the pub, where he'd ordered sparkling water and told her of his drink problem. And she remembered how she'd felt that night after leaving him, convinced already that he was the man for her. She'd been right. He was a great husband and a devoted father. She knew how much he loved her. She knew how much he loved Saffy. 'And I love you too,' she whispered, as a tear slid from the corner of her eye. No matter what's happened, I love you. And I want you to come home.

Much to Claire's surprise, Georgia had taken herself off to her den almost as soon as the last of the guests had left, saying that she was going to have a quick game of Gran Turismo before going to bed. Claire had imagined that she would have wanted to stay up late, chatting about the evening, but Eileen told her that the girl was probably tired out. She had, Eileen reminded her, been on the go all day.

So it was Eileen and Claire who extinguished the almost depleted torches and cleared up the worst of the debris from the patio and garden. And it was Eileen and Claire who sat at the kitchen table and drank the steaming mugs of hot chocolate that Claire made when they'd finished.

'I do believe Dad was a teeny bit jealous,' Claire remarked as she blew on the top of her drink to cool it down.

Eileen grinned. 'Just a little. And that was the desired effect really.'

'I also believe there's a bit of devilment in you, Eileen Shanahan!' Claire grinned at her.

'Nelligan spirit maybe?' Eileen laughed. 'Your dad's happy. Lacey's happy. I'm happy. But if I can spice it up a bit . . .'

Claire chuckled.

'What about you and the man?' Eileen's eyes narrowed. 'You said he was married to that girl, but you spent a lot of time with him nevertheless. And Georgey is right. He fancies you. I saw the way he looked at you. And the way he held you when you were dancing. It's not up to me to interfere, Claire, but your dad's other women made me very unhappy. I don't want someone else going through it when my daughter is part of it.'

Claire put down her mug and explained about Nate's chequered marital history.

'And do you want to go out with him?' asked Eileen.

'I don't know,' said Claire. 'I find him attractive, but I'm not looking for someone. I'm OK the way I am.'

'Have a bit of fun,' suggested Eileen. 'You've gone through a lot.'

'I wish people would stop saying that,' said Claire irritably.

'It's true.'

'Everyone goes through things.' Claire got up and ran her cup under the sink. 'When you're married to a doctor you find out about the sort of things that people go through. I'm luckier than some.'

'You still deserve to have a bit of fun,' Eileen told her.

'We'll see,' said Claire. 'Now I'm going to bed. I'm exhausted.'

'Me too,' confessed Eileen. 'OK, darling, see you in the morning.'

'Goodnight, Mum.' Claire stopped on her way out of the kitchen to hug Eileen. They stayed in the embrace for almost a minute before she went up the stairs.

Faint fingers of light were appearing in the eastern sky when Eavan jerked into wakefulness. She remained immobile in the chair as she wondered what had woken her. And then she thought that it was probably the discomfort of the way that she'd fallen asleep which had been enough to wake her again – she had a crick in her neck and her legs were stiff. She stretched jerkily, her muscles protesting as they unwound themselves from the knots they'd been in. And then she heard the noise downstairs and froze.

Her first thought wasn't that it was Glenn, but that it might be an intruder. Her mouth went dry at the prospect and she shot an anxious glance at Saffy, still out for the count on the bed. But even as she listened, Eavan knew that the sounds from downstairs were being made by Glenn. She sat back in the chair and drew her knees up again, wincing as her joints and muscles protested. She heard the sound of muffled footsteps on the stairs and then of her bedroom door being opened. There was a moment of silence, and then Glenn pushed Saffy's door open.

Eavan peeped through her almost closed lashes at his silhouette in the door frame. Tall, angular, one hand against the frame, the other on the door handle. She remained motionless.

He walked lightly across the room and she could hear the rasp of his breath as he stood by Saffy's bed. She shivered suddenly.

Then he turned towards her. She squeezed her eyes closed, waiting for him to walk away. His breathing seemed to fill the entire room. Then she felt his hands slide beneath her body and scoop her from the chair. She allowed her eyelids to flicker.

378

'Go back to sleep.' His words were clear as she stirred in his arms.

'Glenn . . .'

'Sshh.' He dropped a gentle kiss on the tip of her nose. 'Later. Now – sleep.'

She was going to protest but she didn't. She allowed him to place her in the king-sized bed and pull the covers over her even though she was now wide awake. She listened as he got undressed, hanging up his clothes in the wardrobe as he always did.

Then he got into the bed beside her. She felt as though it was somehow important not to acknowledge his presence, to let him believe that she was still sleeping. He yawned, then rolled over on to his side. For the first time since he'd told her about the loss of his job he put his arm across her body. And even though his elbow was digging into her ribs and hugely uncomfortable, she still didn't move.

Claire couldn't sleep. She tried all of her old tricks but they failed her miserably. The sheep which she tried to count refused point blank to jump over the required fence and huddled in front of it instead, bleating in dissent. Her other ploy, walking down a long flight of stairs telling herself that she was getting sleepier with every step (a technique which Bill had taught her and which was usually quite reliable), came unstuck when she managed to catch her heel in the red carpet of the stairs and mentally bumped down them. Counting backwards didn't help either.

She sat up, punched at her pillows and rearranged them before lying down again.

She wanted to go out with him. She wanted to see what it would be like. If her dates with Gary and Oliver and even with Paul had taught her anything, it was that it was nice to be with an adult male again. But it would be different with Nate. She knew it would. And she didn't know whether she could cope with it when inevitably it would all go wrong and he'd leave her and she'd be left to mend a broken heart all over again. Always provided, she muttered savagely, that she got to the stage where she fell for him properly anyway. Maybe she could go out with him and hate every second of it. Maybe that would be the best thing to happen in the end.

As often happened when she couldn't sleep, the day of the accident replayed in her mind again. She tried to prevent it, but the images were too strong. Swimming out to the pontoon. The diamond sparkling of light on the azure sea. The heat of the sun on her gently browned body. The sense of fulfilment she'd had knowing that she was pregnant again at last. And then the moment when she'd curled her toes around the edge of the pontoon, waited for a split second and then dived into the water . . . the last moment when everything in her life had been right.

'It's not fair,' she whispered in the darkness. 'It's simply not fair.' She exhaled jerkily. She'd never said that aloud before. Eileen had once told her that life wasn't fair and had spoken of starving children and wars and the injustice of great poverty and great wealth in the world, and she'd said that bad things happened to everyone and so you just had to get on with your lot. Claire had done her best to do that. But, she thought miserably, it still didn't make it fair.

Quite suddenly she nodded off. And it seemed to her that she'd only been out for a couple of minutes when she was jerked into shocked wakefulness again by the strident tone of the house alarm as it shattered the night air. She jack-knifed out of the bed, grabbing her T-shirt from the back of the door because she'd elected to sleep naked again that night, and clattered down the stairs, thinking only of Georgia (who was sleeping in her den), feeling almost certain that the alarm was a false one but nevertheless wanting to check that her daughter was all right.

'Claire?' Eileen opened the bedroom door and stepped out on to the landing.

'I'm checking it,' said Claire from halfway down the stairs. 'I'm sure it's nothing.'

She was worried that Georgia hadn't come out of her den at the sound of the alarm. She pushed on the handle and gasped to find that it wouldn't budge. The door couldn't be locked. It was never locked. So what the hell had happened? Claire felt terror mount up inside her. She rattled the handle again and called Georgia's name, trying not to sound as concerned as she felt. Then she heard the jangle of the key in the lock and Georgia opened the door. She too was wearing a T-shirt, her hair spiky and unkempt, smudges of her smoky eye-shadow still around her eyes.

'Are you all right?' asked Claire.

'Of course,' said Georgia. 'I'm sure it was just a gust of wind or something that set it off.'

'Georgey, there isn't a breath of air tonight,' Claire pointed out. 'Maybe it was the cat from next door or something.'

'Probably.' Georgia stood in the doorway, holding on to the half-open door.

'Can I just check the window in your bedroom?' asked Claire. 'I'm always a bit worried because it faces out on to the front . . . I know it might be silly, but I just want to be sure it's all right.'

'I checked it myself,' Georgia assured her. 'I'm fine.'

'All the same.' Claire pushed at the door.

'Mum!' protested Georgia. 'I said it was fine—'

She broke off as Claire stepped past her, then looked anxiously at her mother and at Steve Ó Sé, who was sitting on the guest bed in his olive-green T-shirt and Calvin Klein shorts.

Claire couldn't think of a single thing to say. She stared at the boy . . . young man (she didn't quite know what to call him) sitting on the bed in her fourteen-year-old daughter's room. How the hell had that happened? she wondered desperately. And then – what the hell *had* happened?

'Claire, is everything OK?' Eileen followed her into the room. She too stopped and stared at Steve. Then she turned to look at Georgia, whose face was red. 'What on earth is going on here?' she asked.

'Nothing!' cried Georgia. 'Nothing.'

'Nothing?' Claire didn't take her eyes off the red-headed boy (she'd decided boy was the right word now) on the bed opposite her.

'Honestly, Mrs Hudson, we haven't done anything.' He sounded scared.

'You're the one that Con found kissing her under the apple tree,' said Eileen.

'Yes, well, sure, but that was different,' said Steve.

'Yes,' said Claire acidly. 'You had all your clothes on then.'

'Mum!' begged Georgia. 'You've got to believe us. It's definitely *so* not what you think.'

Claire looked at her daughter. Georgia's amber-flecked eyes were

381

filled with unshed anxious tears. She pushed her hands wildly through her already unkempt hair.

'Well then?' Claire said as evenly as she could. 'If it's so not what I think, what is it?'

'Steve came from Navan,' Georgia told her rapidly. 'But it was late when everyone was leaving. He'd missed the bus. And he didn't have enough money for a taxi. So I told him he could stay the night.'

'You told him this? You didn't think to ask me? When I specifically asked you if everyone had gone home?'

'Well you might have said no,' Georgia said. 'You could've got all parenty about it and we thought it was easier if he just came into the den and waited for me.'

'I don't believe this, Georgia Hudson.' Claire stared at her. 'You think it's perfectly acceptable to invite a strange boy to spend the night in your room!'

'You're making it seem as though I asked him to stay so that I could have sex with him.' Georgia's tone was defiant. 'I didn't. We didn't. It wasn't part of our plan at all.'

'I'm so pleased to hear it,' said Claire angrily. 'I would remind you, Georgia, that it's actually illegal for anyone to have sex with you at your age regardless of whether you think you're mature enough for it or not.'

'I know that,' said Georgia. 'I absolutely do. And Steve knows it too. We talked about it.'

'Then I can't see why you thought it was a good idea for him to stay the night,' snapped Claire. 'According to Dad, you and he were practically eating each other under the apple tree.'

'We weren't!' cried Georgia, her face white. 'We kissed. It was lovely. Steve is lovely. But I don't want to have sex with him and he doesn't want to have sex with me.'

Claire glanced at Steve, whose face was now almost as red as his hair.

'What you want in your mind and what your body tells you can sometimes be two different things,' she said.

'Well they weren't with us!' Georgia retorted. 'OK, maybe earlier a bit, when we were kissing. But not now. You're always telling me that I'm a sensible person. That's because I am. I've had to be, haven't I?' She waved her injured hand in front of Claire. 'I've had to be because this happened to me and because things are different for me than other people even though they shouldn't really be. So I know the difference about what you feel and what you do. Sometimes I think I know a damn sight more about it than you do, Mum!'

'Georgia Hudson!' Eileen intervened. 'Don't speak to your mother in that tone of voice.'

'It's OK,' said Claire. She looked at her daughter, who was blinking back the tears. 'I'm surprised you didn't at least ask me,' she said, and this time her tone was gentler. 'You've always been able to ask me things. You know that.'

'I was going to.' Georgia gulped. 'But you were talking to Nate Taylor and I didn't want to interrupt you. You seemed to be getting on well and I thought . . . well . . . and then I kinda thought about it a bit more and I reckoned you might not approve.'

Claire turned to look at Steve. He was picking at the skin around his fingernails, studiously avoiding the eyes of the women in the room.

'So when you decided to come along today, had you intended staying overnight?' she asked him.

He picked at his nail for another few seconds before looking up at her. 'I didn't really think about it at all,' he said uncomfortably.

'And what about your parents?' she asked. 'Couldn't they collect you?'

'Oh, Steve's parents!' Georgia's voice was scornful. 'They wouldn't know whether he was home or not!'

'Maybe we'd better find that out,' said Claire. 'I bet they do know. And I bet they're worried as hell.'

'Please don't ring them.' Steve suddenly sounded much younger and more frightened. 'They'll freak out. They might not know where I am but they'll sure go berserk if you call them at five in the morning.'

The phone rang, startling all of them.

'That's the alarm company,' said Claire. 'They're checking to see whether it's a false alarm or not.'

'It was me.' This time Steve sounded both frightened and guilty. 'I opened the window. It was very warm. It went off straight away.'

Claire didn't know why it was that she now wanted to laugh. There was absolutely nothing funny about the situation as far as she could see. But there was something about the terrified tone of Steve's voice and the anxious look in Georgia's eyes that made her want to giggle. She went into the hallway to answer the phone and assure the alarm company that everything was all right. In the other room, Eileen, Georgia and Steve waited in silence until Claire came back.

'I have to ring your parents,' she told Steve. 'They need to know where you are.'

'I'm telling you, they don't care,' he said. 'If they wanted to know where I was they would've phoned me, and they haven't.' He took a toxic-green Nokia from the pocket of his jeans, which were hanging over the back of a chair. 'See?'

There were no missed calls listed on the phone, nor any messages. 'They don't give a shit,' said Steve.

'Maybe they think you're at home,' suggested Claire.

'Tell you what,' said Eileen. 'Why don't I make us all a cup of tea? You can ring Steve's parents afterwards, Claire.'

Georgia looked hopefully at her mother.

'Oh, all right,' said Claire. 'But let's all put some clothes on first.'

Chapter 37

Cobaea (Cup and Saucer Plant) – Violet or yellow-green flowers. Quick-growing. Harden off before planting out.

At eight o'clock in the morning, Eavan slid out from beneath Glenn's arm.

'Where are you going?' he asked.

'I didn't think you were awake.'

He sat up. 'I didn't sleep.'

'Neither did I.'

'Bit of a waste, then. Both of us awake and neither of us doing anything about it.'

'What's to do?' Eavan looked at him. 'You don't trust me any more. And you don't think I trust you.'

'I'm sorry,' he said.

Eavan bit her lip.

He held out his hand to her to draw her back to the bed. She looked uncertainly at him.

'Please?' he said. 'Get in. For a few minutes.'

She got back under the duvet.

'I'm a fool,' he said.

She shrugged.

'You've got to understand, I went a bit crazy when I lost my job.'

Eavan said nothing.

'I – well, look, I'm a bloke so I don't really do self-analysis. I did, of course, with the alcohol stuff, but I don't like to think about things too much. I know, though, that a lot of my self-esteem . . .' he made a face at the term, '. . . a lot of it was tied up in the job. Because after coming out of the alcoholism I had to make new things important to me. And the job was. Especially because once we had this house and Saffy it became a big deal. Losing the job made me feel I'd lost part of myself. And that all the things I'd told myself before about being worthwhile and a good person and all that sort of touchy-feely stuff didn't mean shit in the end.'

Eavan bit her lip even harder but stayed silent.

'And so I couldn't tell you . . . I was gutted when you found out even though I knew that you'd have to know sometime . . . and when you got all practical about it and decided we could sell the house and you might get a job – well, it made me feel worse. You were being great and all I did was want to have a drink.'

'You stayed with Saffy and you took her to the pier and she loved it.' Eavan's voice cracked.

'And I made dinner but I forgot the garlic bread and I burned the lasagne.'

'So what? I burn things all the time,' said Eavan. 'But I know I pissed you off by telling you what you were doing wrong.'

'Yes, you did. And then when you told me . . .' His jaw clenched and unclenched. 'I couldn't believe it. I thought I knew everything about you. In my head you always were perfect because you took a chance on me. Suddenly you were telling me that you weren't. And you'd kept it a secret.'

'It was a really difficult decision for me,' said Eavan. 'And I had to live with it. I could only live with it by putting it to the very back of my mind. I wanted to tell you. But the longer time went by without telling you, the harder it was.'

'You never even tried.'

'I was afraid.' Eavan blinked away a tear. 'You always said I was perfect. And I knew that this was so far from perfect . . .'

'I was shocked and angry,' said Glenn. 'And Evs, I was hurt too. But the perfect thing – well, if anything, it kinda helped. Knowing that you didn't get things right all the time after all.'

'But you froze me out,' said Eavan. 'And then going to Claire's . . .'

'That was nothing to do with you,' said Glenn. 'I just suddenly couldn't face it. Not right then. All those people we knew and them knowing I was out of work . . . I didn't want to meet them. I didn't want their damn sympathy.'

'Claire says that sometimes.' Eavan pulled at a piece of fluff on the duvet cover. 'That's the reason she gives for not going places. That people are too sympathetic.'

'Sometimes you're just not ready for sympathy,' said Glenn.

'But you showed up,' Eavan reminded him. 'She called me to say. And she told me that you seemed . . . not yourself.'

'You think I was drunk?'

Eavan sighed. 'I don't want to lie to you. Yes.'

This time Glenn said nothing. He stared across the room before turning to Eavan and taking her hand in his.

'I swear to you I wasn't. I went into a pub. I sat there. I watched people drinking. And I ordered a brandy and port.' He swallowed hard. 'I smelled it. It was wonderful. And I wanted to drink it so much. The same way as the day we argued about the lasagne I wanted to drink the wine. I called one of my mates from AA. He talked the talk. I wasn't listening. I didn't want to listen. I was looking out of the window of the pub and thinking that all I wanted was to go back and drink the fucking drink. And then a woman walked by. She had two children with her. One about Saffy's age. One a little older. She didn't look anything like you, but suddenly I thought of you and Saffy and the kids that we don't have yet. And I didn't want to lose all that. But if I drank the brandy and port . . . yeah, I knew I'd lose it because it wouldn't be just one brandy and port. It was never one drink. So I walked out. I just kept on walking. I ended up going across the river as far as Sandymount. And I sat there for ages thinking that I was a fool. I swear to you, I didn't have a drink. Eventually it started to get dark and I realised that I should go to Claire's. I got a cab across, told him to step on it. Only it was so much later than I thought. You'd gone.'

'You didn't get home till dawn,' she reminded him.

'Yes, well, I decided to walk home too,' he said. 'It's nine bloody miles from Claire's house and I'd already walked nearly as far earlier! I was creased – walking on stumps at that point! I had to stop a few times on the way. But somehow in my head I kept thinking that it was important for me to walk it, not to give in and get a cab. I know

387

it probably sounds crazy. Actually I'm thinking that I might have become addicted to walking by now . . .'

'I thought you might be using it all as an excuse,' Eavan told him. 'I thought maybe you were disgusted by me. Disgusted by the abortion.'

'Oh God, no.' This time he put his arms around her and hugged her fiercely. 'You did what you had to do. You're a brilliant mother to Saffy and the best person I know. You wouldn't have done it unless it was the only choice.'

Eavan started to cry. 'Sometimes I feel as though I should've chosen differently. And if things go wrong I think I'm being punished for it.'

'Don't think that,' he said. 'Never think that.'

He drew her down into the bed beside him. She rolled over on her side to face him and he kissed her. Then she put her arms around him, pulling him closer, running her hands along the length of his body.

We nearly lost each other, she thought as he kissed her again. We came to the brink of it all going wrong and we managed to get it back together again, and it's going to be hard, I know it is. But we have each other. And together we can make it work. We have to.

The sun had braved the horizon but the sky had clouded over, and as Claire, Eileen, Georgia and Steve sat in the kitchen, the rain began to fall again, lightly at first and then building in a crescendo of pellets bouncing off the window.

'Just as well we had the barbecue yesterday,' said Georgia. 'It'd have been a washout today.'

Claire nodded absently. She was trying to think of how she would explain the situation to Steve's parents. Despite what he'd said about their lack of interest in his whereabouts, she couldn't believe that they wouldn't be racked with anxiety. And she wished now that she hadn't agreed to the cups of tea that Eileen was dishing out with such enthusiasm.

'What's your home number?' she asked him abruptly, pushing her half-full cup away from her and picking up the cordless phone. It rang for over a minute before a sleepy voice answered. Claire asked whether she was speaking to Mrs Ó Sé, and when the woman replied that she was, and didn't she know that it was the crack of dawn, and what the hell was she doing disturbing people at that hour of the morning, Claire told her about Steve.

'What!' Gráinne Ó Sé sounded truly shocked. 'I don't believe you.'

'Believe me all right,' said Claire grimly. 'He's in my kitchen. And to tell you the truth, I'm struggling with the idea that you didn't know that your fifteen-year-old son was out all night.'

'He told me he was working at the nightclub,' said Gráinne. 'He does sometimes, helps out with their laser show.'

'Not last night,' said Claire.

'You'd better send him home on the first bus,' Gráinne told her.

'Actually, I was hoping that you or your husband would come and collect him,' responded Claire.

'We can't,' said Gráinne. 'Not right now. Myles is doing a local radio show this morning and he needs the car to get there.'

'I'm sure he has plenty of time to pick Steve up before he goes on the radio,' said Claire.

'No,' Gráinne said. 'It's an early-morning show. He'd hardly have time to get there and back.'

'You know, I can't help thinking that the welfare of your son is somewhat more important than a radio show,' said Claire drily. 'But of course that's entirely your call. In any event, I'm certainly not putting him on the bus.'

'Maybe you could drop him off to us yourself,' suggested Gráinne. 'We'll pay you for the expense.'

Claire felt her grip tighten on the receiver. She couldn't believe how laid-back the other woman was about the whole thing. Or maybe, she thought, maybe I've just overreacted. She didn't think so, though.

'I don't have a car,' she said. 'We'll keep him here until you feel ready to collect him.'

'Grand.' Gráinne breathed a sigh of relief. 'Myles will call to you after the show. He'll go straight there.'

Claire gave her the address and then hung up. She smiled briefly at Steve and Georgia, who were watching her anxiously.

'OK,' she said. 'You're here for a bit longer, Steve. So I suggest that maybe you'd like to have a shower and get dressed properly and wait for your folks to pick you up.'

'Thanks,' he said. He pushed his chair back and left the table. A moment later he poked his head around the door again.

'Up the stairs and to the right,' Claire told him before he spoke.

'Thanks,' he said again.

'Yes, Mum, thanks,' said Georgia.

'I don't approve of what you did,' said Claire sternly. 'You might have thought that you were completely in control of the situation, but sometimes things get out of hand and before you know it you've done something you regret.'

'They didn't get out of hand,' Georgia pointed out.

'I suppose not.' Claire believed her daughter.

'But I'm glad you went a bit freaky,' Georgia added. 'I'd rather have a mother who cared too much than someone like Steve's who doesn't care at all.'

'Soft-soaper!' But Claire smiled as she ruffled Georgia's already messed-up hair. And she smiled again when Georgia gave her a bear-hug of approval.

Despite the rocky start, Claire found herself liking Steve Ó Sé. He had a dry sense of humour which appealed to her, and when he opened up and started talking about his home life she couldn't help feeling a little sorry for him. The boy obviously wanted warmth and approval from his parents, she thought, but they seemed far too wrapped up in their own world to see it.

The impression was further strengthened when Myles Ó Sé finally arrived to collect him. He was abrupt and impatient with the boy, muttering that he had better things to do than come up to Dublin at the drop of a hat. Claire badly wanted to rant and rave at Myles for not having a clue what his son was up to. She wanted to tell him that he could've been doing drink or drugs instead of spending the night in his girlfriend's house – even though spending the night with Georgia wasn't exactly high on the list of things Steve should've been doing anyway!

As he left, Steve extended his hand to shake Claire's and she smiled inwardly at the seriousness with which he bade her goodbye and thanked her for being so nice to him. He pecked Georgia very quickly on the cheek, muttered that he'd text her, then followed his father down the path to the car.

Georgia and Claire stood on the top step until they'd driven out of sight.

'I am sorry,' said Georgia. 'I know we shouldn't have.'

'No, you shouldn't,' agreed Claire. 'But no harm done. And he is a nice boy.'

'He is, isn't he?' Georgia's eyes glowed and her voice was full of warmth. 'I mean, I know he's not The One or anything like that. But he's good to know.'

'Perhaps sometime you can invite him to stay properly,' said Claire. 'Separate rooms, though.'

'I do love you.' Georgia hugged her.

Claire chuckled.

'It was good fun last night, wasn't it?' Georgia went back into the house and closed the door. 'And you were dancing with Nate. I don't want to turn things around on you, Mum, and be super-critical or anything, but I don't think it's a good idea for you to see him any more.'

'Oh?'

'It'd be wrong, wouldn't it? Sarah's nice. It's all very well to say you and Nate could be friends, but you couldn't, if he even barely fancies you. Not when he's married to her.'

Claire hadn't intended to tell Georgia about Nate's divorce but she couldn't help herself.

'But that's great.' Georgia blurted out the words. 'He can date you.'

'I don't know why you're so keen for me to go out with him,' said Claire.

'Oh come on!' cried Georgia. 'From the minute I met him I thought that he was nice. He likes you. And you like him.'

'And it's all so much more complicated than that,' Claire told her.

'I don't see why.'

'People don't just hop in and out of relationships. There are consequences to everything. There are other people to consider.'

'Yes, but he's divorced!'

'Twice,' said Claire. 'And he has a daughter of his own.'

'Oh.'

'I like him,' admitted Claire. 'But we have to live in the real world, Georgey.'

'How old?'

'Huh?'

'Is his daughter?'

'Sixteen.'

'Does she stay with him?'

'Georgey, honey, I don't know. She doesn't live with him because her mother has custody. But Sarah says that they see each other. He was very upset over it.'

'Not like Slimeball Pete so?'

'I don't think Nate would ever be like Slimeball Pete,' said Claire.

Georgia grinned suddenly. 'You told me not to call him that.'

'You're impossible!' Claire hugged her.

'I'm going to my den,' said Georgia. 'I need to think about stuff.'

'OK,' said Claire.

In her den, Georgia took out her diary and began writing in it. She filled the page for the day before with the events of the barbecue and with memories of Steve's kiss. *It was magical,* she wrote. *His lips were way softer than I imagined. And he's the nicest person I know.* She looked at her sloping writing and drew a small heart at the end of the sentence. Then she took out the sheet of paper listing her requirements for Claire's boyfriend. She rewrote the requirements in a long column and wrote Nate's name at the top of the next. Then she surveyed the list and began to write again. When she'd finished, she looked at it thoughtfully.

REQUIREMENTS FOR MUM'S BOYFRIEND
1. *Reasonably good-looking (no facial hair/back hair/not too much chest hair).*
2. *Clean (fingernails especially/also ears).*
3. *Not patronising (no heavy sighs when I say something).*
4. *Money (not rich but well off enough not to freak about price of CDs/DVDs/phone cards).*

5. *Kids (this is difficult. Good-looking son might be interesting tho).*
6. *Interests – music/history/sports (but not bloody football)/fashion (but not pervy).*
7. *Car – something flashy.*

NATE
1. *OK for someone his age – looks good with no T-shirt!*
2. *Cleaned up well tho usually fairly mucky.*
3. *Treats me like an adult – v. interesting talk with him about Mum when he drove me to Tesco!*
4. *Don't know, can't imagine much, but money isn't everything.*
5. *A sixteen-year-old daughter. Would she be a total bitch? Or would she have hints about blokes? Would I get to meet her at all??*
6. *Gardens (good), not bad dancer (a bit embarrassing but could be worse), must be a bit sporty surely, given he's in good condition.*
7. *Drives a van – oh dear.*

Chapter 38

Veronica (Speedwell) – White, blue, purple and pink flowers on tall, narrow spikes. Usually trouble-free but will be killed by winter water-logging.

'I'll call you.'

That's what he'd said. Claire knew that was what he'd said. But almost a week later he still hadn't called and Claire was beginning to feel as though she could release the breath that she'd seemed to be holding ever since the night of the barbecue. It was OK, she thought. He'd thought the better of it and that was definitely a good thing. Especially since she was pretty sure she was over what she told herself was a schoolgirl crush on him. With a bit of luck, she thought, as she lugged one of Eileen's cases down the stairs, our lives will settle back into their old routine again. And that'll be just fine.

She placed the suitcase near the door. Today was the day that Eileen was moving into her new apartment and Alan had offered to drive her there. Her furniture and other bits and pieces which had been in storage for the past couple of weeks were being delivered to the apartment later in the afternoon.

Alan had phoned Claire's house the day after the barbecue, thanked her again for her hospitality and then asked to speak to Eileen. Which was when they'd made the arrangement for him to drive her to her new home. Eileen's cheeks had been slightly pink after the conversation and there'd been a sparkle in her eyes.

'I thought he was just a temporary fixture?' Claire had remarked when Eileen replaced the receiver, and had been rewarded by an even deeper pink in her mother's cheeks.

Alan's maroon Mercedes pulled up outside the house and he walked up the garden path. As always, he was impeccably dressed. Claire couldn't help wondering whether he had any informal clothes at all! She suddenly realised that Eileen had spent some time on her appearance today too – ever since Georgia's restyling of her hair she'd kept to the new look, and today she was wearing a smart periwinkle-blue skirt and jacket that suited her curvy figure.

On hearing the car pull up, Georgia hurried out of her den, still texting on her mobile phone. Claire shot her an exasperated look – her daughter was spending more time than ever sending and receiving messages from Steve Ó Sé. When she'd remonstrated with Georgia she'd simply told her to chill out.

'Have you got everything?' Alan had finished stowing bags in the car.

'I think so,' replied Eileen.

'Let's go then.'

He waited at the car while Eileen, Claire and Georgia hugged each other.

'It was lovely having you to stay,' said Claire. 'I wasn't sure how it'd work out, but it was great.'

'Yeah, Gran, come back and visit soon,' Georgia told her. 'You make it easier for me to stand up to her.'

Claire made a face at Georgia, who chuckled.

'You're sure you want to do all this yourself?' asked Claire. 'Because we could come up on the train later if—'

'I'm fine,' Eileen interrupted her. 'I've enjoyed being with you too but I want a bit of time to myself. And to be honest, I'm excited about getting my stuff delivered. But you'd better visit really soon.'

'Of course,' said Claire.

Georgia's phone beeped and Claire bristled.

'It's only Robs,' Georgia told her. 'Can I go round there for a while?'

'Sure,' said Claire. 'But don't be late home.'

Actually, she thought when both Eileen and Georgia had gone, it was nice to be on her own in the house again. She stood in the kitchen absorbing the silence. It seemed ages since the place had been so quiet. Phydough got out of his basket and woofed at her. She opened a packet of dog food and spilled it into his dish.

'I'm going to do some work now,' she told him. 'I've got hope-lessly behind because it's been so impossible with Mum here. I never thought I'd look forward to shutting myself in the office with the computer, but right now I think I am.'

Phydough ignored her, his head buried in his food bowl.

She'd just sat down at her desk and jolted the computer into life when the phone rang.

'Hi,' said Nate easily. 'Sorry I didn't get back to you before now.'

She stared at the computer screen.

'Claire? Are you there?'

'Yes,' she replied. 'Of course.'

'Well, like I said, sorry I didn't call you. I got caught up in some things.'

'That's all right.' She clicked on a Word document and a tract of incomprehensible information about retroviruses opened up in front of her.

'I wondered whether you'd like to come out with me next Tuesday?'

'I'm really . . . not sure.'

'I've been invited to the opening of an art exhibition,' he told her. 'A friend of mine runs the gallery and I met the artist once before. He seems a nice guy. The paintings are all of gardens. Veronica says they're really gorgeous.'

'Well . . .'

'You won't be late home,' said Nate. 'The exhibition starts at half-six. We'll be there an hour at the most. Afterwards we could get a quick bite to eat if you want. Or not.'

'How . . . where is it?' she asked. I'm not going, she told herself. Say I go and we get on all right, what then? Going out again? Having a relationship? Saying things to each other that we don't really mean simply because I haven't had sex in ages and maybe he hasn't either? Or getting to like each other? But not quite enough, so we make each other unhappy? Or me getting to like him more than he likes me, so I'm the one who's left unhappy? I don't want any of that. I absolutely don't.

'Glasthule,' he replied promptly. 'It's in a lovely location near the Dart station. We can get the train if you like.'

She closed the Word document without doing anything to it. It had all been so different when thoughts of him had been unattainable fantasies. They'd been pleasurable in a guilty way because of her belief that he was married. This was totally different.

'I really do think you'd enjoy it,' he told her. 'And I'd love to have someone there with me. It's such a pain when you go to things and you don't know anyone.'

'You know the owner,' Claire pointed out. 'And the artist.'

'Like I said, I only met him once. But in any event, they'll have to mingle. And I hate the idea of spending ages talking to some art snob about the patina or energy or whatever it is that they come out with.'

Claire chuckled involuntarily.

'So you'll come?'

She swallowed. 'Well, OK. If you don't mind getting the Dart.' Are you mad? she asked herself. You're building up nothing but trouble.

'No problem.' He sounded relieved. 'I'll call for you around six.'

'OK,' she said again. He'll leave you and you'll cry yourself to sleep.

'I'm looking forward to it.'

'Good,' she said.

She put the receiver down then turned the computer off again. She wasn't able to concentrate on working. All she could think about was being alone with Nate Taylor. What on earth would she say to him? What did he really want from her? Would he expect her to sleep with him? And what the hell was she going to wear?

Georgia was an unending source of advice on how Claire should behave with Nate Taylor.

'You've got to treat him right,' she told Claire sternly. 'No being off-hand with him. You've got to show an interest in his interests.' She ran from the kitchen, where they'd been talking, into her den and returned a moment later with a new magazine. 'See – it says so here. Be interested.'

Claire looked at the magazine. She hadn't read any of them since Georgia had come home from summer camp. But they were still full of ways to find the right man.

'I'll do my best,' she told Georgia. 'But we're just going to the art gallery. It's not a big deal.'

'It sounds terribly sophisticated,' said Georgia. 'Though I expect it'll be dead boring really. And maybe the paintings are horrible. You know, the sort of thing I used to do myself when I was four.'

Claire grinned. 'Philistine.'

'I wouldn't have imagined Nate'd be interested in art,' continued Georgia. 'Of course I didn't really know about his hobbies so it's hard to know whether he fits.'

'Huh?'

'My requirements. For your boyfriend. Remember – you read my list?' Georgia's last words had a slight sting to them.

'I told you it wasn't really deliberate,' said Claire defensively. 'What bits doesn't he fit?'

'Driving a nice car,' said Georgia promptly. 'Gran's boyfriend is a much better prospect there. I can't see myself being OK with hopping into a florist's van to get places.'

Claire laughed.

'Having a gorgeous son,' added Georgia. She grimaced. 'I dunno about this daughter thing, even if she does live abroad with her mother. What if she decides to come here sometime? What if she hates me?'

'I really don't think that's an issue,' said Claire mildly. 'We're only going to an art exhibition. Neither he nor his daughter nor anyone else in his family is moving in with us.'

'I suppose not. Being loaded,' Georgia continued. 'I can't see that he's that well off really, and it'd be nice to have someone who handed out cash at every available opportunity. I'm sorry to say, Mum, that Gran beats you hands down there too. Anyone can see that Alan has money.'

'Don't be so shallow,' said Claire.

Georgia giggled. 'I like it that you're suddenly defending him.'

'I'm not!' cried Claire. 'I just don't think that things like cars and money matter.'

'I suppose it'd be a bit pointless him having a top-of-the-range model and you still not liking getting into cars,' agreed Georgia.

'I got that taxi home,' Claire reminded her.

'But you haven't been in one since.'

'No,' said Claire. 'One day maybe.'

Suddenly Georgia hugged her. 'When I pass my driving test you can get into a car with me,' she said. 'And I'll be such a brilliant driver that you won't be able to help yourself.'

On Saturday afternoon Claire and Georgia went shopping in town. Claire kept insisting that she wasn't looking for anything special for her evening out with Nate, but Georgia treated that comment with the contempt she felt it deserved. She dragged Claire into Zara where Claire protested that the fashionable cuts were just too unforgiving for her but where, much to Georgia's delight, she bought her daughter a new skirt, two pairs of stylish trousers, a selection of pretty tops and a fur-trimmed jacket which Georgia raved over, telling Claire that it was totally the thing to be seen in for autumn and that Robyn O'Malley would be pea-green with envy.

Then they went to Debenhams, where Georgia made Claire try on dozens of dresses before agreeing that the first one she'd selected, a dark and dramatic green silk sheath, was definitely the best.

'Green is your colour,' she told Claire. 'It complements your eyes. Makes you look enigmatic.'

'And you think that's how I should look?'

'Definitely,' Georgia said. 'Oh, and look, Mum!' She pointed to another rail. 'This is the most perfect scarf to go with it!' She grabbed the rust-coloured chiffon scarf with green detailed beading and draped it around Claire's neck. 'You look fabulous!'

'Thank you,' said Claire. 'I don't need the scarf, though.'

'Mum!' cried Georgia. 'Of course you do. It makes the outfit complete.'

And so Claire was railroaded into buying the scarf, although she drew the line at the stylish green leather shoes which Georgia tried to persuade her were worth the hefty price tag.

'I've loads of shoes at home,' she told her daughter. 'Enough is enough. And I'd hardly ever get to wear them.'

But she did take Georgia into a hair-dressing salon, where the two of them had a wash and trim. Then they had coffee and cakes in one of the many coffee shops before making their way to the bus stop, laden with parcels.

'Brilliant day,' said Georgia as they boarded the bus. 'And you'll be a knockout on Tuesday.'

'I don't want to be a knockout,' said Claire. 'I just want to be myself.'

Tuesday came around incredibly quickly. Claire spent the weekend catching up with her work, while Georgia got ready for the new school term. On Saturday evening Eavan called to tell Claire that they had a brilliant offer for the house in Howth and that they were going to take it. Despite the fact, she added, that Glenn had gone for an interview arranged by Lacey with a company called Hexagon and that they'd offered him a job at the same salary as he'd earned Trontec. He was starting at the end of the month. They were, Eavan said, going to use the rest of the time to find the right house for them. A less demanding house, she told Claire. Because now all of her bad memories were caught up in the Howth house and it didn't feel the same. It had become a symbol of keeping things from each other. A different house would mean a new honesty and practicality between them.

Claire had been delighted to hear her friend sounding so positive again, and was truly relieved that she and Glenn seemed to have come through their bad patch. Eavan had also told her that although she was going to give up the job at the DIY store once Glenn started work, she would still have something to do. Trinny Armstrong had called to say that there was a vacancy three mornings a week at Locum Libris, and Eavan had decided to take it. She needed, she confided in Claire, to feel that she was doing something else outside the house. Both so that Glenn didn't feel as though everything depended on him all the time, and also so that she had interests outside of home decorating and looking after Saffy. She rather felt, she added, that it was becoming so obsessed with being a perfect wife and mother and having a perfect home that had put so much pressure on Glenn in the first place. He was happy with the idea. He was happy about everything now, and Eavan too bubbled with enthusiasm.

'And what about you?' Eavan had then demanded. 'What about you and the lovely Nate?'

'Lovely Nate?' Claire kept her voice as light as she possibly could.

'I liked him,' said Eavan. 'He asked about you. I told him that he should give it a go with you.'

'You did!' Claire clenched the receiver. So that was what they'd been talking about at the barbecue. Her! She wondered exactly how much information Eavan had given him.

'Ah, Claire, come on. You've changed these last few weeks. You're ready.'

'I'm not,' said Claire. 'You might think I've changed but I haven't. And even though I'm going out with him . . .' Her voice faltered.

'But that's wonderful!'

'Eavan . . . Eavan, if Glenn had left you, would you be rushing to find someone else?'

Eavan sighed deeply. 'Of course not.'

'Well then.'

'But it's been three years. And you're going out with him.'

'Because I didn't know how to say no.'

'You can't stay frozen for ever, Claire.'

'I'm not frozen at all.' And Claire had hung up.

Eavan had immediately called her back and told her not to do anything she didn't want to, and that she was sorry if she'd been instrumental in pushing Claire too far and that she had no right to lecture people on their lives given that she'd nearly fucked up her own.

'You're a good friend,' said Claire. 'Let's get together again soon. Go shopping maybe.'

'In chain stores,' agreed Eavan. 'I'm giving the designers a miss from now on.'

She replaced the receiver and stared thoughtfully at the wall in front of her. Claire was actually going out with this man. And Eavan knew that this was different to her friend's crazy notions of internet dating or going out with people because of Georgia. This was Claire dipping her toe in the waters again and – even though she'd wanted it to happen – Eavan had been so sure of Claire's devotion to Bill's memory that she hadn't really believed it ever would. She hoped and hoped that Claire wouldn't do anything silly to mess it all up. It was time for her to let Bill go. Maybe now she finally could.

*   *   *

401

Now Claire looked at her watch. Five o'clock. An hour to go . . . She opened her mail programme to send the file she'd finished working on. There were four new e-mails in her inbox. One of them had the subject heading 'Soft Cell'.

She clicked on it.

Hi, Soft Cell, she read. *I'm Danno. I'm 36 years old. As you know from my profile, I'm into sports and the outdoor life. I also like good food (I'm a great cook) and Guy Ritchie movies. I have tickets for his latest and was wondering if that would be your thing? We could meet for a drink beforehand and if you don't find me too repulsive we could give it a go. The tickets are for Friday night. How about it? Danno.*

Claire stared at the message. She'd almost forgotten about Danno and Guru. She certainly hadn't expected to hear from either of them. She opened up the HowWillIKnow website and looked at Danno's picture again. He seemed nice and friendly and definitely an outdoors kind of guy. She closed her eyes and tried to imagine meeting him. But the image wouldn't come. Damn it, she thought, as she began to type. I should never have done this in the first place!

Hi, Danno. I'm really, really sorry. I'm seeing someone now. I should've mailed you to let you know but this was my first time on the site and I didn't think. Thanks for getting in touch with me. I hope you find someone a lot better than me. That shouldn't be too difficult. Soft Cell.

She sent the e-mail and closed the program. Then she opened it again and deleted the message and her reply from both her inbox and her sent mail. Although Georgia had her own computer, she sometimes used the ice-white Apple too. And Claire didn't want her to see that she'd lied to a prospective date by telling him she was seeing someone else when she wasn't. Not really.

She got up and went into her bedroom. Georgia was already there, smoothing out the green sheath dress.

'What are you doing?' demanded Claire.

'Making sure you have all the right stuff,' Georgia told her. 'I really wish you'd bought the shoes, though. You have nothing that really wows.'

'I'm fine,' said Claire. 'Actually I'm thinking that this dress might be a bit OTT for tonight.'

'What d'you mean?' asked Georgia. 'Aren't these arty things totally glamorous with lots of celebs?'

'Maybe in Manhattan,' suggested Claire mildly. 'But not downtown Dublin. As far as I can tell, it's just a gang of the artist's friends and a few reviewers from the papers. Artists are notoriously scruffy, so maybe I should just wear jeans or something instead.'

'Don't you dare! cried Georgia. 'You'll look like a model in the dress.'

'It's an art exhibition not a modelling session,' Claire reminded her.

'Actually your only really sexy one is this,' Georgia continued as she took the scorched ochre out of the wardrobe. 'But I think it's a bit low-cut.'

'Do you now?'

'For this event,' Georgia said. 'Other occasions would be different.'

Claire hid a smile. Georgia was taking it all very seriously.

'And I've decided that you can borrow my new eye-shadow,' Georgia told her. 'Tawny Gold. It looks good on me and it'll look good on you too.'

'Will it?'

'Absolutely,' said Georgia. 'I bet he'll be really impressed with you. He fancied you at the barbecue and you'd hardly bothered then.'

'So if he truly fancied me – and I hate that expression by the way, Ms Hudson – but if he fancied me at the barbecue and I was just casual, why on earth d'you think I should bother now?'

'Because this is different!' cried Georgia. 'This is him taking you out. I can't believe you don't understand that.'

Claire sighed. 'I do really. OK, I'll use the Tawny Gold. Now which shoes do you think I should wear?'

With five minutes to go before Nate called, Claire was standing in front of the mirror plagued by doubts. The green dress looked fantastic. The Tawny Gold eyeshadow suited her, making her eyes look bigger and echoing the amber flecks. She was wearing her hair loose – Georgia had spent ten minutes with the straightening iron on it, and now it framed her face in a sophisticated style which (she had to admit) made her look altogether more elegant than the

403

tumbling tresses ever did. It wasn't a look she'd bother with every day but it was definitely very sophisticated for the evening. But she could hardly walk in the high-heeled backless shoes that Georgia had unearthed from the back of the wardrobe and had insisted she wear.

'He's here.' Georgia had been peering out of the window of her den. 'And guess what! He's driving a car, not a van. Nice one too, a Lexus. Must be a few bob in potting plants after all!' She turned to her mother. 'Last-minute check.'

She appraised Claire's appearance and then whistled appreciatively. 'You'll do,' she told her.

'Have you got all your stuff together?'

Georgia nodded. She was spending the evening at Robyn's house and was bringing a selection of PlayStation games with her. Claire had promised to call her on the way home and either collect her or allow Leonie to drop her back to the house. Leonie, when she heard that Claire was going out with a man, offered to have Georgia to sleep over but Claire had insisted that she wanted Georgia back home that night.

'Right,' she said as Nate rang the bell. 'Let's go.'

He was dressed casually as always, but he looked good in chinos and a loose-fitting jacket. His hair was still damp from the shower.

'I'm coming with you as far as the Dart station,' Georgia informed him. 'I'm staying with Robs.'

'And how's the boyfriend?' asked Nate easily as she fell into step beside them, their pace slower than usual to accommodate Claire's inability to stride in the high-heeled shoes.

'He's fine.' She blushed. Nate, of course, didn't know about the drama of Steve staying in her room and she certainly wasn't going to tell him.

His question effectively put a stop to their conversation until they reached the station. Georgia's train arrived first and she waved across the line at them as she hopped on to travel the single stop.

Claire and Nate waited on the windswept platform for another ten minutes before their train came. Claire was worried about the effect the wind was having on her newly styled hair. She patted it to reassure herself that it hadn't turned into a bird's nest.

'You look fine,' Nate said as he noticed her action.

'I'm not used to having it this straight,' Claire confided. 'Georgia went mad with the hair iron again.'

Nate made a face. 'Felicity had one of those. She used to spend hours sitting in front of the mirror with it. I rather think she loved it more than she ever loved me.'

Claire wasn't entirely sure how she should react to that. Then she saw that Nate was grinning, and she smiled tentatively at him.

They travelled in near-silence to Glasthule. Alone with him and having run out of hair conversation, Claire couldn't think of a single thing to say. Nate himself seemed perfectly at ease with no conversation at all. Which could be a good thing, thought Claire, but at this stage in a relationship shouldn't we be chatting about something? Anything? And then she shivered, because she'd thought of them in terms of a couple. Two people, she reminded herself. Two independent people. Not a couple at all.

The Purple Rain Gallery was just off the main street, set back in a small gravelled courtyard in the centre of which was placed a bronze sculpture of a woman with an umbrella, a pile of bronze shopping bags at her feet. The sculpture was so smooth and real that Claire wanted to touch it. But she supposed that people who came to art galleries didn't bother with things like touching sculptures. Maybe they knew how it should feel simply by looking at it.

'She's great, isn't she?' Nate said. 'I always want to give her a hug. I can't help wondering what she's doing standing there in the rain.'

'Waiting for someone to buy her, I suppose,' said Claire drily.

Nate laughed and led her into the gallery. He introduced her to Veronica, the chic and elegant owner, who promptly handed them both enormous glasses of red wine and told them to look around.

The paintings were beautiful. When Nate had said it was an exhibition of garden scenes, Claire had imagined jigsaw-type pictures of olde worlde cottages surrounded by hollyhocks and roses. But these paintings were of overgrown gardens, country gardens, sun-drenched Mediterranean gardens, rain-lashed northern European gardens – even, Claire noted, a quiet and contemplative Zen garden. Some of the paintings were framed behind glass and some of them were uncovered canvases. All of them were wonderful, the vibrant colours leaping off the walls, making her feel as though she could simply step into each one.

She wandered around the gallery while Nate lagged behind, caught up in conversation with various people. But she didn't feel abandoned by him. She was enjoying her time simply gazing at the paintings. Particularly one. Entitled simply *Jamaica Garden*, it was a painting of a pastel-pink house with a corrugated roof set on the edge of a foliage-covered cliff. At the side of the house was a hammock strung between two bending palm trees. A body, impossible to say whether male or female, lay in the hammock, a hat tipped over its face. On the ground beneath lay an abandoned scythe, hoe and trowel. Around the house were flowerbeds crammed with multicoloured tropical flowers. In contrast to the pastel shade of the house, the flowers were a blaze of scorching pinks, reds, oranges and purples.

The painting was impressionist rather than detailed. But as she looked at it, Claire could feel the heat of the Caribbean sun falling on to the garden and sense the languor of the person in the hammock. She could remember the garden of the hotel in Jamaica, where a whole army of gardeners worked to make it both beautiful and colourful and where there was a similar hammock strung up for the use of guests. Bill had fallen asleep in it one afternoon and had said that it was one of the most comfortable experiences of his life. 'When we get home,' he'd said, 'I'm going to buy one of those.'

She'd forgotten that. Completely. Until now.

She walked away from *Jamaica Garden* and looked at other paintings. But that was the one that stayed etched in her mind even as she peered at a much bigger canvas entitled *Scotland Garden* and noted that the price tag was for a couple of thousand. Heavens above, she thought. Maybe I should get into painting instead of editing!

She strolled further around the gallery, her feet now beginning to ache from the height of the shoes. I really wish I hadn't let Georgey persuade me into these, she thought grimly. They were shoved to the back of the wardrobe for a reason.

She looked around for Nate. He was talking to Veronica and a short, balding man with a roly-poly figure and a shining, moon-shaped face. Another man, as tall as Nate but thinner and a little younger, stood beside them. As she watched, Veronica clapped her hands and announced that the exhibition was now being formally opened by Duncan Barrett, the well-known poet and musician.

I'm in culture overload, thought Claire. Artists, poets, musicians . . . She suddenly felt very out of place.

The tall, thin man was Duncan Barrett. He spoke easily and well about the talent of Eamonn Pearse, the artist. Claire found herself nodding in agreement as Duncan suggested that the paintings were like portals into another world. She'd felt that standing in front of *Jamaica Garden*. It had made her feel as though a different world was simply a step away.

When Duncan had finished, the roly-poly man stepped forward. Claire found it difficult to believe that such an ordinary-looking man could produce such wonderful paintings. She knew that it was a stupid way to think, but she'd expected the artist to be the scruffy person she'd mentioned to Georgia earlier, not a man who looked more like a banker or insurance salesman.

Eamonn thanked them for coming, hoped that they'd enjoy looking at the pictures and mentioned that though he hated the idea of selling any of them he needed to pay the bills.

The assembled people laughed. Claire had already noticed that there were quite a lot of little red stickers beside the paintings, indicating that they were already sold. She didn't think that Eamonn would have to worry much about the bills.

Another man, tall, dark and traditionally handsome, presented Eamon with a bouquet of flowers and kissed him on the cheek.

'His partner, Redmond,' whispered Nate, who was standing just behind Claire. 'They're a wonderful couple, been together for absolutely years.'

The crowd swirled around again. A waiter refilled Claire's glass of wine before she had a chance to refuse. She looked around for Nate again. He was standing opposite *Jamaica Garden*. As though sensing her gaze across the crowded room, he turned towards her and smiled.

She smiled too and walked towards him. She wasn't quite sure whether her high-heeled shoe caught on something on the glossy wooden floor, or whether it was the way she'd moved towards him. All she knew was that, quite suddenly, she was shooting forwards,

407

tripping out of her shoe, and shrieking as her full glass of red wine spun out of her hand in an almost perfect arc, so that it landed on the floor in front of *Jamaica Garden* and shattered into pieces. But not before it had liberally discharged its contents on to the uncovered canvas first.

There was a stunned silence in the gallery. Claire got to her knees. The front of her beautiful green dress was spattered with wine. Her hair hung in a tangled sheet in front of her face. Her elegant scarf slid from around her neck and ended up in the spreading crimson pool on the floor.

'Bitch!' cried Redmond in anguish, while Eamon stood beside him in shocked silence. 'Philistine bitch!'

'I'm so sorry,' gasped Claire. 'It was an accident. I really am sorry. Is there anything I can do?'

'Get out!' he cried. 'Get out. You've ruined his work. Months and months of work. The opening night and Eamon's magnificent painting. Both destroyed!'

There was a sudden flash as someone took a photograph. Claire blinked in the unexpected light.

'Come on, Claire.' Nate was beside her, helping her upright.

'That painting is worth millions!' cried Redmond. 'I can't believe it. I really can't.'

Veronica walked over to her. 'Are you all right?' Her voice was frosty.

'Yes. Fine.' Claire was grateful for Nate's hand gripping her arm. She knew that she was shaking.

'It's not worth millions,' he said calmly. 'Only six hundred as far as I could see.'

'Oh but, even still!' Claire was horrified.

'It was an accident,' said Nate. He looked at Veronica. 'Can it be cleaned?'

'Anything can be restored,' she said. 'It's just a matter of how long it takes and how much it will cost.'

'I'm so sorry,' said Claire again.

'Let's go,' said Nate. 'Ronnie – talk to me about the painting later.' He steered Claire back through the gallery, picked up her shoes, and led her out into the courtyard. All the while she could feel the

408

steely glares of the other guests watching her and could hear the enraged ranting of Redmond, still telling everyone that wonderful, wonderful Eamon's opening night had been ruined by her stupidity.

Nate handed her the high-heeled shoes. She put them on shakily.

'Are you all right?' he asked her.

'Are you crazy?' she asked in reply. 'I've just ruined someone's work. I've made a complete fool of myself in front of a hundred people. My clothes are soaked in red wine and I'm wearing shoes I can't walk in. No. I'm not bloody well all right.'

His mouth twitched.

'And it's not funny!' she cried.

'I know that.' But she could see he was trying hard not to laugh.

She walked away from him, out of the gravelled courtyard and into the street beyond. As she went through the wrought-iron entrance gate, she tripped again and almost went over on her ankle.

'Shit!' she cried as she managed to stay upright.

Nate grabbed her. 'You're not safe in those shoes,' he said.

Claire bit her lip. This was all going wrong. She hadn't really wanted to go out with anyone, but she'd come out with him and now she looked like a fool. A fool who couldn't even stand upright in a pair of high-heeled shoes. Nothing like this had ever happened to her before. Had ever happened with Bill.

She couldn't stop the tear from spilling on to her cheek.

'Hey, come on.' He put his arm around her shoulders. 'No need for that.'

'I'm sorry,' she sniffed.

'It's not your fault,' he said. 'And the painting can be fixed. I know it can.'

'Yes,' she muttered, rubbing at her eyes and smearing Tawny Gold eye-shadow and Mocha Brown mascara all over her cheeks, 'but it'll probably cost at least the same again to do it.'

'Don't worry,' he said. 'I'm sure something can be sorted out.'

'Things don't just sort themselves out,' said Claire. 'You have to work to make that happen. And there's nothing I can do.'

'You can't fix everything,' he told her. 'Other people can. Let them.'

'And what happens when I get a bill for goodness knows how

much?' she asked. 'It's not like I'm on the breadline, Nate, but I can't shell out thousands for wine-soaked pictures.'

He laughed. 'It won't cost thousands. Please stop worrying.' He squeezed her shoulder. 'Come on. Let's get something to eat and forget about this for a while.'

She shook her head. 'I'm not hungry.'

'Would you like to go for a drink?'

'No,' she said. 'To be honest, I just want to go home.'

'Of course,' said Nate. 'Let's take a cab.'

'No,' she said again.

He rubbed the side of his nose.

'I don't really like cabs,' she said. 'I don't like being in cars. It's a . . . I . . .' She started to shake beneath his grasp. 'I can't do it.' She started to cry again, but this time big, heaving sobs. 'Look, it was nice of you to ask me out and everything but – but – I'm the wrong person. I don't do cabs and I don't do going out with people.'

He said nothing, but allowed her to cry unchecked. He took his arm from her shoulders as she rummaged in her bag for a tissue, which she used to scrub at her eyes and then blow her nose.

'Regardless of everything,' he told her, 'we still have to get home. So let's go on the Dart again. No problem.'

She nodded. They walked side by side to the station and waited in silence for the five minutes before the train arrived. In the harsh white light of the carriage, the wine stains on Claire's dress looked even worse. And in the window she could see the reflection of her smeared eye-shadow and mascara. She tried to rub at it with the tissue but only succeeded in streaking it still further.

When they got off the train Nate walked towards the house with her. Once again they were walking in silence. Claire was grateful for his tacit understanding that she didn't want to talk. That trying to have a light conversation wouldn't make her feel any better. In the days after Bill's accident people had wanted to talk all the time when they were with her, as though by discussing trivial things they could stop her thinking about it. They'd been afraid of silence but she'd grown to value it, and the knowledge that you didn't have to fill every quiet moment with inconsequential chatter.

When they reached the gate she looked up at him.

'I'm sorry I ruined your evening,' she said. 'I'm sorry I ruined the painting too. When you find out how much it costs to fix, let me know.'

'He's probably covered by insurance.' Nate consoled her. 'And I'm sure it won't be that difficult to fix.'

'Maybe not. But that's not the point, is it? I messed up something he created. He was right to be mad at me.'

'OK,' said Nate. 'I'll let you know.'

'Thanks,' she said. 'Look, I know you asked me out and everything, and maybe the right thing for me to do now is invite you in for coffee, but right now I couldn't handle that. I want to go in, get out of this stuff – I smell like a damn vineyard – and be on my own.'

'Sure,' said Nate.

'So, um, goodnight.'

'Goodnight,' he said. He smiled briefly at her, then got into his car and drove away.

Chapter 39

Catanache (Cupid's Dart) – Daisy-like blue and white flowers which open from silvery buds. Thrives in dry soil.

She threw her wine-soaked dress into the laundry basket although she was fairly sure it was ruined beyond the abilities of even the most determined biological washing powder. She slipped into her cotton pyjamas and ancient red dressing gown. It wasn't cold, but she was shivering. Fool, she thought as she filled the kettle. Fool, fool, fool.

She made a cup of tea and then dialled Leonie's number to tell her she was home. The other woman was astonished to hear her voice.

'It's only nine o'clock,' she said incredulously. 'I thought you'd be much later, Claire.'

'No, it was just this art do,' said Claire as dismissively as she could. 'Look, would it be an awful imposition to ask you to drop Georgey home?'

'Of course not.' Leonie's voice was filled with curiosity. 'Didn't you have a good time?'

'It was fine,' said Claire. 'Not really my sort of thing, though.'

She replaced the receiver and sat in the living room, warming her hands around the big blue mug. Every time she remembered flying headlong across the polished floor of the art gallery she went hot with embarrassment. And her humiliation had been so total, she thought miserably, with all those culture vultures looking at her as though she was a piece of dung that Nate had dragged in on his shoe. It must have been mortifying for him too. The man with the stupid, clumsy girlfriend.

'Only I'm not his girlfriend,' she said out loud. I was right to steer clear of the whole dating scene. It's been nothing but one embarrassment after the other. None of it was what I expected. And tonight – well, maybe it's just as well that this happened. At least this way it's over and done with and he'll never get to leave me and break my heart.

She heard Georgia's key in the lock and put her half-empty mug on the coffee table. Georgia pushed open the living-room door.

'What happened?' she demanded. 'Why are you home so early?' Her eyes narrowed as she looked at Claire in her dressing gown and her hand flew to her mouth. 'Is he here?' she gasped. 'Is he waiting for you upstairs? Oh, Mum, I—'

'Of course he's not here,' Claire interrupted her. 'Don't be so silly.'

Georgia flushed. 'I'm sorry. I know you wouldn't . . . wouldn't . . . not here . . .' She made a face. She liked Nate and she didn't mind the idea of Claire dating him. But Claire bringing him to the house and sleeping with him was something she wasn't quite prepared to accept yet.

'So why are you home?' she asked. 'It's early. Leonie was really surprised. And we only just got to see the end of the DVD we were watching.'

'Things didn't entirely go to plan,' said Claire. 'So we left early and I came home.'

'But didn't you want to be with him for a while?' Georgia looked quizzically at her. 'I thought you liked him.'

'I do. But I'm not sure how much he likes me.'

'He does,' said Georgia confidently. 'It's obvious he does, Mum. And he's nice.' She bit her bottom lip. 'I like him. He's . . . he's kind of strong and silent.'

Claire's laugh was a little strained. 'I know he's nice,' she said. 'But, honey, I really don't want to go out with anyone, no matter how nice. It was enough to have had your dad. I'm fine the way I am. I will go out a bit more, definitely. Just not like this.'

'What happened?' demanded Georgia again.

So Claire told her about tripping on the polished floor and dousing *Jamaica Garden* in red wine, while Georgia's eyes grew rounder and rounder.

'Wow,' she said when Claire had finished. 'I see why you left.' She giggled. 'Expensive date if you have to pay for the painting!'

'I'll have to pay something, I suppose,' said Claire. 'I just hope it won't be too much.'

'Oh, if they can restore Old Masters I'm sure they can dab off a few wine stains,' said Georgia dismissively. 'Don't worry about it.'

'I'm glad you're so relaxed.'

'I'm relaxed about the painting,' said Georgia. 'Not about the fact that your date was a disaster.'

'Like I said, I'm not the dating sort,' said Claire. 'I'm not interested, Georgey, and that's the truth.'

'Not even in Nate?'

'Not even in Nate.'

'Oh well.' Georgia sighed. Then she smiled. 'Even if it was a washout, at least you did it. With those other guys too! And . . . you're different now. Doing more things – like the barbecue. So if you did that, maybe we can have a Christmas party or something this year . . .'

'So that you can invite boys to stay?'

'Oh, Mum!' Georgia made a face at her and then giggled again. 'At least I didn't fall on my face in front of him.'

'Maybe I'm the one who should've been asking *you* for advice all along,' said Claire with resignation. 'I mean, I know I was trying to do it for you, but actually you're far more clued in than me.'

'Not really.' Suddenly Georgia squashed up on the seat beside Claire and hugged her. 'But I have a bit more experience. Because of going to a co-ed school. Because of summer camp. Because me and Robs and the girls share all our info.'

Claire looked into her lovely, fourteen-year-old daughter's shining eyes and earnest face. I'm so lucky with her, she thought. I really am. But the truth is that she's growing up much faster than I ever did. And she doesn't need my advice. Not about boyfriends anyway. She might need my support when she and Steve eventually break up, as they undoubtedly will. She might be miserable for a while unless she was the one who wanted it. But she's a strong person. I'm glad of that. She smiled at Georgia and hugged her in return.

'I wrote stuff down,' she told her daughter. 'All the things I learned. I thought it would be useful for you.'

'Did you?' asked Georgia. 'Let's see.'

Claire got up and fetched her notebook. 'It's all nonsense really,' she said as Georgia flicked through the pages.

'No it's not.' Georgia looked at number 3 on Claire's list. 'Being rejected hurts. You're right. It does.' She bit her lip. 'When Jamesie O'Sullivan ignored me at the céili I thought my heart would break.'

Claire felt the same protective surge rush through her as she'd had the night Georgia had rung to ask about true love in the first place.

'But it didn't,' continued Georgia. 'And I did what you said. I picked myself up and started again.' She glanced at her mother. 'That's what you have to do too, Mum. It's what Gran is doing with her estate agent friend.'

'I'm delighted for your gran. And I'm fine,' said Claire. 'I did pick myself up. I picked myself up off that floor and walked right out of there!'

'Not about that,' said Georgia impatiently. 'Don't get me wrong. About Dad.'

Claire was silent for a minute. 'I've picked myself up over your dad too,' she said finally. 'I've gone out with men, haven't I?'

Georgia shook her head. 'No you haven't. Not really. You went out with those blokes for me, not for you. And so you haven't picked yourself up at all. It's just pretending. And you say not to pretend.'

Claire said nothing.

'About the extraordinary men thing,' continued Georgia. 'That's only partly right. I met Steve in a fairly ordinary place. And he's an extraordinary guy. He's decent and kind and cute . . .' Her eyes twinkled as her mobile phone beeped. 'And he sends great text messages.' She looked at the message and responded to it straight away.

'You're not sending dodgy texts to each other, are you?' asked Claire, suddenly filled with concern.

Georgia handed her the phone and Claire pieced together the consonants, turning them into a sentence which read. 'Just finished economics homework. Wish I was with you instead. Love and kisses. Steve.'

Claire handed the phone back. 'Sorry,' she said.

'Ah, you're all right.' Georgia grinned at her. 'You're a parent. You read the papers and listen to the news and live your life in a whirl of horror about what could happen to me. And so far it's all turned out OK.'

'Fortunately for me,' said Claire. 'You know I nearly went nuts when I found him in your room. But you're right, he's a nice boy.'

'And he comes under heading number six,' added Georgia.

'Men have feelings too,' read Claire out loud.

'Sometimes I think that girls don't realise how upset blokes get about things,' Georgia said. 'Sometimes we think too much about how upset we are and forget about them.'

Claire nodded. 'Good point.'

'Like you,' Georgia said ruthlessly. 'You don't really care about Nate at all, do you? Not how he feels. Only how it affects you.'

'Georgia Hudson!' Claire looked at her angrily. 'I do care.'

'Do you?'

'Of course I do. Nate – well, Nate's a nice guy. And I wouldn't want him to believe I thought anything else.'

'But you don't love him?'

'Georgey – of course I don't love him. I hardly know him.'

'Thing is, I don't mind you going out with him,' said Georgia with feeling. 'I like him too.'

'Listen, matchmaker, even if it was the thing I most wanted in the world, the chances of him going out with me again are fairly minimal,' said Claire forcefully. 'Men might not be the shallow, vacuous creatures we sometimes make them out to be, but they'd rather go out with someone who doesn't make a show of them in public.'

'That's partly my fault,' said Georgia mournfully. 'I shouldn't have made you wear the shoes.'

'It's more my fault,' said Claire. 'I shouldn't have chosen red wine.'

Later that night, when Georgia had gone to bed and was sound asleep, Claire wandered into the garden again. The solar lights which Nate had arranged in the flowerbeds glowed gently with a soft yellow light. The coloured electric lights in the rockery also gleamed through the branches of the apple trees. The fountain in the rockery gurgled quietly as water recycled over the stones.

416

It was a peaceful place again. If Nate had done nothing other than transform the garden for her, it had been worth knowing him. She absent-mindedly dead-headed the garnet penstemon. And maybe some day, far into the future, when she was properly ready, she might find someone else. Someone who couldn't take Bill's place. But someone she'd be able to allow into her life.

The sound of the door bell carried into the night air. She dropped the faded red flowers and hurried into the house, her heart beating rapidly. Nobody called at this hour of the night with good news. Her fingers trembled as she opened the door.

'Hello,' said Nate. He looked at her pyjamas and dressing gown and frowned. 'I'm sorry, I didn't mean to get you out of bed.'

'I wasn't in bed.' Her heart was still racing. 'But it's late. What do you want?'

He regarded her thoughtfully from his odd-coloured eyes.

'I wanted to talk to you. But I shouldn't have come at this hour. I didn't realise how late it was.'

'No.' She opened the door wider. 'It's OK. I'm sorry. I got a fright when I heard the bell.'

'Sorry,' he said. He followed her into the kitchen. Phydough, who'd stayed in his basket while Claire had wandered around the garden, now got out and stretched. He padded up to Nate, who scratched him behind the ears.

'I brought you something.'

For the first time Claire realised that Nate was carrying an oblong parcel. He put it on the table. She took the scissors out of the kitchen drawer and snipped the Sellotape that held it together.

'Oh.'

It was *Jamaica Garden*. It looked perfect.

'It's an oil painting,' explained Nate. 'As soon as we left they got to work on it. It wasn't so difficult. Looked worse than it was at first glance.'

'Why have you brought it here?' she asked.

'A gift,' he said.

She stared at him. 'I can't accept this. It's worth six hundred euros!'

'A pittance in the art world,' said Nate cheerfully.

'Maybe, but it's not a pittance to you or to me. Nate, it's lovely and a really nice gesture, but—'

'You spent ages looking at it,' said Nate. 'I was watching you. You were looking at it as though you were standing in the garden itself.'

'It's a beautiful painting,' she admitted. 'And it reminded me of the last holiday I went on with my husband and Georgia.' She swallowed. 'The one where he was killed.'

'It must have been the worst thing in the world,' said Nate. 'Georgia told me a lot the day of your barbecue when I gave her a lift in the van. She told me how awful it was for you and how she didn't speak afterwards . . . she told me how great you were and how hard you've worked—'

'Georgia talks too damn much,' Claire interrupted him.

'She told me about your fear of cars too,' continued Nate. 'I shouldn't have suggested that cab to you tonight but I thought that maybe you were so upset over the painting you might not even notice you were in one. I thought it might be helpful. Stupid, I guess. And maybe bringing a painting set in Jamaica wasn't the most sensitive thing to do either . . . but you seemed to like it so much.'

'Oh, it was a lovely thing to do,' she cried. 'But I still can't accept it.'

'OK.' He scratched Phydough behind the ears again.

'I'm sorry,' she said, after a moment's silence. 'It must seem really rude of me not to take it. And I'm sorry about making a fool of myself at the gallery too.'

He smiled. 'No problem either way. If you don't want the painting I'll keep it. Eamonn's getting good reviews. It'll be an investment. As for making a fool of yourself, well, all I can say is that it was the best opening of an exhibition I've ever been at.'

She made a face at him. 'It was my one and only art experience.'

Phydough trotted out of the open kitchen door and into the back garden.

'It looks good at night,' remarked Nate as he looked out into the night.

'Yes,' she agreed. 'Everyone at the barbecue thought it was wonderful.' She turned to him. 'It *is* wonderful. I love it.'

'Mind if I look again?' he asked.

She shook her head. He stepped out into the night. She hesitated and then followed him.

He walked right around the garden, stopping from time to time to check the various bushes and flowers. Claire sat on the wooden bench and watched him. Georgia had said that he was strong and silent. She was right. He was strong. And he understood the value of silence.

She imagined his arms around her. Not casually, as they'd been earlier, but passionately. She closed her eyes and let herself think of what it would be like to have him hold her and then kiss her. She thought of what it would be like to have him leave her for ever. Her heart was racing again.

'You OK?' He sat beside her and she snapped open her eyes.

'Sure.'

'I hesitate to ask, but would you like to come out again some-time?' He looked enquiringly at her.

'I don't really see the point, do you?' she asked.

'I enjoy your company,' he said.

She got up from the bench. She still wanted him to kiss her. But she wasn't going to let that happen. He could kiss her and hold her and say all the right things, but how the hell would she know whether he meant them or not? And if he did – it didn't mean he'd mean them for ever.

She sensed him behind her and her body tensed. She expected to feel the touch of his hand on her shoulder but she didn't. Instead she heard him say that it was getting late and he'd better go. Part of her wanted to tell him not to leave. But instead she nodded.

'Don't forget the painting,' she said.

'I won't.'

'It was a really nice gesture.'

He shrugged. 'I'm good at gestures. But, like I said before, not so good with women.'

He strode up the garden ahead of her. As he hurried up the steps into the kitchen, he collided with Phydough, who'd bounded play-fully after him. Claire watched in horror as Nate stumbled, almost regained his balance and then, with a startled cry, tottered off the steps and landed with a resounding thud on the patio.

'Oh, hell, are you all right?' She ran up the garden while Phydough stood over Nate and licked him.

'Get off me!' Nate pushed at the dog. 'I said you were a mutt before and you sure are!' He pulled himself into a sitting position and yelped.

Claire hunkered down beside him and looked at him anxiously. 'I'm so sorry!' she said. 'It wasn't Phy's fault. He didn't mean it.'

'Do you train him to do that?' demanded Nate. 'I've lived with dogs in the past. He's the only one who's ever knocked me down. Twice. Of course he gets it from you, doesn't he? You did it once! I'm beginning to feel there's a conspiracy thing going on between you.'

'I'm sorry,' she said again.

Phydough licked Nate's face again in apology.

'Ow, don't!' cried Nate. He grimaced as he felt his ankle. 'Ouch.'

'Phydough, sit!' commanded Claire. The dog looked at her ruefully then plonked himself beside Nate and licked him quickly on the hand.

'Did you hurt yourself?' asked Claire.

'Yes,' said Nate irritably.

'Where?'

'My ankle.' He grimaced again. 'It kind of went from under me as I fell.'

Claire pushed up the leg of Nate's jeans and ran her fingers over his ankle. It was already beginning to swell.

'Hang on,' she said. She went into the kitchen and came out with a bag of frozen peas and two plump cushions. She helped him to sit on one of the patio chairs and put the cushions on the other. 'Now put your foot on the cushions,' she told him.

He did as she asked and she put the bag of peas on his ankle. He looked at her askance. 'And this will help?'

'Absolutely,' she said. 'It will stop the swelling. Always ice a twisted ankle.'

'And how long am I supposed to sit like this?' he asked.

'For a little while,' she said. 'Will I make a cup of tea?'

'You know, I rather feel we've done this already,' said Nate. 'You rushing round me like a ministering angel.'

She chuckled. 'I guess. Would you like the tea anyway?'

'I know it's good for shock. But any chance of something a little stronger?'

'Whiskey?' she asked doubtfully. 'I think I've got some in a cupboard somewhere. Or brandy?'

'Whatever,' he said.

She disappeared inside the house and came out again a few minutes later.

'I'm really sorry,' she said. 'I only have beer. It's not exactly what they recommend as a restorative.'

'Beer is good,' he said.

She handed him a tin of Bud, which he took gratefully. Claire contented herself with a glass of sparkling water.

'Maybe there's something wrong with both of us when we get together,' she said after she'd taken a sip. 'Every time we meet we seem to have some kind of disaster. Between me and Phydough we've knocked you over three times now. Plus Georgia nearly killed you with the peanut butter sandwiches. And I ended up on the floor tonight too. There's obviously some malevolent force going on here.'

He smiled at her, then winced as he moved his foot a little. 'Not necessarily a malevolent force. Haven't you ever heard of falling in love? Or being bowled over?'

'I don't think it's meant to be literal,' she remarked.

'No. But it's happening all the same.'

She stared at him.

'Don't worry, I'm not in love with you yet,' he reassured her. 'But I – I'd like to find out if I could be.'

'Oh, Nate—'

'I know there are all sorts of issues going on,' he told her. 'Everyone says that you and your husband were the perfect couple. So you've had that good relationship and anything else might be a let-down. Me and Felicity, on the other hand, were walking hell. Me and Sarah should have been great, but it was a complete disaster. I'm not saying that me and you could be anything. We'll never know until we try, though.' He looked hopefully at her.

'I have more issues than you could possibly imagine,' she said hastily. 'I still miss Bill. Sometimes I'm doing something and I think of him and it's like it only just happened. I get panic attacks every time I get into a car because it brings it all back – even though the accident didn't happen in a car. I'm a single working mother who's so concerned about her daughter that I tried dating men to learn about them to give her hints, and I'm afraid . . . I'm afraid of being left on my own again . . . Nate, these are not the actions of the kind of woman you want to go out with.'

'Of course they are,' he said robustly. 'Why shouldn't you still miss your husband? Why shouldn't you worry about Georgia? Why shouldn't you get panicked about things?'

She sat in silence, her elbows propped on the patio table, her face in her hands. He wanted to go out with her again. He wanted them to have a relationship. He wanted to see if there was something more. He was talking about falling in love. How the hell could she fall in love? She was still in love with someone else, wasn't she?

'I can't replace him.' Nate's voice seemed to come from a million miles away. 'I don't want to be another Bill. I don't want to be another anyone. I'm me and we might not make anything work out. I know that. But what's the harm in trying?'

She looked up at him. He wasn't Bill. Bill had never said that sort of stuff to her. Bill hadn't needed to.

'Is your ankle any better?' she asked.

'No,' he told her.

She rearranged the frozen peas and suddenly started to giggle.

'Claire?'

'I've never had anyone talk to me about love like this before,' she told him. 'And certainly not while they're balancing a twenty-five per cent extra free pack of frozen peas on their leg.'

He grinned. 'I'm not your average sort of bloke.'

'No.'

'And I'm sorry if I embarrassed you or made you feel uncomfortable,' he added. 'But I needed to tell you this stuff. So that it's perfectly clear. I like you. I want to go out with you. But if you don't want to, that's fine.'

She bit her lip. 'I keep thinking about how I'll react when it's over,' she said. 'How I'll feel when someone else walks out of my life.'

'From my point of view, I'd be going out with a woman who can stick a needle in my thigh and frozen peas on my leg without even thinking about it,' he told her. 'I wouldn't have the nerve to walk out!'

She smiled faintly. 'But it might not work out. And so either of us could walk.'

'You can't stop taking risks,' he said gently. 'You can't tell yourself that you'll never do something again because it hurt you in the past.'

'It hurt so much.' She closed her eyes. 'When it happened. When I saw him. They'd done their best to make him look normal but how the hell could they? And when I came home and he wasn't there . . .'

'You can't feel guilty for ever either,' he said.

She swallowed hard. She didn't know whether she'd ever stop feeling guilty. And going out with someone else – well, it was hard not to feel guilty about that too. But if she let Nate go now, how would she feel about that?

She cleared her throat. 'From my point of view there was only ever Bill. I don't know what sort of deal it'd be with someone else. Nate – I really do like you. But I'm not sure . . .'

He reached out across the table and closed her hand in his. His grip was firm.

'Nobody knows until they try,' he said.

She got up from the seat and stood beside him. She leaned towards him and looked into his odd-coloured eyes. Then slowly, uncertainly, she kissed him on the lips.

Rule 8, a kiss is just a kiss, she told herself as she felt him put his arm around her. It doesn't have to mean anything more. He pulled her closer to him. Neither of them noticed as the packet of frozen peas slid gently to the ground.

Claire didn't wake the following morning until Georgia rushed into her room and asked her what the hell Nate Taylor was doing in the house. He'd spent the night in the guest bedroom – *her* guest bedroom, Georgia reminded Claire. So she should've been consulted before anyone slept in it. What the hell was going on?

Claire pushed her hair out of her eyes and was astonished to realise that it was after ten. But it had been late when she'd finally gone to bed because she and Nate had sat together in the garden until dawn. Some of the time had been spent kissing. Claire had now decided that a kiss wasn't always just a kiss. But most of the time they'd spent talking. It hadn't always been deep and meaningful stuff. A lot of it had been light-hearted banter. And Claire had realised how much she'd missed this kind of chat with someone special. But she wasn't ready to sleep with him. She'd thought about it when they went back into the house and then told him that if she ever did it wouldn't be when Georgia was there. He'd smiled and nodded and told her that he probably wouldn't be much good if he thought there was the slightest chance Georgia would hear them anyway. He was, he told her, loud and lusty in bed. And when he said that, she laughed.

Now Claire explained to Georgia about Nate coming round with the painting and about Phydough knocking him off the steps and him twisting his ankle.

'Gosh, Mum, you two are a disaster area,' she said.

'We concluded that ourselves,' agreed Claire as she got out of bed and pulled her dressing gown over her pyjamas again.

Nate was sitting at the breakfast table when they arrived downstairs together.

'I put the kettle on,' he said. 'I hope you don't mind.'

Claire shook her head.

'I'll give Sarah a ring and ask her to collect me,' he told her. 'She can drive me back to my place. I'm only five minutes from here in the car. I could probably hop if I really put my mind to it.'

'You don't live together?' asked Georgia.

'Of course not.' He looked appalled. 'We work together. That's enough. Besides, we nearly killed each other when we lived together. We're far too different for it to work.'

'You and Mum have a pretty good chance of killing each other too,' said Georgia cheerfully.

'I know.' Nate's eyes twinkled at her. 'But we're prepared to take the risk.'

'I'm glad,' said Georgia. 'Has she given you my list yet?'

'List?'

'Requirements for any man that goes out with her.'

424

He looked aghast. 'She didn't tell me about any list.'

'I didn't want to terrorise you any more than I had already,' said Claire. 'Don't worry, I'll give you the list.'

'Are you two always going to gang up on me?' he asked.

'Always,' Georgia told him. 'But because you've got a sore ankle I'll get you the phone so's you can call Sarah. Never let it be said that I don't care for the infirm.'

Nate laughed and she winked at him.

'I'll drive you.' The words were out of Claire's mouth before she could stop them.

Nate and Georgia stared at her.

'I'll drive you,' she said again more confidently. 'If you've got comprehensive insurance, of course. I have a driver's licence. I can do it.'

'I came here in my car, not the van,' said Nate.

'I know,' said Claire.

'Mum, are you sure?' Georgia looked anxious.

'Do you want to come too?' asked Claire. 'Keep an eye on me?'

'Yes.'

Claire laughed. This time Georgia's look was of astonishment. She couldn't remember the last time Claire had laughed like that. A free and easy laugh. A laugh that reminded her of another Claire in another time.

'Let's have breakfast first,' said Claire. 'And then I'll drive Nate home.'

And so, after muffins and coffee, with Nate in the passenger seat and Georgia behind her, that's exactly what she did.